FERGUS THE

FERGUS THE SILENT

a novel

MICHAEL MCCARTHY

YOUCAXTON PUBLICATIONS

ISBN 978-1-914424-38-0
Published by YouCaxton Publications 2021
YCBN: 01

YouCaxton Publications
www.youcaxton.co.uk

For Flora, Seb and Hugo

...there may be still "some happier island in the watery waste" to which the Penguins of the western seas may have escaped; but then, we may rely upon it, there is left a scanty remnant only.

Alfred Newton, 1861

PART ONE

1

People said there was treasure on Lanna; not a soul guessed what it really was.

I see the island so often in my dreams now that I fall asleep expecting it to appear and so it does, materialising out of a squall the way Jenny and I first saw it from the boat, the gauzy curtains of grey rain parting to reveal emerald slopes and white breakers in a royal blue sea. We gasped at its beauty. Even Jenny, determined to be in control and unimpressed, could not help herself. And in my dreams I am still stunned, still taken aback by that first wild fresh unforgettable sight of it. In the good dreams.

It was the remotest of the Hebrides, the farthest-flung of all the British Isles apart from Rockall, remoter than North Rona or Sula Sgeir, farther out even than St Kilda – 62 miles west by south of Barra Head with nothing but a stormswept ocean between its improbable green ramparts and Labrador. But it was more than that, it was more than remote: it was the purest of the Western Isles, in fact I sometimes think it was the purest of all islands anywhere, it was the very ideal of the purity of the natural world, for it was wholly untarnished by humankind. Its seabirds, the countless thousands of seabirds which thronged its cliffs and slopes, bred and fished and squabbled and died unhindered; the small flowers of its astonishing rain-fed greensward bloomed unpicked; the fish in their millions and the dolphins and porpoises, the orcas and the great whales which circled about it did so freely, uncaught, unharassed, as they had always done, since before the ascent of Man.

Its purity was such that it seems to me now, looking back, that Lanna deserved its secret; if it's not merely whimsical to say so, I feel that it was a worthy bearer, as so few places anywhere might be, of something quite so momentous, almost as if it were a temple enshrining an unseen holy of holies. Is that whimsy? Perhaps. Yet it remains the case that it was an extraordinary place in which this extraordinary secret was held, the secret which so profoundly changed the lives of all of us who came into contact with it, most of all of Fergus, the man who discovered it, and who, for all the long age of his adulthood, told no one.

It has taken several years to write this down. It took a long time even to begin. In the end it was part of a coming to terms with everything, with the scarcely believable calamity of what happened – I still struggle to accept it took place – but also with who we are, with the moral choices we make, and with one great moral choice in particular. Yet the hesitation was simple: why would you write something which you know no one will believe? Why write something which not only invites disparagement or even snorting ridicule but which, in the very act of a public telling, in the straining for credibility, somehow diminishes itself? So this is a private account, looking to persuade no one of what occurred, but intended merely to order and set down for myself the remarkable events of that summer, the summer of the Millennium, on what the satellites show as an isolated, inaccessible dot in the Atlantic.

That this dot was said to hold fabulous riches, that it was supposed to be a Treasure Island like Robert Louis Stevenson's, complete with buried Spanish gold, has always seemed to me the most perfect irony. It arose from the final episode of the island's history – for despite its isolation, Lanna did indeed have a history, one as notable as its beauty or its purity, which lasted a thousand years, began with a martyrdom, and ended with a curse. The island was the site of a monastery, which for its scarcely credible location was throughout the Middle Ages one of the wonders of the Celtic world, and which endured from the time of St Columba until all of Scotland's religious houses were abandoned in the Reformation.

Right at the end of its years of human settlement, when a handful of former monks were still eking out their existence there, Lanna collided with other great events. It was the summer of 1588, the year of the Spanish Armada, when Medina Sidonia led his defeated galleons back to Spain on the heroic voyage around the top of Scotland, and one of them – historians dispute whether it may have been the *Santa Barbara* or the *San Maria del Junca* – was wrecked seeking shelter on the island. The legend had it that somehow, the last islanders got hold of its treasure and fought over it to the death, until there was but one man left; and he, facing death himself, hid the treasure, and in his final written testament, cursed his island home.

(margin note, handwritten) Rules / lack of belief / that he will not / be believed

(margin note, handwritten) Story history of having

This curse was said to have a most peculiar and sinister supernatural effect: that as you approached Lanna, *it would disappear.* Well, I myself have seen it 'vanish' suddenly in a squall, one of the unending squalls out there in the Atlantic storm zone, and before the days of radar you might as well have given up the island for lost if the weather closed in like that, and then you could really be in trouble, a full day's sailing from the nearest haven. But to the men from Lewis and Harris, from the Uists, Benbecula and Barra, it wasn't a matter of weather: the curse to them was real, and they called Lanna *An t-Eilean Air Chall*, The Lost Island, and avoided it entirely – they wouldn't fish around it and they wouldn't take visitors – and so for four centuries, through all the turbulence and tumult of modern history, Lanna remained in quiet on the edge of the world, forbidden, secluded and quarantined.

This quarantine was interrupted but once. In the summer of 1939, as Europe prepared for war, an Edinburgh lawyer published a history of the island and told the tale of the treasure – that is, he told it in modern English, for the first time. The effect was electric: following an article about his book in *The Scotsman*, given a sensational twist by the *Daily Express*, there was a gold rush. Treasure hunters from far beyond the Western Isles flocked to Lanna – they had to provide their own transport as the islanders refused take them – and began to tear at its ruins and its green slopes, a dozen, two dozen, then scores of them in a mad summer saga until Lanna's owner, a Scottish nobleman, the Earl of Kintyre, gathered an army of his estate workers and freelance roughnecks, sailed across in a convoy of small boats and threw the treasure hunters off.

Lanna, he announced to the world, was henceforth CLOSED. To make his point he fixed chains across the narrow defile between the cliffs which led to its remarkable sheltering harbour, and closed Lanna remained, for year after year, until it entered our lives.

The bad dreams I have come to terms with now, or rather I should say they have grown less frequent, although their content is always the same: the burning cross. In the early days they were terrible and I would wake with a cry and find myself sweating, and sometimes even now I have to leave the calming embrace and the whispered comfortings and pull on a sweater and go down to the shore, and walk along the edge of the sea, the dark sea, occasionally putting up a pair of oystercatchers which flee with a startled *Puhpeep!* I walk until the beat of my heart matches the rhythm of the lisping waves and that will restore me.

Yet some of the <u>dreams are hopeful</u>, most of all the dreams of the other cross – the <u>giant Celtic cross on Lanna's peak</u>, the cross which the pilgrims would see at the end of their perilous voyage. This is the part of Lanna's history to which I am really drawn; to be honest I think the buried treasure bit is so much stuff and nonsense, but the saga of the abbey which went before it is glorious, even if it is now forgotten.

From the earliest days of the Celtic church Lanna housed its monastery, one which eventually became Scotland's great pilgrimage centre, a Santiago de Compostela of the sea, second in importance as a sacred site only to Iona itself. It was dedicated to St Corman, an early prior martyred by the Vikings, and held as its much-revered relic one of his hands, which was said to be capable of miracles. But more miraculous still was the very presence of this institution, which only Celtic Christianity could have produced, with its stone-built church and its working, praying, singing community of monks, on the most wind-whipped, wave-pounded, isolated outcrop in all the British Isles. Men marvelled at it; and thinking of those who should naturally be there, they called it *Abaid nan Ròn*, the Abbey of the Seals.

It was owned and supported by the Lords of the Isles. Who now remembers the great days of the <u>Clan Donald</u>, when for three hundred years they ruled the western seaboard of medieval Scotland? There's another empire long forgotten. But an <u>empire</u> it truly was – making war, making peace, ordered from their castles at Finlaggan on Islay and Ardtornish on the Sound of Mull through their sea power, though the reach of their birlinns, their open highland galleys.

<u>Lanna with its abbey</u> was that <u>empire's greatest possession</u>. It gave the Lords of the Isles a sense of spiritual as well as temporal dominion and it also gave them substantial revenue, for every summer when the sailing season arrived it was Clan Donald birlinns which carried the shivering pilgrims, for a fat fee, on their hazardous voyage to St Corman's ocean shrine. They would board in Loch Aline, under the lee of Ardtornish, the Lords of the Isles' summer residence, to be rowed up the long Sound of Mull and then out, against wind and tide and current, over a hundred miles of untamed Atlantic which even in summer could turn murderous. I often think of them. I've often imagined just how thankful they must have been when the great Celtic cross on Lanna's peak at last began to come into view, and how they must have fallen down to kiss the cherished earth as soon as they set trembling foot back upon it. That's what I see in the good dreams, the sight of the cross and the

More history here

PART ONE

pilgrims getting closer to it, and the reason, the reason I suppose my mind returns to them so much, is because I too first went to Lanna on pilgrimage.

Like them, I went seeking expiation for my sins. Like them, I went hoping for redemption. But I did not start from Loch Aline; I started out on the platform of Oban station, the moment I caught sight of Jenny, struggling with her holdall in the melee of rucksacked hikers plopping one by one off the Glasgow train. I was almost speechless with elation after waiting so long and hoping so hard, and it must have shown in my face as I bumped through the backpacks towards her calling 'Jenny!' because the instant she saw me her own face set like concrete; she stood, put her holdall down, and waited for me to come up, impassive.

I said: 'Jen!' Marvelling at her, entranced by the real presence at last instead of the imagined one.

She said: 'Yeah. Hello, Miles.' Her face and her voice were neutral, but there was something coming off her – I started to realise it was a weird sort of hardness, something I had never seen in her before – which held me back from attempting to kiss her on the cheek or touch her in any way. I said: 'You're here!'

She said: 'Not for very long, prob'ly.'

'What d'you mean?'

She held something up, a pale card. 'See this?'

'What is it?'

'Day-return ticket. Takes me back to Glasgow in an hour and twenty minutes from now.'

'I don't follow.'

'I've come, Miles, but I still don't think you understand the basis I've come on. I told you, but I don't think you were listening. And I want to be straight with you, not mess you around or raise your hopes or do to you any of what you did to me, so if you don't like it or accept it, and you probably won't, I'm going straight back.'

I said: 'OK.' Puzzled, but wanting to sound willing.

'I shan't have lost anything. I quite enjoyed the journey. There were waterfalls and stuff, and a funny paddle steamer going down the Clyde, and my distant cousin Georgina's in Paisley, so I'll go and see her. But first I need to make sure you do understand it, and offer you the choice, so let's go somewhere and have a coffee, shall we?'

I was knocked off balance. This wasn't the reunion I had increasingly allowed myself to picture, the one with the kiss of

5

greeting which dissolved into a long embrace. But I said 'Sure,' and I took her bag – I insisted – and we walked out into the town, that odd mixture of seaside tattiness and Victorian granite grandeur, and ended up sitting at a formica table in a place called Hamish's Kitchen. She said not a word until the coffee was before her, in a transparent plastic cup, I remember, and she had stirred it several times. Then she looked up.

She said: 'Miles. Do you really think I would ever come back to you? That I would ever seriously consider it, for a second?'

I swallowed. I said: 'I don't know. I suppose I, I mean obviously I can see why you wouldn't, of course, but I suppose I would hope there might be a chance that, that you might.'

'Why would I do it, Miles? I mean, just from a practical point of view. What would be in it for me?'

I said nothing.

'Put yourself in my position. Why on earth would I give you the chance to screw me up again? Have I got STUPID stamped on my forehead?'

'Well I've changed, Jen.' I heard myself say it. It sounded feeble. It sounded pathetic.

She shook her head. 'Doesn't matter if you've changed. Doesn't matter if you haven't, because whatever I might have felt for you once is dead. And it's not only dead, it's worse than dead, it's hatred now, Miles, a real, nice, proper, festering hatred. After what happened, after – after something I can't forgive myself for, and never will, well I'm going to forgive you for it even less, you understand that?'

The hope I had been allowing myself to harbour had been like the warmth of an open fire; now I started to feel a chill wind blowing. I said: 'Then why are you here?'

Jenny took a sip of her coffee. She said: 'Seeking closure. That's the phrase everyone uses nowadays, isn't it?'

'What d'you mean?'

'Look Miles. You've made me an offer which is carefully crafted to appeal to a particular side of me, a side of which you have personal knowledge because I let you into my life, sucker that I was. And you must be betting that it *would* appeal to me, and that it might, how shall we say, do the trick?'

I said nothing.

'So you know what? I will accept it. I will come with you to your island. I will spend three or four days in your company on the most amazing island anyone has ever set foot upon, the way you tell it, and I will do it just to show you that *even that makes no fucking difference.*'

I was taken aback by the vehemence.

'But I'm not going to con you, like you did me, I'm going to be upfront with you, and if you don't want to accept it, fine. But that's the deal.'

'You'll come, but just to show you don't want me?'

'Got it in one, Miles.'

Something sagged in me then, and I listened sort of helplessly as she went on, only half hearing her as she said that then I really would understand, and she would have proved something to herself, and maybe watch me squirm a bit along the way, she didn't mind admitting that, it wasn't very pleasant, but that was the deal.

Our whole existences sometimes turn on certain moments, certain decisions, do they not? I could see that I'd been fooling myself. I understood that there really was no more hope, and I could see too that the best thing to do now was to get out with as much dignity as I could muster, and say, OK, Jen, if that's the way it really is, goodbye and good luck, but I want you to know I will always wish you well.

Yet there was something deeper than that stirring inside me, something deeper than just keeping my dignity, something to do with knowing now what was the right thing to do, even if it wasn't the best thing to do. After all the months of thought and of beginning to understand who I was, and seeing how wrong I had gone, it was something to do with accepting my fate, going with the flow of my fate, even if that fate was losing Jenny. And after what may have seemed an inordinate amount of coffee-stirring time for her, I simply said: 'I accept.'

'You know I'm not going to change, don't you?'

'Yes.'

'Very well, Miles.'

She was stiff. She seemed slightly … put out? I'm not sure. As if she hadn't expected it at all. But there it was; and with that bizarre bargain sealed in Hamish's Kitchen – a trip together to prove I wasn't wanted – we walked back out into Oban, and crossed over to the port, and found the *Katie Colleen*, the old trawler which was the boat of the Balnay Estate, and said hello to Murdo the skipper and his young nephew Donald the deckhand, and boarded and stowed Jenny's bag, and then gave them her camera. I had told her she couldn't bring a camera, but she'd forgotten.

No cameras, was the deal with Kintyre. God knows why, but that was the deal, and Jenny's mood was certainly not improved by that. Nevertheless, we set out then, in the early evening of that sunny breezy day in the first week of June, and headed south down the channel between the mainland and the long green island of Kerrera, bound for Lanna – Jenny wrapped in her anger, myself despairing, and both of us on course for an encounter, with Fergus and his secret, whose consequences we could never for one moment have imagined.

Religious overtones - beauty purity of island. Sins redemptions. p1, 2, 5. title.

Miles has good & bad dreams - crosses Jenny - agrees to go to island p3. to prove she doesn't love him.

2

How do we define what a tragedy is? Words loosen over time, do they not, and now we might use the term merely to denote any disaster, any catastrophe, or indeed any happening with major injurious consequences, although I think we still generally tend to reserve it for circumstances involving loss which is particularly sad or distressing. But over the years I have been writing this, I have found myself increasingly focusing on the original, classical meaning of the term, which refers to the narrative of a noble figure brought low by some aspect of their own character, as I have wrestled with how to set down this story, the story of Fergus Pryng and the momentous decision he took, to keep hidden from the world what he had found on Lanna.

In setting it out it I have been guided by one principle in particular: to suspend judgement. This is a new experience for me. I am a man who has had two lives, and in my earlier incarnation I was quick to judge people always, usually negatively; for being a believer in intellectual excellence, and sure that I possessed it myself, I found condemnation fall naturally from my lips. Yet in becoming the person I am today, I have begun to understand, among much else that was hitherto foreign to me, the ambiguities of moral choice, and to realise that judgement of people can be a dodgy business, full of pitfalls; and that it is by judgement's suspension that the real truth of a matter, and especially of an individual, can sometimes be more nearly approached.

It is a fitting approach in the case of Fergus. What he kept secret was explosive, and had he ever disclosed it, the world would have been amazed – it would have gone round the globe in a flash – but his decision to stay silent was momentous most of all because of its ultimately disastrous consequences; so his story is not only sad in the extreme but it is one where moral judgements might seem hard to avoid. Had it ever emerged, had the full set of circumstances ever been publicly made known, I think that accusations of irresponsibility, greed, egotism, special interest and God knows what else would have been readily levelled at him and hard to rebut – not to mention sheer craziness – despite the fact that Fergus himself was a deeply moral man, and his own severest critic. But such accusations will not come from me. Indeed, I think I would characterise this epic, this still-secret epic which has come to dominate my life, as much by the difficulty of judging its rights and wrongs, as by the wonder which lay at its heart.

Yet in setting it all out, there is one harsh judgement I cannot avoid passing: the one upon myself. For I was led to Lanna and to Fergus by a quest to atone, an attempt to repair the hurt that I had caused to my former partner Jenny Pittaway – a wounding so savage and extreme that I shudder to think of it even now. That I was capable of it, today leaves me aghast, but at the time, it caused me to lose not a wink of sleep; and so writing this is an exercise not just in grappling with the story of Fergus, but in coming to terms with what led me into his world, and that means facing up to the exceptionally unpleasant person that I was, before I changed.

It's all part of the same saga, anyway, it all blends into one, but to sum it up, to pass that judgement which I cannot avoid passing upon myself: these events took place because I was an academic, a brilliant and ambitious young research scientist, with all the worst traits of the type – haughty, dismissive and snobbish, and possessed of a great store of intelligence, with no wisdom whatsoever. Most of all I was selfish, pursuing my ambition ruthlessly and sacrificing without a thought anyone who got in the way, such as Jenny.

I had jilted this woman, who loved me, who had given me her whole heart, with a cruelty which had effectively destroyed her happiness, probably for good; and she understandably saw my attempt at a reconciliation in Hamish's Kitchen as outrageous. She was not aware that in the intervening time something unusual had happened to me, a sort of spiritual earthquake, I suppose, which began with finding the body of a bird on a beach and climaxed at a human deathbed. It was a great shift, in which I had perceived who I was and what I had done, and who she was and her true worth; and as a result I had resolved to live a different life, one whose principal purpose would be to make up for the hurt I had caused her, if that were possible, and if not, at least to hurt no others.

Of course she could not know this, but she would not have cared anyway: the wound was too deep. Looking at her as we left the harbour, planted with her back to me in the bows of the *Katie Colleen*, it seemed that the anger was coming off her in waves –

perhaps he flatters himself

anger not only with me, but with herself too, perhaps, for agreeing to the trip in the first place; for really, despite her understandable motive of wanting to make me squirm, or proving her point, or whatever, what good could come of it, for her? Wasn't it just an impulsive piece of gesture-politics? Maybe we should have gone our separate ways from the Oban café after all, I thought, feeling fully the hopelessness of the situation, as she stood there in the bows a pillar of defiance, letting the wind buffet her face all the way down the Sound of Kerrera until Murdo Macleod, the skipper at the wheel, murmured to me: 'Your colleague is going to get wet.'

'What?' I said.

'We'll be coming out into the Firth of Lorn just now,' he said. 'It's the open sea. The swell will be bigger and it may come over the bows,' and as he spoke seven gannets in line astern came looming low towards us, as if to announce the advent of the ocean proper, and a minute later we started to pitch up and the swell began to make its presence felt: the third wave dumped a shower's worth of water over Jenny and she reluctantly retreated, striding down the deck to the other side of the wheelhouse from me. But she had adjusted. She was back in control. 'Well then, skipper,' she said to Murdo. 'Tell me about your boat.'

I gazed at her. There she was before me, the love that I had lost. I understood entirely now what she had given me, and what I had thrown away, and that there was no hope of recovery. I think it was the most miserable moment of my entire life. But what else could I expect? There was no mitigation I could plead. There were no excuses whatsoever for the way I had acted – there never could be.

Yet I do think this: there were reasons, there is a background which is germane; and since, as I said, this is not just the narrative of what happened on Lanna itself, but an attempt to understand what led up to it, then the background is relevant too. The key to it all was my ambition, which was fierce in the extreme, and it was that which Jenny fell foul of; it was to my ambition that she was sacrificed. For it was not a normal, realistic scientific ambition, of hoping to make discoveries and receive recognition in mid-career; I wanted success as quickly as possible, so that I could surpass my father.

That was a pretty twisted objective, really; but then, my father was a pretty twisted guy. He was an academic like I was, Andrew Bonnici, but not just any old lecturer: he was a Nobel Prize-winner. Professor of Physics at Imperial College, London. Fellow of the Royal Society. Leading British expert on the laser. Discoverer of the 'Bonnici effect', which made so much modern laser technology possible, and consequently won him his Nobel. Famous public figure. Reith lecturer. One of the first 'media scientists' and eventually, National Treasure, in an abrasive, cantankerous sort of way, the subject of a 1,200-word obituary in *The Times*. And nasty, self-centred, heartless, hopeless apology for a husband and father, who so oppressed me with an unrelenting refusal, all through my youth, to acknowledge that I had any worth whatsoever, that in the end I felt that only by actually overtopping the bastard, in eminence and distinction, could I force him to recognise that I had value as a person (and just as important, could I reassure myself that this was the case.) I see him now as irretrievably spoilt, the only son of indulgent parents, the Italian café owner and his wife, who doted on the young mathematics prodigy they had so unexpectedly produced in their Croydon bungalow (and he repaid them with scant kindness in their old age, I have to say.) He was devoid of empathy. Other people tended to be blurs at the edge of his vision. I was one. That was the problem.

It went right back to the beginning. He constitutes my earliest memory, from when I must have been four or five. I remember going up to him at the breakfast table; he was eating (probably toast) and reading (probably Physical Review Letters or some such.) I had done a drawing of a double-decker bus. I held it up.

He took no notice.

I continued to hold it up, moving into his line of sight.

Eventually he said: 'What?'

'It's a bus, Daddy.'

'What?'

'It's a bus.'

'Can't you see I'm reading, Miles? Haven't you got a toy or something to play with?'

'It's a bus.'

'I'm busy.'

'It's a bus, Daddy.'

'Go away.'

'It's a bus.'

He lowered his head, ran his hands through his hair, and gave an exaggerated sigh. Then he carried on reading.

I said: 'It's a bus. I drawed it.'

He sprang to his feet, this big, bespectacled man, tore open the kitchen door and shouted in a colossal voice: 'Will someone take this bloody child away from me?'

Bump, bump, bump, the words go in my brain, even now,
bringing back the terror that seized me as I fled like a cat from a
firework to the farthest corner of our house, our big old house in
Wimbledon, where my mother came and found me, and took me
in her arms, and murmured for the first time her consoling mantra,
so often to be repeated: 'Daddy's got important work.'

I'm sure he did; but to me and my younger sister Lotte, he
was a tyrant. From the moment we could first comprehend it,
he made it clear that we might be seen, if that were wholly
unavoidable, but most definitely should not be heard. We were
to make no noise, ever, outside his study. We were to speak only
when spoken to, at family meals. We were to be entirely obedient,
to be always polite, neat and tidy, and we were to work tirelessly
at our schoolwork and at the piano practice that was thrust upon
us both. There was no caressing from him, no tousling of the
hair, no physical contact at all, in fact – no fun, no advice, no
encouragement; just the rules.

I did not demur. His explosion had made me terrified of his
censure. And yet things were more complicated. As time went by
I began to feel not just a desire to avoid his anger, but a longing for
his approval, and that was grounded in admiration. I was aware
of and proud of his distinction (even if a little confused initially
about its true nature.) I remember talking to my first friend in
school, Charlie Prince, about what our dads did. We were about
eight, I suppose.

'My dad's an accountant,' Charlie said.

'What's that?' I said.

'He counts up people's money for them, when they've got too
much to count themselves,' Charlie said. 'What's your dad do?'

'He knows about lasers,' I said.

'What're lasers?' said Charlie.

'Death rays,' I said.

Charlie's eyes widened.

'Like you have in a ray gun, you could shoot people with,' I said.

'Has your dad got a ray gun?' Charlie asked.

'It's a secret,' I said. 'I'm not supposed to talk about it.'

'Ah, tell, tell,' said Charlie. 'What's it for?'

'All right,' I said. 'But you promise you won't tell anyone?'

'No-one at all,' said Charlie, 'Cross my heart and hope to die.'

'It's for shooting down flying saucers, if they attack the Earth,'
I said.

Charlie's eyes widened still further.

'See,' I said authoritatively. 'Flying saucers're too fast for bullets. If you shoot bullets at flying saucers, they can just fly out of the way. But they can't get out of the way of death rays. That's lasers. That's what my dad does. But listen, you're not to tell, right?'

'Wow,' said Charlie.

'You're not to tell anyone, 'cos we would be arrested, see?'

'Wo-ow,' said Charlie.

As I began to understand it properly, the sense of his distinction only increased: I was eleven when I watched him on TV receive his Nobel from the King of Sweden, resplendent in white tie, and I swelled with pride. And feeling more strongly than ever the yearning for his approval, I hit upon a way I thought would guarantee it: I would be clever. Exceptionally clever. I was bright, I knew that. Now I vowed I would apply myself to my studies so diligently that I would reach peaks of achievement which would prove me a truly worthy son of a Nobel laureate, and entitle me beyond all argument to his warm regard. I would reach a state where commendation was unavoidable.

It got me nowhere. I was top of my class every year from eight to thirteen, and he never once congratulated me. He didn't bother with the details of our education, beyond specifying to my mother the very academic institutions he wished me and Lotte to attend, and providing the funds; he left minor items such as praise and encouragement to her, along with the ironing of our shirts and blouses. I suppose I sort of got used to that, like a dull background ache, but I began to resent it more actively when I got a scholarship to my new school, at thirteen.

No praise for achieving that. My first report, at the end of the first term, was very good: no praise for that either. My mother left it for him to read; he never did, or if he did, he passed no comment. Exactly the same thing happened at Easter with the second term's report. The final report at the end of the year was even better: the word 'outstanding' was actually used of my performance and by now I was desperate for him to see it, and to give me the acknowledgement I felt so strongly was my due. It was a feeling intensified by the fact that he had just delivered his controversial Reith Lectures on BBC radio, *In Defence of Excellence*, and was temporarily one of the most celebrated figures in the land; being prouder of him than ever, I prevailed upon my mother to ask him, specifically, if he would read my report and comment upon it, and with irritated reluctance, he agreed.

When the moment finally came I remember the three of us sitting at the kitchen table. There is a tension in the air. The report is passed to him by my mother. She has already congratulated me on it, fulsomely.

My father takes it in an off-hand manner, with a sort of brusque half-interest. I know what he will read first, the comment from my housemaster, Mr Cogan: 'Miles has been a positive pleasure to teach. He is a hard worker with an enquiring approach to his studies who produces impressive work for class assignments and writes with authority and imagination on a range of subjects. He has had a quite outstanding year and is a credit to College. He is to be heartily congratulated.'

But does he remark on that, or even affect to notice it? No. Instead, he flicks through the subject reports until he finds a comment under Chemistry which he reads out: *He works assiduously in the laboratory but perhaps he might concentrate more on how he manipulates and interprets the data he collects.*

He says: 'Explain that to me. Explain this lack of concentration.'

'But … but I got the top mark in Chemistry, Dad.'

'Is that all you have to say?'

I was taken aback. I was dumbfounded. Somehow I lost the power to defend myself.

He continues to flick through and finds this under Maths: *Miles might do better to show more of his working-out of problems in full. Simply presenting the correct answer is not always enough.*

He says: 'That sounds like a pretty basic flaw to me, young man. Is it not?'

'But … I was top in Maths too, Dad.'

'You are not answering me. Is there not a serious flaw in your work being highlighted here? How d'you explain it?'

I didn't know what to say.

'Hmph!' he grunted.

My mother intervened. 'Oh Andrew, that's not fair. Mr Cogan says he is a credit to College, and Dr Rae says almost the exact same thing. In his comment at the front.' She reached for the report to show him but he held it away from her.

He was riled.

'Muriel. I am commenting on the boy's performance in mathematics, for which I like to think I am professionally well qualified. Are you so qualified?'

My mother reddened.

'Are you?'

'No, Andrew.'

'No. Are you in fact professionally qualified to comment on any of these subjects? Physics? Latin?'

My mother lowered her eyes.

'No. Indeed not. Then I will thank you to hold your tongue and leave these matters to those who know best.'

He finds two more tiny, qualified criticisms in what was in actual fact a series of glowing tributes to my youthful ability, and harps upon each of them, as I sink further and further into myself, and finally slaps the report down on the table and remarks: 'No, a pretty poor show, all in all.'

I was speechless.

He rose to leave. 'I think you had better buck your ideas up, young man. Muriel, if Peter Medawar telephones, inform me instantly.'

As I sat there, burning like a flare, I didn't hear my mother's clucking, after he had gone out, *Oh, your father, Miles, he can be such a funniosity sometimes, when he's got a lot on, take no notice love, it's a marvellous report …* But then, I mostly didn't hear her. I had picked up early on his ability to dismiss her as of no consequence.

Yet I say now, if my childhood did not twist me more than it did, if there was any gleam of hope for me, she was responsible. She was a wonderful mother, to me and Lotte both, as I now acknowledge with all my heart – too late! She strove to make up for my father's tyranny, which she could never quite openly oppose, with a sort of underground resistance based on love, supplying endless sympathy for what we were doing at school and with our friends, commemorating the smallest achievement or anniversary with humour and warmth and cards and presents (contributing no doubt the ones supposed to be coming from him), and providing constant physical affection. In so far as I had a normal childhood at all, it was down to her, to her covering me with love and attention and regard.

But it was his regard I craved! It's hard to put into words how screwed up his perverse dismissal of my report made me feel. He was famous, his judgement was monumental, everyone respected it, I more than anyone, and here he was setting me at nothing, his own son; I had striven so hard to win him over and I had done so well and he was saying: *You are worthless.* Hard to take, at any time. Very hard to take when you are fourteen, from your own father. I left my mother and I went out into the garden and paced up and down, I paced up and down the lawn breathing heavily and pounding my right fist into my left palm, and then I swung round and walked over to the garden shed and fired my fist into the window which shattered and ripped open my knuckles and the back of my hand with its splintering shards. Blood spouted. My mother heard the crash from the kitchen and rushed outside and I still remember the look of horror on her face as she beheld me, the tears running down my cheeks and the blood running down my upheld arm. 'Miles, Miles, love, what have you done?' she cried, and I cried back to her: 'He will have to respect me one day, Mum, because I will be better than him.' She folded her arms about me; her white apron grew red.

That was the moment, on an early evening in July, in London's southern suburbs, when resentment finally overcame the admiration and the desire to be loved; when the hate for him was born in me, and when my early life received its organising principle: *I would surpass him*. Inside the brilliant physicist there was something weird and warped and I knew instinctively then that he would never acknowledge my worth, however sterling it became – and indeed he never did; and I knew too that the only way I could refute his unbearable dismissal of me, in a way he would have to concede – or at least, in a way I would believe in myself – was to transcend, objectively, his own achievements. He got a First? I'd get a better one. He wrote a dazzling doctorate? Mine would be more dazzling still. He was an FRS at forty-five? I would be a Fellow at forty. I would climb to the very topmost peak of the scientific establishment, look down upon him and pronounce from on high the words that would enable me to have self-worth: *Fuck You*.

For a long time I took it for granted I would be a physicist like him, but at seventeen I stumbled across the different discipline which I would surpass him with: evolutionary biology. I chanced upon *The Selfish Gene* and was bowled over by it: like everybody else I was captured by the rhetoric, and by the brutal simplicity of the central idea, that our bodies, that we ourselves, are merely survival machines for our genes. The way Richard Dawkins told it, Darwin's theory of evolution by natural selection was reductionism taken to the ultimate power: it explained every single thing about us, and not only our bodies' hairlessness, or our upright stance, or our opposable thumbs, but the way we behaved towards each other. Only those aspects of us are present, which in the past have aided survival. Everything else has been selected out. It was convincing. And you could see that it might well be true.

But then, with wider reading, I saw the implications, and with them, the arguments. If evolution explained everything, if it was the reason why everything about us was there, then maybe evolution *justified* everything. Like aggression. Or racism. Or even rape. And I discovered the man who best articulated the worry, Stephen Jay Gould – and there were the 'Darwin wars', waging before me.

I was riveted. It seemed to me truly a clash of the titans, the opposition between these men with such formidable intellects, with such passionate yet conflicting beliefs about what makes us who we are. Fired by the sort of enthusiasm that used to affect intellectual teenagers who had just discovered Marxism, I threw myself into neo-Darwinism and modern evolutionary theory, and read everything I could with increasing excitement; and when the time came I applied to read zoology at Oxford, where Richard Dawkins reigned in state, knowing full well that both aspects of my choice would royally piss my father off. He thought Oxford a frivolous place in comparison to Cambridge, his own alma mater; and arrogant physicist that he was, he deemed zoology beneath contempt.

'Zoology? For your degree? Are you serious, Miles?'

'I'm going to do it, Dad.'

'You might as well study bird-watching.'

'I'm going to do it.'

'Are you by any chance contemplating a career as a zoo-keeper?'

'I'm going to do it.'

I was hardened now: his derision bounced off me, though it still stung that he uttered not a word of congratulation when I won my place at Pembroke – my mother was full of delight and even Lotte congratulated me heartily – but from him, not a syllable. OK. Fine. Fuck you. *Fuck you, fuck you, fuck you*, I thought, the sentiment which sustained me for three years of immersion in the world of animal behaviour seen through a Darwinian lens – behavioural ecology, the British term for it. It was a monkish existence which involved little social life, but which culminated in my First, and the Gibbs Prize in Biological Sciences, both achievements my father could ignore; and he did. Yet with my postgraduate research, I began to climb towards a place where ignoring the success of his son was, for Andrew Bonnici, going to become more problematic.

My field of postgrad study was sex. I chose it because I sensed that any discoveries I might make would prove to be of wider public interest than most of evolutionary biology, since only specialists care about optimal foraging, or predator–prey interactions, but everyone in the world is interested in sex. Though I didn't stay in Oxford; I went off to the pint-sized university of Aberfair in West Wales, where an exceptional young professor, Callum McSorley, was carving out a fascinating research area for himself, into how sexual behaviour had been moulded by evolution, and in particular, the uncovering of just how frenzied, unrestrained and pitiless was the pursuit, by most creatures, of reproduction.

It was a novel and exciting field, partly based on that famous leap forward of the 1980s, DNA fingerprinting, which, along with enabling us to catch criminals, had revealed there was much more furtive shagging going on in the natural world than anyone ever suspected. For DNA testing enabled us for the first time to assign paternity. That meant that in a blackbird's nest of six chicks, say, we could tell exactly who the father was of each one; and frequently, it turned out, the male bird who was helping the mother feed them, was not, poor sod, the father of them all.

Hanky-panky. Naughty nookie. Infidelity. Extra-pair copulation is the scientific term. We had long assumed that because birds lived in pairs they respected the pair bond; now DNA analysis was revealing that promiscuity, on a scale never hitherto imagined, was the true order of things in the animal kingdom, since extra-pair paternity was ubiquitous. Everything was at it! The biological world was astounded. Birds and other organisms might be socially monogamous, but sexually monogamous, they were not. It was one of the great biological breakthroughs of the 1990s.

Callum ran a research station on Skarholm, *Skahrum* as they pronounce it, one of the big rocky islands off the Pembrokeshire coast – that was why he had gone to Aberfair, which was nearby – and his studies of sexual behaviour focused mainly on its guillemots, those penguin-like cliff-nesting seabirds, because they were easy to observe, sitting together in long lines on their narrow breeding ledges. In the final year of my degree I spotted a research objective I thought might be carried out there, which was to prove that all this newly-discovered promiscuity in birds was not just random or casual, as one might suppose, but had a definite purpose – the begetting of more offspring.

It was an idea fitting neatly into the great shift in understanding which *The Selfish Gene* had popularised: that creatures evolved above all to get more of their genes into the next generation, and that the great evolutionary prize was survival. Where a piece of behaviour had evolved which actually aided survival of the genes, it was termed an evolutionary adaptation, and the word *adaptive* was used in a special sense to mean, giving a better survival chance. The idea that extra-pair copulation – sexual infidelity to one's mate – was adaptive in birds, I thought, might be proved in the guillemot colony on Skarholm, for the first time.

Which, in my world, would be a big deal.

When I talked to Callum and he realised I had perceived this, as a mere undergraduate, he was stunned, and at once offered to take me on as a doctoral student, although there were conditions: to work with him on the sea cliffs of Skarholm I had to be not only intelligent, but a competent climber and a good swimmer, and possess also some further indefinable quality – *not being a wanker*, he eventually explained it to me – which he judged I had when he took me during the Easter holidays to the island, and showed how in the summer we would be catching young guillemots, and ringing them, and taking blood samples to extract their DNA, all on the vertiginous cliffs. So while others of my year were beginning postgrad research in Oxford itself, I left it all behind, the dreaming spires, the dazzling lawns and the dazzling minds, and off I went to Aberfair, finding a settlement so parochial Dylan Thomas might have used it for the sequel to *Under Milk Wood*. The Co-Op supermarket on Dragon Square, it seemed to me, was the liveliest place in town, unless it was the Taj Mahal Tandoori House on a Friday night.

It mattered not. My intent was sufficient unto itself. I took up climbing. Weekends were for pitons, cams and carabiners. I took up running and serious swimming. I swam every morning, and I took a special interest in life-saving: one day, someone next to me might fall off a cliff. I was not quite so monkish as I had been at Oxford; I had three affairs in my time there, although to me they were diversions of absolutely no consequence, but apart from that I led a largely solitary life, content with my own company and my CDs and my piano on which I practised the forty-eight preludes and fugues, music being my principal pastime; the other Aberfair postgraduates thought me stuffy and standoffish and a stuck-up Oxford snob. I was. And for the next three years I threw myself into my research, trying to prove that infidelity in guillemots produced offspring – you might well assume that, but *proving* it scientifically was a different matter – and discovered Arty Booboo.

Oh Arty, what a role you have played in my life! He was a guillemot, but not just any guillemot; he was an avian Casanova. His name came from the combinations of coloured leg rings we employed to identify individual birds on the breeding ledges: the code letters for his rings were R and T on his left leg – R was for red, and T was a technical ring – and Bu Bu on his right leg, Blue and Blue. He was RTBuBu, soon converted into a proper name, and he was one of the birds in my study group of 100 pairs, all identified not only by their rings, but more deeply by their DNA samples. And at the end of the first breeding season we took DNA samples from the 100 chicks which the 100 pairs had produced – guillemots just have a single chick – and matched the chicks up to the parents.

In the vast majority of cases the chick had been fathered by the male bird which cared for it with his female partner. So most male birds had just the one chick, within the pair bond. But there were a small number of extra-pair paternity cases where male birds had fathered extra chicks, with females other than their regular mate. Three of the males out of the hundred had fathered a single extra chick. Arty Booboo, however, had fathered four, plus his chick with his own mate, for a total of five. *Well well*, I thought. *What a lad.*

The next year I focused on him more closely, trying to observe his infidelities, and I witnessed eleven extra-pair copulations or EPCs, and I almost certainly missed a few; and when the time came to check, we found that these had resulted in a total of six offspring, including the one he had fathered with his missus, as it were. It was enough to make my case, and over the third year I wrote it all up as my doctoral thesis; and then, greatly helped by Callum, turned it into a scientific paper which we submitted to *Nature*, and which to my astonished and unbounded elation, was accepted.

When it eventually came out, Callum bumped into me in the corridor. He said: 'Hey, bonny prince. There's a copy of *Nature* in the common room. I think ye should go take a look.'

It was on one of the coffee tables and as I got closer I began to realise with trembling excitement what I was looking at: a photo which I had managed to snap with a long lens of Arty Booboo engaged in a fluttering mounting of a female on his Skarholm cliff, under the headline: *Extra-pair copulation in a seabird is adaptive.*

We were the cover story.

Not only that. I turned to the paper itself and saw, underneath the title: *M S Bonnici and C P McSorley, Department of Life Sciences, University of Aberfair.* Callum, who had actually constructed the paper, had put my name first.

You cannot imagine, unless you are a research scientist, what it means to have not only a paper published in the most prestigious scientific journal in the world, but to have it on the cover: everyone in science, right across the globe from San Francisco to Shanghai, suddenly knows your name. My career had lifted off. There seemed to be scores of people who wanted to get in touch with me; there were invitations to speak at conferences; most of all, there were opening doors, especially of journals, and the next three research papers I produced all landed in very respectable ones. But there was something more for me in this. I did not just rejoice: on a whim I sought out the original paper in which my father had announced the discovery of the Bonnici effect in laser science, and I found that that too had appeared in *Nature*, in November 1977. However, for some reason the editors had not quite grasped the full implications of it at the time, and it was not actually mentioned on the cover. Fantastic moment! And I was wondering what to do with this information when, as chance would have it, he suffered the stroke which was to finish him.

It left him half-paralysed and robbed him of speech, and he lingered for three weeks before a heart attack carried him off. I came back from Wales to Wimbledon to see him; my mother had been told he was unlikely to speak again and was greatly distressed, and Lotte was distressed for my mother, but I had other feelings swirling around when I went with them to the hospital. He was in a side room off the main ward; I saw he had suddenly aged and the left-hand side of his face seemed to have dropped. He could say nothing but his eyes were alive and followed us.

My mother said: 'How are you, darling?' She mouthed the words for him to understand. 'Have you managed to eat anything?'

He seemed to shake his head faintly.

'Is there anything we can get you?'

Another faint shake.

'Is that nice nurse still looking after you? The Irish one?'

He blinked.

She said: 'Miles is here, Andrew.' She motioned for me to approach the bedside. 'Miles. He's come from Wales. He's come to see you. It's Miles, Andrew.'

I said: 'Hi, Dad. How are you?'

His eyes moved over me.

'I'm sure they're doing all they can for you, Dad. I'm sure you'll be on the mend soon.'

He seemed to glare.

I said to my mother and Lotte: 'Look, d'you think I could possibly have a few minutes with him by myself? I sort of … want to say a few things to him. That I think I ought to say.'

My mother bestowed on me a look of understanding and even of pride, at my filial devotion. 'Of course, love,' she said. 'We'll wait outside.'

'Sure, Miles,' said Lotte.

When they had gone I reached into the inside pocket of my coat and brought out the copy of *Nature* with my cover story.

I held it up, like all those years before I had held up to him the picture I had drawn of the double-decker bus.

But this time he could not destroy me.

'See this?' I hissed in his ear.

I opened it and found the page with my paper. 'See?' I whispered. 'Miles Bonnici. Lead author. See?' Then I turned back to the cover. 'And see *this*? It's the cover story. The *cover* story. On the *front*. You didn't have that, did you? With your precious Bonnici effect.'

His eyes seemed to flicker rapidly at me.

'No you didn't, because I've looked it up. You were *inside*. Whereas this is the cover story. And it's gone round the world.'

The flickering continued.

'And you know what it means?' I whispered. 'Know what the meaning of this is?'

I stood back from him.

We looked at each other.

I leant in again to his ear.

'It means FUCK – YOU,' I whispered as distinctly as I could, to my dying father. 'FUCK – YOU.'

Father distant, critical, unloving - a git
Mother kind
He gets his revenge.

23

3

I know what I think now about my behaviour then, at my father's deathbed: I think it was monstrous. It was grotesque. A clash may be natural between fathers and sons, but Andrew Bonnici's non-acknowledgement of me did more than leave me bruised or resentful, like many unhappy offspring; it left me warped. It skewed my whole outlook on life, my obsession with surpassing him replacing any sort of moral compass I might have acquired, and eventually leading me into a sort of madness, of which Jenny Pittaway was the victim. But in the meantime it continued to fire my ambition and drive me forward at a frenzied pace, until three years later, after producing three more well-regarded scientific papers in Aberfair, I was back in Oxford with an ever-expanding sense of self-importance, a new research project, and a well-reviewed book, just published.

My book was a synthesis of all the literature emerging on the weird and inventive ways of promiscuity in animals, which had become a flood. I hit upon an engaging title for it: *Everything Except Seahorses*, which referred to the curious reproductive arrangements of those charming small creatures: the female seahorse's eggs are transferred into the male's brood pouch before he fertilises them, so that there is no chance another male could get his own sperm anywhere near; for seahorses, therefore, promiscuity is not an option. But for everything else, I was implying – including humans! – promiscuity was the natural order of things, and here was the evidence, with the sexual exploits of Arty Booboo on Skarholm featuring prominently. I suggested it to Oxford University Press and they loved the idea. Sex always sells. Even when properly scientific.

My new research project was to look at promiscuity in the female of the species, since we were starting to realise that females might be sexual adventurers as much as males, and might solicit or initiate infidelities, with a real evolutionary purpose – to obtain better genes for their offspring, from fitter males than their partners. If you could prove that – in effect that *adultery pays* – once again, it would be a big deal in my world; and it was Callum McSorley who suggested I go back to Oxford to do it, as a Royal Society Research Fellow at the Niko Tinbergen Institute, the NTI, the part of the zoology department named after the great Dutchman who had come to Oxford and founded the science of animal behaviour. Callum had done his own DPhil there. I applied and was accepted, by the Royal Society and the NTI both; and the day at last came when I left my rented cottage in Aberfair and transferred my CDs, my upright Bechstein and my framed copy of the Arty Booboo *Nature* cover to the small Victorian house in Jericho which I had bought with the legacy from my father (money that had actually come from my mother; the miserable bastard left nothing directly either to me or to Lotte).

But coming back was more than a functional move: it was symbolic in every way. Oxford with its zoology department was the supreme stage on which anyone in my field could shine, and when I returned, in September 1997 after six years in Aberfair, I returned in triumph, as I saw it, for I not only had a peerless *arrogant* academic publishing record for someone my age, but *Everything Except Seahorses: New Light on Promiscuity in Animals and People* had just come out, to enthusiastic notices, thus confirming my opinion of myself, at twenty-eight, as the hottest young evolutionary biologist on the planet.

There was just one tiny cloud in the sky, one teeny smudge on my perfect halo: Oxford University Press had deemed *Seahorses* not important enough for a launch party. I had strongly wanted one. It didn't have to be much, just a small reception. But it would be a formal moment where my success would be underlined by ceremony and I could say in my mind to my father, *Look, you fucker, did you ever have this? Did you? No you fucking didn't!*

My publicist in the marketing department at OUP, Celia Thornberry, a science-minded matron whom I had had come to like and respect, tried to get me a launch, but the suits were adamant: the funds weren't there. She was really sorry. But then, a few days later, she called me.

'Listen Miles,' she said. 'In the week before term starts we are having a launch party for Dominic Makepeace.'

'Why?' I asked petulantly. 'What's he written that's so fantastic?'

Sir Dominic Makepeace was one of the zoology professors, an entomologist by training, who had made his name not so much as a research scientist as an administrator, both within the university and outside. For several years he had been Vice-Chancellor, and he was known as a formidable fund-raiser. For years he had kept his hand in, as far as his teaching responsibilities were concerned, by giving a course to first-year undergraduates entitled *Zoological Perspectives*, which I had attended. I thought that academically, he was second-rate, and pompous into the bargain.

Celia said: 'He's written a sort of popular account of zoology called *The Pageant of Living Things*.'

'Sounds like his undergraduate lecture course,' I said.

Celia coughed. 'It is, actually.'

'What?'

'He's turned his lectures into a book.'

'Jesus. So why are you giving him a launch?'

'Makepeace knows everybody. He can pull more strings than anyone in Oxford. He's owed a thousand favours, and he's called them all in.'

I snorted.

'Miles, listen,' she said. 'Point is this. Would you like to come?'

'Why on earth would I?'

'Because it's going to be as fairly major social event and everybody who's anybody in your field will be there. Dawkins. Robert May. Maye even William Hamilton. I might be able to make some introductions. What I'm offering you is the chance to mix with them more or less on equal terms, not just as a researcher, but as a published author.'

I saw what she meant. 'OK,' I said. 'I will. Thanks Celia, You're a brick.'

A consolation prize it might be, yet I was excited about it; it would be my first appearance on that stage, the true stage of my destiny. I would be joining the great actors. And rightly so, for I deserved it, didn't I? I was going to be one of them. And looking back on it now I see that party as the beginning of everything, as the start of the long road to Lanna, for it was there, at the peak of my pomposity, that I met not Richard Dawkins and his storied colleagues, as I was hoping, but Jenny.

The Makepeace launch was being held in the Founder's Library of New College, and I planned to get there just ten minutes after the start, to miss nothing but avoid seeming over-keen. Yet at 6.40 p.m. I eventually found a room which seemed to me not nearly as full as I might have expected; there were gaps in the company, and in one of them I caught sight of Celia. She waved at me frantically to come across and said: 'Miles, Miles, where have you been? It's nearly over.'

'I thought it had just started.'

'It started at half-five. You've missed the speeches.'

'Christ, I thought it was half-six.'

She saw me looking round, 'They've all gone, all the big hitters have gone. Dawkins, Bob May, Richard Southwood. And Bill Hamilton was here. Oh, Miles.'

I felt an intense rage. I looked about me again, futilely. So even my sodding consolation prize was ruined, I thought, as I half-heard Celia say to a man standing next to her: 'This is another of our authors, Miles Bonnici, he's just done a brilliant book on reproductive behaviour' and I was about to stalk off when Celia said, 'Miles, do let me introduce you to a fellow OUP author, this is Terry Bunce.'

I saw a plump, youngish man, about my age, with long greasy hair and a wispy beard. He held out a grubby hand. I took it.

'Terry has a book out as well.'

That sparked my interest slightly. 'Oh yeah,' I said. 'What on?'

'Annelid worms,' he said. 'The cladistics of annelid worms.'

'Cool,' I said. 'What's it called?'

'*The Cladistics of Annelid Worms*,' he said.

'Right,' I said.

He smiled at Celia complacently. 'It's quite a radical take on things,' he said. 'I like to think it's rather daring, in fact, we fear it may be too daring, don't we, Celia? We fear it may excite controversy.'

'Controversy where?'

'In the annelid community. You see, it proposes that the polychaetes and the oligochaetes should not be viewed as separate groupings, but that the oligochaetes should be viewed as a sub-group of the polychaetes.'

I realised I was desperate for a drink. I started looking around for the drinks table. Then I realised I was expected to say something. 'Er, you been reviewed?' I said.

'Well I haven't been yet, but I'm sure I will be. In *Annelida*. They can hardly ignore it.'

'In what, sorry?'

'*Annelida Analytica*.' And to my blank, none-the-wiser face, 'It's the journal of the Annelid Society.' He smiled again at Celia.

'Miles's book is called *Everything Except Seahorses*,' she said.

'Seahorses?' he said. 'Ah. And have you been reviewed?'

'Uh-huh.' I nodded.

'Anywhere interesting? Is there a seahorses journal?'

'Usual places. *TLS. London Review of Books. Spectator.* Plus a few others. You know. The dailies. *Times* itself. *Guardian.* It may be serialised in the *Telegraph.* We're still talking about that aren't we?'

Celia nodded.

'And the *New York Times* have asked for a review copy. Although the American deal hasn't been tied up yet.'

I saw his eyes widening but I'd had enough. I'd come for winners. I wanted no part of losers. I didn't even want to be polite, I was about to excuse myself brutally and walk off to get a drink when a voice at my shoulder murmured: 'Bonnici, is it not?'

I turned. 'Oh hello, Dr Maunder.' He was an ancient geneticist, short, dapper and bow-tied; he was the world expert on the genetics of butterflies and moths. I had taken one of his courses. And he knew my father.

'You are back amongst us?'

'I would appear to be.'

'Excellent. Excellent. I heard you were coming. And how long has it been, your exile?'

'Six years.'

'Six years! Oh my! Six years of hard labour in the provinces, eh, breaking intellectual rocks. And where were you again? Kidderminster? Hartlepool?'

'I was in Wales. Aberfair.'

'Aberfair! Ah yes! You were with McSorley. Well, he's all right, I suppose. Bled him dry, did you?'

'I learned a lot from him, yes.'

'You did rather well, in fact, didn't you, with that doctoral thesis of yours. The cover of *Nature*, Bonnici! Not just *Nature*, but the cover! Not seen that done before with a D.Phil. thesis.'

'Yes, I was very fortunate.'

'There are people in the department who have never made it into *Nature*, you know, who would lie, cheat, steal or kill to get a paper into *Nature*, and you get the cover! Barely out of short pants, as it were. That was noted, I can tell you. Rather jealously, in some quarters, perhaps. Not by me, of course.'

'Of course not, Dr Maunder.'

'No. I merely congratulate you. But tell me, Bonnici ...'

Uh-oh, I thought, *here it comes* ...

'Your work was excellent, but when I read the paper, I thought, wasn't there rather a lot of DNA banding to be done?'

'There was, yes.'

'Do it yourself, did you?'

'No, I had an assistant. A lab technician.'

'And yet, you see, this occurred to me when I read your paper, there seemed to be only two names on it, yours, and McSorley's, of course. Did I miss another name?'

'She got a box of chocolates.'

'She! She! Where would we be without the ladies, eh? Eternal helpmeets that they are! Their aid at every opportunity. Their asking for nothing in return. Happy, was she, with her box of choccies?'

'There was a misunderstanding. I may have been at fault. I apologised.'

'I'm sure you did, Bonnici. But perhaps it was for the best. The fewer names on a *Nature* paper, the better, wouldn't you agree?'

I found myself shaking my head and laughing, in spite of myself.

'And now! The boy is not only back, but the boy is back with a book! And one which is well-reviewed, in all the right places!'

'Yes, I've been fortunate again.'

'Indeed you have. You come back amongst us crowned with laurels. But I would mention some other plants to you.'

'Other plants?'

'Besides the laurels.'

'And what would they be?'

'Poppies, Bonnici! Tall poppies! Remember, this is a society full of chaps who chop. Chaps who like to chop tall poppies down.'

'I'm aware of that.'

'I wonder if you are really aware of just how pervasive the instinct is.'

'I think so.'

'I would watch your step.'

'I shall.'

'You should. You have by no means reached the level where one is unchoppable. Like Richard, of course. Or that old fool Makepeace over there.'

I followed his gaze and saw Sir Dominic at the head of the room, laughing. He was clearly enjoying his party.

'A living example of how a second-rate mind can rise to eminence through assiduously pursuing the administrative minutiae with which no one else is concerned. Publishing his undergraduate lecture course! The nerve of it!'

'I sat through it in the first year.'

'I'm surprised you see fit to come here and take his wine.'

'I was invited by OUP.' I suddenly felt pathetically like confiding my frustration in someone. 'A sort of consolation prize for not having a launch party of my own.'

'What, to let you meet and mingle with the great and good?'

'Sort of. I seem to have missed most of the great and good, though. I got the time wrong, I got here an hour late.'

He looked at me. 'Want to meet Makepeace?'

'Sure.'

He led me across the room calling out, 'Dominic, Dominic!'

Makepeace, a rotund figure, paused, full of beaming benevolence. 'Yes, Marcus?'

'Dominic, I have someone here you must meet. This is Miles Bonnici. He's Andrew Bonnici's son.'

'Really? Well, well. How d'you do, young man?' he said, shaking my hand. 'I sat with your father on the Save British Science committee in the '80s. When the Iron Lady was taking her axe to everything.'

'I remember all that vaguely,' I said. 'I was at school.'

'Young Bonnici here is a fellow author, Dominic,' Maunder said. 'He also has just been published by OUP. But he's not grand enough for a launch party of his own. He's reduced to attending yours.'

Makepeace smiled. 'Really?' he said. 'What have you published?'

'It's a thing on reproductive behaviour,' I said. '*Everything Except Seahorses.*'

'It's been reviewed everywhere,' Maunder said. 'Glowing, glowing reviews. The sort I'm sure you'll be having, Dominic.'

Makepeace's eyes narrowed. 'Ah, so that's you, is it?' he said. 'I hadn't made the connection.'

'You've read it, Dominic?' Maunder said.

'I've glanced through it, yes,' he said. 'So much crosses one's desk, of course ...'

'I hope you like what you glanced through,' I said.

After a pause, to signify that a formal judgement was coming, in which he looked at the floor and looked back up again, he said: 'I thought it, ah, a *clever* little book. You aim at the trick of walking the tightrope between academic seriousness and popular accessibility. The *Selfish Gene* trick which Richard so brilliantly executed. But perhaps it takes a Dawkins to do it properly. A near miss, I would have said.'

You patronising shit, I thought. Maunder was smiling and making a gesture of a man with shears and mouthing at me:

Chop chop. Out loud I said: 'And your own book, how is that doing, may one ask?'

'Oh it's only just hitting the shops,' he said. 'So no sales figures yet. Do take a copy from the table. I'm sure in your case OUP can run to that.'

'Well thanks, but I won't need one,' I said.

'You have it already?'

'I've still got my lecture notes.'

He stared at me for a second, taking in what I had said, then his benevolence vanished and his face tightened. 'Yes, well I'm sure you have someone you want to talk to,' he said, and turned his back, so abruptly that he almost barged into me.

Maunder was still smiling, and now wagging an admonitory finger.

I didn't care. Sod him. Sod them all. I was fed up, and I still didn't have a drink, and by now I was desperate for one, so I threaded my way through the room to the drinks table at the other end, and asked for a glass of white wine, and then there were two young women by my side.

One said: 'You're nice. What do you do?' And before I could reply she said to her companion: 'He's nice, Treen. Waddya think he does?'

'Search me, Jen,' said her friend.

'You think he might be a don? One of those Oxford dons? His name might be Don. He could be Don the don.' She turned to me. 'Are you a don? Don?'

I looked at her. There was an accent. Australian? Short-haired and boyish; she seemed to sway ever so slightly. I sipped my wine and said: 'I'm a behavioural ecologist.'

She looked at me wide-eyed, and hiccupped.

'Although you could say I'm a functional ethologist,' I said. 'At its simplest, I suppose for the past few years I've been a seabird biologist.'

She turned to her friend and hissed: 'Wossesay Treen? Seagulls?'

'Not just gulls,' I said. 'Sea*birds*. Auks in particular. Guillemots a speciality. Although I do razorbills, puffins, you name it.'

'What have you got against seagulls?' she said.

'I have nothing against seagulls,' I said. 'Long live the Laridae, say I.'

'They do a very good job,' she said. 'Eating bits of burger. You know?'

I shook my head. *uni, famous science dad* *being a mean,*

'At the seaside? Those bits of burger people throw away. You get bits of the bun and bits of the meat as well. Seagulls eat'em. Great job they do. What have you got against the poor little bastards? You bastard. You seagull hater.'

I affected a wan smile.

She peered at me. 'Nice smile he's got though, Treen,' she said, 'For a man who wants to kill seagulls.'

'I don't think he actually wants to kill'em, Jen,' said her friend.

'What's your name, seagull killer?' the first woman said.

'I'm Miles,' I said. 'Miles Bonnici. And you must be, Jenny? And Trina, is it?'

'Jesus, Treen, he knows our names.'

'He seems to, Jen.'

'What else d'you know about me, seagull man? What have your gulls been telling you?'

And then before I could think of a reply, she caught hold of my shoulder, slumped against me and said: 'Oh Jesus Treen, it's all going round. I think I need the smallest room in the college.'

'Will you excuse us?' said Trina, detaching Jenny from my shoulder and bearing her off.

'Be my guests,' I said.

'So long, seagull killer,' the one called Jenny shouted over her shoulder. I didn't even think about it. I was consumed with the inequity of the world, with how Sir Dominic bloody Makepeace, look at him, laughing there, great fat fool, with how he might have a launch party at which great names paid him tributes, all for reproducing his undergraduate bloody lecture course, while I, I who had produced something new and original and widely praised, I was offered no such ceremony, no such mark of distinction by Oxford bloody University Press.

Who exactly in OUP takes these decisions? I wondered. Who exactly decides, *he* gets a launch, but *he* doesn't?

And who's above them? Who is there you could appeal to? If you knew them? I had to get to know more people in OUP. That was it. That was the way. I started to drain my wine.

Or maybe, get an agent. I didn't have an agent. I had negotiated the book by myself. I ought to get an agent.

Or maybe get to know more people in OUP.

Maybe both.

I had to do something.

Shit.

I slammed my glass down on the table, pissed off to the back teeth, and left without even saying goodbye to Celia – I did apologise to her later – and brooded on it for the rest of the evening, the unfairness of it, the injustice of it. I went to bed thinking about it. I woke up thinking about it. In fact, I was still thinking about it at ten the next morning when my office phone rang and a voice said: 'Dr Bonnici?'

'Yes?'

'This is Jenny Pittaway at Oxford University Press. I think I was briefly in your company last night. In fact, I fear I was.'

'I'm sorry?'

'I am told I subjected you to a drunken tirade.'

My memory stirred hazily. 'Oh. That was you, was it? The woman who assaulted me?'

'Oh God, I didn't, did I? I didn't actually lay hands on you? And you're one of our authors. God. That compounds the offence.'

'You work for OUP?' A light went on in my brain.

'Not for much longer if I carry on like this.'

'What department are you in?'

'SciMed. Science and Medecine.'

'Are you now? Do you know Celia Thornberry?'

'It's Celia who's just told me what I did.'

'Who else do you know?'

She seemed puzzled by the question. 'Well I suppose I know most people, but not all that well. I haven't been here that long.'

I started to see a way forward. I started to see a contact that might be very useful. So when she said, 'Look Dr Bonnici, I owe you a thousand apologies. I would think of an excuse but I have none, other than chardonnay. So a craven apology it is. I will just have to swear off alcohol,' I said: 'Should we have a drink on that?'

She laughed, surprised. 'That would be very nice.'

'How about this evening?'

'Er, yeah, OK.'

'D'you know Le Petit Blanc? In Walton Street, in Jericho?'

'That's just up from the office.'

'There's a little bar in there.'

'I know it.'

'I'll see you there, at, what? Shall we say seven-thirty?'

'Yeah, OK then, sure,' she said. 'See you there.'

A book launch. Mills meets Jenny – can use her

4

Women had never constituted a major presence in my life. I liked well-bred girls who were presentable, and they seemed to gravitate to me since I was one of their kind, and I wasn't needy and was presentable myself. Now at twenty-eight I had prematurely lost the hair at the front of my head so I cut the rest of it very short, but otherwise I passed muster: I was slim and fit from staying in condition to go up and down the cliffs of Skarholm ringing seabirds without getting killed.

But I'd never been in a serious relationship. In my six years at Aberfair I'd had three girlfriends – I imagine they were the only three Sloaney undergraduates who appeared in the place during my time, two of them doing History of Art and the other doing French – and in each case the liaison followed the same arc, beginning with the start of the academic year in October and coming to an end when I went over to Skarholm for the guillemot breeding season in April, staying through to July. This ending was not always immediately perceived as such by the other party – Tamsin, Ginny and Allegra, in date order – but the three months' island-bound absence, which I was careful to maintain with minimal communication, was invariably enough for my current inamorata to find someone else, or eventually get the message that she'd be better off doing so.

Skarholm was a blessing: the perfect excuse. There was simply no place in my head for anything serious with a woman. Serious was reserved for my work and nothing would get in the way of that; the idea of a partnership in which I would have to make compromises, slacken my focus, was out of the question, while the idea of a pram in the hallway was the ultimate horror. So when I dated, I did so virtually at one remove, offering intelligent company in return for arm candy and sex, but tendering no passion, above all no commitment: I grew adept at diverting commitment requests, direct or disguised. I had never known love, and never wanted to. Still less had I ever known rejection. It was I who did the rejecting.

Strange as it may seem, then, I really was seeking nothing from Jenny Pittaway that evening other than inside information about her employers, information which should not take long to procure, which was why I'd arranged to meet her in the bar of the restaurant for a drink rather than book a table for dinner; but a couple of surprises awaited me, the first almost the moment she came through the door, in a yellow tailored suit.

'Dr Bonnici?'

I stood up. 'It's Miles.'

'Jenny Pittaway.'

We shook hands. 'I really do have to apologise profoundly once again,' she said sitting down. 'I would say I dunno what got into me, except that I do. Chardonnay. 'Tis an ignoble grape.'

I said: 'It wasn't anything, forget it. You're from Australia?'

'New Zealand.'

'How long have you worked for OUP?'

'Nine months, going on.'

'And you're on the science side? Strange I haven't seen you in there. I think I would probably have noticed you.'

For that was the first surprise. I hadn't taken it in the night before, but she had a fresh youthful beauty that a certain tomboyish spirit only added to. It didn't set my heart racing – nothing did – but she was certainly good-looking. I nodded to the barman. I said: 'You're very brown.'

'Just come back from holiday.'

'Where've you been?'

'Lipari.'

'Where's that?'

'You know the Aeolian islands? The home of the winds?'

'Where are they?'

'In the Med, north of Sicily. Lipari, Stromboli, Vulcano ...'

'Never heard of them, I'm afraid.'

'Not many Brits have. Germans have, though. Full of Germans. And Italians, of course.'

'And are they, erm' – I waved my hand – 'attractive? *Nice*?'

'Oh, they're wonderful. You like islands?'

I smiled faintly and shook my head. 'Too much of a busman's holiday for me. I've spent much of the last six years on one.'

'Where was that?'

'Skarholm.'

'*Skahrum*? Don't know it.'

'It's off the coast of Wales.'

'What's it like?'

'I don't know that it's *like* anything. It's just a lump of rock in the sea. To me, it's just a laboratory work bench.'

'It must have some distinguishing characteristics.'

'Well, it has cliffs, that seabirds breed on, and it has a house where the researchers live. People such as myself. And the boat comes out from the mainland on days when the weather permits.'

'Doesn't it have a *feel*?'

'A feel?'

'A special atmosphere. Most islands have a special feel, an atmosphere of their own.'

'Why're you so interested?'

'I love islands. I sort of collect them. I more or less island-hopped my way to Britain at the start of my OE.'

'Your what?'

'Sorry. Kiwi expression. It's our Overseas Experience. It's what we all feel we have to do back in New Zealand before we settle down to become farmers' wives.'

'And where did you hop to?'

'Let me see, Bali. Penang. The Maldives. Zanzibar. Then to Mykonos, and a whole pile more in the Aegean. I had the idea of doing all the islands in the Odyssey, finishing with Ithaca. I'd really like to go to Ithaca. I've got a lot of sympathy with Penelope. But I never got round to it.'

I wasn't really interested in all this. I said: 'Tell me about OUP. You like it?'

She said: 'They're pretty good employers. It's a very interesting place to work. It's one of the world's great imprints, after all.'

'Where are you in the organisation?'

'Pretty junior. I'm an editorial assistant. What I want to do, is make the jump to assistant commissioning editor. Then I'll have my foot on the ladder.'

I said: 'Take me up the ladder. Tell me who's who at each stage.'

So Jenny delivered as best she could a verbal organigram of OUP, from her own level right up to that of the Secretary, as the Chief Executive was historically called, and I made a careful mental note of who seemed to be the key figures, and who might repay some cultivation, and then she said: 'What's your own experience of them been? I'd be interested to know.'

'They've been OK.'

She said: 'Well I think they've done you proud with your book. It looks great. I enjoyed it, by the way.'

And that was the second surprise. 'You've read it?'

'I have, yeah. I liked it a lot.'

'What did you like about it?'

'The subject was absorbing. I had no idea there was that much freelance shagging going on in the world. And you write entertainingly. I think you got the balance just right between the serious, I mean the academic, and the popular.'

I looked rather more closely at her. 'That was the whole idea. Except that prat whose party we were both at last night said just the opposite.'

'Well he's a nonentity, isn't he, Makepeace? We're only publishing him because of his connections. That's common gossip in the office.'

I said: 'Look, we could have dinner if you like. If they've got a table. Looks like they might have.'

'That would be lovely,' she said. 'But first I must find the loo.'

Contemplating with approval her retreating form, I began to think this might turn out to be more than an information-gathering exercise, so when we were seated, and we had the menu, I said: 'Shall we have a bottle of wine?'

'I dunno. Wadda you think?'

'Why not?'

'As long as it's not chardonnay, then, which is a detestable grape. Smells of peas. I didn't want to drink it at all, last night.'

'Why did you?'

'Wasn't anything else.'

I laughed. 'Then what would you like?'

'Well if they've got a Kiwi white sauvignon that'd be great. You realise my little country makes the best white sauvignon in the world? Goodbye, Sancerre. Hello, Cloudy Bay. You ever had Cloudy Bay? If they've got that on the list, that would be terrific.'

They didn't, but they had another one, and when we had ordered, and the sauvignon had been sipped and I had agreed it was excellent, Jenny said: 'Someone in the office said your dad was a Nobel Prize winner.'

'He was, yes.' I told her about Andrew Bonnici, about his glittering career at Imperial, and the Bonnici effect and his Nobel, and his Reith lectures which made him a national figure.

She said: 'But what was it like to have a Nobel Prize winner as your dad?'

I paused. I measured my words. 'Good and bad, I suppose.'

'Why good?'

'Because I...I admired him. He was the reason I became a scientist.'

'Did it help with your career?'

'Not really. I'm in an area he knew nothing about, animal behaviour. He didn't see it as important. He thought physics was the only real science. He would have preferred me to become a physicist.'

'Why didn't you?'

'I suppose I might well have done, but I stumbled across evolutionary biology. It just seemed a whole lot more exciting. The gene-centric revolution. The paradigm shift. Physics sort of seems to be finished, don't you think? Just discovering tinier and tinier particles, unless they can make fusion work, which doesn't seem to be possible.'

Jenny said: 'What was the bad side? Of your dad being a Nobel winner?'

I weighed the words again. I wasn't going to say what I really felt. I said: 'I suppose... he wasn't fantastic at... parenting, really. Always in his lab, or at meetings, and when he was home he was reading papers. So it was my mother who more or less brought us up.'

'Us?'

'I've got a sister, Lotte.'

'How old's she?'

'Twenty-five.'

'Same as me,' said Jenny. 'What does she do? She a scientist too?'

'Far from it. She's a...sort of singer? But she does...she recites things, as well. Comic songs. She writes them. I don't quite know how to describe it properly.'

'She got a recording contract or anything?'

'Not that I'm aware of. I think she's more or less a struggling performer. I'm not that close to her, to be honest. What about you, your family?'

She said: 'What about your mum?'

'She's just my mother. She's always been there. Tell me about you.'

Jenny told me she came from Auckland, her father was a family doctor, her mother was a teacher who had grown up in England, and she had a brother who was twenty-two. They were all passionate sailors. 'We're yachties,' she said. 'Half of Auckland is. We sail every weekend. I miss it a lot. I like Oxford, but the thing I don't like's being so landlocked. Suppose that's one of the reasons I love islands. There's sea all around you. In Auckland, you're on an isthmus, you've got an ocean on each side.'

She told me she had a science background: she had done a biological sciences degree at Auckland Uni and had nearly gone on to do a Master's but at the last minute decided to go travelling instead. After her island-hopping she had come to London – 'to a house in Shepherd's Bush with 16 other Kiwis, get back after midnight and somebody new was in your bed' – and had got a job as a copy editor with a small scientific publishing company; eventually the opportunity with OUP came up, and it was too good to miss, even though it meant leaving friends in London.

Then she asked me about my own time at Oxford, and I told her about being an undergraduate, and now being back as a Research Fellow, and dinner came, and it was good, and we drank down our bottle of sauvignon, which Jenny couldn't help but drink rather more of than me, which in turn started to free her from any inhibitions with which she might have started the evening.

In particular she was fascinated by the tale of Arty Booboo.

'Arty Booboo the supershagger,' she said. 'Wow. What an idea. Fantastic. And you spent how long watching him?'

'Six years.'

'Didn't you get horny watching all that sex?'

'My dear Madam, it is not really possible to get horny, as you put it, in a wooden bird hide on the top of a 200-foot cliff.'

'I wonder,' she said, smiling. 'So what's he like, Arty? Is he a good-looking guy? I mean, if you're a guillemot girl – has he got what it takes?'

'Undoubtedly.'

'You got a photo?'

'Not on me. Maybe I should have. But I've got a photo of him on the wall, at home. Just round the corner, in fact. You like to see it?'

It was the moment where things shifted. But she didn't miss a beat. 'Sure,' she said.

We walked back together in the cool night air and she asked me how long I had had the house and I told her I had bought it in the summer when I knew I was coming back to Oxford and had only moved in three weeks earlier.

While I was making the coffee she noticed the piano. 'You play?' she called, fingering the keys.

'I do, yes,' I said as I came in with the tray. 'That's the one thing my sister and I have in common.'

Jenny said: 'So where's Arty?'

I pointed to the chimneybreast and the framed picture, hung in pride of place above the mantelpiece.

She peered. 'But that's the front page of *Nature*.'

'That's right. He's the cover story.'

She read the headline: *Extra-pair copulation in a seabird is adaptive*. 'So you wrote a paper about him?'

'Sure did.'

'And it made the cover?'

'Well it was pretty ground-breaking, really. It proved all sex had a purpose.'

She gazed on him.

I came up by her.

'So that's Arty Booboo?'

'It is.'

'The champion shagger?'

'That is indeed him.'

She turned to me with mischief in her eyes. 'And how do you compare?'

'What d'you mean?'

'In the shagging department.'

I said: 'Would you like me to show you?'

We fell together on the sofa, hungrily locking mouths, grappling with buttons and zips, and I slid down the skirt of that yellow tailored suit and her tights and I slid into her quickly and she cried out, and then I whispered 'Let's do this properly' and I picked her up and carried her to the bedroom, and finished what I had started, to my entire satisfaction. Then we lay there, and sleep descended.

In the morning I realised that Jenny Pittaway was very self-possessed, because I found she had gone, without waking me. She left a note which said: *Thanks both for a great evening (you and Arty B)*.

I looked at it with complacency. Yeah, I was cool. And she recognised that. Perhaps I would see her again. Although I don't think I'd have been as keen to learn that Jenny was not as impressed with me as I was myself.

She referred to me, to her friend Trina, a secretary at OUP who also came from New Zealand, as 'Captain Seagull.'

'Guess what I did last night, Treen?' (She told me this much later.)

'What, Jen?'

'Only the deed of darkness with Cap'n Seagull.'

'You never?'

'I did too.'

'What was it like?'

'He's got a nice body, he keeps himself fit, but I'll tell you, for someone who's making a name for himself writing about shagging, he could do with a few lessons in that department.'

'Yeah?'

'Talk about over quickly! A girl is left panting for more.'

'You tell him?'

'He's not really the sort of bloke you can say that to. He's all brain. But he's got nice manners, I'll give him that. And he's probably gonna be famous.'

'You think it's going anywhere, Jen?'

'Nah. Just a one-night stand. Bastard's too pleased with himself.'

I think she was surprised therefore, when I rang her three days later and said, 'Look, there's a concert on Friday in the Holywell Music Room, it's the Vivaldi concerto for two mandolins which is very appealing. I wondered if you might like to come?'

She said: 'Yes, I would, Miles. Yes. Thanks very much.'

And we went, and we enjoyed it, and we went for a pizza afterwards, and talked some more, and we went back to the house in Jericho and went to bed in a civilised rhythm this time, and made love, and she was sweet to me, and did not leave in the early morning, and we spent Saturday together, and arranged to meet the following weekend; and so, as autumn came to Oxford, and the honeyed stone glowed in the soft October sun, Jenny Pittaway and I started to go out together.

Miles meets Jenny

5

The notion of riding for a fall was one which in all my life had never occurred to me; the very concept was alien. The value I held highest was intelligence, and I had a supreme confidence in my own, so there were no cracks whatsoever running through my self-belief. That I might be about to topple over a cliff into a psychic chasm was not only something I did not expect, it was something I was simply unable to conceive of; and in such cases, of course, the toppling is the more precipitous, the chasm all the deeper.

Certainly, there was no sign whatsoever of precipices when Jenny and I began dating, that Michaelmas term, for it all proceeded smoothly enough: I would ring her on a Thursday, and we would go out on the Friday night, to a concert or a movie and then to dinner, and Jenny stayed over; we would sometimes spend the weekend together, driving into the Cotswolds in my Mini Cooper. Neither of us made demands on the other. I suppose the way I saw it was as a working exchange: Jenny was offering me her beauty and her sexuality, which were considerable, and in return I was offering her my status, which wasn't a bad status. *Seahorses* sold well; the American publishing deal was done; and as I got down to work at the Niko Tinbergen Institute and started to plan my research project on female promiscuity. I realised I could make it the basis for a follow-up book on female sexuality in general, which would be another great success and further confirm my position, as I saw it, as the hottest young evolutionary biologist on the planet.

But there was something else as well: I offered Jenny Oxford. For I was not simply stuck in the small office I had been granted in the zoology building; I had renewed my acquaintance with my old college. I had applied for and been granted a Junior Research Fellowship at Pembroke, which was non-stipendiary – there was no money attached – but it did give me dining rights, for lunch in the Senior Common Room and dinner in hall. It meant I could show Jenny Pembroke, and hence Oxford, from the inside, and she loved it. I showed her everything: I pointed out the high window of my undergraduate rooms, and told her how cold it was in the winter and how I had huddled next to the electric fire writing my essays on group selection and kin selection for John Krebs my tutor, and how it looked out at Tom Tower in Christ Church across the road. I showed her Pembroke's ancient quads and its baroque chapel and its Victorian gothic hall, and told her of its alumni, with Dr Johnson of course the most celebrated, but also John Pym who had started the Civil War and Michael Heseltine who had brought down Margaret Thatcher and JR Tolkien who had written the first two books of *Lord of The Rings* when he was a Pembroke Fellow (and I made her laugh when I told her of CS Lewis's legendary response to the second volume, as in Not Another Fucking Elf.) I showed her the Turf Tavern where Bill Clinton did not inhale, which to my astonishment she had never discovered, and which she took to instantly. Most of all I delighted her when towards the end of term I took her as a surprise to Formal Hall – as a guest to dinner at High Table with the Fellows, myself included, in our gowns, and the Latin grace, and the college silver glowing in the candlelight, and the white Burgundy and the Claret and at the end the decanters of Port and Madeira and Sauternes and the snuff in its silver box passed around the table under Dr Johnson's portrait, and she talked about New Zealand wines to the world expert on slime moulds who was sitting on one side of her, and about the Middle East peace process to the young woman Arabist on her other side. I think she felt then that despite her position at OUP, she had seen an Oxford she would never have experienced without me, and she repaid me when I took her to the zoology department Christmas party the following week and in that gathering of t-shirts and jeans she turned every head in a simple but stunning dress of cobalt blue, and had people looking at me in a different way, thus gratifying my self-regard even further (although I have to say everybody liked her).

We left the party and went back to bed that night the nearest we had been, I suppose, to being openly happy together. Not that I had the slightest inclination to say so. Yet there was a warmth in our lovemaking that was perhaps something more than the formal sexual intercourse we – maybe that should be I – had been engaging in for the previous eight weeks. Perhaps it was the fact that she was leaving the next morning to spend Christmas with her family in New Zealand, which gave the moment a different dynamic. Perhaps it was her own gratitude for an entertaining autumn (Jenny was always big on gratitude.) Perhaps it was my own sense of boosted self-esteem.

But that was it, that bit of warmth. In the morning we exchanged Christmas presents and wished each other well, in the friendliest way possible, and Jenny went off for her thirty-hour flight and I went back to my home in Wimbledon, and we agreed we would meet in the New Year. There were to be no missing-you phone calls. Not even on Christmas Day.

Looking back, I think it was all – how can I put this? – curiously poised. I had enjoyed Jenny, but only as I had enjoyed every other woman who had come into my life: superficially. I had no intention of allowing things to deepen, and in the back of my mind I was already starting to envisage an exit strategy. Yet Jenny was no more needy and no more seeking involvement than I was, she was just taking everything as it came, and watching, and waiting, and what she was perhaps waiting for arrived in the New Year when she came back two days early – she found her ticket wouldn't let her stop off in Singapore as she had hoped – and in the Pizza Express in Oxford city centre she saw me with Poppy McLennan.

I had been a nerdy undergraduate and had by no means been considered cool by Poppy, in my year at Pembroke reading English, who was as cool as they come, outspoken, brilliant and a beauty who did not let her radical feminism get in the way of showing off her legs, which were sensational. But things had changed. As Poppy had got her First and then, like me, her doctorate, and now was a lecturer with a Pembroke English Fellowship, we were colleagues in the SCR and broke bread together; and she saw that I was a different proposition, with a book out which was a critical success, from the geek of six years before. Over the Michaelmas term a frisson grew up between us, the beginnings of a flirtation; and while (as I thought) Jenny was still away, I took it a stage further with an invitation to lunch. Would it have led to anything? I don't know. It didn't that day, but I can't put my hand on my heart and say it was innocent. It was an option for the future. Certainly, as a lunch it was flirtatious, its terms underlined by Poppy's garb, a long dark Russian greatcoat which she discarded to reveal a miniskirt making her famous legs visible from the moon, it seemed to me, and they were visible at once to Jenny when she came into the restaurant with her shopping bags and caught sight of us from the porch, without being seen herself, and took in the body language and the frisson, instantly and unmistakeably.

Some women might have launched into a confrontation, there and then. Jenny knew a better way. She slipped out, still unseen. And (she told me much later) she phoned Trina.

'Trouble with Captain Seagull, Treen.'

'What's that then, Jen?'

'Bastard's cheating on me. Thought he might, sooner or later. Saw him in town all lovey-dovey with some tarty-looking bimbo.'

'Really? What you gonna do about it?'

'His balls, Treen.'

'Yeah?'

'They'll have to come off.'

Trina said: 'What a girl's gotta do, a girl's gotta do.'

She waited in perfect equanimity for two days until the Thursday, when I called her as arranged, and when we had said Hello, and Happy New Year, and I asked where she would like to meet up for the weekend, she said: 'Sorry Miles, can't make it. I'm doing something else.'

I was surprised. And irritated. I said: 'What are you doing that's so special then?'

Jenny said: 'Not doing anything special, I'm just doing something different from seeing you.'

I was put out. I said: 'Well, shall I call you next week?'

Jenny said: 'Miles, listen. Please don't take this the wrong way. But – well – at the end of the day I don't think you're really my type of guy.'

'What d'you mean?'

'Well, I look for certain things in a guy, and it's just, you're not for me, that's all.'

'What things?'

'Well, I wouldn't want to go into all that.'

'So – so – what are you saying?'

'I'm saying, Miles, I think it's time for bye byes.'

'You mean – you think we should finish?'

'That's the general idea.'

I was taken aback. I said: 'This is a bit sudden, isn't it?'

'These things are best that way, don't you think?'

Jenny could hear my astonished silence, and into it she said: 'No point in agonising about it, is there? So long, Miles, and er, thanks for all the fish, as it were.' Then she hung up.

I called back five minutes later.

I said: 'Jenny, this is somewhat premature, surely? I thought we were rather enjoying each other's company? Weren't we?'

'All good things must come to an end, Miles.'

'I thought we had the beginnings of a good relationship there.'

'Did we?'

'I mean, have I done anything to, to spoil it?'

'I don't know, Miles. Have you?'

'Not that I can think of.'

'Well there you are, then. You don't need to blame yourself, do you? It's purely me. I just feel like a change, old boy. You can understand that, can't you?'

'Well no I can't, actually.'

'I can't do anything about that, Miles.'

'Is there…is there anybody else?'

'Ah come on, Miles, that's hardly a fair question, is it?'

I said: 'Will you reconsider?'

Jenny said: 'Fraid not. These conversations don't go anywhere, you know. They just go round in circles. So all the best now, and thanks.'

Bewildered, I said: 'Yes. Very well.'

She called Trina.

'Cap'n Seagull's balls, Treen.'

'Oh yeah?'

'Snip snip.'

'They're off?'

'Certainly are.'

'How's he taking it?'

'Not a happy bunny.'

Trina said: 'Nice one, Jen.'

At that moment, although I didn't realise it immediately, my life, my carefully-planned and hitherto efficiently-directed life, came off the rails. After putting down the phone I felt strange. Something had ceased to be right in my head, as if there were something I had forgotten, but I couldn't remember what. Or, it felt as if there were a stone in my shoe. Which I couldn't remove.

Or something in my eye.

Or something.

I paced up and down and found I was breathing heavily, and then I found I was sweating, and this shocked me and made me more unsettled still. I sat down in front of the TV and flicked through the channels and switched it off again. I did not like television. I liked music. I went through the CDs until I found

Schubert's 5th and put on the first movement, which was the most serene and calming piece of music I knew, and after about a minute I got up and turned it off and went into the kitchen to make myself a coffee. As the kettle boiled I realised I did not want a coffee. I wanted a whisky.

I went to the pub on the corner and ordered a double whisky and drank it off, and then another, and then a third, and then I went back home and sat down on the sofa, trembling. I remember looking at my shaking hand. And I got up and went back to the pub and drank more whiskies until I lost count and staggered back and fell onto the sofa into a coma.

The next day I woke late, almost at noon, and after a few seconds I realised there was something wrong, and at first I could not remember what; and then I remembered that what was wrong, was that things were not right. I felt I could not raise my head, as if I had been sapped of all my strength; it was as if I had flu. Eventually I forced myself up and stood under the shower for five minutes and I got dressed and walked in to the department.

I had important work to do: at the start of the following week was the NTI conference. In January every year the Niko Tinbergen Institute held a symposium on animal behaviour which attracted specialists from far and wide and was very popular with the zoology undergraduates. This year the focus of attention was on me; on the basis of my work and the synthesis of it that *Seahorses* represented I had been asked, as a new member of the NTI, to give the opening address.

It wasn't terribly difficult but it was a signal honour and it was something you had to get right; you were being judged by a very critical audience of your peers. I was going to present an overview of the latest studies on extra-pair copulation in apparently monogamous creatures – on animal adultery, if you like – and indicate where the research might be heading. I had most of the talk sketched out but I hadn't yet done the introduction, and this is what I sat down to begin, that morning, with my head in a strange place.

I opened up the PC and I began to write: *Of all the developments in animal behaviour studies in recent years...*

I paused.

I typed: *Jenny.*

I looked at it.

Then I copied it and rapidly pasted it five times.

Jenny.

Jenny.

Jenny.
Jenny.
Jenny.
Then I deleted it.

I got up and went out into the corridor. I walked down to the common room and got a coffee from the machine, and I bumped into Roger de Vries, the professor who was the NTI director, and he asked me how things were going and I said OK, and he said: 'You all right, Miles? Look a bit distracted.'

'I'm OK. Bit under the weather. Bit fluey, that's all.'

'Be all right for Monday, I hope? Counting on you to give a stellar performance.'

'I'll be fine.'

Back in my office I sat down at the PC. Then I stood up. I walked around the room and sat down once more. I said out loud: 'Come on. For Christ's sake. Get a grip.' I started again and began to write: *Of all the developments in animal behaviour studies in recent years, one of the most important has been the discovery, through the use of molecular techniques, that extra-pair paternity is very prevalent even amongst apparently monogamous organisms.*

Then I wrote: *Jenny.*

And I did it again:

Jenny.
Jenny.
Jenny.
Jenny.
Jenny.

I stood up. I said out loud: 'This is no fucking good. Sod this.'

I shut the PC down, took my coat and I headed out of the building, meeting Roger de Vries on the way again who said: 'Hey Miles really, are you OK?' and I said I was feeling a bit grim, fluey, you know, and I was going home to shake it off.

'You do that,' he said. 'Go on. You go home and get better for Monday.'

I walked, then. I walked in a great clockwise parabola around Oxford, down St Cross Road and Longwall Street and then along the High and up Cornmarket Street to the Randolph Hotel, and then on past Worcester and up Walton Street and although part of me pretended I was walking aimlessly just to get my head straight, really of course I knew I was never going anywhere other than the great classical façade of Oxford University Press, where I stopped and gazed and a voice in my head said: *Jenny is in there.*

I stood in the street for fully twenty minutes watching people come and go and the voice in my head said, *Jenny might come out and you can talk to her.* But it was mid-afternoon. The staff weren't leaving. And gradually on that darkening winter's day the cold got to me, and hunger, as I had had nothing to eat for twenty-four hours, and some sort of rationality returned and I muttered to myself, What are you doing, standing here like a dork? For Christ's sake, Miles, get a grip. And I went back home, which was only ten minutes' walk away in Jericho, and made an omelette and forced myself to eat it.

I think that if at that moment I had someone I could talk to, things might have been different. But I didn't do friendship. I never had. I had colleagues and acquaintances, but I had not a single true friend with whom I might have talked about what was afflicting me; so then began a struggle of a kind I had never encountered before, in which I was alone.

I sat down on the sofa and tried to make myself think it through.

I felt very...troubled? Was that the word for it?

Why did I feel troubled?

Because Jenny had ended it with me, obviously. Without giving any good reason. Why didn't she give me a reason? Maybe she was seeing someone else.

That thought was suddenly intolerable, and I jumped up and walked around the room, breathing heavily.

Then I sat down again.

Come on, Miles.

I thought it through. We were OK when she left, weren't we? We were fine. And she had only just come back from New Zealand. The very night before. She wouldn't have had time to meet someone else, surely?

Then why?

But it didn't matter, did it? What mattered was, what was I going to do about it.

Well, I couldn't ask her again. I had already asked her twice and she had said No. So I was stuck with it. I was stuck with it, and I had to beat it, and not let it beat me.

I said out loud: 'Come on, Miles. You have to beat this.'

And I began, then, that Friday evening, a mental effort like no other mental effort I had undertaken, which essentially was the use of my intelligence to overcome my emotions. I swore I would be single-minded in the enterprise, and I made a conscious decision that I would not go back to alcohol, that I would simply live with the ache, the great ache that seemed to infuse itself through my spirit, and over the next two days by sheer willpower I managed to get back to work and I wrote out the introduction to my conference address, and by the Sunday evening I knew I would be OK.

It had been touch and go at times.

But I'd be all right.

There were lots of familiar faces the next day at the conference registration session and the morning coffee which followed it. There was Crispin Timmins from Cambridge, who was emerging as the guy to watch in dung fly studies, and Axel Christiansen from Copenhagen who had proved that, against all expectations, mute swans when pair-bonded really were faithful to each other – that had made everybody sit up and take notice – and most notably there was Jasper Bakker from Groningen who had done fascinating work on great tits and was the nearest thing I had to a direct rival.

He was tall, and a natty dresser in black-rimmed square spectacles; he was only a couple of years older than me, and had been the young prince of evolutionary biology until I came along, so naturally he hated me, although he was far too smooth to be open about it. False bonhomie was his speciality, at our every meeting. 'Miles, Miles!' he gushed, slapping me on the back as we bumped into each other by the coffee table. 'Just one success after another! The rest of us can't keep up!' We shook hands, and he said, there's talk you're doing something on female mate choice and I said, you don't want to believe everything you hear, Jasper, and under my breath, *you sneaky shit.* There were many more academics, as well as what seemed like the whole student population of the zoology department, pale-faced and earnest, and people said Hello, or Hi Miles, and if they were generous-hearted they said congratulations on the book, and if they were jealous or mean-minded they didn't, although even if they didn't they of course all knew about it, and had almost certainly read it, and wondered why they hadn't thought of doing it themselves.

I was amongst my peers. My hyper-intelligent, my hyper-ambitious, my hyper-critical peers. And at five to ten we all trooped chattering into one of the zoology department lecture theatres.

I had forgotten how deep it was. It was a pit, with rows of seats climbing steeply up in a semi-circle from the platform at the bottom. I had sat there as a student a hundred times and never really registered this depth because I was above, looking down, but now that I was on the bottom looking up, sitting on the platform with Roger de Vries who was speaking to open the conference and open the meeting and introducing me, it seemed… a little daunting.

All those faces. Looking down at me. I could see Jasper Bakker, near the bottom, with his bespectacled eyes. They seemed to be boring into me.

Anyway.

'So we've asked him if he can start things off,' Roger de Vries was saying, 'by giving us an overview of his area, which focuses on sperm competition in pair-bonded organisms. Miles, over to you.'

Everybody clapped, and I stood up. I said: 'Thank you Roger, for that generous introduction, and let me say that being asked to give this presentation is indeed a privilege. First, though, I would like to echo what Roger has just said about the value of the NTI conference as a potential source of opportunities for future research, because one of these meeting sparked my own post-graduate career when I heard a presentation from Callum McSorley of Aberfair about guillemot reproductive biology on Skarholm. Callum can't be here this year, incidentally, because he's in Antarctica looking at penguins. He can't keep away from the cold. Maybe cos he's a Scotsman.'

The audience smiled.

I took a sip from the glass of water on the lectern.

I looked at the expectant faces.

And I began.

I said: 'Of all the developments in animal behaviour in recent years, and there have of course been a great deal, one of the most noteworthy, and most important, has been Jenny.'

I stopped.

I tried to get my head around what I had just said.

I was confused.

Somebody in the audience said: 'What?'

Roger de Vries was looking at me and mouthing: 'You OK?'

I said: 'Sorry. Sorry Roger.' I had started to sweat. I laughed. I took a gulp from the glass of water. I said: 'Sorry everybody. Bit of a brainstorm. Let me start again.'

I looked at the rows of faces. They were boring into me, indeed.

I cleared my throat and I said: 'As I was saying – of all the developments in animal behaviour studies in recent years, and there have of course been many, one of the most significant and noteworthy has been the *discovery*, through the use of molecular techniques, that extra-pair paternity is very prevalent even among apparently monogamous organisms' – that was better, getting into my stride now – 'in fact far more so than was suspected even by such well-known pioneers of sperm competition studies as Bob Trivers, Geoff Parker and Jenny Pittaway.'

Jasper Bakker said: 'Who?'

I had begun the next sentence, saying 'The full force of this discovery...' when I registered the whispering: somebody was hissing 'Who's he say?' and somebody else was saying 'What?' and a restlessness was running across the audience like a wind across the surface of a lake.

I stopped.

'What?' I said, looking around me. My mouth felt dry.

Roger de Vries was himself loudly whispering to me 'Miles, ARE YOU OK?'

'Sure,' I said. 'Be fine. Be fine.'

I took another drink. I looked up and said: 'Sorry about this. Third time lucky, eh?' I cleared my throat and I said rapidly: 'Of all the developments in animal behaviour studies in recent years and there have of course been many one of the most significant has been the discovery through the use of molecular techniques that extra-pair paternity is very prevalent even amongst apparently monogamous organisms in fact far more so than was suspected even by such well-known pioneers of sperm competition studies as Bob Trivers, Geoff Parker and Callum McSorley.' I took another sip of water. Should be all right now. I went on: 'The full force of this discovery is being widely felt and is causing a revolution in our thinking, in fact it is putting a very significant question mark over the whole notion of her ending it, without giving any good reason.'

I stopped again. I sensed I had said something wrong, without being quite sure what.

What had I said, exactly?

A muttering was growing in the audience.

Roger de Vries was on his feet and he came over to me. 'Miles,' he said.

'Hot in here,' I said.

He took my arm. 'Miles, I don't think you're quite up to this, are you? Let's go outside and sit down.' And he said quickly into the microphone: 'I'm sorry about this, ladies and gentlemen, but I happen to know that Miles was quite ill last week, and I think it's obvious he might have come back a little too soon. We'll resume in a few minutes.'

I still remember the embarrassed murmur that accompanied our leaving the platform and the lecture theatre. It was the worst sound I had ever heard in my life.

Outside Roger sat me down. He said: 'Miles, you're really not well, are you?' He was kindly, and concerned.

I was sweating, and breathing heavily. 'Jesus, I'm sorry Roger,' I said. 'Reckon it's this bug. Thought I'd shaken it off. Obviously haven't.'

'Don't worry about it, Miles. Forget the conference. These things happen. Go home and get well, and don't come back to work until you feel absolutely OK. You want me to get you a taxi?'

'No thanks, I'll be fine. I'd rather walk. It'll clear my head.'

'You sure?'

'I'm sure.'

As Roger de Vries slipped back into the lecture theatre and I remained outside with what he was telling the bemused audience was my flu, I felt for the first time in my life something approaching panic.

It was not just that I had screwed up in public, and I would be an object of derision, or even worse, an object of pity for my peers; it was that I had lost control. I had tried to conquer my emotions with my intelligence, and the emotions had won, and they were trampling all over me and I did not know how to fight them any more. It left me feeling that I was tumbling, tumbling wildly downwards, and as I staggered out of the zoology building into the rainy January morning and headed back to Jericho I knew what I wanted more than anything: for the pub to open at lunchtime. When it did, I drank three double whiskies in quick succession, and then slowed down with a sandwich, and drank steadily until closing time at 3pm and went home and fell onto the sofa and slept.

I woke in the middle of the night. I opened a bottle of wine and drank it and fell asleep until lunchtime the following day, when I went back to the pub and drank myself silly once again. It was midnight when the phone started to ring. I gradually started to hear it. I had been sick down my shirt and peed into my trousers. I looked at the vomit on my shirt front. The phone kept ringing. I tried to grab it, and knocked it over. Then I picked it up and said: 'Yeah?'

'Miles?' A distant, crackly voice.

'Yeah?'

'It's Callum. Callum McSorley.'

'Oh hi, Callum.'

'What happened?'

'What?'

'What happened? At the NTI? Ah heard it all went wrong. Somebody thought I ought to know.'

'Where are you?'

'I'm on the fucking Antarctic peninsula, laddie. On the sat phone. Haven't got long. Tell me what happened.'

'I screwed up, Callum. I screwed up my presentation at the conference.'

'Why?'

'They think I've got flu.'

'And have ye?'

'No.'

'So what's the problem, then?'

'It's a girl, Callum.'

'A girl?'

'A girl who left me.'

'Ah didn't think you were ever that bothered about women.'

'Spose this one's different.'

'So what's the situation now?'

'I've been drinking. Ever since I screwed up.'

'But what's the situation with the girl?'

'I dunno.'

'Have ye talked to her?'

'No.'

'Why not?

'Don't think it's any use.'

'Miles, if she means that much to you, ye've got to talk to her, you hear me? Can ye hear me?'

'I can hear you, Callum.'

'Listen Miles, will ye talk to her?'

' 'F you say so.'

'I do say so. Ah want ye to talk to her. And I want ye to stop drinking. Can ye do that? Can ye do that for me?'

'Yes, Callum.'

'And listen Miles. This is important. Ah want ye to remember this. You're one of the best young scientists in the world. OK?'

'OK.'

'Ah mean it. You're one of the best young scientists in the world. What are you?'

'One of the best young scientists in the world.'

'That's right. You are. Now will ye stop drinking?'

'Yes.'

'And will ye talk to this girl?'

'I will.'

'You promise?'

'I promise.'

'I'll see you when ah get back. Will ye remember what ah've said?'

'I will, Callum. I will.'

That was the turning point; that was the lucky break which I had done absolutely nothing to deserve and owed entirely to Callum McSorley and who he was. But it was enough. His words, and I suppose, the fact of his concern, penetrated the fug of my feelings, and I got up and sat in the bath for half an hour, periodically running a cold shower over my head; and then I shaved, and put on clean clothes, and made myself beans on toast, and tried to think straight.

I would approach Jenny. I would. I felt that in a sense I had nothing more to lose because I had lost everything, certainly in terms of self-control. But if I was going to do it, I wanted to talk to her properly. I didn't want to ring her and have her just hang up the phone, and I didn't want to go to her flat and have her not let me in. So I would approach her in the street. I would meet her as she came out of OUP after work. At about 5.30. I would do it the very next day, which was Wednesday.

But Jenny wasn't there. At 4.45, as dark fell, I planted myself outside the Corinthian columns of the gatehouse, shivering with nerves on the other side of the road, and waited till 6.15 as scores and scores of OUP staff came out, but no Jenny Pittaway. I did it on the Thursday, even more nervous, with the same result, and I started to feel very upset; and I did it on the Friday, and something unpleasant happened. At about 5.30 a police car drew up and a young PC – he seemed to be about 12 – got out and came over to me and said: 'Excuse me, sir, what are you doing here?'

'I'm waiting for someone,' I said.

'What's your name?' he said.

'Miles Bonnici.'

'What d'you do?'

'I'm an academic. At the University.'

'Got any ID?'

'Not on me.'

'You've been here for several nights, haven't you?'

'I have, yes.'

'We've had a report that you're acting suspiciously.'

'I'm just waiting for someone.'

'And who are you waiting for?'

'Miss Pittaway.'

"And who is she?'

'She works in there.'

'And does she know you're waiting for her?'

And it all happened in an instant: before I could answer him I saw her, I saw Jenny come out of the gate and I cried: 'She's there!' and I darted across the road crying 'Jenny!' with the PC in tow and she stopped and turned and said, 'Oh hello Miles.' The policeman came up. He said to Jenny: 'You know this man, Miss?'

'I do, yes.'

'Everything all right?'

'Everything's fine, officer.'

'OK,' he said, looking at me suspiciously. 'OK then.' And he walked back to his car and drove away.

'What was that about?' said Jenny.

'I've been waiting for you,' I said. 'For the last few nights. I think somebody rang them up.'

'I've been in Edinburgh,' she said. 'So why have you been waiting for me?'

'I wanted to ask you something.'

'What?'

'Will you come back to me?'

Jenny seemed startled. She stared at me, she stared at me hard, and did not reply.

I wasn't at my best. I said: 'I haven't been sleeping. I can't work. Everything has fallen apart. All I can think of is you. Will you come back?'

Jenny said: 'Well I don't know, Miles. I don't know.'

'Then can we talk about it? Can we have a proper talk?'

'I'm not sure.' She looked around her. I sensed she was starting to move away.

'Jenny. *Please.*'

Begging is awful, but it's hard to ignore. She said: 'I can't talk now.'

'Then tomorrow.'

'I'm away tomorrow, Miles.'

'Then when?'

She took a deep breath. 'I'll be here on Sunday.'

'OK, Sunday then, I was going to go home but I'll cancel it. Where can we meet?'

Jenny said: 'You were going home?'

'Just for Sunday lunch. I promised my mother.'

'I thought you never went home. Apart from Christmas.'

'I go a few times a year but it doesn't mean anything. I'll cancel it.'

'Don't cancel it on my account, Miles.'

'But I've got to see you, Jenny.'

Jenny looked at me. And to this day I still for the life of me don't know why, but she said: 'All right then. Why don't I go with you? On Sunday.'

'To my home? To Wimbledon?'

'Yes.'

'You'd be bored out of your brain. It's just my mother and my sister, she'll be there too. There'd be nothing for you there.'

'Well I can't make tomorrow, Miles, and I wouldn't be the cause of you missing an engagement with your family, so realistically, if you want to meet, it's that or nothing.'

I agreed to it. I'd have agreed to anything.

On Sunday morning I picked her up at her flat in Summertown and as soon as she got into the car I started to say, 'Jenny, I really, really want to …' and she held up a hand and said: 'Miles, why don't we just take the day as it comes? You know, you can ruin things by talking about them. Why don't we not talk, and just listen to the radio, eh?'

So we set off down the M40 more or less in silence, and eventually hit London, and the first thing she said was, as we were coming down the hill from Wimbledon Common, 'Can we find a florist? Will there be one open?'

There was. She bought a bunch of tiger lilies. They were spectacular and expensive. She said: 'D'you think your mum'll like these or will she think they're over the top?'

'I've no idea.'

'What does she like?'

'I don't know.'

'What d'you normally take when you go home?'

'I don't take her anything.'

Jenny looked at me and shook her head.

My mother liked the tiger lilies. In fact, she was astonished by them. 'Oh, dearie me, they're gorgeous,' she said. 'What on earth must they have cost you? That is just so kind, let's put them in water at once' and she led us through into the kitchen where Lotte was bent over the sink, peeling potatoes.

'Jenny, this is Lotte,' my mother said. 'She's an actress, a sort of actress. She does er, monologues, and singing and things. She has a funny name for it she likes us to use.'

'A *diseuse*,' Lotte said, drawling out the word and nodding hello to Jenny, sizing her up with a polite smile.

'You mean like Joyce Grenfell?' Jenny said.

'You know La Grenfell?'

'We had her records at home. In New Zealand. They reminded my Mum of the old country. We had them all, the kindergarten, the whole bit.'

Lotte looked at her in a new way, drying her hands. 'Well, well,' she said. 'Here's somebody different from your usual run of totty, Miles.' She said to Jenny: 'Most of them have been brain-dead. Posh, but no evidence of intelligent life.'

'Oh for God's sake, Lotte,' I said, and my mother murmured 'Lotteee' in an admonitory tone, but Jenny was already smiling and she said: 'So do you do something in the Joyce Grenfell line?'

'I'm trying to take over where Her Grenfellness left off,' Lotte said. 'In my own humble way.'

'I'd love to see your stuff,' Jenny said. 'You haven't got a video or anything, have you?'

'I could show you one but I could also show you my holiday snaps.'

'I mean it, I'd really love to see it.'

'OK. But in the meantime, you don't seem to have a drink. Has my ignorant swine of a brother offered you anything?'

'I could kill a glass of wine, actually.'

'He gets no better. Miles, don't be a complete wanker, there's a bottle of Chablis in the fridge, do the honours for Christ's sake.'

We went to the sitting room to drink our wine and Lotte was persuaded to put on a video. She said: 'This is from Edinburgh last August. From the festival.'

It showed her sitting at a piano, wearing a hat with an enormous feather, and lurid red lipstick, which highlighted her slightly horsey but very white teeth; and she announced that the song she was about to play was called 'Suede High Heels'.

It had a bouncing rhythm and it began:

I'm going on
The town
This evening;
Cos I'm dressed
All in
Me bes';
I've got me hat with the ostrich feathah
And me new cock
-tail dress...

It went over my head completely, but when it got to the end, Jenny laughed so hard that she reached out to put her wine glass on the table and slipped sideways off her chair.

I couldn't see what the fuss was about.

Lotte was delighted. She went over and helped Jenny up, beaming at her. 'I've had a few laughs but you're my first actual falling-off-a-chair,' she said. 'I think this calls for a proper celebration. Feel like some champagne?'

'God yes. That'd be great.'

'Make yourself useful Miles, go round the corner to the offy and get us a bottle of fizz. Go on, you can treat us, with all that money the sodding Royal Society is paying you for chicken sexing or whatever it is you do.'

As I came back in I heard Lotte say: 'All the others have had the cheeks of their little arses sewn together. Here he comes now, Mr Three Brains.'

I smelt something. I realised they were passing a cigarette to each other. 'Is that cannabis?' I said.

They fell about giggling.

'Sod the fizz, Miles,' said Lotte. 'Jenny had something better in her handbag.'

'That is against the law,' I said.

The two women began laughing again.

'Hey bro!' said Lotte. 'Take a chill pill, huh?'

'Yeah Miles, take a chill pill,' said Jenny. 'Better still, take two. Better still, have a toke.'

'I'm driving, aren't I?' I said. 'Where's Mum?'

'Having her bath,' Lotte said.

My mother was old-fashioned in the matter of Sunday lunch: she took it seriously and dressed for the occasion. I was surprised at how well she seemed to get on with Jenny, who spoke to her, I noticed, in a different tone, with a reserve and a softness I did not realise she possessed.

She said: 'I imagine being the wife of a Nobel Prize-winner wasn't all plain sailing, Mrs Bonnici.'

'It's Muriel,' my mother said. 'Well, it had its moments. Though as I'm sure you realise, Jenny' – with the barest hint of a glance at me – 'good scientists tend to have a lot of things on their minds, a lot of the time. But we shared a passion for music. And these two, they've inherited the musical genes. They both got their Grade Eight. Lotte went on to the Guildhall. Eventually.' She smiled at her daughter. 'And Miles is a fine pianist too, you know. Have you heard him play?'

'I haven't, but I've seen his piano. Do you play yourself?'

'A little. I've had a different pastime for the last couple of years.'

'Watercolours,' said Lotte. 'Mum's a whizz. She's absolutely brilliant. She paints like a dream. You must see them.'

And after lunch Lotte persuaded my mother to bring out her painting portfolio and I saw them for the first time myself, or rather, noticed them, the watercolour landscapes she had been painting on Wimbledon Common, and they were good. One in particular, of the sunset, was stunning, I had to admit myself.

Jenny was very struck by it. 'I think it's absolutely gorgeous,' she said. 'The light – it seems to be glowing.'

'That's a watercolourist's trick,' my mother said. 'It's the paper. You let the luminosity of the paper shine through the paint.'

We went for a walk on the Common then, and actually saw the winter sunset, which made me realise once again how good my mother's depiction of it was, then came back for tea, Earl Grey and Madeira cake, and Lotte and my mother asked Jenny about her family and they seemed unusually interested, it seemed to me, far more so than in any of my previous girlfriends. In fact they seemed positively regretful when the time came for us to make our goodbyes, and my mother had something for Jenny wrapped in cardboard and brown paper.

It was the painting of the sunset.

Jenny said: 'I can't take this from you. I can't possibly take this.'

My mother said: 'Jenny, it's been such pleasure meeting you, it would mean so much to me if you would. As long as you like it.'

'I love it.'

'Why don't you have it, then? To remind you of our lunch, perhaps.'

'I'll treasure it,' she said.

As I was moving towards the car, my mother said something else to Jenny, quietly, which I couldn't hear, and Jenny suddenly looked taken aback. Then she smiled, and said goodbye.

Driving away she said to me: 'Why didn't you tell me your family were like that?'

'Like what?'

'They're just terrific. Absolutely terrific.'

'Are they?'

'Aren't you aware of it?'

'Well I suppose they're all right. They're just Mum and Lotte. I don't really have a lot to do with them.'

'Were you closer to your dad?'

'Well – more … involved with him. He was … a pretty big character.'

Jenny said: 'What did they think of him?'

'Mum was very loyal to him. I don't suppose he was all that nice to her, really. Lotte and he clashed ever since she was little. They had ferocious battles.'

As we drove back up the M40 she was quiet.

I was still desperate.

I said: 'They didn't bore you, though? You didn't think they were boring?'

'I didn't think they were boring.'

'My mother's just a housewife. She goes on and on about stuff. Lotte goes on about her stuff, singing and stuff.'

'They didn't bore me.'

Silence fell between us then, and I slowly started to sense what was happening: she was making up her mind. And when eventually we got to her front door in Summertown, I knew the moment had come. It was the end, or not; it was truly poised, and if I had tried to tip it my way, if at that moment I had asked, had begged her, she would undoubtedly have said No; in some way, she would have had to say No. She was weighing it up. I quickly half-glanced at her, my hands on the steering wheel, and I used my last bit of strength to force myself to say nothing. I looked straight ahead. And eventually she said: 'D'you wanna come in then?'

I merely nodded, and we got out and collected our things, slowly, deliberately, as if in a dream. I knew I must ask for nothing more, make no moves, make no grabs, but I knew then it would happen, in an utterly calm way, almost floating, even as she asked me if I would like some coffee, even in the casual conversation that followed about the day, through which she was finally deciding and through which my heart pounded so hard I could hear it as well as feel it – until at last she said, with all the insouciance in the world, 'Shall we go to bed then?'

In the dark she said: 'You're trembling.'

I could not speak.

She took my head in her hands and kissed it all over and whispered: 'Stop trembling.'

Then she came down to me.

In the night I clung to her, like a drowning man clinging to a log, scarcely believing I might have her back, she whose dismissal had so shattered me, and in the morning when I woke I was overcome.

'I love you,' I said, kissing her. 'I love you, I love you, I love you.'

'Miles,' she said, laughing and pushing me away, 'Do me a favour.'

'What? I love you.'

'No you don't.'

'What d'you mean?'

'Course you don't love me. You barely know anything about me. You've never been interested enough to want to find out.'

I was exasperated. 'Well what am I feeling then?'

'You've been in dump-shock, mate. The feeling you get after somebody dumps you. Not good. You strongly wish to be un-dumped.'

'Oh.'

'What you are now experiencing is un-dump euphoria.'

I thought about it. 'All right, Jenny,' I said. 'All right. But look. What can I say? I am serious about wanting you. Totally serious.'

'Yeah, OK,' she said, smiling and conceding the point.

'And ... if we're here together, you must be prepared to at least consider ... having another try ...'

A pause. 'And?' she said.

'Will you come and live with me?'

She said: 'I'll think about it.'

She moved in a week later, keeping her Summertown flat on as an insurance policy, but bringing into my life many adjustments of taste and style, the most notable of which was the dethroning of my framed *Nature* cover, with its photo of Arty Booboo, from its place of honour on the chimneybreast (replaced by my mother's watercolour of the sunset over Wimbledon Common).

'Miles,' she said, 'I really do not want to be looking every day at a poster shouting how clever you are, without any hint of irony. And that sex-mad little penguin makes me nervous. I feel like he's sizing me up for a shag.'

'He's not a penguin,' I protested. 'A guillemot is an auk.'

'Doesn't matter if he's an auk or a fucking bird of paradise,' Jenny said. 'He's gotta go.' And Arty was banished to the wall of the upstairs loo.

I didn't care. I had forgotten my career. I had forgotten the burning desire to surpass my father. I had forgotten scientific renown. The fervent purpose which had animated my psyche for more than a decade seemed to have vanished overnight, replaced by a purpose even stronger, by a true passion: to win Jenny Pittaway once and for all.

People call this love and maybe for some it is, but for me, then, it was at base an overpoweringly strong need not to be destroyed once more by Jenny leaving me. I was desperate to avoid that happening

again, and to be sure of avoiding it I had to be sure of her. I needed
Jenny to love me, I needed her to say she loved me, so that I could
be back up as her equal again, or better still, back on top, when I
would no longer live in the terror of rejection. This feeling was at
the heart of everything that followed, and that spring in Oxford
it filled me entirely, although to tell true it was a genuinely happy
time (and my mother and Lotte were thrilled and delighted at
Jenny's arrival.)

The sex was wonderful. She was very sweet and generous to me,
even if early on she felt obliged to offer me some technical advice.

'Miles,' she said one night, as we lay in bed after a lovemaking
session which from my own point of view had been entirely
satisfactory, 'Have you ever heard of the myth of the vaginal orgasm?'

'Er, I don't think so,' I said.

'D'you know what the clitoris is?'

'Well of course I do.'

'D'you know what it's for?'

'D'you mean its evolutionary purpose? Its adaptive significance?'

'Aargh,' she cried, 'Sod its adaptive fucking significance, you
great nerd, d'you know what it's for as far as I'm concerned?'

'Er, not really,' I confessed.

'Look,' she said. 'Comere. Gimme your hand. You take your
fingertips and you do, this. See? Like this. See? Unnngh.'

She may have been frustrated (although with her ministrations,
that ended soon enough), but she wasn't half as frustrated as I
was, in seeking to win her heart. For she gave me everything, bar
that. She was delightful, huge fun, considerate and loving, but her
interior surrender was not on the horizon. I knew from the way
she teased me that she liked me – Jenny only teased people she
was fond of – and she was enjoying our time together, but there
was an unshakeably firm holding back. After each lovemaking I
would say, I love you, Jenny, and she wouldn't tell me she didn't,
she merely kissed me and said *Sssh!*

She was most elusive about what you might call her internal
life, vague in particular about previous boyfriends: there had been
a couple in London, both just affairs which 'sort of ran their course,
really'. Back in New Zealand there'd been 'nothing special'. I met
Trina McVeigh, her Kiwi friend from OUP, but only the once, and
before I ever had the chance to get her on her own and talk about
Jenny, Trina's Overseas Experience had come to an end and she
had gone back home 'to marry a farmer's boy in Wairarapa,' Jenny

said, laughing, with Trina protesting that Stanley was actually an agronomist. (That evening the pair of them got drunk and repeatedly sang *Pokarekare Ana* to me, tearful and embracing.) She gave the distinct impression that life, or at least love, had not really touched her deeply, and definitely wasn't to be taken too seriously, as if there were no deep side at all to Jenny Pittaway; or at least, not one she was going to show me.

What she showed me freely was her madcap side. It could be pretty mad. I remember one night after dinner we were sitting by the fire reading; we had drunk a bottle of Kiwi sauvignon and she had had most of it. I looked up and she was staring at me. I looked up again and she was still staring at me, and then she said, for no apparent reason: 'Yoooou little shit.'

'What's that for?'

She didn't answer. But when I looked up again she was still focused on me. She said: 'Yoooou little *worm*.'

I shook my head and went back to my reading, but felt forced to glance up once more. She was still looking at me, and she said: 'Yoooou little *wanker*.'

I closed the book with a slap. I said: 'Is this the sort of after-dinner conversation you generally enjoy in Kiwi land then? When you're not discussing having carnal relations with sheep?'

'You thin' that's what we talk about?'

'D'you talk of something else?'

'Listen sonny. Greatest 20th century work of philosophy in English was written in New Zealand.'

'What was that then? The Sheepshaggers' Guide?'

'You don' know, do you? You little shit. You really don' know.'

'Go one then, tell me.'

'*The Open Society and Its Enemies* was written in Christchurch. In 1943.'

'What was?'

'Ha!' She was triumphant. 'You might be able to tell one seagull from another, but you've never even heard of Karl Popper! Ha! Miles Bonnici, the Big research scientist! Never heard of Karl Popper!'

Laughing, I picked her up and put her over my shoulder. She weighed nothing.

'He's never heard of Karl Popper, but boy, can he tell one seagull from another!' she shouted, beating at my back with her fists.

I carried her up the stairs.

'He's going right to the top! Professor of seagulls in the University of Oxford!'

I surged along the landing to the bedroom.

'Professor of the Public Understanding of Seagulls! Fellow of the Royal Fucking Society! Mister Big, here!'

I threw her down on the bed and tore at her clothes and she fought me, for a second or two.

Later, as we lay entwined together, I said: 'That was all right, wasn't it?'

'It'll do, you little shit.'

'Don't you love me yet?'

'*Shhhh*!'

It was mid-April before I found a clue to what made Jenny tick. It was a Friday; she had a day off from work and came with me to Wytham Woods, the piece of ancient forest west of the city which generations of Oxford zoologists have used as a laboratory to study animal behaviour. I explained to her my research project on female infidelity: to test the proposition that the female of a pair of birds might actively seek copulation with an extra-pair male, sensing that he had better genes to pass on to her offspring, than her regular partner.

I was going to test it on the woods' population of blue tits, I told her: I was going to trace the paternity of all the chicks in a series of clutches, and try to follow them, and see if chicks which had been fathered by males other than the male on the nest, actually did better than their siblings, in terms of survival.

'What would be the object of that?'

'To prove that the mother's promiscuity actually gave these, er, 'illegitimate' chicks a better chance in the world.'

'You mean like, Ladies! Cheat on your husbands and more of your kids will live longer!'

'Exactly so. Or as we would put it, that female promiscuity is adaptive.'

'That's intriguing,' said Jenny.

'There's another book in it,' I said. 'And I'm going to write it.'

The project was based on 60 nest boxes scattered throughout the woodlands – nesting time was just beginning – and I was checking them all. We spent more than two hours going from tree to tree, sliding off the front panel of the box and often finding nests, cups of green moss mixed with grass or bark, and lined with feathers or badger hair for insulation. In many there were the first eggs: three or four exquisite tiny ivory pebbles with reddish-brown spots at the blunt end.

Jenny was fascinated by it all. She had brought her camera – photography was a big thing for her – and she took dozens of pictures, delighted when in one box we found a large hornet, and in another, three small bats, fast asleep. She adored the woods; they were truly beautiful that day, with a green mist of young leaves enveloping the trees, and the yellow flashes of the primroses on the ground and the brimstone butterflies in the air, and over it all a universal shower of birdsong, from the heart of which eventually there came a special sound.

She caught it as we sat finishing our picnic, having expostulated at length on the beauty all around us while I went over my data. She suddenly broke off, stood up and whispered: 'Listen!'

'What?'

'What's that?'

Two clear, liquid, descending notes, distant but distinct, sounded through the woodland.

'There!'

'It's a cuckoo,' I said. 'It's just a cuckoo.'

'Just a cuckoo?' cried Jenny with mixed irritation and delight. 'Waddya mean, Miles, just a cuckoo?'

Cu-cu! called the bird, closer now, unmistakeable.

'A real cuckoo! That's fantastic!'

I smiled, as to indulge her.

'I grew up reading about cuckoos in New Zealand but I never thought I'd hear a real one. Listen!'

Cu-cu! called the bird.

I shook my head, smiling.

'You know, Miles, I don't care, you're not gonna spoil it with your Mr Cynical-I've-heard-a million-cuckoos routine. That is one fantastic cuckoo.'

'I'm glad you think so,' I said.

She growled, though she was too good-humoured to be angry. Yet she came back to it later, as we sat outside the pub in Wytham village, with the evening sun lighting its honey-coloured stone and the first swallows swooping about its roof.

'You know, you're wrong about the cuckoo,' she said. 'It was a great cuckoo. But you can't see that, can you?'

'It was just a cuckoo,' I said.

'You're missing the point. You work in a fantastic, wonderful place, Miles, these woods, this village, yet you don't seem to realise what a wonderful place it is.'

'Is it?' I said.

'Like your island that you worked on, all that time – what's its name again?'

'Skarholm.'

'*Skahrum*. I bet that's wonderful too.'

'It's just a seabird breeding station two miles off the coast of Pembrokeshire.'

'You know, Miles, I'm sure you're missing something. It can't be as prosaic as you make it sound.'

'Why can't it?'

'Because islands are special. All islands have something.'

'Yeah, they're surrounded by water.'

She squinted at me, head cocked sideways. 'Know what?' she said. 'You're clever, Miles Bonnici. Really clever. But you're not wise. Anyone ever told you that?'

'You're the first,' I said. 'But be my guest.'

'D'you really not see that islands are among the world's most, most magical places?'

'I don't see that at all. Islands are boring places. There's nothing to do on them, you're cut off from civilisation and if you spend weeks at a time on one like I have, you just can't wait to get off.'

'So you don't think islands have anything special about them?'

'Nope.'

'Nothing about islands that could ever excite your interest? That could really grab you?'

'Sorry.'

She drained her glass, put it back down on the table, and looked at me. 'Well it just shows how fucking stupid you are.'

'Why?'

'Because islands are the way to me. That's what you're chasing and can't find, isn't it, me bucko? And if you want to win me, Miles, you'll have to win me with an island.'

'What?' I sat up. 'Win you with an island? What on earth d'you mean?'

'Oh no. You get no more, sonny boy. You want any more, you'll have to work it out for yourself.'

And then she clammed up, resisting all entreaties to explain; the following day she laughed it off, denying she had said it.

Yet said it she had. I was baffled. That lumps of rock surrounded by water – the way I'd always thought of islands – might in some way offer a key to Jenny Pittaway's inner life, I found the weirdest notion. Certainly she saw something, otherwise she would never have used the phrases that hung in my mind, *win me with an island*

and *the way to me*. But what was the way to her? What on earth did *win her with an island* mean? Give her an island? Buy an island for her? In a sort of panic I reached out for the only island I had available, and realising I would shortly be going back to Skarholm to check on how my guillemot research was being taken forward by a new Ph.D. student, I asked her, a couple of days later – as casually as I could – if she would like to come with me.

Her face lit up. 'I would love to, Miles.'

Loss of J affects his work.
Wants to win J back so he can
continue work
J. knew how to get him back p45
Rankles that J ended relationship
M. cocks up his lecture
Callum says M needs to get
   J back p54
M + J vist his mother + sister
She won't say she loves him
In Wytham Woods – M can see
the science but not the beauty
J – M is stupid
Win her with an island.

6

Jenny Pittaway's passion for islands, which eventually led us to Lanna, took me a long time to understand; and I did not work it out on the Skarholm trip, which in fact was nearly the end of us.

We crossed over on a late afternoon of perfect spring sunshine and Jenny was captivated by the place from the moment she stepped off the boat, bounding up the steps from the jetty like a deer, as if her giant rucksack were weightless. I showed her to the house – Aled the warden was out, and there was no sign either of Russell, my postgraduate successor – and we dropped off our gear and then sat at the wooden table outside with mugs of coffee, looking back at the distant hills of Pembrokeshire over the glinting waves.

'And you were here six years?' she said.

I nodded. 'Mid-April to mid-July each year.'

'Must have been a wonderful place to work.'

'Well you're seeing it in favourable conditions. Weather's often very different from this. But from a scientific point of view, no, there isn't anywhere better, not for what I wanted to do.'

'Which was?'

'Watch guillemots copulating. You want to watch guillemots *at it*? You want to watch 'em shagging, having it off with each other, morning, noon and night' – Jenny was giggling – 'this is the place to come.'

'And of course it has Arty Booboo. The champ.'

'Indeed it does.'

Jenny said: 'D'you think I could I see him, Miles?'

'Course you must see Arty. If he's still around. We'll have to check. He's on a cliff on the other side called Craig Yr Adar. The guillemots breed on its ledges and we've got a hide that overlooks it from the cliff opposite, so you can see everything that goes on.'

Arty was so much a part of her life, she said, with his photo in the loo – 'Every time I take a pee that boy is watching' – that she couldn't wait for the chance of seeing him in the flesh; so after I had picked up my telescope and binoculars we set out to cross the island over its higher central core, striding up over the tussocky grass, and Jenny bounded ahead of me once again until she got to the crest of the rising ground when she stopped dead and screamed.

'Oh!' she cried. 'My God!'

I ran up beside her.

I looked.

'Oh,' I said. 'It's just the bluebells.' They stretched away for hundreds of yards in an unbroken glowing prairie, an airfield-sized, shimmering plain of intense lilac blue. I was used to it, but I suppose if you hadn't seen it before ...

'I've never seen anything like it in my life!' Jenny cried, and before I could reply, she ran straight into the millions of blooms with the urge of someone running down the beach into the irresistibly-inviting sea, splashing through the bluebells as you would splash through the wavelets, running with her arms stretched out in aircraft fashion and then pirouetting, her slight figure in her white T-shirt backgrounded in blue for all the length of her dancing run, and while part of me was entirely bemused by this performance, and came close to disapproving, another part of me, I should record, was struck dumb with desire.

She hurtled back towards me with her arms outstretched and I caught her and she collapsed at my feet, laughing fit to burst, and eventually she stopped and looked up at me, panting, and then exploded with laughter once again. I started to say something but she put her finger to her lips. 'If you say, "it's just the bluebells" one more time,' she said, 'I will cut your cock off.'

We moved then through the gull colony, the lesser black-backed gulls whose nests were all about us in the grass, and as we picked our way gingerly between them the nearer birds left their nests to mob us, briefly revealing their clutches of mottled eggs or fluff-covered chicks, all to Jenny's fascination, and finally we came to the flower-covered clifftop where we could see below us Craig Yr Adar's jutting basalt mass: it was abuzz with birds, not just guillemots and razorbills coming and going but kittiwakes and fulmars wheeling in white, and at its base, cormorants and their smaller cousins the shags arrowing darkly over the surface of the water, while as we watched, a peregrine falcon floated across our line of sight and I pointed it out.

'It's just full of life, isn't it?' Jenny said, marvelling. 'The whole place.'

'You know what?' I said. 'I think it's full of data.'

70

I explained how dangerous the cliffs were and how she should follow me carefully down the path to the hide, putting her feet where I put mine, as there was a 200-foot drop just beneath it; and I explained also that Russell the new researcher would probably be inside, and he was chronically shy, so not to worry if he didn't say a word. But when we got there, we had the hide to ourselves.

She was surprised at how robust it was, this small shed with a bench inside into which four people could just about squeeze, perched on its narrow plateau of flat cliff. 'This,' I said, 'is a small marvel of wooden engineering. You wouldn't want it to collapse on you here, would you?' And I opened the window flaps,

'Wow,' said Jenny.

She looked out and down directly on to the Craig Yr Adar rock faces, which were jam-packed with birds, in lines snaking along the narrow ledges; birds standing upright and clustered together like queues for a sale in a department store. There was a blast of noise, of their growling calls, and a burst of acrid smell, of their guano.

'They're guillemots,' I said, handing her my bins while I began to get out the scope. 'Nearly all of them, anyway. Few razorbills in the odd corner, the ones with heavier beaks with a white mark on. See?'

Jenny scanned the rows and rows of birds. 'And the great Arty Booboo is one of these, is he?' she said.

'Should know in a minute,' I said as I brought the scope to bear and began to focus, muttering to myself. 'Down below the overhang. Then along. Along, Along. Well, well. Son of a gun. There he is.'

Jenny put the binoculars down and looked at me, her eyes widening. 'Can I see, can I see?'

'Sure,' I said, moving away and letting Jenny up to the scope. Her eyepiece filled with a bird with a long dark beak and a smooth chocolate-brown head and back, contrasting smartly with his white underparts.

'Fantastic!' she cried, 'Hey. He's beautiful. Arty Booboo the champion shagger. We meet at last. G'day, Arty boy. Who you been shagging?'

I took up the binoculars.

'Well, his mate's not there,' I said. 'She'll be away fishing. Building up the big egg inside her. They'll all be laying, any day now.'

'You think he's been screwing anyone else, Miles?'

'Maybe. Often happens in the early morning. Maybe one of the birds in the group around him. Have a look at the others.' I moved over to her and lessened the magnification of the scope so the eyepiece held the birds on either side.

'The one next to Arty's sort of bending down on his tummy,' she said.

I took up the bins.

'That's not a him,' I said. 'That's the next-door female. She's inviting copulation. You're going to see a guillemot mating. Watch. Her male will jump on her back. The one on the right.'

'Isn't that Arty moving to her?' she said. 'On the left?'

'Jesus,' I said.

'He's jumped on her!' she shouted.

And we watched as Skarholm guillemot, RTBuBu, flapping his wings to keep his position on the back of the crouching female next door, swung his tail underneath hers so that their cloacas were touching, and wiggled his bottom from side to side and shuddered, three or four times, as he shot his sperm into her, with the next-door male, who had been too slow, vainly trying to push him off.

'Go Arty!' Jenny cried. 'Yes! Go boy!'

'Well I'll be damned,' I said. 'Hardly ever seen it at this time of day.'

'That's fantastic!' Jenny said, as the cuckolded male finally succeeded in dislodging his cuckolder, alas for him, too late, and the other guillemots on the surrounding ledges all watched, calling out and stretching their heads to see.

'A perfect EPC,' I said. 'A perfect data point. I shall twit young Russell about him missing this.'

Jenny was laughing. 'What a chap,' she said. 'Is that how he does it, Miles? By being quick like that?'

'That's typical,' I said. 'Opportunistic. But also, if you look at him closely, he's a little bit bigger, a bit stronger, than some of the others. You saw, he kept the other male away, for just long enough. He's quite a specimen.'

'He's gorgeous,' she said. 'And you tell 'em apart by the rings on their legs?'

'That's right. All of the birds you can see around Arty are ringed and we know who they are. Let me have another look.'

We changed positions and watched for several minutes until a fresh bird landed on the ledge. I squinted and I said: 'Hey, she's back.'

'Who's back?'

'Arty's mate. Wytrog. WTRG. White, Technical, Red, Green.'

'His mate? You mean his female? Can I see?'

I let Jenny in and took up my bins again.

'The bird on the left in the scope,' I said. 'Arty's next to her on the right. She's just come back from the sea. They're greeting each other. See them, billing and cooing?'

'They seem to be really affectionate.'

'Well they've been together for years.'

We watched.

Jenny said: 'The one on the left, she's ... going down on her tummy. Like the earlier bird.'

'I don't believe it,' I said.

'She is, look.'

I was looking. 'God Almighty, it's not been ten minutes since the last one.' And we watched Arty Booboo once more hop up on to a female back, this time of his regular partner, holding her down with his feet and flapping his wings for balance as she threw back her head and opened her bill in ecstatic surrender, and we watched him once more swing his tail underneath hers, cloaca to cloaca, and wiggle his bottom and shudder his being and force his sperm inside her.

'Fantastic!' shouted Jenny. 'Fantastic! Go, Arty! You know what he is, Miles? He's a life force, that boy.'

'He's just a data point as far as I'm concerned.'

'No, look, there in the open air, it's like, it's life being created, right in front of us. It's visible. The life force is visible. Look at the way he does it. The sexy beast.' And she murmured, so I only half-heard: 'I wouldn't mind being taken like that.' And she said: 'Can't you see it, Miles? That's what we all should do, make love in the open air like that.'

'Sure, Jenny.'

'Can you really not see it?'

'I see a pair copulation, which has just followed an extra-pair copulation.'

Jenny looked at me. She said: 'You know what I think, Miles?'

'What?'

'It's not really the scientist in you, is it? Makes you talk like that.'

'What then?'

'It's your inhibitions, isn't it, Miles me boy? Your little old gentlemanly English inhibitions about sex.'

'Jenny,' I said, 'What nonsense you do talk.' I was still looking through my bins.

'You ever done it yourself?'

'Done what?'

She nodded towards Craig Yr Adar. 'Made love in the open air? Like Arty?'

'Well, I dunno. Probably,' I said, going back to the binoculars.
'I don't think you have.'

'Jenny, you do go on.'

'And you know what I think? I think you need to do it.'

'Yeah, yeah, yeah.'

'I mean, I think you need to do it *here and now.*'

'What?'

'Come on,' she said, moving over to me, 'Why don't you take me? Right here. Get rid of those English inhibitions and take me from behind like Arty Booboo.' She was reaching for my cords. '*Forcefully*, Miles.'

'Don't be bloody ridiculous,' I laughed, but she had caught me off guard and was pulling my zip down before I could stop her. 'Get off, you crazy woman,' I cried, 'You can't do this in a bird hide!' but Jenny already had her hand inside my pants and brought my cock out and planted her mouth on me and fired me up instantly in spite of myself, shuffling down her own jeans as she did so. For several seconds I gasped as ecstasy made me helpless; then she turned, holding my cock, and backed herself on to me and took me into her and began to slide up and down on me and in spite of all my inhibitions, which she had identified entirely correctly, and which were screaming at me to desist, the deep urge consumed me and I held her hips and took her vigorously, as she wanted, harder and harder until she came, and cried out, at the same moment as I did myself.

We half-collapsed on the bench and the shelf of the hide.

We were both gasping.

'Jesus,' I said.

'See Arty,' she called, laughing. 'You're not the only one can do it on a cliff.' Then she freed herself from me, and turned, and held my head, and kissed me warmly.

I kissed her back.

'You're a sweet boy,' she said, 'To give a woman what she wants.'

'You're a total fucking loony,' I said.

Jenny took my hand as we walked back; she pressed against me and nuzzled my neck. She was very happy that evening, and I started to wonder if indeed it was something to do with her being on the island, for it seemed to make her completely ... completely open, somehow, completely friendly with others, as if there were no evil in the world and no artifice in the human character. It was a trait that quite disarmed both Russell the lanky inhibited Ph.D.

student and Aled the irascible warden, the first as she chopped onions on the outside table for the giant spaghetti bolognese she insisted on making; I had met Russell three times and been in his company for several hours and had never heard him utter a word more than was absolutely necessary; but then, I had never asked him about himself, as Jenny did, in the most natural way possible, as soon as they met; and over a beer he told her about his parents who had been missionaries in the Sudan, where he had spent part of his youth, and his younger sister Adele who had cystic fibrosis and probably would not live to be twenty-one. I was astonished. When she went back into the kitchen he looked at me. He was about to say something, then stopped. Then he said: 'She's nice, isn't she?'

'She is, yes,' I said.

Aled I would have thought a much tougher nut to crack – he was an unreasonably short-tempered man and he was only on civil terms with me because I had actually been a Skarholm resident longer than he had – but she worked a similar unaffected charm on him while the four of us ate her spaghetti, lubricated with the Chianti we had lugged over, at the table outside, as the sun sank with all guns blazing into the western sea. She got out of him that he had qualified as a marine biologist and had done a thesis on the dolphins of Cardigan Bay, and when she told him that she had spent a summer surveying Bryde's whales back in New Zealand, he was actually interested – a unique event in my experience, as the herds of research students who came to Skarholm were ignored by him entirely – and he was even more pleased at the fact that she was a Kiwi, as he had a favourite cousin in Wellington. When she went off to our chemical loo he grunted, nodded, and said to me: 'She's all right.' He said: 'Show her the Manxies, why don't we? Surprise for her, that'll be, eh?'

'Yeah, OK,' I said, smiling at the thought. 'Why not?'

'Bit of fun, eh? Great night for it. No moon. They'll all be coming in. Out there just after eleven, we want to be.'

As darkness fell we moved back into the lamplit house for coffee and when we had done the washing-up Jenny looked over the books in the bookcase while Aled and I had a large scotch from the bottle I had brought him, which was a sacred duty, and caught up on Skarholm life, not that there was much to catch up on. Russell had gone to bed, for he started his observations at dawn.

Jenny said: 'What's this thing in the little glass cabinet on the wall? The thing that says *Remember* underneath it?'

'Belongs to Callum, that,' Aled said. 'Coming tomorrow.'

'My old boss,' I said. 'Callum McSorley. The professor at Aberfair. Guy who's in charge of all the research here. Coming tomorrow to give Russell the once-over.'

'What is it?' she said.

'What d'you think it is?'

'I dunno. It looks old. Like a little curved, er, stone knife blade. The blade of a prehistoric penknife, maybe?'

'Not quite that old. But maybe we'd better let Callum tell you tomorrow,' I said. 'A story goes with it. He likes to tell people the story himself, doesn't he, Aled?'

'Yeah, goes on about it, he does,' said Aled, and he stood up. 'Shall we go for a walk?'

'What, now?' said Jenny.

'Eleven o'clock walk's a tradition on Skarholm, isn't it, Miles?' Aled said, winking at me. 'Never know what we may come across.'

His timing was spot-on, for the first unearthly, strangulated cry exploded next to our ears less than five minutes later as we walked along the pitch-black clifftop with our torches, causing Jenny to grab my arm and hiss: 'What in Christ's name was that?'

But before I could reply another howl from hell burst out just behind us and then something hit her square in the back and she let out a shriek of her own. 'Christ all fucking mighty, what is this?' she cried.

I put my arm around her, laughing, and said: 'It's all right. It's just the Manxies,' and I shone my torch at her feet. 'Look.'

She put both hands to her face: 'Oh my God. It's a bird.'

It looked like a small pigeon with long wings, ponderously trying to crawl away over the grass tufts, having to use beak and wings as well as its feet to move.

'Pick it up, why don't you?' Aled said, as another gurgling screech ripped the night air and something flashed through my torch beam. 'Careful it doesn't give you a nip.'

She caught the bird and held it lovingly, gazing at it in the torchlight and feeling its beating heart, entranced to be so intimate with such a wild being. 'God, it's beautiful,' she said. 'What is it?'

'A Manx shearwater,' I said. 'It's a seabird, but it's breeding in a burrow in the grass here. Somewhere around our feet.'

'Its mate's sitting on the egg, waiting to be relieved, see?' Aled said. 'This one will feed the other, and they'll change over.'

As Jenny released the bird there were more violent shrieks in the darkness. I shone my torch. Shearwaters were flapping on the grass. 'What d'you think of the call, then?' said Aled. 'There's lively, eh?'

'Terrifying.'

'Know what?' I said. 'It's supposed to be the only thing the Vikings were afraid of. They thought it was ghosts, or trolls, or whatever.'

'You would.'

'But it's the just the call they make to let their mates know they're coming in, see,' Aled said. 'Only come in at night, they do, and has to be a dark 'un, doesn't it, 'cos you can see how vulnerable they are on land.'

He shone his torch. 'See? Can't hardly walk. Predators could pick 'em off easy. But over the sea, well, they're fantastic flyers, low down, right next the waves.'

As we walked back to the hut with the Manxies shrieking in the dark all about us and birds falling into the grass every few yards, Jenny linked her arm in mine, and when we got ready for bed I saw she was smiling at me, and shaking her head.

'Miles Bonnici,' she said. 'Your boring island.'

We squeezed into one bunk. Jenny snuggled her head into my shoulder, which she always did when she was happy.

'You like it, then?' I said.

'Oh yes, I like it, Miles.'

'Well, good.'

'It's like your family.'

'How d'you mean?'

'It's another part of you that's marvellous, that you don't appreciate in the slightest. That you don't even realise you've got.'

'Does it get you any closer to loving me?'

'I'll tell you what it does do, Miles, it gets you a proper thank-you. So c'mere.'

It was on the second day that things went wrong, when Callum McSorley came: we had our first row, one so explosive it nearly finished our relationship.

The day itself was fine: Jenny spent it roaming the island with her camera, while Russell and I passed several hours in the hide, observing the guillemot colony with Callum, who arrived after lunch. I had told Jenny quite a lot in advance about my doctoral supervisor, this exiled Celt, a Scot in a Welsh university. I did not tell her how he had rescued me from the pit into which I had fallen after she dumped me, but I did explain that he was an intellectual powerhouse, although different from me in that he was passionate about the wildlife we both studied, whereas I was only interested in it in so far as it enabled me to test scientific theory; its conservation left me cold. While Callum was a naturalist as well as a scientist, I was not.

'Really?' said Jenny. 'Seems a shame.'

'We just disagree about it,' I said. 'But you'll find he's a very good guy.'

In the event, they got on famously, Jenny and Callum; a little too famously even, for my liking, because I sensed quite quickly that there was a physical spark between them, even though both were far too decent to do anything like openly flirting. Looking at him, it dawned on me for the first time what an attractive man Callum must be, divorced, in his early forties but with his frame still lean and wiry, and his sandy hair, and his quiet sardonic take on life which his Scottishness and his roll-up cigarettes somehow both enhanced. And Jenny for her part was just the sort of woman Callum would respond to, not merely for her beauty, as any man might, but for her lack of ego and her intelligence and her strength: I suppose really I mean the way she carried herself, under the zany surface. I knew at once they saw these things in each other, I knew as only a lover can know, even though the conversation between us all was happy and normal and full of laughter; and for the first time in our four months together I felt the prickle of jealousy.

It was kept at bay at first because Russell was part of our company (Aled having gone to the mainland) until nearly the end of dinner, which we moved inside for, as the weather was breaking and there were the first spots of rain, and talk was generalised; but when my young successor had sloped off to his bunk for his dawn start, Callum and Jenny began a more personal and animated exchange about Kiwi wildlife – he had visited New Zealand, on his recent trip to study penguins in the Antarctic – and how much of it had been decimated by introduced predators such as cats and stoats, including the kakapo, the giant flightless parrot which was nearly extinct.

To Jenny's surprise I had never heard of it – 'Course the boy has nae heard of it,' Callum said. 'Ah keep telling him, take a bit more interest in other species, will ye for God's sake Miles take some interest in the natural world, but will he listen to me?' – whereas they both seemed to be intimately acquainted with the bloody thing, and quickly cast me, or so I felt to my irritation, as the idiot ignorant of kakapos. But at least they moved on then to discussing other flightless birds and how vulnerable they were, particularly the dodo, and why it had disappeared, and I suggested to Jenny that while they were on the subject of flightless birds going extinct, she should ask the professor about the small object in its case which she had wondered at the night before.

Callum got up, and stepped over to the glass cabinet bearing its *Remember* legend, unlocked it, and took out the object inside. He handed it to Jenny, saying: 'What d'ye think then?'

She weighed it in her palm. 'Looking at it last night, I thought it was maybe a little stone knife, but is it stone? It's much lighter than stone.'

'It's not stone, no. It's organic. It's from a living thing.'

She examined it closely. 'Is it a bird's beak?'

'Aye it is. Half of one.'

'Where's it from?'

'An island off the coast of Newfoundland. Funk Island.'

'And what was the bird? Whose beak this is?'

'A great auk.' Callum rolled the *r. Grrreat och.*

Jenny said: 'And isn't that … extinct as well?'

'It is.'

'But it lived on this island?'

'Oh aye. In thousands. Tens of thousands. Maybe even hundreds of thousands, originally.'

'What happened to them?'

'They were wiped out. Every one. By a ruthless introduced predator they had nae evolved with.'

'Which predator was that?

'Man.'

There was a clap of thunder, a long loud rumble, and rain started to beat against the windows.

I said: 'Legendary bird, Jen, the great auk. Like a huge guillemot. A very big Arty Booboo. And you know what? It was the original penguin.'

'Eh?' said Jenny.

Callum said: 'The first sailors in the New World, cod fishermen mainly, they called it The Penguin, which was a Welsh name, 'cos it had white on its head in the breeding season, and the Welsh for white head is *pen gwyn*. And later they just transferred the name to the proper penguins, which looked very similar, when they found them in the southern hemisphere.'

Jenny said: 'So was it just on this one island then?'

'Not at all,' said Callum. 'It spanned the ocean. Found all round the North Atlantic perimeter. Even in Britain. And it was flightless, like the dodo. Wonderfully well adapted to live in the sea, could dive and swim at a fantastic speed, but on land it was more or less helpless. Could nae run, could only waddle very slowly, and once it came into contact with man, it was doomed.'

'Why?'

'It was very meaty. There was a lot of meat on a great auk. And they bred in large numbers together, in big colonies on islands, especially off Canada, so European sailors, when they first got across the Atlantic they discovered the breeding colonies, and they started raiding them for provisions, and they couldn't stop killing them. Funk Island was probably the biggest colony and the scale of the slaughter there was unimaginable. These guys, Jesus, they would land and just start clubbing left, right and centre, killing every bird within reach. They built stone pounds and they herded the auks into them so that they could be more easily killed. We know because the pounds are still there. You can see them.'

'You've been to Funk Island?' said Jenny.

'I have.'

'What's it like?'

'A charnel house. Full of guillemots and other things now, but underneath … it's covered in bones. Bones of great auks. Millions of bones. Ye're holding one of them in your hand.'

Jenny looked at it. She said: 'So when did they die out?'

'On Funk, about 1800, probably. No one knows the exact date.'

'And it was also in Britain, you said?'

'Aye, they bred around the coast of Scotland, in the remoter parts. They were on Orkney, and on St Kilda, but they died out too, although we don't really know when or how. Except, we do know the last great auk in the British Isles was killed on St Kilda in 1840. Ye know St Kilda, Jenny?'

'It's an island?'

'Small archipelago. Four islands. Wonderful place. Just so beautiful. Ye must go. The remotest islands in the British Isles. Next to Lanna, that is, which is even further out, but it's uninhabited and ye can't get on it, 'cos that nutter owns it, the Tiger Laird. But St Kilda, ye can visit St Kilda, and it had people, there was a community there for centuries, you can still see their houses. Strange bunch. Lived off seabirds and their eggs. Hard, hard life. Finally gave up in 1930, the remaining souls, asked to be taken off and they were brought back to mainland Scotland.'

'And great auks bred there?'

'They did. We know that from a guy called Martin Martin who visited in 1690-something and wrote an account of it, and they were almost certainly exploited by the St Kildans for hundreds of years, along with the other seabirds. But exactly how they went extinct there, we just don't know.'

'But you said you know about the last one?'

'We do, aye.'

'It had a tragic end,' I said.

'Certainly did,' said Callum. 'Three guys caught the poor beastie on a big sea rock called Stac An Armin, and kept it alive for a few days, and then a storm blew up and they decided it was a witch and had caused the storm, so they beat it to death.'

We laughed, exasperation's mirthless guffaw.

'And that was the end of it all?' said Jenny.

'Not quite. There were still a few birds left in Iceland. On small remote islands off the coast. Last ones were on a rocky islet called Eldey. Problem *they* had was, they'd become sought after. By European collectors. Ornithologists. Ornithology was all based on skins and stuffed specimens in those days, and 'cos of the great auk's increasing rarity, the price had shot up. Ironic, eh? People who should have the biggest interest in keeping ye alive are the ones driving ye to ya final disappearance.'

'And that's what happened?'

'Yeah, guys from the mainland started making trips every year out to Eldey, even though it was dangerous, get a few auks and eggs for collectors in places like Denmark or Germany. Price was so high they could nae resist. And soon enough, they were all gone.'

'Do we know when?'

'Well,' said Callum, 'We think it was in June 1844. We're not certain. We only know because some years later, it was 1858 if you want to be precise, two English ornithologists, they were called John Wolley and Alfred Newton, they made a trip to Iceland to find out if there were any great auks still alive, and they found that there didn't seem to be, but they stayed with the very guy who had organised the last trip to Eldey that ever found any. Guy called Hakonarsson. He reckoned it was the beginning of June 1844 when they'd gone. But he hadn't kept precise notes, and for all anyone knows, it might have been 1845. Or 1843. Not that it matters. They still wiped them out. They rowed out in a big rowing boat, a group of them, and when they got to Eldey they spotted two great auks at their landing place, just the two, so three guys scrambled ashore, in pursuit. You want their names?' said Callum. 'They live in infamy. Alfred Newton wrote it all down. It was Jon Brandsson, Sigurdur Iselfsson, and Ketil Ketilsson. And Brandsson got hold of the first bird, and the other two chased the second, which nearly got away after Ketilsson slipped, and it was on the point of jumping into the sea when Iselfsson grabbed it.'

'What did they do with them?'

There was an enormous clap of thunder right above us, so loud that Jenny and I jumped, and didn't hear Callum's reply.

'What?' Jenny said.

'They strangled them.'

We fell silent, then, the three of us in the room. Jenny handed Callum back his beak, and he took it to its small cabinet and replaced it.

Jenny said: 'And were they the last? The last great auks?'

'They were, aye. I mean, maybe not the very last. Maybe a handful more lingered on for a few years somewhere else. Nobody knows. But in effect, that was it. And that's our dodo. The dodo of the northern hemisphere. Except it's a much bigger loss, really, because the dodo was just on Mauritius, and the great auk covered a whole ocean.'

I poured us all another glass of wine. I said: 'Callum wrote a book about it. It's called *Remember the Penguin*.'

Jenny said: 'What does that mean, Callum? What … what exactly do you want people to remember?'

'That it was us.'

'Sorry?'

'You're a biologist, Jenny. How do creatures usually go extinct?'

'Loss of habitat?'

'Yep. And pollution, and the effect of invasive species. But the great auk was driven directly to extinction by Man. By human beings. We hunted this bird out of existence. *We* wiped it out, *we* drove it off the face of the earth. It was vulnerable, sure, but only to us. If we'd left it alone, it would be living still. So this is a bird whose fate tells us a lot about ourselves.'

'I'd love to read it,' Jenny said,

'Ah'll send ye a copy.'

'It's a really good book,' I said. 'Callum wrote it for the 150th anniversary, the anniversary of the extinction. That's what? Four years ago. It got great reviews.'

It was indeed a good book, *Remember The Penguin: The Great Auk and Extinction*. I had read it and admired the writing, and my opinion was honest, even if natural history was simply not my thing. But I was also offering up the comment as a sort of peace offering, something to do away with my nascent jealousy, so that we would all three simply be on good terms; and I took it badly, therefore, when Callum at once responded: 'I'm just sorry you don't share the sentiments, Miles.'

Maybe it was all the Chianti we had drunk, but it seemed so needless to say it. Fuck it, I thought. 'Why?' I said. 'You still upset I'm not a birdwatcher, Callum? Does it really bug you that I don't get myself an electronic pager and rush off after some bar-tailed godwit? Me being a research scientist on the cover of *Nature* not enough for you?'

Callum was rolling himself a cigarette. 'Nah, it's no that,' he said, perfectly calmly. 'Ah just think ye might take a bigger interest in conservation, that's all.'

'There's plenty of people taking an interest in conservation. Plenty of second-rate minds.'

'Don't knock conservationists, Miles,' said Jenny. I didn't notice her tone. Looking back, though, I can hear it now.

'Why second-rate minds, Miles?' Callum said. 'Ye don't think conservation's important? Ye don't think it deals with really difficult problems?'

'You know what?' I said, 'I think conservationists make it out to be a lot more important than it is. No doubt so they can secure their funding.'

'Miles, you're talking nonsense,' said Jenny.

'So ye don't think the *Sea Empress* was important?' Callum said, sealing his roll-up and feeling for his matches. The *Sea Empress* was a tanker which had run aground at the entrance to the Milford Haven refinery complex two years earlier and spilled a huge amount of crude oil into the sea. It was less than 20 miles from where we were sitting, but Skarholm had been very lucky: the wind and tides at the time meant that the island and its own birds escaped more or less unscathed.

'Didn't affect us,' I said, entirely disingenuously.

'What bollocks ye do talk sometimes,' Callum said, lighting his cigarette. 'There were thousands of other birds killed, and you would have seen that for yaself had ye deigned to come down and help with the clean-up, like I asked ye, but ye couldnae find the time, could ye?'

'I was doing other things, that were more important to me,' I said.

'You ever seen an oiled seabird, Miles?' Callum said, blowing out smoke.

'I don't need to see an oiled seabird.'

'Oh, but I think ye do, bonny lad, because here ye are saying conservation's not important, but set eyes on an oiled seabird, a badly oiled seabird, and you will change ya mind. Don't tell me it's not important.'

'I'm not saying it's not important. It's just not important to me.'

'Why not?'

'Because it's not enough of an intellectual challenge.'

'You saying conservationists are stupid?'

'I don't think they're necessarily the brightest minds on the planet.'

'Miles,' Jenny said, and she was getting distressed, I realise now. 'Please, don't knock conservationists like that.'

'Ye're basically saying they're stupid?'

I was somewhat drunk. I was riled. I resented him pushing me. I said: 'Well if you want to know what I really think, then yeah, I think conservation is basically just doing birdwatching for a living. Conservationists are just one step up from birdwatchers—'

'Don't *say* that, Miles,' cried Jenny.

'And birdwatchers, birdwatchers are basically just one step up from stamp collectors, and I think that—' But Jenny had stood up, and she shouted, more than that, she screamed at me, she screamed in my face: 'Well I've *known* conservationists, Miles, and some of them, some of them are more of a man than you will ever be!' and she fled to the door, and slammed it behind her as she ran out into the rain.

I was open-mouthed.

It was the first hurtful thing she had ever said to me.

Callum too was taken aback. After a few moments he said: 'Hey er, look, Miles, never mind that, the lassie's upset, people say all sorts of things when they're upset.'

The thunder rumbled, distant now.

I was at a loss for words.

So was Callum.

He stood up. 'Ah think ah'm gonna leave ye to it,' he said. 'Ah'm gonna turn in now. Gotta be up at four to go out with Russell. But ah'll see ye before ye go, hey?'

'Yeah, OK,' I said.

'Goodnight now, Miles.'

'Goodnight, Callum.'

I sat in the quiet of the room. The dagger of scorn which Jenny had suddenly plunged into me left me more than wounded, it left me profoundly shocked. It felt as if she had suddenly become a different person, a Jenny I had no notion of. I wondered whether to go after her. But somehow I felt paralysed. I simply sat there.

She returned after about ten minutes, her hair wet and her face haggard: she had been crying. But she must have taken in from the look on my own face how shaken I was, for her expression changed. She softened. She went into the kitchen and got a glass of water. Then she came and sat next to me.

At length she murmured: 'I'm sorry for what I said.'

I looked at her.

'I was very upset and people say things when they're upset that they don't mean.'

I said nothing.

'Miles?'

I said: 'Well. I'm trying to work it out. There's two things. There's pride. And then there's common sense. And pride says, I should just walk away. It's a pretty strong feeling. Insistent, even. But I've wanted you so much I suppose I could put pride aside. Guys do, don't they? Women too.'

Jenny waited.

'But common sense is different. Common sense says, that if underneath, after these months together, what you really feel for me is contempt, then it's a waste of time, isn't it? Of my time and your time. Can't be anything else. And we should end it now.'

Jenny shook her head. 'I don't want to end it, Miles.'

'But it cannot work on the basis of contempt.'

'I don't feel contempt for you.'

'You said I could never be a man in your eyes, Jen.'

Her face darkened; she took my hand in both of hers. 'Miles, listen to me. I got very upset. Because of things in my life, things that are, that are buried deep in my past. You weren't to know. And when people are that upset, they lash out, don't they, they use whatever comes to hand, whatever feelings, whatever insults, but it does not mean that at the end of the day, that's what they really feel, and I swear to you, Miles, look at me, I swear I do not feel contempt for you.'

I looked at her. I looked at her full in the face as she looked at me, and I knew that Jenny Pittaway when she was serious about something was not capable of lying, and so in spite of myself, in spite of the evidence to the contrary which I had just been so forcefully presented with, part of me, at least, believed her.

I said: 'Then why were you so upset? It was only an argument about conservation.'

Jenny seemed to wrestle with her feelings. She said: 'I just – I can't talk about it, Miles, can you accept that? Please?'

I shrugged. I nodded. 'Yeah, all right.'

'I know it might seem a lot to ask. Especially after what you've given me here.' She looked around. 'I've loved your island. I can't tell you how grateful I am to you for bringing me to Skarholm. It is truly the most marvellous place. I've enjoyed every second of it and I really don't want this to, to sour it all. To affect the memories of it. Which are fantastic.'

'OK.'

She kissed my hand. She said: 'You know what I think – I think maybe if we just, let it mend, it will be all right.'

'OK.'

I reached forward and kissed her forehead.

She smiled at me. It was a weak and wintry smile, but a smile nonetheless. She said: 'Thank you for that.' Then she reached forward herself, and kissed my cheek, and ran a single finger down it.

So it did not end, on Skarholm, though I think it came close. But it changed. You cannot lash out and stick a knife into somebody and there not be a scar. For the first time I was wary of Jenny; I did not entirely trust her. It was as if our innocence had gone, that time from when she moved in when I was Mr Serious, pursuing her, and she was Ms Madcap, teasingly rebuffing me, but we were just ourselves, not trying to be anything, not calculating. Now, although I still wanted her more than anything in the world, something in me drew back, and the first time we made love again, I did not cry out my passion for her at the climax as I had on every previous occasion. Nor did I subsequently.

There was a distance between us.

Jenny took that in her stride, and did not lessen her warmth for me, which was terrific of her, looking back. She was on a healing mission. That did not mean she was about to give her heart to me out of guilt – never in a million years, and I had enough sense not to use any temporary moral superiority I might have felt to try to bring that about, which would have ended everything, in short order – but it did mean she wanted to mend the hurt. And so as the summer came on, and I busied myself with my blue tits project from the nestboxes of Wytham Woods, Jenny and I moved forward stiffly: walking wounded.

But we couldn't go on like that; it was no basis for future togetherness. I was still desperate to have her, and I began to realise that in some way I would have to force the issue now, I would have to bring it to the proof. Her words about winning her with an island still echoed around my soul like an unceasing peal of bells, but I knew I could not take her to island after island, year after year; realistically, I sensed, I would get one more shot at it, and it would either happen there, or it wouldn't happen at all.

So as that summer advanced, I began to search for the island, the miraculous island that would compel Jenny Pittaway to surrender her heart to me. I searched the whole world, surfing the infant internet. I searched the temperate zone and the tropics, I searched the Caribbean and the Indian Ocean, I went from the Baltic Sea to Micronesia, I looked at the celebrated and the obscure, the placid and the edgy, the luxurious and the rough-and-ready, and it was weeks before I suddenly thought I had found it, and got Jenny to agree to go on a mystery holiday, one whose destination she would discern only on arrival.

To Skokholm. He sees copulation
She sees shagging in open. Says
he's inhibited.
p76 Shearwaters (Warden Fled)
p79. Great Auk beak.
p84 M thinks conservation not cmp.
conservationists are bit thick.
They fall out - come together -
M starts to look for an island
for J.

7

We left Oxford at four in the morning to get to Gatwick for what was meant to be a 9 a.m. flight: we had foolishly drunk the evening before, not a lot but we had hardly slept and Jenny was grouchy. We joined the check-in queue well before seven; I pointed to the flight on the departure board which was labelled *Kefalinnia* and said: 'That's us.' Jenny had to think for a minute: 'That's Cephalonia, isn't it?' she said. '*Captain Corelli's Mandolin*. OK, fine. Never been. Now I just wanna get there.' I thought she might guess our real destination, but the Ionian islands were a part of Greece she had never visited and she didn't have a map in her head.

It was the start of a trying journey. Boarding was delayed for several hours, and then we had an argument with a stroppy woman about moving her bag in the overhead locker so we could get ours in. Two rows in front of us, a woman was carrying a baby, which started screaming and sent heartbeats up all through the plane; we both put headphones on and turned the music channel up full but it was no use, the screams got through and they lasted, and I timed it by my watch, an hour and twenty minutes till the little monster fell asleep. I said to Jenny: 'We can't shut it out because it's a sound we're programmed to respond to.' She said: 'Know what? I can see Herod's point.' When we landed, with the hot day winding down into evening, Jenny was so tired and stressed that she felt ill.

But things improved. Yiannis, the driver from the private tour company which had organised the holiday, took one look at Jenny and said: 'Bad flight? You go in back by yourself, lie down' and as we skirted Argostoli the capital and headed north, she stretched out and slept in the back of the Mercedes for more than an hour until we came to the end of the now-darkened road, when I called out to her; and as Yiannis stopped she opened her eyes and stretched and yawned and avowed she felt better.

'We there?' she said.

'Nearly,' I said.

'Where are we?'

'Fiskardo.'

'I go find Socrates with bags,' Yiannis said. 'You go have a drink.'

We wandered through to the harbour and found a bustling, restaurant-fringed waterside that was lit with lanterns in the warm night. 'Oh, this is lovely,' said Jenny, and we sat down in one of the tavernas and ordered a plate of bread and oil and a flask of retsina, and Jenny said, as the life started to flow back into her, 'So come on, Miles, where we staying? We staying here? This'll do, old lad. This looks great.'

'Not quite,' I said.

'We've farther to go?'

'Yes, but not a lot. We're going to another island.'

I was sure she would guess it then, but she didn't, she just said, 'Well, well. OK,' and after a few minutes Yiannis came along with his friend Captain Socrates the boatman, and Socrates, who wore a peaked sailor's hat, indicated his boat down the quay and I got up and whispered to him, 'Don't say where we're going, OK?' and pointing to Jenny, 'It's a surprise.'

By the time we boarded she was wide-awake and back to her best, delighted with the sparkle of Fiskardo harbour at night as we left it behind and chugged out to sea, the pair of us standing next to Captain Socrates in the wheelhouse. When we got beyond the harbour lights into the true darkness we realised there was a full moon, a huge creamy harvest moon, and as we rounded the headland we saw that the channel in front of us, the whole sea, was lit by the moonlight, every wavelet sprayed with silver, as was the towering land mass opposite.

'Jesus,' said Jenny. 'Will you look at that.'

'That's where we're going,' I said. 'The silver island.'

'What is it?' she said. 'Come on Miles, tell me now. What, what, what?'

'Socrates?' I said.

'I tell now?' he said, smiling.

'You tell.'

'*Itharki.*'

'What?'

'Ithaca.'

It was a moment before she took it in. Then a great smile spread over her face and she curled her arms about my neck and murmured, 'Miles Bonnici, you little fucking beauty.'

'Not little shit, then? Not little wanker?'

'Come here,' she said, and brought her lips to my mouth in what was the most smouldering kiss I had ever received, something that in its soft yielding went far beyond affection and promised complete sexual surrender. 'You little fucking marvel,' she whispered.

She stood with her arms around me and her head on my shoulder as we began to head inshore, and gradually a cove opened out to us with lights at its end. 'This here Polis Bay,' said Socrates. We found that the holiday organisation was still working because there to meet us was another driver, Costas, and he loaded our bags into his Toyota and drove us up the steep hill from the harbour to a village, which he announced as: 'Stavros!' There were lighted restaurants and old guys outside a café playing chess. We headed downhill again, and after a few minutes came to another restaurant-surrounded small harbour, which Costas announced as: 'Frikes!' Then he drove along the coast a few minutes more until we encountered a final settlement, announced by Costas as: 'Kioni!'

'This is us,' I said.

'You want harbour first?' said Costas.

'No, go straight there,' I said, and he drove uphill to what we could see in the shadows was a villa, and he let us in, and checked that we had everything we needed and told us he would be back in the morning with our hire car, and bade us goodnight; and Jenny skipped around and liked everything she saw and then found the balcony, and from it we could see the lights in the harbour below but more than that, the full moon high above the distant mountains of Greece across the water, lighting the land and lighting the sea, lighting the whole damn world.

She took my hand. I had got it right, although I did not realise then just how right I had got it. Thinking though everything she had said about islands, I registered that she had spoken more than once of Ithaca, in an animated way, and I had simply taken the chance that it might be special to her. I had no idea how special, nor that at that moment she was experiencing a turbulent mixture of emotions.

The one nearest the surface, though, was simple gratitude, for my showing her, with a gift so carefully chosen, that after our time of distance the injury of Skarholm was fully healed; and Jenny was always big on gratitude. It was that which lit her warmth as she turned towards me and brought her arms up about my neck, and it was gratitude which charged her kiss, her kiss of fire, and her giving of herself to me during the night that followed, when everything seemed slower, floating, endless, when every touch felt new, and when the darkness and the silence were everything you ever might want.

But I had got it right in other ways. I had not only found the island which echoed Jenny's imaginings – as I was to come to understand – I had unwittingly found a corner of it, a corner of the world, which we both found … overwhelming, really. Kioni, in the brochure I used to book the holiday, had seemed agreeable enough, very pleasant even; but having arrived in the dark, neither of us was prepared for what awaited us in the light.

Jenny encountered it first; she woke at seven, and stretched and yawned, and wandered out on to the balcony and looked down. Then she called: 'Miles. Miles!'

'What?' I grunted.

'Come and look at this.'

I dragged myself out of bed, and stumbled sleepily to her side and looked: my own eyes opened wide. There below us was a miniature gulf of perfect electric blue ending in a tiny harbour, with at the water's edge bright white houses with terracotta roofs, and above them a dark green wooded hillside. It was so faultless, its colours and its beauty so intense, that I had the feeling for the first time in my life that I was looking on something no painter could improve upon, that even the most inspiring rendition of it would only make you want to go back to the place itself.

Seen from above, at that moment of early morning stillness, it was dream-like; and it continued to seem so as we wandered down into it, hand in hand and heady from our lovemaking, both Jenny who had seen so much of the Greek islands and I who had seen nothing, looking about us, scarcely believing its perfection. Around the harbour were four tavernas and a couple of cafés; one of the cafés was open and we sat outside it with bread and coffee, watching the yachts and fishing boats that were tied up bump gently in the clear water, with the dark blue sea beyond and the pale blue sky above.

Jenny said: 'Would have been worth it, wouldn't it? Odysseus's journey from Troy. To come back to this.'

'This is where he came to?'

'No idea. I don't know anything about the island. It was always just somewhere I imagined.' She smiled. 'As you clearly realised.' And she kissed her fingertip and touched my hand with it.

'What did you imagine?'

'Penelope, mostly. Odysseus's wife.'

'You'll have to remind me.'

'When Odysseus goes off to Troy with the rest of the Greeks he leaves Penelope behind, here on Ithaca. And the war lasts ten years, and it takes him another ten years to get home, 'cos he's taken prisoner by the sea-nymph Calypso and stuff. So he's away twenty years. Pretty long time, eh?'

I nodded.

'And Penelope waits for him, all that time, even though he might well be dead, and there's a whole gang of suitors, eligible young men, hanging around Odysseus's house, badgering her to marry one of them.'

I considered. I said: 'So what were you thinking about her?'

'Whether she was right to wait.'

'And what do you think?'

'Well, I suppose, all things considered, she was probably right. Given her circumstances.'

'Where did it all … actually take place?'

'Dunno. But we could find out, couldn't we? You brought a guidebook?'

'I have. You want to do that today? We could go for a tour, when the hire car comes. Nine o'clock, Costas is bringing it.'

'You know what, Miles, I think I'd rather swim in this sea before I do a single other thing.' She looked at the yachts in front of us. 'Jeez, wouldn't it be fantastic to have a boat here?'

'We get one,' I said.

'What?'

'We get a boat as part of the deal. Along with the hire car.'

She looked at me for a second, as if not believing what she had heard, and then she exploded into laughter, holding on to her chair as the convulsions shook her, and finishing with a coughing fit.

I was bemused. 'Why's it funny?'

'It's just you,' she said, pointing at me, shaking her head and still laughing, wheezing now. 'Nerdface. Supergeek. Weird … seagull man.'

'What?'

'It's the idea of you …' Her features dropped down into a smile. 'Nothing. Nothing at all. I just laugh like that when I'm happy.'

The boat was a small dinghy with an outboard which we picked up from Yorgios who ran the boat-hire business, and we took our snorkeling gear and the guidebook to the Ionian islands and *Captain Corelli's Mandolin* for me, which I thought I ought to read, and a parasol and beach mats from the villa, and a picnic from the little

Kioni supermarket; and in high good humour we set out from the harbour and the miniature gulf with its three white windmills on the right-hand arm, into that bluest of seas, and south down the coast which was entirely wild and untouched by human activity; and we found a cove, a completely isolated, exquisite cove with a pebble beach and limpid, crystalline water where we anchored; and we spent the day alone, swimming and diving and looking at the fish and the starfish and the sea urchins – Jenny was a wonderful swimmer – and eating our picnic of feta and loukanika and tsatsiki and olive bread and lemonade, and lying in the sun, in and out of the parasol shade, with Jenny glued to the guidebook, drinking in all she could about the island, the real Ithaca, in place of the one of her imagination, until the fiery ball started to dip and we headed back.

We showered then and dressed to step out, laughing as we formally admired each other, and we took a glass of wine on the balcony as the lights came on in the harbour below, and we wandered down to it once more in the balmy dusk and took our choice of the tavernas: Jenny decided on the one called Kalypso. We sat outside and ate grilled sea bream and lemon rice and drank a white wine called Tsandas, I remember, as the skinny restaurant cats prowled about our feet and a fat moon climbed up again over Greece in the distance and its creamy reflection trembled in the water a few yards away. Jenny wore a white muslin dress and seemed to me lovely beyond description. She talked animatedly of her summer crewing yachts in Greece, the summer before she came to London, saying it had been a crazy time, and she was drunk or stoned for much of it, but she had learned a few things, such as enough Greek to make herself understood, and she started to laugh and told me of a fellow Kiwi crew member who had just arrived and got mixed up between *kalimera*, which means good morning, and *kalamari*, which means squid, and spent his first few days cheerfully saying 'squid!' to every Greek he encountered – it was too wonderful to correct, and she and the rest of the crew encouraged it, shouting 'Kalamari, mate!' to Andy every morning. It had all been in the Cyclades, she said, Mykonos and Paros and Santorini and the rest, which were beautiful. Then she looked at me. 'But not as beautiful as here, Miles.'

Was this it, then? Was this indeed the island I would win her with? Funny. I was relaxed about it. I knew I could not make it happen, I could only try to set up the circumstances and let events take their turn. Since Skarholm I had stopped telling Jenny I loved her, but it had to be clear to her that <u>Ithaca was a declaration</u>, the most obvious bid for her commitment there could possibly be; and so although for two days more I said nothing about what was at the forefront of my feelings, and Jenny said nothing either, I knew she would have to make up her mind eventually. And on the fourth day, she did.

I had already begun to notice odd moments about her that were … darker, somehow. Not troubled, exactly, but pensive. I caught her a few times deep in thought: in one of our swimming coves, when I was dozing under the parasol, I opened my eyes and noticed she was looking out to sea and turning a pebble over and over in her hand, and for fully ten minutes I watched the expression change on her face like the shadows of clouds on the land; a number of times her lips moved soundlessly; once she bit her lower lip, for several seconds. I said nothing.

On the fourth day, in the morning, she said: 'What d'you say we go find Odysseus?'

'Sure,' I said.

Some of the main Homeric ruins, the guidebook told us, were quite nearby, above the village of Stavros which we had gone through on the night of our arrival; we drove up to it and eventually set out walking up a minor road for what the guide said was a site called the School of Homer.

We found it on a rocky eminence among olive groves high above the sea: I realised we were there when I suddenly saw a grey-bearded man in a straw hat sitting on a stool, his arms folded, looking at something. As we got closer we saw that there were awnings stretched from the rocks to the olive trees to provide shade, and underneath them, people were working: the bearded man was overseeing it all, shouting the occasional direction. Under the first awning, a group of people were trying to raise a large white boulder with a block and tackle attached to a big olive trunk; under the second, a burly muscled guy with a mattock was breaking up the earth, and after each of his strikes, a young man and young woman got down on their knees and began to search through the loose soil with scrapers.

We approached.

The man on the stool glanced up.

'*Kalimera*,' said Jenny.

'*Kalimera*.' He nodded.

'*Milaste Angliká?*'

'Yes I do,' said the man, looking more closely at Jenny, and half-smiling. He was taken with her.

'Is this ... the School of Homer?' Jenny said.

'So it is called.'

'Might we ask ... what you are doing?'

'We are searching for the Megaron of Odysseus.'

'Sorry, the what?'

'The Megaron. You would say in English, the Great Hall. The Great Hall of his palace.'

'Ah. The place where—'

'Where he held his feasts.'

'Where he shot the suitors with his bow and arrows?'

The smile broadened. 'Perhaps. Indeed.' He stood up. 'You know *The Odyssey*?'

'In English only.'

'That is more than something. Allow me to introduce myself. I am Thessalitis Papandreou. I am Professor of Archaeology at the University of Ioannina.' He gave a slight bow.

Jenny beamed back at him and said: 'I am Jenny Pittaway, and this is my friend, Doctor Miles Bonnici. From the University of Oxford.'

'Oxford?' said the Professor, delighted. 'Then you must know John Boardman! How is he, Sir John? He is Emeritus, now, of course, and Bert Smith, how is he?'

'I'm sorry,' I said, shaking my head. 'I'm afraid I'm not an archaeologist. Not even a classicist. Just a humble biologist.'

'No matter, no matter, you are welcome,' said the Professor. 'Would you like to see our operations?'

We said we would, and he led us over to the dig under the nearer awning, and introduced us to his doctoral students, Nikos and Eleni, although he did not bother with the workman, who stood by looking bored. 'We are searching for the Megaron's outlines,' said the Professor. 'We have not found them yet, but we are hopeful because we are finding other things, which make it clear this is a Homeric site.' And as if on cue the young man handed the Professor a small dark object he was holding, speaking in Greek and then saying to us: 'We have just found this.'

The Professor scraped some soil off, then held it out. It was a small rimmed pot. It was beautiful.

'You could drink coffee from it, couldn't you?' he said. 'Or tea. Yes, I think we are in the right place.'

Jenny said: 'And where would Penelope's apartments be? Where she retires with her women?'

'You are interested in Penelope?'

Jenny said: 'I see *The Odyssey* as more about Penelope than about Odysseus ... I'm afraid.' Suddenly aware of her boldness.

'Really? Do not be afraid, my dear. That is a perfectly respectable view, in fact, more and more so. Perhaps you should speak to my wife.' He called out: 'Hera! Hera!' and added something in Greek, and a woman in dark blue overalls with a pale blue scarf at her throat detached herself from the group at the farther awning and came towards us. She was taller than her husband, statuesque, almost, with a dark sensual face of big eyes and a wide mouth.

'She is Professor of Comparative Literature,' the Professor said, and to his wife as she came up: 'We have English visitors, my dear, this young man from Oxford and his young friend, it is ... Jenny, you said?'

Jenny nodded. 'And this is Miles.'

'Miles, yes, and this is my wife, Hera' – we all nodded and smiled and shook hands – 'and Jenny feels, she feels, my dear, that really the point of *The Odyssey* is not the story of *the quick-witted Odysseus*, and his adventures on the *wine-dark sea*, but the story of *the prudent Penelope*.' He opened his hand out to Jenny in an invitation to speak.

Jenny blushed. 'Well it just seems to me,' she said, 'that if the twenty years after the fall of Troy are difficult for Odysseus, they are even more difficult for Penelope.'

Hera said, in a perfectly friendly way: 'Do you not think the poem recognises that?'

'Yes I do, but I think the way the story has passed into popular culture, it's about Odysseus's wanderings, and not Penelope's waiting.'

'You identify with Penelope, perhaps?'

'Yes. Well. Perhaps. A bit. Sometimes.' She briefly bit her lip. Somewhere in a far corner of my brain, I wondered why.

'I think a lot of us do. Would you like to take a glass of lemonade? It is hot out here,' and she indicated a third awning behind us with a table underneath it which was clearly where the team took their lunch, and we said that was very kind, and the Professor excused himself and we thanked him, and sat down with Hera and she poured us a glass of lemonade from a bottle kept in a cool box – I remember how delicious it seemed – and she said: 'Feminism has of course changed the way we see Penelope. We pay more attention to her now. But that is not the same as saying that Penelope should be seen as a feminist. Or even a proto-feminist.'

Jenny said: 'Yes. No. I mean, I understand that.'

'She is a powerful woman, and she holds her own in a world of violent men, but she does it by acting cleverly in a womanly way. Entirely within the way that women were expected to behave, at that time.'

'No, I don't see her as a feminist,' said Jenny, 'Although you can see her as a feminist icon, can't you? But the thing that interests me is her actual waiting. Waiting for him all that time. For Odysseus.'

'What about it?'

'I wonder if she had a choice.'

'That is an interesting question.'

'Because if she didn't have a choice, her fidelity to Odysseus is … worth less, somehow. Isn't it?'

'Let us examine it,' Hera said. 'After twenty years, the probability must surely be that Odysseus is dead. Even in those days, it would take a few weeks at most to sail from Troy back to Ithaca. So there are lots of arguments for marrying one of the suitors. She would have protection, at once, in a violent world. And she would end the, the depredations of the suitors on the estate, which is being ruined.'

'Would she be condemned, if she did it?'

'Well, probably not by the Ithacans. It would seem a reasonable thing to do. But I think she would be condemned by someone else.'

'Who?'

'By the poet. Homer is very attached to the idea of loyalty, is he not? When Odysseus finally returns, if you remember, Homer writes warmly of those who have remained faithful, like Eumaeus the pig man, and Eurycleia, the nurse. And if you remember also, for those who have not been faithful, he reserves the cruellest punishments. The twelve slave-girls who have slept with the suitors are hanged. And you remember what they do to Melanthius the goatherd.'

Jenny nodded, pensive.

I said: 'What do they do to Melanthius the goatherd?'

'They cut off his nose and ears,' said Hera, 'and then his genitals, and then his hands and feet.'

'Oh,' I said. 'Right.'

Jenny said: 'So you're saying that Penelope is stopped from having a choice by … the story itself?'

'In a sense. It would be a very different Odyssey, wouldn't it, if Penelope had married again, and then Odysseus arrived home. But my own impression is that Homer is portraying a woman who is truly loyal. She does not marry again because she is loyal in her heart. For twenty years.'

'Is that a good thing?'

Hera laughed. 'What a strange question! Do you think it is not?'

'But what if Odysseus *was* dead,' Jenny said. 'What if he had died, say, a year after leaving Troy. The next nineteen years of loyalty would have been futile. A wasted life. Penelope would be denying herself her chance of being happy again.'

'But her heart belonged to Odysseus.'

'But that,' said Jenny, quickening her speech, 'giving your heart to someone, if it's somebody it looks like you'll never have again, isn't that ... hopeless?'

'You think so?'

'I didn't use to. I used to think Penelope was wonderful, because she kept the faith. But what if the faith leads nowhere? Should you still keep the faith?'

Hera looked at her pointedly, glancing quickly at me. 'Are you perhaps keeping the faith, my dear?'

Jenny bit her lip.

It went over my head completely. I was still thinking what it would be like to have your nose and ears cut off, then your genitals, then your hands and feet.

Wow, I was thinking, that was somewhat excessive, wasn't it?

'Listen,' Hera said, 'what we must remember is that Penelope simply did not *know*. She did not know what had happened to Odysseus. She kept the faith because there was still a chance that he was alive. But if she *had* found out that he was dead, and there was no possibility of having him again, the situation would have been different, would it not?'

'You think then she would definitely have married one of the suitors?'

'I think, very probably. The advantages would be overwhelming.'

'Right.'

'But I have to say to you, Jenny, in so far as I think of Penelope as a real character and not just a literary construct' – she laughed – 'I do think it is also possible – not likely, but possible – that she might *still* have kept the faith. Penelope might still have remained faithful to her first love, Odysseus, and not married again. I think we owe her that.'

'Should we be faithful to our first loves?'

'What do you think?'

'If a first love is so much, if it's absolutely everything, the whole world to you ... it's very hard to let it go. But what if that means that you're sort of trapped? Just trapped in the past? And

you can't move on to other things that might be worthwhile?
What should you do?'

'I can only tell you what my mother once told me,' said Hera.
'And she was a wise woman.'

'What is that?'

'Look in your heart.'

Jenny's eyes filled with tears. Thinking back, I registered that
somewhere in my brain, but I was being particularly dim. My
thoughts had drifted off to the bay I could see in the distance; I
was wondering if we could bring the boat round to it.

Jenny said: 'Thank you so much, Hera. I'm sorry we have taken
up so much of your time.'

'No, it's been a pleasure,' Hera said. 'A pleasure to meet you
both.' And we got to our feet, and shook hands. Jenny started to
say something else to Hera, but she thought the better of it.

Hera said: 'Jenny?'

'Yes?'

'Remember, eh?'

'What?'

'Where to look.'

Jenny said: '*Efharisto poli*, Hera.'

Hera beamed. '*Parakalo.*'

Leaving the School of Homer, as we picked our way along the
track in the rising heat, I said I thought it must be pretty tough work
being an archaeologist, mustn't it, unless you were the professor
and other people did the actual digging for you, although I don't
suppose Hera did any actual digging either, and she was pretty
cool, wasn't she, for an archaeologist but then she wasn't one, so
I suppose archaeology was a bit of a sideline for her but it must
be worth it for when they make their actual discoveries, like that
cup ... Jenny?

I turned to her and saw she was biting her bottom lip again.
She was distressed.

'Jenny, what's the matter?'

'Miles, I don't know what to do.'

'Do about what?'

'Do about us.'

So the moment had come.

I was calm about it.

There was an olive tree nearby and I said, 'Shall we sit in
the shade?'

So we sat down under it, and I remember I could see Cephalonia in the distance, across the channel, and Jenny picked up a pebble, and turned it over and over in her hand, thinking, until after a minute or so I said, as gently as I could: 'What d'you mean, that you don't know what to do?'

She said: 'With the others it was easy.'

'What was?'

'With Kevin on Kos it was easy. And with Gareth on Minorca.'

'What was easy?'

'They failed the test.'

'What test?'

'The island test.'

'What on earth is the island test?'

She looked at me and seemed unable to speak.

I was exasperated. I said: 'Jenny, will you for God's sake please now tell me what this is, this thing with you and bloody islands? What is it? Please?'

She said: 'It goes back a long way. To when I was a child.'

'Then will you tell me about it now, Jen? I think the time has come.'

She smiled at me, a faint smile. 'Yes, I suppose it has, hasn't it?'

She grew up in Auckland, she said, which as she had already told me was a city full of yachties, and the Pittaway family had a yacht of their own, a much-loved sloop called the *Windwhistle*. Every weekend they sailed her on the east side of Auckland in an area of sea called the Hauraki Gulf, and the Hauraki Gulf was full of islands, and the Pittaways sailed around them all and would explore them, the ones they could tie up at, and Jenny got to know them pretty well, Rangitoto, Motutapu, Waiheke, Kawau, Rakino, all of them, and she would take photos and when she was about twelve or thirteen she started a book on them, a big scrapbook. It was known in the family as *Jenny's Book of Islands* and was kept under the TV. She was sort of collecting them, she said, because she had started to feel they all had different personalities, as if each island had a soul, and she started to dream about them. Some young girls might dream about being princesses or pop stars, she said, but she dreamed about islands, islands where she would have adventures, islands that hadn't been discovered, islands with secrets, most of all, she dreamed that there would be a truly special island, where something amazing would happen to her.

She paused.

'And?' I said.

'There was.'

There was a longer pause. And then it dawned on me. Finally.

'Was it with a guy?'

She nodded.

It had simply never occurred to me before.

'The bastard,' she said, 'the blond-haired, blue-eyed, idealistic bastard.'

I realised she was crying.

And that was how I leaned about Shane.

Shane Peberdy was the year ahead of her in the Biological Sciences department at Auckland Uni, but he was twenty-eight, a mature student who'd already had a full life; he'd been a fisherman and then an activist with Greenpeace but his really big thing was cetaceans: whales and dolphins. He wanted to go into cetacean conservation full-time, so he was doing a marine biology degree and Jenny and her girlfriends all thought he was gorgeous; with blue eyes, long blond hair and a permanent tan from his time at sea he looked like a Californian surfer, only he was more natural. He wasn't a poser. He was a bit of a mystery. He didn't chase girls like he could have done, and he could have had any girl he wanted, Jenny said. He didn't go out with anyone in the department but seemed to have his own life, outside.

Jenny got to know him in her final year when Shane was doing his Masters, a study of Bryde's whales in the Hauraki Gulf, and he needed an assistant to drive his inflatable, and because Jenny was hoping to do a Masters herself the department suggested she apply for the job; and that summer, in the November, she went out to work with him on Great Barrier Island, the farthest island out, where the department had rented a holiday home in Tryphena, the little harbour; they shared it, but she had her own room and everything, and Shane was perfectly gentlemanly and didn't try it on with her in any way. And Jenny said she began to enjoy that, the fact that he wasn't interested in her romantically; it was liberating, she suddenly felt freed from all the games that men and women play, and she started to enjoy him and admire him for who he was, a really interesting guy, deeply committed to conservation.

I saw it: 'Is that why you were so upset on Skarholm, when I … when I was disparaging about conservationists.'

'It was, yes.'

I nodded.

'And I am truly sorry that I hurt you the way I did. And I do not think the things I said.'

'I know that. Go on.'

They had a purely professional relationship for the first three weeks of Shane's surveys, Jenny said, but things changed between them because of the accident: they were in the fizz boat one day – 'that's the inflatable,' she said – heading back at high speed and they hit something, something big and solid, which wasn't a rock. They never found out what it was. Shane's best guess was a dead whale. But they hit it and the inflatable flipped over and threw them out and what must have been the fibreglass hull caught Shane on the head and knocked him senseless.

Jenny swam over to him and managed to get him to the upturned rib and they hung on to the grab handles, with Shane not quite unconscious but very groggy, and as luck would have it a boat came out of Tryphena and spotted them and got them back. I asked her how long they were in the water and she said two hours, maybe three, it was nearly dark when they found us, and I looked at her and marvelled at the things you don't know about people. I said: 'And it changed between you after that?'

It did, she said; their time in the water, when they might have died, had in some way bonded them deeply; and they became lovers.

Could I understand this, she said, from the very beginning, from the first moment, they were in love. It wasn't about sex, although the sex was great. She loved him for who he was – she loved him for being strong and beautiful, sure, but she loved him most of all for the way he cared about things. Like, she asked him what attracted him so much to whales and dolphins and he said, their dignity, which made her stop and think. And she said, I flatter myself that he loved me in the same way, in fact, I know he did, and she didn't think it was possible to love anyone more completely than they loved each other. But what intensified it was the time and the place. Their summer, on the Barrier. Waking up with him to such crystal mornings, and the golden evenings, and the beauty of the ocean all around them, their love on their island; she had always dreamed there'd be a special island for her, and here it was, it seemed fated, she knew she would love him always, whatever happened, and I said, what did happen and she said, he was married, Miles, and I said, Ah.

No, she said, it wasn't like that, Shane wasn't cheating on his wife. He was separated, he'd been separated for over two years, although he hadn't told her and she thought he should have done.

The problem was his wife, Sylvia, had been in London but she came back; it had gone wrong for her in some way. Jenny thought she'd had some sort of breakdown, though Shane wouldn't give her the details, all he said was that she needed him, and he had to go back to her. It was at the end of the wonderful summer, in the February, they were getting ready to return to Auckland and Jenny was going to start her own Masters and they were going to live together, and a week before they were due to return Shane said to her that there was a problem.

She told me of her amazement. Of her protests. Of the ashtray she threw at him and then the vase, when she saw he was serious, and of his own protests that he would always love her and it was tearing him apart but he had to do it, and of her realisation that he had to do it because of who he was, which was why she loved him, so she was caught every which way, wasn't she; and of the last night she would never forget, making love with the tears streaming down her face before getting the ferry back to Auckland the next morning and collapsing into the arms of her mother.

She said: 'I cried for a whole day. Maybe two. Maybe more. It's all a blur. You know, I didn't believe it was possible to hurt so much. I sort of understood why people kill themselves. Cos what are you gonna do with the rest of your life if what you cherish most in your life has been lost?'

She was saved by her best friend Lisa, she said, who had a trip planned to Europe and persuaded Jenny to accompany her, so she jettisoned her planned Masters and off she went on this island-hopping itinerary Lisa had planned, ending in the Med – and eventually, on Mykonos, she told Lisa she had to be alone now and Lisa understood and went on to London while Jenny got the job with the sailing company, for the summer, for the European summer, that she'd already mentioned.

She said: 'It was June by now. And the shock of it all had died down, and I realised that I hadn't stopped loving Shane and I would never stop loving him. And I thought, I would wait, just wait, for however long it took. And that's when I discovered *The Odyssey*. There was a tatty Penguin edition on one of the boats and I started reading it 'cos I was bored and I stumbled on Penelope, waiting for twenty years. I was electrified. There it was – the way to think about it. I was Penelope, and Shane was Odysseus – I could easily see Shane as Odysseus – and bloody Sylvia was Calypso, keeping him from his rightful love. But it didn't matter because I would wait for as long as it took. Penelope, that would be me.'

She told me that she went on to London to join Lisa, but when Christmas came she returned home to New Zealand and made a critical discovery: Shane and Sylvia were going to have a baby. She knew then that she could never get him back while he had young children, she would have to rebuild her life, even if it was Shane Peberdy who held her heart. So she returned to London in the New Year and got her job, and after a few weeks she started to go out with one of the editors at her firm called Kevin, Kevin Blackstock, nice guy and it was going well, they liked each other's company, but he wanted more and she wasn't sure about that, until they went on holiday. They went to Kos. And then she was sure. 'Because all I could see, on an island with Kevin, was that it wasn't anything like being on an island with Shane.'

'That was the island test?'

'Yup.'

'And Kevin failed it?'

'He did. I just thought, what am I doing with this bloke? And when we got back, I ended it.'

'Was he upset?'

'Pretty much.'

'Did he … pursue you? Er, like I did?'

'Yeah.'

'But that made no difference?'

'Well, no.'

I realised how close I had come.

'And then there was another guy?'

Gareth, she said, Gareth Lightbound, banker and rugby player, well-off and good-looking but a pompous arse really, so eventually she set up another island test, deliberately this time, and that was Minorca, a sailing holiday, and Gareth failed it too.

'You finished with him as well?'

'Yup.'

'And how did he take it?'

'Well with Kevin, I just had to change jobs, but with Gareth, I had to leave London.'

'Really?'

'He went nuts. He started stalking me.'

'Was that when you came to Oxford?'

'It was, yes.'

We looked at each other.

'So now, Miles Bonnici, you know everything.'

I let my gaze wander out over the sea to Cephalonia; there was a big white ferry ploughing up the channel between the two islands. I said: 'You said when we started talking, you didn't know what to do. About us.'

She nodded.

'But if *I* had failed the island test, Jen, you would know what to do. Wouldn't you?'

She bit her lip.

'Then why don't you know what to do?'

'Because ...' She looked up. 'I want you, Miles.'

'So what is the difficulty?'

'I don't know if I can give my heart again.'

I gazed out to sea once more. It was calming, somehow, it helped me think. I said: 'Look. When Kevin and Gareth failed the island test, they failed it because they weren't Shane, really, didn't they?'

'Yes.'

'But I'm not Shane, am I? And the next guy's not going to be Shane, nor the one after that, and no one is ever going to be Shane, so what you're doing is, you're cutting yourself off from your whole future, by being so attached to your past. Don't you think?'

'Maybe.'

'I'm sure Shane was everything you say he was, but I can't really see how you would keep your heart *entirely* for someone you very probably will never have. If you had a chance of happiness elsewhere. And I flatter myself in saying that.'

Jenny said: 'You're not flattering yourself, Miles.'

'Do you not want to have a future? Do you only want to have a past?'

Jenny struggled to speak. At length she said: 'There's something else.'

'What?'

'I'm afraid.'

'What are you afraid of?'

'If I give myself again, I'll have no defences left.'

I said: 'That doesn't sound like the Jenny Pittaway I know.'

'No, it's true. My heart was broken once and I got through it, but I couldn't survive a second time, Miles, if I were to give my heart to anyone and they left me again, I wouldn't know how to survive.'

I said: 'Left you again? But Jenny, I love you. You know that.'

It was the first time I had said it since our falling-out on Skarholm. She looked at me with what seemed like astonishment on her face, and then she fell against me, clinging tight to my shoulder.

I kissed her hair, many kisses.

I kissed her forehead.

I brought her face out from my shoulder, and I kissed her eyes, and her cheeks, and I kissed her mouth.

I nuzzled her nose with my nose, like a cat does, and I said: 'I love you, Jen.'

And her eyes met mine, then, and I saw the strength in them, and she said: 'And I love you, Captain Seagull.'

Jenny's happiness, in the remaining days of our time on Ithaca, was overflowing. It let her look at the world afresh, as if its beauty were new-born, as if all its value were there to be rediscovered and cherished; and in our final days on the island she took intense delight in everything it had to offer, from our trek to the mountain monastery of Panayia Katharon with its stupendous views over the deep blue gulf as far as Vathy, the island capital, and beyond, to the corny joviality of the bazouki music in the little Kioni bar, Spavento, where one night she actually got me to my feet to dance, and the simplicity of the cold retsina, and the freshness of the fish in the habourside restaurants.

Most of all, she delighted in the beauty of Kioni itself, privileged, she said, that we might have found love in such a setting; and on our final evening, as we had dinner once more on the harbourside with the gently bumping boats, the trembling reflection of the by-now waning moon and the restaurant cats prowling about our feet in the glowing dusk, she said to me she felt she had come home – *like Odysseus came home here after his wanderings, Miles, like he came home at last to Penelope, I have come home to you.* And she began to cry then, the tears flooded down her cheeks, and I said what, what is it Jen, and she said she was crying for all the people who could not have the happiness she had.

In the night, in the dark, in our embrace, I told her again that I loved her and she whispered to me: 'Miles, I will love you all my life.'

And yet, within a year, I had smashed this love to pieces.

Greek island. Discussion about
Penelope faithful to 1st love.
Past boyfriends failed to island test. p100
She wants M (I'm not sure why)
afraid of pain separation

8

When I consider it now in the cold light of day it seems too astonishing almost to be believed, this savage act of mine which is at the heart of this whole saga, and which eventually led us to Lanna, and to Fergus Pryng and everything that followed; it seems to me, given the circumstances which had preceded it, one of the most egregious examples of human cruelty you could ever imagine, and although there are no mitigating circumstances about it whatsoever, it does denote the extent to which my youthful psyche had been twisted by my relationship with my father.

For that was what lay at the heart of it. My problem was, as Jenny once remarked, that I was clever, but not wise: in the considerable corpus of knowledge I might possess as a brilliant researcher, self-knowledge did not feature. I never acknowledged consciously the real nature of my pursuit of her, which was, of course, to reverse her rejection of me and then to reach a point where such a calamity could never happen again. I suppose I was aware of this instinctively, but I presented the emotion to myself as being deeply in love, not registering that my 'love' was in essence simply a commanding need, and when it was fulfilled, when at last Jenny had lost her heart and become dependent on me and our positions were reversed – when I was back on top – my ardour for her might begin to cool.

She understood something of these matters, though, and I'm surprised, looking back, that she took a chance on me; I could so easily have gone the way of Kevin and Gareth. That I did not was partly her meeting my family, and the whole-hearted sympathy that sprang up between her, and my mother and Lotte; and I think it was partly too that she was becoming tired of living in the past with the memories of Shane, and she wanted to have a future once again (and as I was to discover, sensed the ticking of that most clichéd of timepieces, her biological clock).

It might not have mattered. Rejected men do win women back – and vice-versa – and then live happy lives together, I don't doubt;

but Jenny's misfortune was that she had a formidable rival for the key position in my soul: my ambition, my towering ambition. It had been on ice for months, whilst I pursued her, but once the pursuit was achieved and Jenny was won, it emerged from its cold storage to make itself felt once more.

After Jenny surrendered her heart, therefore, I rejoiced as she did, but my own reason for rejoicing was fundamentally different from hers. What I had been seeking was security – security against ever being shattered again by her leaving me, which was the worst thing that had ever happened in my life – and I had found it; and I was filled with an intense happiness, just as she was, and an exultant haze enveloped us both during the last days on Ithaca and our return. And we flew home holding hands, and went to Wimbledon the next day and showed off our gladness as if we were showing off a new baby, and my mother and Lotte could see it clearly and were thrilled. We drove back to Oxford that evening in deep contentment and the next day woke with a kiss and laughed at breakfast and parted with a kiss, and Jenny went off to OUP, and I went off to the zoology department, and opened up my office and sat down at my desk, and I began to take stock.

It was quiet: the students would not be back for nearly a month. I sat with a coffee, idly tapping my desk with a pen, and I thought about things. My pursuit of Jenny: what a saga, eh? And how it had all come right in the end, thank God: the gnawing fear of being dumped again was over at last. It was a hugely satisfying feeling. But it had taken time and effort.

I thought about how long it had actually taken.

Best part of nine months.

Remarkable. All that time had been taken up with Jenny Pittaway, in place of my previous purposes and aims: that was certainly new.

Beforehand, my ambition had been my only purpose. I thought back to my triumphant return to Oxford and the specific plan I had then. I was ploughing ahead with the research project, the project on female infidelity with the blue tits of Wytham Woods, but also I was going to accompany it with a new book on female sexuality that would be a sequel to *Everything Except Seahorses* and would create even more of a stir. I registered the fact that over the previous nine months I had been so obsessed with Jenny that what I had done about the book amounted to precisely nothing.

Shit.

Nothing.

For nine months.

I took a piece of paper from the printer tray and wrote on it in pen: *Female infidelity.*

Then I added: *In animals and people.*

I drew a circle around the sentence.

How could I have done *nothing* for nine months?

I tossed the paper on the desk.

The point was, the two complemented each other perfectly, the research and the book. The research finding, which I was pretty confident of getting, would show that young birds born from infidelities which their mothers had freely initiated were tougher and had more of a chance of survival than their siblings, fathered by the 'husbands'; because it was with stronger, fitter males than their regular partners that the mother birds had chosen to be unfaithful.

It would show, in effect, that female infidelity was worth it.

Boy, that would shake people up.

Get your morality around that one, folks.

But it would be the *book* that would bring the finding to wider public attention, beyond the specialists that a scientific paper would reach. It would look at female sexuality in general and female infidelity in particular, in women as well as in non-human animals, and it would plaster me all over the media. I needed both to keep my career on track, to stay on my soaring trajectory and stay on course to outstrip him, the man who filled my being, the man who swam into my mind even then and I heard myself internally shouting, Oh no, you don't get away with it just because you're dead. Oh no. FUCK YOU. It doesn't end just because you're not around any more. I'm on track. Or, I will be. Because, to be honest, it had stalled, somewhat, hadn't it? The soaring trajectory. But I would get it back.

That evening, over dinner, I told Jenny I was going to write another book, this one about female infidelity.

'Bit hard on us lot, isn't it?' she said.

'I don't think so,' I said. 'It's paying women their due, which has never really been recognised. It's showing that female choice is a key determinant of reproductive behaviour. In other words, that the females are in control. As you know only too well, my dear.'

She grinned. 'And what's it to be called?'

'At the moment it's provisionally entitled *Female Infidelity in Animals and People.*'

'God, that's boring. Sounds like a medical manual.'

'Well, what would you suggest?'

'It's about female choice, you say?'

I nodded.

'That the females of the species are … doing the deciding?'

'Yes.'

'Then why don't you call it *Sisters Are Doin' It for Themselves?*'

'What?'

'It's the song. The famous song by Annie Lennox. Of the Eurythmics? The nearest thing we've got to a feminist anthem, Miles. You must know it.

I thought about it. 'Sisters are doing it for themselves?'

'*Doin'* it, Miles. No g on the end.'

'I can't just rip off the whole song title.'

'All right. Just call it *Doin' It for Themselves*, then.'

'But no one will know what that means.'

'Miles, I think every feminist in the world, every woman with any feminist sympathy at all, will know instantly what it means.'

'You really think so?'

'Trust me.'

How was he qualified to write this

So *Doing It for Themselves: Female Infidelity in Animals and People* – I didn't really think I could drop the g – indeed became the working title, and I put together a formal proposal and once more approached OUP about it and they were enthusiastic, and agreed to take it on, and they gave me a moderate advance with a provisional deadline of two years, and I began work. I started with a substantial search of all the scientific studies of female extra-pair copulation in socially monogamous animals, and in addition to that, all the sociological studies of infidelity by women. At Jenny's suggestion I broadened the latter inquiry to include classical literature, beginning with *Anna Karenina* and moving on to *Madame Bovary* and even *The Graduate*: I started to become an expert on unfaithful wives and lovers and the reasons for their straying. It was a major project, and the more my dormant ambition reawoke with it, the more I had a sense of needing to catch up, to get back on the track that would overtake my father, to get a move on, properly. So although I could do a certain amount of the research and the writing in the office, I tended to bring it home in the evenings, which meant that after dinner, during which I would not drink – so Jenny, who enjoyed wine, had to drink alone – after dinner I would retreat to my desk in the spare bedroom, and leave her downstairs to read or watch TV by herself.

I don't think it was quite how she imagined our life would be after we returned from Ithaca. I think she thought we would become

more intense in our togetherness, not less: for example, she finally
gave up her rented flat in Summertown, which she had been keeping
on as an insurance policy against us splitting up, and began to pay
half the mortgage on my Jericho house; while from me, I think she
may have thought, even if only half-consciously, that after we got
back there might be some sort of equivalent gesture in respect of
our permanent union, something to mark the significance of her
surrendering her much-defended heart.

Such as the buying of a ring, perhaps.

Not that it was essential, no, no, no, she was a thoroughly
modern young woman and her commitment to me was in no way
dependent upon anything as old-fashioned as me asking her to
marry her.

But I think she noticed.

I mean, that I hadn't asked.

I hadn't even hinted at the idea.

In truth, the thought was nowhere in my mind, and the reason
was that Jenny had ceased to be my purpose. Now my purpose had
returned to academic achievement and the overtaking of my father,
in general, and getting *Doing It for Themselves* written, in particular.

She did not see this, of course; she saw the writing purdah into
which I retreated as not fantastic, but unavoidable. It was part of
the deal, the deal of me. She accepted it was something I had to do
and treated it with great generosity of spirit and good-humoured
resignation, sitting alone on the sofa in the evenings with her glass
of sauvignon blanc and a book in her hand or the TV news on while
I tapped at my laptop upstairs, and she was still happy, and full of
love, and there was no friction between us until the question arose
of where we were to spend Christmas.

It was about the third week of October. She said: 'Miles, can
I ask you something? Will you come with me to New Zealand for
Christmas, to meet my family? I would really, really like it if you
would. I've told them so much about you and I'm dying for them
to meet you at last.'

I hadn't considered this but I instantly saw it would involve
at least a two-week break in the writing, maybe even more. The
book was going well. There was no way I could spare that. So I
said, thinking quickly, 'Ah but Jen, Mum's dying for you to spend
Christmas with us, the four of us, in Wimbledon. It would mean
so much to her.'

I saw the conflict on Jenny's face.

She bit her lip.

She struggled.

She was desperate to show me off back home and desperate to see her family again. But she loved my mother dearly and would not do the tiniest thing to hurt her.

'I mean, it's up to you,' I said, 'but I think she'll be really upset if we don't go to Wimbledon.'

Jenny breathed in deeply. She said: 'OK.'

'We could go to Auckland later,' I said encouragingly, though not, of course, specifying when.

'OK,' she said.

But she was not happy. It was the first cloud. She brooded on it, and her sense of natural justice told her that after Ithaca, and the nature of our commitment to each other, I should have been willing to go and see her family, I should have realised what it meant to her; yet she was prevented from complaining or protesting, she was silenced, by the idea of my mother's disappointment – which I had introduced. Even if she couldn't quite articulate it, she began to feel something was not right about this, and her bullshit detector began to beep.

Not loudly, at first, because Jenny had given her heart to me and she ardently wished to make it work. But the matter festered for weeks, it rankled with her, even more because she was unable to say anything, and it finally erupted in the form of a protest about something else, when my writing commitment pushed me into taking one liberty too many.

We were due to go and see a movie on a Saturday evening in early December. We were to leave at 7.30; I had spent all afternoon working on the book and it was going swimmingly and as the time to go approached I found I very much did not want to interrupt my flow, so I came downstairs to Jenny, who had already had a glass or two of sauvignon, and said, 'Look, Jen, I'm really sorry about this, but I think I'm going to have to give the film a miss, I'm right in the middle of something and I can't really afford to break off.'

'What?' she said.

'I'm going to have to give the movie a miss,' I said.

She looked at me blankly. 'Why?'

'So I can carry on writing.'

'So you can carry on writing?'

'Yes.'

'So you can carry on writing, you're going to fuck up our evening?'

'Well, don't say it like that.'

She shook her head decisively. 'No, Miles.'

'What?'

'The answer's no. No, mate. No can do. No can miss movie.' Shaking her head.

'I'm sorry, but I'm going to have to. I'm right in the middle of a passage and I can't lose my flow.'

'It's our one night out this week.'

'We can go out next week.'

'But I want to go out *tonight*. You know I do. I've been looking forward to it.'

'We'll go next week. I promise.'

Jenny said: 'Miles. This matters to me.'

'Sure, but we'll go out next week.'

'Uh-uh. Look at me, Miles. Read my lips. *It matters to me.* Do you understand what I'm saying?'

'Sure, but look, Jen, I just need to get this bit of writing done.'

Jenny was incredulous. 'You're going to insist? After what I've just said to you?'

'Fraid so. I need to do it.'

She looked at me. She took a breath. She said: 'That your last word?'

'I just need to get it done.'

'OK, me bucko,' she said. 'This is my response.' She turned on her heel and walked into the kitchen, and after a second there was a crash. Then another. I ran in. She had a glass in her hand, one of my best wine glasses, which were expensive, and she was hurling it to the stone floor where it shattered, after the two she had already smashed. Now she took yet another and looking me in the eyes, smashed that to the floor, with truly vicious force, and while I was still mesmerised at the sight of her, she reached into the cupboard and took a fifth and smashed it down, and then a sixth, just reaching in deliberately and hurling them to the floor, and she was reaching for a seventh as I cried, 'Jenny, Jenny, stop!' and tried to grab her arm but she pushed me away and then she reached into the dresser on the other side and took hold of one of my best dinner plates, they were expensive too, and she brought that above her head with both hands and with all her might she hurled it to the floor as well, where it splintered into shards in what I remember as a grenade-like explosion, and then she did exactly the same with another as I tried again to reach her until I finally managed to enfold my arms about her, calling softly, 'Jenny, Jenny, Jenny.'

She was in floods of tears.

I brought her back into the sitting room; we sat on the sofa and she buried her head in my shoulder, still crying, and I stroked her hair, and kissed it, and eventually I brought her face up to mine and nuzzled her like a cat, like I had done under the olive tree on Ithaca, and kissed her on the lips and told her I loved her, again and again.

Jesus, I thought, this is going to take some managing. I can do without this. To write I need peace and quiet.

At length Jenny said: 'I'm sorry, Miles. I'm sorry I got so upset. It's just that – we don't seem to have had a lot of time together, recently, do we? Like we used to. I'm sorry.'

I knew the game was up, for the time being. I had learned a lesson: there would sometimes be limits on how far I could presume. 'No no,' I said. 'My fault, Jen. My fault entirely. I was completely thoughtless. I was so bound up in my stupid book.'

'It's not stupid, it'll be a great book, Miles. I don't mind you doing it. You know I don't. I'll support you all the way. It's just that we've got to have *some* time together, haven't we?'

'Course we have,' I said. 'So come on, shall we go and see our movie now?'

'I don't mind if we just stay in, to be honest. Long as we're together.'

'Why don't I cook dinner for us, then?'

'Yeah, that would be nice.'

So we cleared up the mess of glass and china in the kitchen, laughing ruefully about the expense of it, and I cooked us pasta with tomatoes and olives and put candles on the table, and I joined Jenny in drinking the sauvignon and was warm and attentive to her and she was happy again, and later we went up to bed and came together in the sort of truly explosive sex which she could conjure up, with a sort of thrilling hard-faced impersonality, when she seriously put her mind to it. Especially if she was feeling grateful. As she was. And we went to sleep in each other's arms, which had by no means been the case every night, in previous weeks.

For her, it was a renewal, of sorts: she put aside her doubts about us and went into Christmas in Wimbledon in a generous spirit, despite the fact that being apart from her own family tested her severely. (My mother had asked me if I was quite sure Jenny wouldn't rather be in New Zealand with her family; I said, no Mum, she wants to be here with us, only don't mention anything about it or she'll be embarrassed.) But she made the best of it; and after her tearful ten-minute phone call to Auckland on Christmas morning, during which I said hello to her parents for the first time, she and Lotte cooked a goose together and the pair of them got drunk on champagne and teased me mercilessly, as sisters-in-arms, my mother beaming benevolently; she was deeply happy. As was Lotte. They both loved Jenny; they felt she was the best thing that had ever come into the family from the outside, and the best thing that had ever happened to me, by a country mile.

For my part, I saw Christmas as an opportunity to get time on my own for the book; I had brought my laptop home with me. To try to make Jenny's stay as entertaining as possible, my mother had bought four tickets for matinee performances of *Cats* and *Les Misérables* between Christmas and New Year, to each of which we were to go as a party; I managed to cry off both, appealing to Jenny to back me up and say how important *Doing It for Themselves* was to me and my career, which she loyally did, with a rueful laugh.

What I couldn't get out of was our New Year's Eve, when we all went to see Lotte perform in a rather louche cabaret club in Islington. (I had given one hint at being excused from this as well but Jenny had said, in a tone which brooked no argument, don't even think about it, sunbeam.) So off we all went, to hear what again seemed to me Lotte's strange songs, and they all went over my head like most of her stuff, but Jenny and my mother seemed to like them enormously and laughed and cheered with the rest of the audience; and when midnight came the four of us held hands for 'Auld Lang Syne' and Jenny embraced my mother, then Lotte, and then me, with a deep and smiling look directly into my eyes, saying, 'Well, Bonnici, here's to the future.'

'Here's to the future,' I said, thinking of my Fellowship of the Royal Society.

You would have thought it was a picture of family happiness that was complete and entire.

But the next morning my mother said to me: 'Miles, will you tell me something?'

'Sure.'

'Are you going to get married to Jenny?'

She had come into my old bedroom, where I was working on the book. Jenny and Lotte had gone in to London for the New Year's Day sales.

I turned abruptly in my chair. I said: 'What on earth's brought that on?'

'Well are you?'

'Haven't got a clue. Never given it any thought.'

'Don't you think you should? I mean, give it some thought.'

'Why?'

'Don't you think Jenny might like to get married?'

'She's never mentioned it. Not once. Never said a word.'

'But she can't, can she? It's not for her to mention it. It's for you, son.'

'Why would she want to get married?'

'Most young women want to get married. Deep down. Whatever they say. They want to settle and raise a family.'

I didn't at all like the direction in which the conversation was heading. I said: 'Jenny's not like that. She's a modern woman. She's perfectly happy as we are.'

'How do you know?'

'I can tell.'

'Miles, remember when you came back from your holiday in Ithaca, and you came here for Sunday lunch the next day? You wanted us to see you together, and even though you didn't say so specifically, Lotte and I got the very strong impression that you, you had committed yourselves to each other.'

'Well, that'd be fair enough to say, I suppose.'

'Jenny had committed herself to you?'

'Well, yes.'

'That's a very big commitment, Miles. Don't you think she deserves a commitment in return?'

'I'm as committed to her as she is to me.'

'Yes, but women need a bit more. Some women are more vulnerable, and they need security.'

'She's got all the security she could want with me.'

'Miles, let me ask you frankly. Are you sure you're not neglecting Jenny? You're spending an awful lot of time on that blinking book of yours.'

'No, Mum. Not at all.'

'How long have you been together now?'

I thought back. 'Living together? A year, later this month.'

'Are you going to mark your anniversary?'

'Am I going to mark our anniversary?' I said, voicing a thought which had until that instant never entered my head. 'It's already planned. It's going to be very special.'

Yet it the event it wasn't special at all; merely expensive. I took Jenny on a Saturday night to a famous restaurant in the Oxfordshire countryside, The Old Stables, which possessed a Michelin star;

we were staying over as well, and it cost so much I had to take the money out of my building society account. But I saw it as an investment. My mother's mention of marriage had alarmed me, and I realised that to make sure Jenny was content with the status quo I would have to be pro-active, not just wait till she got upset and then mend her feelings: I would have to actually *do* things from time to time to make her feel I cared about her, throw her the odd bone. Otherwise she would complain, and there would be rows, and my writing would be interrupted just when I didn't need it; for to write I had to have peace. The Old Stables would fit the bill as a start; with Jenny being so big on gratitude I reckoned it would keep her happy for maybe even six weeks, which would be six weeks of writing peace, and so would be money well spent.

But she didn't enjoy it. The place was luxuriously appointed to an almost foppish degree, as were the guests; I was pleased, because I thought it was a sure sign of how much I was spending on her, but something jaundiced got into Jenny's view of it all, which extended to her opinion of the food (and objectively, it was very good). In the end I suggested we cut the evening short, and she did not demur.

As we got ready for bed I felt aggrieved. I said: 'You didn't really enjoy it, did you?'

'It was fine.'

'Yes, but you didn't really, actually *enjoy* it. Which is a bit of a, you know, disappointment, really, considering all the money it's costing.'

Jenny looked at me. 'Well if you want to know, Miles, that's why I didn't enjoy it.'

'What d'you mean?'

'You're marking our anniversary with money. With a big dollop of dosh.'

'So? I wanted the best for you.'

'Yes, but the best doesn't have to be the most expensive, does it? There might be other ways, there might be better ways, maybe even more loving ways of marking our … our togetherness.'

'Such as?'

'Well use that famous brain of yours, Miles. What d'you think?'

'I don't know.'

Jenny shook her head. She climbed into bed and pulled up the bedclothes, and lay facing the edge, so her back would be to me. 'Then I can't help you, sonny boy.'

'Well, come on, Jenny, what?' I said.

She said nothing.

'What? What? Tell me.'

She snorted and sat up. 'Well don't you think, Miles, we might be able to put down a few markers for our future?'

'What d'you mean?

'Don't you think we might be able to sketch out our future a bit more definitely? At the moment it's all very vague, isn't it?'

'Sketch it out how?'

'Well for Christ's sake, you know, start to think about what our future together might involve.'

'Such as what?'

'Well, I dunno. Whatever. The obvious things.'

'Such as?'

'Well, children, for example.'

'*Children*?'

'Yes, Miles. Children.'

I felt a chill steal over my soul. 'Why on earth would I want children?'

'Why would *you* want children?' said Jenny, raising her voice. 'Isn't the question, why might *we* want children?'

'I've never given it a thought.'

'I've been thinking about it more and more.'

'But I don't want children.'

'Why ever not?'

I was still getting over the shock.

'Why, Miles? Why wouldn't you want children?'

I said: 'I can't think of anything worse. I *hate* children. I hate the very idea of them. Little monsters. Demanding, yelling, getting in the way. Awful, awful. Appalling.'

'Miles, that's ridiculous.'

'I'd sooner have a dog. And I don't want a dog. I'd sooner have a pet rat than have a child.'

Jenny was taken aback. She said: 'But Miles. It's the completion. It's the completion of two people who love each other.'

'No it isn't.'

'It is.'

'Why does that have to be the completion? Just because it's traditional or whatever, because society says so. You can have love without children.'

'I don't think you can, ultimately.'

'Plenty of couples can't have children.'

'That's different.'

'And plenty of couples choose not to have children. They just want their lives to take the course they are planning. Children knock you off course. They stop you doing what you're trying to do. What you've worked for, for years.'

'They don't have to do that.'

'Anyway, it's not a crime not to like children. If it comes to that, *you* don't like children.'

'What are you talking about?'

'You said.'

'Said what?'

'On the plane. Going to Cephalonia. There was that ghastly baby yelling its head off right in front of us and you said you could *see Herod's point*. Remember? You hated it just as much as I did.'

Jenny's eyes filled with tears. 'How can you say that, Miles? How can you come out with shit like that?'

'It's true.'

'How can you say such fucking shit? That's about the most hurtful thing anyone's ever fucking said to me.' She was crying. 'You total bastard. You know I didn't mean it like that.'

'Then how did you mean it?'

'I was just irritated by a crying baby like all the other passengers were. You must know that. How can you twist it? Why are you being like this?'

'I'm just saying, you don't like children, when they're like that, any more than I do.'

'But I do want children, Miles. I do. I long for children. I want them to be the completion of us.'

'Well I don't.'

My words hung in the air.

Jenny was breathing deeply. She stared at me. She said: 'So that's it, is it? That's the end of the discussion?'

'I'm just saying what I feel.'

She said, slowly: 'Well, maybe now's a good time to get that learnt, isn't it?' And she got out of bed, and began to get dressed.

I watched her.

I think I was as shaken as she was, although for opposite reasons. *Children.*

Hadn't seen that one coming.

I thought I had everything sweet, but that changed things. *Children. No way.*

When she had finished dressing, she began to throw her things into her overnight bag. I said: 'What are you doing?'

'I don't want to spend another second here. I think I hate this place more than any place I have ever been to in my entire life.'

'Hang on, don't just leave. This is costing us a fortune.'

She zipped up her bag.

'Don't just *go*. Don't be silly. We can talk about this a bit more. Jenny.'

She looked at me, and shook her head, and picked up her bag, and turned on her heel and left.

I stared at the door, letting the silence wash over me. I sat in an armchair of unprecedented depth and softness, a chair of quite preposterous comfort. And I realised I'd made a mistake.

I had said too much.

I'd been taken by surprise and had let Jenny see my real feelings.

It was a mistake which if I wasn't careful, was going to threaten the peace I needed to write.

I would have to think very hard about the future with Jenny Pittaway. Because I certainly wasn't going to have the wrong future. A future that would screw up my life and my purposes with some ghastly baby in some ghastly pram in the hallway. I was not going to do that.

But I realised, this was the wrong time for a split.

I wouldn't be shattered by a split now, it was Jenny who would be shattered, I sensed that instinctively; she had given her heart, and the power had shifted to me. But it was the wrong time, even if I could ride it out, because it would still be a substantial disturbance in every way, and I needed calm around me to write the book.

It would have to wait until the book was finished.

Another year, maybe. Maybe less.

Do it then.

So in the meantime, I thought, I had better mend things, try and get them back on an even keel.

It took a day and a half. I found Jenny had left the hotel by taxi, but I had drunk too much to drive home that night and I thought it was a waste of money to take a taxi after her. When I got back on the Sunday she was nowhere to be seen and though I tried several times during the day, she didn't answer her mobile. But I didn't think she would go far.

Where could she go?

So on the Monday morning at 10 a.m. I rang her office line at OUP, where she wouldn't see the incoming number, and when she answered: 'Jenny Pittaway,' I said: 'I've been a dork, haven't I?'

There was just the sound of her breathing.

I said: 'Put it down to arrogance, or put it down to stupidity. Either will do, really, won't it?'

Still just the breathing.

I said: 'Which would you prefer? I'll own up to both.'

She said: 'You better had, you bastard.'

I said: 'I can say sorry, now – I mean, I do say sorry, now – but if I met you at lunchtime and bought you a sandwich, I could say sorry, properly. Which will take a bit of time, really. Won't it?'

I waited.

I said: 'Jen?'

'What?'

'Buy you that sandwich? Any filling you want.'

A long pause. Then: 'Yes.'

'At lunchtime?'

'Yes.'

'One o'clock at your main gate?'

'All right.'

'I love you, Jen.'

'Hmmm.'

She was angry, though she was more shaken; and I was at my most emollient. I told her that what she had suggested about children was completely new to me, which was why I had reacted in the way that I did, for which I fulsomely apologised; but it was an idea I thought I could get used to – given time.

I did not mean it. I was lying. I had no intention of having children with Jenny Pittaway.

But that is what I said. With time, I could get used to the idea. Say, when I had finished the book. In a few months. Then we could consider it again.

Could she live with that?

She could. She clutched at it. It was enough for her. And with renewed professions of love, and a grasping of hands, we made up.

I said: 'Where did you go, anyway?'

'A hotel. Place on the ring road.'

'What was the idea of that?'

'I was going to leave you. I was so upset. I felt I had no choice.'

'You silly sausage. Where were you going to go?'

'I suppose I would have found somewhere. But I dreaded it.'

'You don't still want to leave, do you?'

She shook her head vigorously, still clutching my hand.

I smiled at her. No, Jenny Pittway wasn't going to leave me, it was I who was going to do the leaving, in about a year, probably, when I had got my manuscript finished and the blue tits experiment sorted out, and when the question of children raised its head again in a way that could not be resolved: then I would be off. There it was, the end of Jenny Pittaway, now in view. The bedroom argument in the hotel had precipitated things; in thirty-six hours I had decided it all, I had made the mental shift: she was history. Scientific ambition was my life's purpose and nothing would stand in the way of it, certainly not some screaming brat in a pram. Though in the meantime I would keep Jenny sweet, so our lives could be calm and my writing could flow without interruption over the following months.

But it didn't work out like that. I met with disaster.

In which he's a shit and she's a fool to stay with him.

9

Truly ambitious scientists are often haunted by the notion of coming second, in so far as coming second in science means you are nowhere. For a single-minded researcher, the most terrible of fates! Like many evolutionary biologists I had pondered the story of Alfred Russel Wallace, the impoverished, self-taught, lower-class naturalist who, quite independently, worked out the theory of Natural Selection at the same time as the rich, privileged, gentleman thinker, Charles Darwin. I was gripped by the fact that Wallace, when he was collecting butterflies for a living in the South Seas, wrote to Darwin with his idea; and all that did was spur the leisured gentleman, who had long kept his own theory private, into writing *On the Origin of Species* in less than eighteen months, so that by the time Wallace got back to England, Charles Darwin was the most famous scientist in the world, while Alfred Russel Wallace was but a butterfly collector still. He was Mr Nobody!

No, for coming second in science, you got a bit fat Nothing, and this idea always hovered around my ambition: my *Nature* paper had been a stunning first, which was why it was on the cover, and I fully intended my blue tits project to be a similar revelation, telling the world that the female of the species was more deadly than the male, but in a way no one had ever realised before.

I had reckoned without Jasper Bakker, the Dutch researcher who was my rival.

His bomb detonated in my life late on a Friday afternoon at the end of April. My blue tit work was going forward, and although it was too soon even for initial results from Wytham Woods, I was confident we would get there in the end; the book was progressing; and life was stable enough, until Callum McSorley phoned me from Aberfair. After the briefest of pleasantries, he said: 'So how's the female infidelity study going, with ya blue tits?'

'Er, OK. Too soon to see a pattern emerging yet.'

Callum said: 'Look. Have ye seen the paper in *Science*? The current issue?'

'What paper?'

'The paper by Bakker from Groningen. And his mate, Holstege.'

I started to feel strangely nervous.

'No, I haven't. Why?'

'It's in your field, Miles. Smack bang in your field. Ye need to see it, right away.'

When I found the latest edition of *Science* I stared at the cover: the covers changed colour every week and this one – I shall never forget – was purple. There was no sign of Bakker on it, thank God for that at least, but then I started frantically thumbing through the Reports section at the back, and I found it, at the bottom of a left-hand page, the headline: *Female birds' preference for higher-quality extra-pair males is adaptive.* And reading down from the asterisk, I took in the authors' details: *F Jasper Bakker and Marius P Holstege, Animal Ecology Group, Centre for Ecological and Evolutionary Studies, University of Groningen.*

I focused on it, and with a sort of disbelieving horror I read the abstract: *We tested the hypothesis that females of a socially monogamous species, the Great Tit* Parus major, *actively engage in extra-pair copulations with socially dominant or more attractive males to gain fitness benefits. Molecular parentage analyses of the Great Tit population (N = 300 families, 600 individuals) of a section of the Hoge Veluwe National Park, The Netherlands, revealed that extra-pair offspring had a significantly higher overwintering survival and higher reproductive success than within-pair offspring.*

And then, with my heart racing, I read the terrible final sentence, which it seemed Bakker must have written in whooping triumph, specifically for me to read: *This study provides the first unequivocal evidence that extra-pair copulation behaviour is adaptive for female birds.*

Have that, Bonnici!

There it was. The conclusion. The striking conclusion which would go around the world: *Women! Infidelity pays! Be unfaithful to your partner and more of your offspring will survive!*

My conclusion.

The conclusion I'd come back to Oxford for. The conclusion which was the whole basis of my future.

Mine no longer!

I had come second!

I was Alfred Russel Wallace! I was Mr Nobody! And Jasper Bakker, Jasper fucking Bakker, smiling behind his black-rimmed glasses, was Darwin!

I think in some way, at that moment, I went mad. By that I mean that what had happened was an event which the reasoning part of my brain simply could not cope with, so I left reason behind. All there was, was distress: everything seemed to be blown to bits, most of all my lifelong purpose, to achieve an eminence to surpass my father's: my whole identity resided in that. Now it was gone, and wherever he was, he would be shaking his head in smug triumph: *That boy was never up to much.*

I heard his contempt! It rang around my head!

Pretty poor show, all in all ...

You had better buck your ideas up, young man ...

It was unbearable.

And what I did then, in my anguish, was find a scapegoat, and lash out: I blamed Jenny. Because she was what was different from my ambition, wasn't she? She had toppled it from its place as my principal purpose. She was The Other. *It was her fault!*

First, however, I dialled Callum's office number, with fingers that were trembling uncontrollably.

He said: 'McSorley.'

I said: 'I am fucked, Callum. Completely. I am completely fucked by that bastard Bakker.'

'Miles?'

I was barely articulate. 'Everything gone. Everything. The, the, the purpose, the, whatever. My father. All gone. Fucked. Years of work. All fucked. What am I going to do, Callum?'

He took a breath. 'The first thing, Miles, is to calm down.'

'It's all over, Callum.'

'What's all over? Ya life? Ya career? Bollocks. Get a grip, man.'

'They are, Callum, they're finished, it's like, it's like falling off a cliff.'

'It is not, Miles. It – is – not. We need to talk this through. If ye want, ye can come and see me, if that would help.'

'Can I come right away?'

'Ye mean, just now?'

'Yes, can I come now. Please, Callum.'

A brief pause. 'All right. Yeah, ah suppose ye better had. Ah'll put somebody off. How will ye get here?'

'By car. I've got it here with me. At the department.'

'How long'll it take ye?'

'Four hours, about. Bit more.'

'All right, come for dinner. We'll eat together.'

'Thanks Callum. Thanks so much. Be there ASAP.'

I took my jacket and was shutting down the computer when the phone rang.

I grabbed it and said: 'Yeah?'

'It's me.'

'What?'

'It's me, Jenny.'

'Oh. What do *you* want?' I felt a surge of anger. *It was her fault. She did it. If I hadn't spent all that time pursuing her, and lost my sense of purpose, I would have beaten Bakker.*

She said: 'You all right, Miles?'

'Why wouldn't I be?'

'Oh. Well. Look. I was just ringing to remind you about tonight, that's all. Not to be late.'

'What?'

'We've got Corinne coming round, from work. With her husband? For dinner? Remember?'

'Can't do it.'

'What d'you mean, you can't do it?'

'Something's come up.'

'What has?'

'Something with work. Gonna have to go to Aberfair.'

'When?'

'Now.'

Jenny said: 'You can't go *now*. We've got guests coming, for God's sake. It's all arranged. You know that.'

'I'm gonna have to go.'

'You can't, Miles.'

'Have to.'

'Well what is it, that can't wait?'

I said: 'It's just, a thing. About a thing.' I had taken the decision, already, that I was not going to confide in my companion, my partner, my lover, about the worst event ever to occur in my career; I was not going to tell Jenny Pittaway, who should have been my greatest comforter, about my downfall, my disaster. Jenny was history. *It was her fault. She did it.*

Jenny said: 'A thing about a thing? What on Earth's that mean?'

'It's just a thing. Look, I've gotta go, OK?' And I hung up the phone.

It rang back but I didn't answer: I was closing the door and running for the car park, where I had left the Mini Cooper that morning when I brought a pile of books back to the department;

as I got behind the wheel, my mobile rang, and I saw that that was Jenny too, so I switched it off and gunned the car out into the Oxford rush hour traffic.

It was 217 miles to Aberfair; by the time I got to Callum's house it was dark. We sat with a large Scotch each and he said: 'Well, bonny prince. Ye never saw it coming then?'

'Not a clue. Had no idea he was even working on it. Slimy Dutch toad that he is.'

'So ye think he's wrecked ya life, do ye?'

'Well, it's blown apart, isn't it? It's like, the bridge to the future has collapsed.'

But over the next fifteen minutes, Callum persuaded me I was wrong. He pointed out what a remarkable reputation I had for someone my age, but it was based not so much on my research papers, as on *Everything Except Seahorses*; and that it didn't necessarily have to be with discoveries, that you made it as a scientist. Wasn't *The Selfish Gene* largely a synthesis of other people's work? And wasn't I working on my next book, about female sexuality? And infidelity?

I nodded.

'Got a name for it yet?'

'It's called *Doing It for Themselves*. You know the song? 'Sisters Are Doing It For Themselves'?'

Callum smiled. 'Clever title.'

'Just came to me one day.'

So which did I think would have the bigger impact on the world at large, he said, Bakker's paper at the back of *Science* saying something which, at the end of the day, was pretty technical – or another *Seahorses*, about an issue which everyone was fascinated by?

I started to see a chink of light.

If female infidelity was adaptive in birds and it let their chicks survive better, he said, why did I have to be the guy that proved it, to write the book? 'Ye can just build ya book on the back of Bakker. Like Dawkins did on the back of Hamilton. And as a bonus, when it's a success, as ah'm sure it will be, ah would imagine Bakker himself will freak out.'

I looked at Callum open-mouthed.

'So all ye have to do with the book ...'

The light flooded into my brain. ' ... is do what Darwin did with *Origin*, when he got Alfred Russel Wallace's letter ...'

Callum nodded and smiled.

'... and finish it quickly. Of course!'

'This isnae the end of the world, ye see that now? You can still come out on top.'

'Callum, you're a genius.'

'Nah. Just common sense. You'd have seen it yourself, soon enough. All ye have to do, is get that book done now, quick as you possibly can.'

I nodded my head, thinking. 'Except, I've got a problem there.'

'What's that?'

'I can't do it with *her*. Jenny.'

'Seemed to me on Skarholm you were ... pretty happy with Jenny.'

'Maybe. Once. But it's ... it's all gone wrong.'

'How's that then?' he said. 'If ye don't mind me asking.'

My upset, my need to complete the book as quickly as possible, and my blaming of Jenny for Jasper Bakker's triumph, had all coalesced: now I wanted to finish the book by getting away from her, and I effortlessly constructed a new narrative to support that.

I even believed it.

I'd gone mad.

'It's just – she resents me doing it. She says I don't pay her enough attention, and she's nagging me and we're bickering all the time, so it's hard to get the peace to write. But it's worse than that. She gets these screaming fits.'

Callum looked at me.

'When they happen, they're uncontrollable. One time, we have a minor argument about a movie, about what film we were going to see, and she ends up going into the kitchen and smashing all the wine glasses. One after another, screaming and hurling them down on the floor. Can you imagine? Another time, we had another row, I can't even remember what it was about now, and she went into the kitchen and started smashing all the dinner plates. Holding them up above her head, and screaming and smashing them down with both hands. It was all I could do to stop her. She's very, very hard to live with.'

'Doesn't sound like the girl I met on Skarholm.'

'Doesn't, does it? But I suppose people aren't always the way they seem at first. I think finishing the book quickly is going to be impossible if I'm still with her. Gonna have to get away.'

'Just from Jenny? Or, d'ye mean, like, leave Oxford?'

'Well I haven't given it any thought till right this moment, but I suppose that the one really means the other. Cos anyway, everything's changed, in research terms, with the Bakker paper, hasn't it?'

Callum mused. 'Maybe, yeah.'

'I went back to Oxford for the research. Now Bakker's beaten me to it with his fucking great tits, there's no reason to stay.' I gave a half-laugh. 'Know of any jobs going, anywhere else?'

Callum looked at me. He gave me a very hard, long look. The person I am today would not have liked that look, but I was indifferent to it then. He was weighing up, whether or not to say anything. At length he said: 'Ah may know of one.'

'Where's that?'

'It's in Scotland.'

Whereabouts?

'Aberdeen.'

'And what is it?'

'You heard of UKOCA?' He pronounced it: You-coke-ah.

I shook my head.

'The United Kingdom Offshore Conservation Agency. Fairly new. They've created it to coincide with devolution in Scotland and Wales, so there'll still be a body that looks at marine biodiversity with a whole-UK remit.'

'Oh yeah?'

'Small but interesting. Run by a friend of mine, Ramsay Wishart. We did zoology at Glasgow together. He's another seabird specialist. Good guy. He's the first Director.'

'And?'

'He's looking for someone to run a major research project for him. Ideally he wants a bright, energetic young post-doc, about your sort of age.'

'What sort of research?'

'The environmental impacts of fisheries. Like, the damage done by trawling and deep-sea fishing. To fish stocks, to the sea bed, the lot.'

'I don't know anything about fisheries, Callum. But then, it can hardly be that complex, can it?'

'Wouldn't have thought so. He'll be interviewing soon. It's a public process, so ye could enter for it. Ah suppose I could put a word in for ye, if ye wanted.'

'Would you do that?'

'Ah could. If ye're really sure you would want to do this. Are ye? Go all the way to northern Scotland? If ye got the job, that is.'

'Don't see why not. I can make my bed anywhere. And my research has come off the rails for the time being, has it not?'

'Aye, laddie, for the time being, I suppose it has.'

I said: 'And my relationship is coming to an end, Callum.'

He looked at me. 'Ye know, I really find that hard to believe, Miles.'

'Oh yes,' I said. 'It is. It definitely is.'

Jenny was hopping mad at my fleeing from the dinner party. She was also disturbed, because she couldn't make sense of it, she couldn't understand what had happened; but that was an underlying feeling. On the surface she felt anger more than anything else, that I had ruined a long-planned evening for three other people, and resented it strongly. When, the next morning, I switched my mobile back on, I found she had tried to ring several times; and eventually she had left a message. She said: 'Miles, I've no idea why you're doing it, but you're acting like a total shitbag. So you can fuck off. You can just fuck right off. I'll see you when I see you.'

That was OK. That wasn't a problem at all.

I slept late at Callum's because we had drunk a bottle of Beaujolais to go with his boeuf bourgignon and then hit the Scotch again, and I was in no hurry to get back. When I eventually did Jenny was nowhere to be found, and there was no sign of her on the Saturday evening, or all day Sunday, so she had clearly gone off somewhere. That was all right, as well. I didn't ring her, and she didn't ring me. Instead, I started studying the web page of UKOCA in Aberdeen; the deadline for applications for the research post was the following week, so I began to sketch out mine.

I was ignoring the script. The script said that I knew Jenny would have to be back at her desk at OUP on the Monday morning, so I should ring her then, be all apologetic and lovey-dovey; but I wasn't following it any more. When I didn't ring, her anger began to morph into anxiety – something might have happened to me, after all – and eventually, at four o'clock on the Monday afternoon, she yielded to it and she called my mobile.

I answered.

She said: 'Miles! Where've you been?'

I said: 'At home. All weekend. Well. Since Saturday afternoon. Where've you been?'

'I went to London to see my Kiwi mates. To get pissed with them, actually. Cos I was so pissed off with you.'

'Well, yeah, I'm sorry about that, something came up and I had to shoot off to Aberfair in a hurry.'

'But you ruined the evening, Miles. You completely fucking ruined it.'

'Yeah well, I said, I'm sorry.'

Jenny breathed out. She couldn't quite get her bearings. She said: 'What was it that was such a big deal that you had to drop everything and go to Wales, even when we had guests coming?'

'Ah, it was just something that came up at work.'

She paused. She didn't quite know what to say. 'Where are you now?'

'In the office.'

'Well, do you want to have dinner together, this evening?'

'Sure. That would be nice.' Throwing her a bone. Might as well keep up the pretence till the actual moment came, so it was a moment of my choosing.

'I could get some lamb steaks, if you like.'

'Yeah, do that, I'll pick up a nice red.'

'All right, then. I'll see you later.'

'See you later.'

She hesitated. She said: 'Love you, Miles.'

'Love you too.'

My departure from the script had unsettled her; my failure to placate, beg forgiveness, or apologise profusely, was unexpected, as was, most of all, my failure to call her on the Monday. That night at dinner she found it hard to work out where we were, not least because when we met again, I had not covered her with kisses but had been, instead, perfectly friendly. She began to doubt herself, to think that she was being pathetically needy and clinging, to feel she wanted a greater reassurance of my affection; but feel it she did. It disarmed the resentment and anger she would otherwise have directed towards me about my behaviour, which of course, had been atrocious. Instead, she was forced into a new mode of interaction with me, the superficial: I willingly repeated my apology for disappearing so suddenly but continued to hide the cause, while she for her part gave me an account of her Kiwi girls' night out in the West End on the Saturday, full of cocktails and aren't-men-shits, which I listened to with every sign of interest, and laughter at the appropriate places.

At length she said: 'Didn't you wonder where I was?'

'I guessed you'd be off seeing someone. I don't blame you. I reckon I would have done the same myself, in your place.'

There was a pause. Jenny said: 'I feel a bit strange.'

'I'm sorry.'

She thought. She was going to say something, then stopped. She bit her lip. Then she said: 'Miles?'

'Yeah?'

'Can we make love?'

'Make love?' I laughed. 'Sure, if you want. Of course. Absolutely.'

Just because I was going to leave Jenny Pittaway, I saw no reason not to enjoy her body, which was formidably enjoyable, and that night she displayed her sexual talent to the maximum, hoping to bind me to her with it; and I think that had I cared a lot about sex, I might indeed have been affected and thought, do I really want to give this up? But sex was a glass of wine to me, as it always had been, to take or leave, and I was going to leave it.

Jenny for her part also craved the physical contact with me, as she felt that the emotional contact had in some weird way become mislaid, although on the surface everything was … perfectly friendly. And as she came, she cried out 'I love you Miles' just exactly as I had cried out 'I love you Jenny' a year before.

But whereas she had only sssh'd me, then, I kissed her and whispered, 'Love you too.'

Another bone.

Why not? Didn't cost me to be nice.

And she buried her head in my shoulder, and held me in a tight embrace.

I had established a new relationship. It was one I was in complete control of, one which Jenny felt unable to protest against for fear of seeming needy, as I was careful to be consistently thoughtful and considerate in my behaviour towards her, giving her everything she required except that which she now most needed: the convincing reassurance that my heart was still hers. That, I had withdrawn; and Jenny sensed it, or at least she felt she sensed it, but there was no obvious sign of it, so, as she had never been selfish or demanding, she told herself she was imagining it.

Although of course, she was not.

She turned again to sex for reassurance. It was now her only way to intimacy with the man she loved, so she invested invention in it – and that was quite something – hoping perhaps it would bring back the thing that had gone missing which she couldn't even name. It was intense and exciting and regular, there had never been so much sex, which of course can have consequences, while I, what I did was send off the application form for the vacancy at the UK Offshore Conservation Agency. It was for a year's contract for a senior researcher; and a week later the invitation to interview came, and I flew up to Aberdeen, telling Jenny I was going for a meeting.

I was interviewed by Ramsay Wishart, Callum's friend, who was short, but somehow possessed of a gritty and determined air; he was a dapper dresser, grey-haired with a neat grey moustache. I quickly saw what he needed, which was basically a literature search of all the damage commercial fisheries were doing to the marine environment, so that a system of marine protected areas could be sketched out for the UK; and I feigned a lively interest in it, and we had an animated conversation and I had a sense, from Dr Wishart's warmth when I left, that I might have succeeded, and so it proved; for a week and a half later I duly received the offer of the job. I flew to Aberdeen once more, for two days this time, telling Jenny there was a mini-conference at the University, and saw Ramsay again, and we shook hands on my appointment – 'You come highly recommended,' he said, and we both smiled – and I found a flat in an area called Rosemount, and took a year's lease on it, and hired a piano, having agreed with Ramsay on a starting date. Which of course, meant a leaving date with Jenny.

And the madness came to its climax.
I find this really hard to write down.
Anyway. Get on with it.
There must be fifty ways to leave your lover, sang Paul Simon, but I could think of only one: cut and run. I hated the idea of argument, I wanted it to be over, and it dawned on me that the argument would come, not just from Jenny, of course, but also, and powerfully, from Lotte and my mother, so I resolved to be ruthless in cutting them all off. Otherwise, I thought, I would never get away.
As for the ending itself, there was an undeniable yellow streak in me: I quailed at the idea of the confrontation. With my three girlfriends in Aberfair I had used my exile on Skarholm to let each relationship merely wither on the vine, and a big part of me wanted to leave a note and just be off, but after everything that had happened there wasn't really any way around it. I would have to tell her to her face. Yet I determined it would be quick and clinical: I wanted just to get out and go somewhere a long way away and start repairing my life and my life's purposes, get it all back on track, while Jenny could do whatever she wanted – she could carry on living in the house, for the time being, anyway – as long as it didn't involve me.
Yes. It would be over in five minutes, the whole thing.
Like an execution, I think now.

It fell on an early Friday evening in June. I had made all my preparations, without Jenny having an inkling: I had resigned my Research Fellowship and handed over my blue tit project to Lars, the Swedish post-doc who had been helping me and who had agreed to take it on; I had covertly packed everything I needed and stowed it in the Mini Cooper. I was just going to up sticks, and go. As chance would have it, Jenny too was thinking of a getaway: she had become somewhat exercised about our summer holiday and she had brought a pile of brochures home and dumped them on the kitchen table, and said, come on Miles, we've got to talk about this properly because everywhere will be booked up. She made a pot of tea and poured out two mugs.

She said: 'D'you want to go back to Greece? Because we could, couldn't we? I mean, we don't even have to go to an island, there are great places on the mainland, there's that area in the south, one of the, you know, like fingers of the Peloponnese?'

I was thinking, Now. Got to do it now.

'On the other hand though, we could maybe try Italy, say. What d'you think? Miles?'

'What?' I was trying to screw up my courage.

'What d'you think about Italy? Maybe Tuscany, though it's expensive. Corinne at work swears by the Marches. Le Marche. That's on the other side, the Adriatic side. Lot cheaper. How would you feel about that?'

I stared at her.

'Miles?'

My head felt as if it would burst.

'Miles? What's the matter?'

'I've got a job.'

'What?' said Jenny.

'I've, er, got a new job.'

'In the University?'

'No.'

'Then – who with?'

'With the, er, the government. Well. A government agency.'

'Oh,' said Jenny. She put down her mug, which she had been gesturing with. She said: 'You've haven't told me anything about this.'

'Well, no. I wasn't sure I would get it.'

'And now you have?'

'Yes.'

'And who's it with?

'It's with a body called the Offshore Conservation Agency. The UK Offshore Conservation Agency. UKOCA.'

'And is that – here in Oxford? London?'

'No. Neither.'

'Where is it?'

'Aberdeen.'

'Aberdeen in Scotland?'

'Yes.'

Jenny said: 'What's this about, Miles? What does it mean?'

'It … means what it means.'

'You're going to *Aberdeen* to work?'

'Well, er, sort of, yes.'

'For how long?'

'Not really sure.'

'But for some time?'

'Mmm-hmm.'

'More than, more than a week, say? Or, more than a month?'

'Mmm, yeah.'

'And you're going without us having discussed it? Without having even mentioned it to me?'

'Maybe I should have done. I probably should have done.'

Jenny looked at me. She said: 'I can't believe I'm hearing this. You've taken a decision to leave our home, is that what you're saying?'

'It's just going to Aberdeen for a job, really.'

'And d'you expect me to follow you? To give up my own job and follow you, just like that?'

'Not necessarily.'

Jenny's eyes widened. 'What do you mean, *not necessarily*? What the hell does that mean? Do you want us to finish?'

I said: 'Just, maybe we should have a break from each other. For a bit.'

She sat down. She said: 'I don't understand. I don't understand what you're saying.'

'Well it's like I said, I've got this job.'

'And it's hundreds of miles away? Why do you want to go hundreds of miles away?'

'I just think we should er, we would benefit from having a bit of time apart.'

'But why?'

'Get things clearer. In our heads.'

'Get what clearer?'

'What we want.'

'What do you want?'

'That's what I want to think about.'

Jenny said: 'D'you not want me, Miles?'

'I want to think about it.'

Jenny flinched backwards, as if she had been struck a physical blow. She said: 'You're saying you want to leave me?'

I didn't like being put on the spot.

'Miles. Are you saying you want to leave me?'

'Have some time apart, maybe.'

'But *why*?'

I didn't reply.

'I thought you wanted us to spend the rest of our lives together. We've been happy, haven't we? This has been the happiest time of our lives. Hasn't it? You said it was for you, and it certainly has been for me. What's changed?'

'Well one thing is, I need to write the book.'

'But you're writing the book.'

'I need to finish it.'

'How am I stopping you? In any way? In any way at all? How am I doing anything other than helping you?'

'I just think I would be able to finish it quicker if I, er...if I went to Aberdeen.'

'What on earth can you do in Aberdeen that you can't do here?'

'Able to concentrate more.'

'But that's crazy. It doesn't make sense.'

I shrugged.

Jenny seemed wholly bewildered. She said: 'No no. Don't be silly. I think this is just a brainstorm, Miles. It's just a mad idea. I don't believe you can really mean it. It'll pass. It's a nonsense. I mean, when would you be proposing to do all this?'

'Well, er, sort of now.'

What d'you mean, now?

'Now – like, now.'

'Now this minute?'

'Well, more or less, yeah.'

'You mean, you're just going to walk out of here? *Right now?* And...fuck off to Aberdeen?' She was incredulous.

I shrugged agreement.

'And when are you coming back?'

'Well, whenever. At some stage, probably. Maybe.'

'But what about your research? Your big experiment with the wossnames, the blue tits in the wood?'

'That hasn't worked out. I've given it up.'

'What about your position in the university? Your fellowship?'

'That's been sort of put on hold.'

'Then what about this house, and everything?'

'You can carry on living here. Long as you like. I'm fine with that.'

There was a silence for second or two. The whole world turned in it. She said: 'You mean this? You really mean it?'

'Mmm-hmm.'

She stared at me. Then she shook her head. She said: 'No.'

'No what?'

'I won't let you do it, Miles.'

'What d'you mean?'

'I won't let you go.'

'Well, I've got to sort of, go now, really.' I stood up.

'No, Miles.' Jenny stood up too. 'You can't.'

'I have to go,' I said, moving towards the door. Jenny got there first. She spread herself across it. 'No, Miles, no. You can't.'

I tried to reach for the latch. She took hold of my arm and pushed it back. 'Why are you doing this, Miles? Why? Tell me why. What have I done?' We were wrestling. It was unreal. 'Is it because I went to London to see my mates when you rushed off to Aberfair? Because I felt after that that things had somehow changed. But why would that make a difference?'

'Look I have to go,' I said, reaching again for the latch. I managed to grab it and open the door. She took hold of my arm again and this time held it tight, with both hands. 'Don't do this Miles, don't do it please.' I squeezed through the door into the street with her hanging on to me. 'You don't really want to do this, do you? After Ithaca? After what we promised each other? You said you loved me and you would always love me and I said I would always love you and I will and I do, and you still love me really, don't you?'

'I have to go,' I said, dragging her down the street with me, trying to detach her hands from my arm as her voice rose, 'No, don't Miles, please. Please. Please don't go. Don't do it, Miles, don't leave me, please.' The loaded Mini Cooper was a few paces away and I managed to get its door open with my free arm but she pulled me back crying, 'Please Miles. Don't. Don't do this.'

I pushed her then, I pushed her hard, and she stumbled and fell backwards onto the pavement, and I did not go to her aid, or help her up … and I see it still, I see it now, it will never leave me until

I die ... *the look on her face* ... and I swung myself into the driving seat and slammed the door and started the engine as Jenny cried out at me, 'Miles, don't you understand, if you do this I won't be able to stand it, I told you on Ithaca, I wouldn't be able to survive it a second time if I gave my heart a second time!', as I put the car into gear, and as she struggled to her feet she was crying, 'Don't you understand, I've got no defences left!', as I moved off from the kerb, and Jenny screamed: 'Miles!'

I was on the ring road in ten minutes; in twenty, I was on the motorway. It was 500 miles to Aberdeen, almost exactly, and I wanted to get into Scotland before halting for the night, so I had booked a hotel in Gretna. I felt exhilarated, heading north in the long June evening: I was driving into my freedom, I was driving back to my purpose, and my identity.

It was after midnight when I finally got to the hotel and switched on my phone: there were five messages.

The first was from Jenny. She was crying. She said: 'Miles, please call me. Please.'

The second one said: 'Miles, will you call me, will you please.'

The third one said: 'Miles, I beg you please to call me, I beg you, please, it doesn't matter when, just call me.'

The fourth one was from later and said: 'Miles, it's Lotte, what the hell're you playing at? Jenny's in bits, she says you've walked out and gone to live in Scotland, what the fuck's this about? Call us, please. Come on, call us, soon as you can.'

The fifth one had only been left a few minutes earlier. It said: 'Miles, it's Mum here. It's Mum. What are you doing, son? Jenny says you've walked out on her. She's here with us and she's quite distraught. I don't understand, at all. Please call us as soon as you can.'

I didn't answer any of them. I switched my phone back off, and I slept soundly.

In the morning I set out again for the 200 miles remaining; I arrived in the early afternoon and picked up the keys to the flat. When I had unloaded the car I went for a walk to check out the Rosemount shops and then went back and opened up the laptop, and spent the rest of the day working on the book. I got quite a lot done.

At midnight I decided to switch my mobile back on. There were several missed calls, from Jenny and Lotte, but only one message left, from 7.30 p.m. It said: 'Miles, it's Mum here. This is wrong. This is quite wrong. You cannot behave like this, Miles. What on earth has Jenny done to deserve it? She loves you. She is immensely distressed. Lotte has taken her to the cinema to try to take her mind off it all but she is very very upset, as we all are. You must talk to her. You cannot simply hide behind your mobile phone. That is a coward's way. I never thought I would say that to you, I have loved you since you were born and believed in you all your life, but this is dreadful, Miles. You must not behave like this. You must call us or preferably call Jenny as soon as possible. Goodbye.'

I had prepared myself for this, so I was hardened to it. Got to be ruthless. With them all.

I switched the phone off and went to bed.

The next day was a Sunday, with little traffic, so I drove into the city centre to get a feel for Aberdeen; the agency occupied a nondescript seventies office building between the harbour and Union Street, the main drag. It was a fine day and I felt good. I went back to the flat and got out the book again and worked on it till nearly midnight when I switched the phone back on.

There were three more messages. The first was from 3.55pm. It said: 'Miles, it's Lotte. Just what in God's holy name is this all about? What on earth are you doing, and why? Jenny is beside herself. She's just gone back to Oxford and she's in no fit state to, but she's insisted. Why are you making her so unhappy? Will you just for Christ's sake call her, please.'

The second one was from 4.35pm. It said: 'Hi Miles, Ramsay here, Ramsay Wishart. Hoping you arrived safely and looking forward to seeing you tomorrow at nine. Any problems, give us a call.'

The third was from just after 10pm. It said: 'It's Jenny here.' Her voice was trembly. She said: 'Will you call me please, Miles? Would you, please?'

That was it.

The next morning I started at UKOCA. I was located on the first floor: the layout was open-plan, except that at each corner of the building there was an enclosed office, and to my great gratification I was allocated one of these, probably because Ramsay Wishart thought the quiet would help me think, and indeed it did: my own small kingdom with its own door, where I did not have to talk to colleagues, where thankfully no one could look over my shoulder and see what I was working on, as it might not be anything to do with offshore conservation or fisheries, it might well be my book. It was pretty basic, just a desk with a computer and a phone, and a chair and a filing cabinet, but it was ideal. I sat down and got myself registered with the IT system and got an email address, and I began, I embarked upon my mammoth literature search about damage to the environment caused by fisheries, and the phone rang.

Jesus, I thought, busy already. I picked it up and said: 'Miles Bonnici.'

'It's Mum, Miles.'

'Oh,' I said. I was caught entirely off guard.

'Why, why are you behaving like this? Why have you done this to Jenny? You've devastated her. You told me yourself you were committed to her. Why won't you at least talk to her? None of us can understand it.'

I didn't know what to say. My strategy had been to flee, not to argue. I had no cogent arguments.

'Well?'

'I've got my reasons,' I said at last.

'What are they?'

'They're ... my reasons,' I said, retreating into defiance. 'I don't have to explain them.'

'Yes you do, Miles. You most certainly do.'

It hung in the air.

'Well?'

I did not reply.

'*Well?*' my mother demanded with an unaccustomed ferocity. '*Well?*'

I gave in. 'Well it's about the book,' I said.

'That blessed book,' said my mother. 'I always felt it was trouble. Why on earth has it made you act like this? Like, like a *scoundrel?*'

'Because I've come up here to finish it,' I said.

'Don't you love Jenny any more?'

'That's ... private.'

'So what's changed, Miles? What has she done to deserve this?'

I didn't answer.

My mother said: 'Miles, listen. You must talk to her. You must. If you want to split up, well, so be it, Lotte and I both think it would be a most dreadful thing, a ghastly mistake, but if it is to be so, then there it is. But you have to talk to her, Miles. You simply cannot do what you did on Friday, walk out of her life with five minutes' notice, after she has given her heart to you. It is not only cowardly, in a way I never imagined, ever, you might behave, and I have to say it breaks my heart to see it, but it is grossly cruel. You cannot do this, son. It is wholly unacceptable. Do you not see that?'

I said nothing.

'Do you not *see* it, Miles? Answer me. Do you not understand that you simply cannot behave like this, in this wholly inhuman way?'

'I'm going to have to go,' I said. 'Got a meeting.'

'Miles!' cried my mother.

I hung up.

I went and found the telephone room then, and spoke to the middle-aged woman telephonist. I said: 'I'm the new guy, Dr Bonnici.'

'Hi,' she said. 'Ah'm Kirstie.'

I said: 'Kirstie, d'you mind me asking, did you just put a woman through to me just now?'

'Aye. Said she was your mother, so she did.'

'She's not my mother,' I said. 'This woman's crazy. She's a friend of an ex-girlfriend who's been stalking me. Another friend of hers pretends to be my sister. It's a real problem. If it continues, I'm going to have to get a court order. But look. Would you mind, if any women come on for me, any at all, no matter who they say they are, would you mind not putting them through? And don't give them my extension, either. Just say I'm out or whatever, and take a number, and say I'll call them back. Would that be OK?'

'Ah suppose so,' Kirstie said, giving me a curious look.

No more calls got through, although several were made. I thought then I had built impenetrable barriers of distance and inaccessibility and behind them I was safely cut off, although I did fear that Jenny might make the trip to Aberdeen and ambush me outside work, as I had ambushed her outside Oxford University Press. But she did not appear.

Instead, just over a week later I received a curious letter from her (email was just taking off then, and letters were still being written.) It said: 'Dear Miles, I wasn't going to bother you ever again, but something has happened. I don't want to say what it is, because you might think it was a way of trying to get you back and it isn't. But I do feel, I do have to ask you one more time, will you come back to me, please? Can you let me know by the end of the week? It's hard to think straight. But can you let me know by the end of the week? I still love you. Love, Jenny.'

I had no idea what she was talking about. I didn't bother replying.

At the end of the week, on the Friday, I got another letter, posted first class the day before, which said: 'Can you let me know by the end of Friday? I still love you. Will you come back to me? I have to know. Love Jenny.'

I didn't reply to that, either.

And I thought no more about it until ten days later, when, in the late morning, the UKOCA front desk rang my extension and said someone was in reception for me, and I asked who it was and they said it was my sister, and I said, will you tell her I'm not here, and I heard the receptionist say, he's not available, and I heard Lotte shout, oh yes, he damn well is, and the receptionist said, Madam, you can't go up there, and then the receptionist said to me, she's coming upstairs, and in less than a minute I saw Lotte on the floor and someone pointing her towards my office, and she was marching towards me, and she saw me and she shouted, Miles! and her face was fury and I knew I would have to talk to her so I motioned her into my office and closed the door, and she said to me, she hurled it at me: 'Just how unhappy do you think you have made Jenny? On a scale of one to ten?'

'Lottee,' I growled in irritation.

'Eight? Nine? How about the full ten, Miles?'

'What's the point of this, Lotte?'

'I'll tell you what the point of it is, Miles. Let me ask you, would it have made any difference to you when you abandoned her to know she was carrying your child?'

'What?'

'It was an accident. But it was the symbol of her love for you. Although I daresay to you, it would have been just a restriction on your freedom, isn't that right?'

'What?' I said. 'What? I ... Jesus I ...'

'Yes, well,' she said, raising her voice into a weirdly chilling tone I had never heard before, 'you don't need to worry about that any more, you unspeakable bastard. She's had it aborted.'

Someone does same research e gets
papers in dournal.
He can write book on back of research
Gets fisheries job
↪ Her abortion.

10

You can talk about guilt, but it's much more than guilt. It is part of me forever now, what I did to her.

It is in my movements and my stillness, my speaking and my silence, my waking and my sleep.

It is in the growth of my hair, in the flaking of my skin, it is in the lines that will appear on my face as I move towards old age: a part of me which is terrible, and can never be erased or covered over, or forgotten or forgiven. And such was its nature, I thought, as we left Oban harbour on that June evening, bound for Lanna, such was the awful reality of what I had done, that maybe I should never have tried. Maybe my relationship with Jenny Pittaway was always going to be beyond repair. And yet I did try, because I changed.

Change in humans is difficult and rare. Profound change, of the essence, is such a wholly exceptional event that we memorialise it, like St Paul on the Damascus road. Yet it happened to me. In the great central event of my life I broke out of the personality my childhood had shackled me with, seemingly for ever, and cast its bonds aside. That I was able to do this, that I might shatter the spell of my twisted father, has long seemed like a miracle, and indeed it was a sort of spiritual upheaval, a sort of earthquake of the soul. And as such, it was necessary. For I believe that in a case like mine, a case of selfishness so extreme as to be impenetrable, a person cannot half-mend; there cannot be a promise to be good, a resolution to be, er, *better*, that sort of thing. For real change to happen, there can only be a complete collapse of what has gone before; and so it was with me, leading to horrified understanding, and unrelenting remorse, and the hunger for atonement, and eventually, to the island, where Fergus Pryng stood, watching over his unique and remarkable business, single-minded and indomitable.

But not at once. No. Of all my transgressions against the love which Jenny bore me, the worst, the most merciless, was now to follow: it was that in learning what she had done in her misery and her despair, I turned my back. When Lotte stormed into my office her announcement stunned me, certainly, it rocked me back on my heels, but as soon as I had recovered from the shock, I saw it in a flash as the ultimate blackmail. It was the concerted effort by the three of them, girlfriend, sister and mother, to force me to alter course, to give up my freedom to pursue my life's purpose and return to … incarceration. And once the astonishment was over, which took but a few seconds, I snapped shut my mind to Jenny's plight and I said *No. No, I will not*. I didn't just say it, I shouted it at Lotte, I shouted No! at her, No, No, No! and she shouted back at me You've got to! You've got to come back and see her! Can't you imagine what it's like for her? She's in pieces! and I shouted I will not! and she shouted you monster, you vicious cold-hearted monster, you're not even human and I shouted back at her, what's it got to do with you, anyway, why don't you sort out your own life, and she screamed at me Just what does that mean Miles and I shouted at her it means what it means, sort your own life out Sister and don't try to sort out mine and she started to hit me then crying Bastard! Bastard! Bastard! and I caught her arm and wrestled with her and people were alarmed at the shouting and came to the door of the office and Lotte saw them and realised there was nothing to be done and she turned, in tears, and she fled.

A thousand-mile round trip. For a two-minute shouting match.

I was breathing heavily. I said to the people who had gathered, with anxious faces, it's OK, I'm very sorry. It's er, a personal thing. Sorry.

Ramsay Wishart called me into his office twenty minutes later.

He said: 'What's all this about, Miles? Some woman screaming at you in the office? Some of the staff are quite disturbed. This is a bad business. We cannae have this.'

I apologised profusely. 'It's like this, Ramsay,' I said. 'Before I left Oxford I had a relationship which broke up, you know, the way relationships do, and the woman concerned has been following me, ever since. Stalking me, if you like. And that was her.'

'But this woman told reception she was your sister.'

'That's what she says, sometimes. So she can get access to me. I'm really sorry. I, I very much doubt she'll be back.'

'I hope not, Miles. We don't want any more of this.' He chewed a nail, and I noticed all his nails were bitten down to the quick: strange, I thought, for such a precisely-dressed individual. 'No. We don't want any more of it at all.'

Lotte did not return. Instead, she sent me a letter. This one said: 'Miles, You have destroyed Jenny. She is broken in her spirit. She has given up her job and gone back to New Zealand. Mum is beside herself. You have broken her heart too, she is sick with anguish and not well at all and I have not even told her what happened with Jenny at the end, as I think the shock of that would kill her. You are the most despicable human being I have ever encountered. I never wish to speak to you again about anything whatsoever or have anything to do with you. You are beneath contempt. I renounce you as a brother.'

I threw it in the bin.

A couple of days later my mother sent me a letter of her own, saying much the same thing, bewildered and shocked. That went into the bin as well.

I had steeled myself to it. It was as if I had become a husk, empty of anything but my cursed ambition. For that was still festering nicely, my father-complex. FUCK YOU. Oh yes. The book was going well, and I would get there, as long as I remained focused and self-disciplined about the writing; so every evening after work I went home to my flat and made my dinner – I had decided to take up cooking seriously and I always had something interesting or expensive, sea bass, porterhouse steak, asparagus, which I enjoyed, which I felt I was entitled to – and then spent three or four hours on the laptop. For relaxation, there was the piano, the small upright which I had hired, and Mahler's symphonies on CD and I started getting into Bruckner, and I began swimming and running again, discovering to my surprise that Aberdeen was a city with a beach, two miles of it, which made running a pleasure.

Yet that was all I absorbed of my new country. Great events were happening in Scotland, a Scottish Parliament had just been elected for the first time since 1707, and on 12 May, which I now realise was the day of my initial interview with Ramsay Wishart, it reconvened on The Mound in Edinburgh after the 292-year-gap; but the occasion passed me by entirely.

I took nothing in of Scotland, indeed, I took virtually nothing in of the city, this ancient metropolis which was now the oil capital of Europe; I had the same interest in Aberdeen, as a place, as I had had in Aberfair, that is to say, none whatsoever. And this indifference extended to my work colleagues, the decent, soberly-mannered conservationists surrounding me, just as it had, in Wales, to my fellow post-graduates, but even more so: in Aberdeen I had no desire to be one of them, to be part of their office community, to know them or interact with them. I had no small talk beyond what was necessary for work; I who was devoid of empathy anyway had become even more estranged, not just from those close to me but from all people, and indeed from something profounder, which is probably best described as common decency.

Yet I was the object of speculation. The row this new guy had. With the woman who stormed in, d'you hear it? Amazing. Going at each other hammer and tongs. His ex, it was. I thought it was his sister. No, he told Ramsay it was his ex. Said she was stalking him. Wow, really? He came from Oxford, didn't he? Yeah, evolutionary biologist. Seems a bit on the snooty side. Well they're probably all like that in Oxford, aren't they, ivory tower, you know....and as the cool summer of north-east Scotland turned into the even cooler autumn, and I made steady progress with the book, and my mother wrote to me again and once more I binned her letter, several members of the staff of the United Kingdom Offshore Conservation Agency made friendly approaches, and I rebuffed them all. Twice in the canteen, where invariably I sat at lunch by myself, reading (I was going through *Anna Karenina* and *Madame Bovary* as part of my infidelity studies), people came across from other tables and said, Miles, is it, would you like to join us? and I politely declined. Twice I was invited for after-work drinks, and once for a Sunday afternoon party to celebrate the arrival of a new baby: in every case I made excuses.

People began to comment on this. They began to drop their voices when I passed and direct sideways glances in my direction; and then, one Thursday afternoon in late October, Ramsay put his head around the door of my office, in a sort of semi-formal way and said: 'Hi, Miles. How's it all going? Just, in general. You know.'

'Fine, thanks,' I said.

'Getting on with people all right?'

'Yes, thanks, no problems, no problems at all.'

'What is it now ye've been here, four months, nearly?'

'About that.'

'And ye've settled in? I mean, socially and everything? Making friends?'

'I'm fine, thanks, Ramsay.'

'Good. Good. Because, look, on Friday nights, me and a few of the others, some of the more senior ones, sometimes we go to an old bar round the corner called The Grill. Bit of an Aberdeen institution. Nothing major, just a wee dram. Come and have a drink with us tomorrow night.'

'I'm a little busy tomorrow night, Ramsay.'

'What're ye doing?'

'Well,' I said, not being able to think of a convincing excuse on the spot, 'I was going to catch up on my work.'

Ramsay shook his head. 'Nah. That can wait. Come and have a drink with us in The Grill, OK? Bout seven.'

'Well—'

'What I'm saying is, Miles, ah'd like you come and have a drink with us, all right?'

'Yes, all right.'

'Good. Good. Seven o'clock at The Grill. Only round the corner.'

When the next evening I walked in at seven-fifteen through The Grill's strange windowless front, having left it as late as I reasonably dared, I found a long, packed bar containing – I noticed at once – no women. There were just men, standing and drinking and many of them smoking, and through the resultant fug I spotted Ramsay halfway down the bar at the centre of a group of four: around him were a middle-aged man with unkempt white hair and a cigarette on his lower lip, a tall bulky guy with a black beard just starting to go grey, and a bull-necked, stocky young man about my age, with red hair cut very short. He appeared to be gesturing at Ramsay, with some animation.

'Ye've had a tip about it?' Ramsay was saying as I came up.

'From ma guy, aye,' said the bull-necked young man. He was a Scot, with a noticeably thicker accent than Ramsay's.

'Your guy in the DTI?'

'That's right.'

'And what's he say again?'

'That Lanna'll be in the next oil licensing round, when they release it in March.'

'Lanna itself?'

'Aye. That's what ah'm sayin'. The actual block the island's in. It'll be up for auction, can ye believe it?'

'Well that's pretty grim, if it's true,' said Ramsay.

'And what ah'm sayin is, we've gotta start planning now. Do the survey. Like we shoulda done the last time.'

'Kenny, ye know perfectly well, we couldnae do it the last time because the island is closed to outsiders, and Kintyre denied us access.'

'Aye well, this time he winnae be able to, will he?'

'Why not?'

'Cos of the land reform bill. In the new parliament. There's gonna be a legal right of responsible access to all land, and about time too. Was the first thing Donald Dewar said, in June when he read out the bills. So ye winnae be able to close an island to the public, any more than ye'll be able to close a sporting estate. It'll be illegal to do it.'

'Miles, hi,' Ramsay said, noticing me. 'Come into the body of the kirk. Just having a wee discussion here.' He turned back to the man he called Kenny. 'Ye think this'll go through by the spring?'

'Should do, aye.'

'But what if it doesn't?'

'We should go anyway, because we know the legal right of access is in the pipeline. We'd have a moral right.'

'Kenny, that'd be completely outwith our powers. And anyway, look, it's not just a question of legality, with Lanna it's a question of practicality. Sorry, Miles, this is Kenny Lornie, who's acting head of marine industry' – indicating the bull-necked young man who'd been speaking – 'this is Fraser Muir, who's my deputy' – indicating at the tall guy with the beard, who was another Scot – 'and this is Sidney Jeffries, who's head of seabirds,' nodding at the middle-aged white-haired guy with the cigarette. 'Miles is researching conservation policy on fisheries.'

We all said hello, and Ramsay was about to ask me what I wanted to drink but before he could, Kenny Lornie said to him: 'What d'ye mean, practicality?'

Ramsay said: 'On Lanna there's only one landing place, and Kintyre has this guy there, what's his name, Sidney?'

'Fergus,' said the white-haired guy, seized with a fit of coughing. 'Kintyre has this guy Fergus there, who keeps it closed.'

'How's he do that?' said Kenny.

'Sidney?' said Ramsay. 'You've been there, have ye not?' He waved at one of the barmen.

'Aye,' Sidney said, finishing his coughing. He was English, from the north, somewhere. 'There's a natural harbour, but the only way in's through a narrow gap in the cliffs and they keep it closed with chains. Chains held up by buoys. Fergus mans the chains.'

'What, ye mean he lives there? On the island?' Kenny said.

'In the spring and summer, certainly.'

'By himself?'

'Seems to. In the seabird breeding season, anyway. He's sort of, Kintyre's warden. Very big bloke. I mean, enormous. We went there once for a look, just a good look at the birds from the boat, team of us from the old NCC, few years back, and the weather turned, and we tried to get in for shelter and he wouldn't let us. Stopped us at the chains, at the entrance.'

'Really?' said Kenny.

'Came down in his rib to the other side of the buoys and more or less told us to bugger off. We wondered about legal action. I mean, a prosecution, if he was committing an offence. We actually looked into it. But there's no automatic right to use a private harbour, and there's no legal right of shelter, it's just a maritime custom.'

'But he denied you shelter? From a storm?'

'He did.'

'That is just fuckin' outrageous,' Kenny Lornie said.

'We weren't too happy,' Sidney said. 'It were a long way back to Barra in a Force Seven.'

'Closing an island, the very idea of it.' Kenny shook his head. 'The fuckin' landowners. The liberties they take. Parasites on the body of Scotland. Sooner they're cut doon tae size, the better.'

'You really don't like the lairds, do ye son?' said Fraser Muir, smiling.

'Nor would you, Fraser, if ye'd had the experiences ah had with some of the Highland estates, when ah was a young birder, when they try and throw ye off when all ye're trying tae do's see a golden eagle, which they're probably trying their best tae poison anyway, cos it takes a few grouse for its chicks'

'Did they succeed?' Fraser said.

'In what? Poisoning the eagle?'

'Throwing you off.'

'With difficulty, Fraser. With difficulty.'

'I can imagine that.'

'Ah didnae go quietly. I objected. Ah generally object to being pushed around, ah have a constitutional problem with being told what tae do. One keeper in particular laid hands on me, and regretted it, and ah was only eighteen then. But ma real objection's deeper than that.'

'Yeah?'

'Ah took the view that I might be a boy from Sighthill, but these were my Highlands as much as anybody else's. They belonged tae all o' Scotland, and all o' Scotland should enjoy them. They didnae belong just tae the lairds, parasitic bastards that they are.'

'Steady on, Kenny, these are people we have to deal with,' Ramsay said. He waved at the barman again.

'Come on, Ramsay, most of them dinnae even live there, they live in London half the time. They're not even Scottish.'

'Some of them are OK,' said Sidney Jeffries. 'Some of them are quite conservation-minded in my experience. Buccleuch's all right.'

'Aye well, that's as may be, but your man Kintyre's not one of them,' said Kenny Lornie. 'Fuckin' Tiger Laird. A' that stuff about captive breeding, away tae fuck wi' that. He's just a fat cat with a private zoo, and we need tae confront him now over Lanna.'

'We need to do no such thing, Kenny,' Ramsay said. 'We're not in the business of confronting anyone.'

'Yeah, but look Ramsay, what happened before was outrageous, he kept us off the island, we couldnae put up a proper objection and now we've got an oilfield less than fifty miles from one of the best seabird stations in the Atlantic. Ye cannae allow it tae happen again, man, even closer.'

'We won't allow it to happen again. I promise you.'

'But what do we do when the block is offered for auction and Kintyre tells us again to get fucked? Next thing ye know they'll be spudding a well a mile from Lanna, probably right next to the gannetries. You gonna allow that, Ramsay? Are ye? We need to take him on. We need to take him doon a peg.'

'What we need to do, Kenny, listen to me,' Ramsay said, 'is keep our personal opinions out of our work, OK? If what your guy says is true and the Lanna block is in the next round, we will take a very serious view of that, and we will do what needs to be done, to stop it. Dinnae fash yaself. We will. But we won't do it by letting personal animosities get mixed up in it, and anyone who does that, let me tell you Kenny, is not going to be involved in the process. Am I clear?'

There was a pause, slightly uncomfortable.

'Well,' said Kenny Lornie at length, 'you're the high heid yin.'

'Aye,' said Fraser Muir, laughing, 'he's the high heid yin, all right.'

'Aye Kenny,' said Ramsay, 'I'm the high heid yin….'

I had no idea what they were talking about. I wondered how long all this was going to go on for.

'And what I say is,' continued Ramsay, 'that that's enough talking shop. We have a guest here. So let us talk about something else, gentlemen. Sex. Football. Anything you like.'

Fraser said: 'Och, never football. Dinnae get him started.' He turned to me and indicated Kenny. 'He's a mad Jambo, this lad.'

'I beg your pardon?'

'He's a big Hearts fan. It's the triumph of hope over experience. Is it no that, Kenny? Whereas I follow the Gers, and have something to celebrate noo and then.'

'Ye're just a glory hunter you,' said Kenny. 'Ye're from Dumfries, man. Ye should support ya local team, ye should be following Queen o' the South, ye shouldnae be at Ibrox at a', ye should be at what's the place, Palmerston Park. Ah went there once for a cup tie. Nice wee ground. Ye're a traitor tae ya home toon, Muir, that's what ye are. Where you from, Miles?'

'I'm from London. To be precise, I'm from Wimbledon.'

'Wimbledon? The crazy gang and a' that? They were some antics, eh? D'ye follow them?'

'I'm afraid I don't follow them, no.'

'D'ye follow anyone?'

'You mean in football? Not really.'

'Not even Man U? A wee bit?'

'I'm afraid I have no interest in it whatsoever.'

'Oh. Well. Right then.'

'Miles, welcome to our watering hole,' said Ramsay. 'What d'you think? It's pretty much unchanged since 1926.'

I peered through the nicotine miasma down the mahogany bar. 'There don't seem to be any women,' I said.

The men grinned.

'There don't, do there?' said Ramsay. 'Although women are perfectly welcome.'

'They didn't use to be,' said Sidney. 'They didn't have a ladies' toilet in here till last year. They're welcome more in theory than in practice.'

'Quite wrong, Sidney, quite wrong,' said Ramsay. 'Miles, what will you have?'

'I'll have a glass of white wine, please. A Pinot Grigio or something.'

Kenny Lornie and Fraser Muir glanced at each other and stifled a laugh, it seemed to me.

'You'll be lucky,' said Sidney Jeffries. 'All you'll get here's a dram.'

'I'm sorry?'

'This is a whisky bar, Miles,' said Ramsay. 'It's famous for its single malts. It's got more than 500. Let me suggest you try one from Speyside, they're more lightly peated than the Islay malts.'

'Yeah, don't touch them, whatever you do,' said Sidney Jeffries. 'It's like drinking bloody medicine.'

'What are you on about, Sidney?' said Fraser Muir. 'Pay no attention, Miles. The Islay malts are wonderful. Sixteen-year-old Lagavulin, that's pure nectar. And Ardbeg Uigeadail, och, that sets off taste explosions in ya head.'

'Don't listen to him,' said Sidney. 'It's like drinking cough mixture.'

I was persuaded to take a glass of fifteen-year-old Glenlivet, and while Ramsay was ordering it, Fraser Muir said to me: 'So how are you finding it up here?'

'Fine, thanks.'

'Interesting time to come to Scotland.'

'How d'you mean?'

'With devolution. The new parliament and everything.'

'Right.'

'If you think having a Scottish Parliament's going to make a difference to most ordinary people, you're sadly mistaken,' said Sidney, coughing. 'It'll be just another talking shop. Waste of time and money.'

'Not at all,' said Kenny.

'Why not have a Yorkshire parliament then? Or a Lancashire parliament?'

'Cos Yorkshire's just a county, like Aberdeenshire, ye dismal wretched Sassenach. Scotland's a nation with its own proud history.'

'What do you think, Miles?' said Fraser.

'I haven't really formed an opinion, I'm afraid,' I said.

'See much of Scotland?'

'Hardly any.'

'How're you finding Aberdeen?'

'It's fine.'

'There you go, Miles,' said Ramsay, gesturing to a small glass on the bar with a water jug beside it. 'Glenlivet 15-year-old. Take just a wee drop of water, it releases the flavours.'

I did so, and sipped, and Kenny Lornie said to me: 'Where ye living? In Aberdeen?'

'Rosemount.'

'That's quite trendy, isn't it? Where d'ye drink?'

'I'm sorry?'

'Where d'ye go for a drink? There's a nice wee pub up there, isn't there, the Queen Vic? D'ye go in there?'

'I don't really go for a drink.'

'What, not ever?'

'Not really, no.'

'Then what d'ye do in ya spare time? D'ye go birding? Cos you're a seabird specialist, aren't ye?'

'I did my doctorate on guillemots, but it wasn't ecological. It was a behavioural study.'

'That was under Callum McSorley in Wales, he's an old friend of mine,' said Ramsay.

'Whereabouts in Wales?' said Sidney.

'Skarholm.'

'The colony on the cliffs there? Craig Yr Adar?'

'That's right.'

'I know it.'

'I spent six years there.'

'Then Miles wrote a book about it,' said Ramsay.

'Is this the book about sex that that I've heard tell of?' said Fraser.

'In so far as it was a book about extra-pair copulation being adaptive in socially monogamous organisms, yes.'

'Oh. Right,' said Fraser.

'We've got a fantastic guillemot colony just along the coast here, at Fowlsheugh,' said Kenny. 'It's forty thousand pairs, plus twenty thousand pairs of kittiwakes. Just past Stonehaven. I could take ye, if ye like.'

'I can't think of anything I'd like less,' I said.

Kenny Lornie fixed me with a look. 'Suit yaself then, pal,' he said.

'I spent six years of my life staring at birds on cliffs and I'll be quite happy never to stare at another one.'

'You suit yaself.'

'But you've been in Oxford the last few years?' Sidney Jeffries said.

'I've been a Research Fellow, yes.'

'At the NTI?'

'That's right.'

'Roger de Vries still the head of it?'

'He is.'

'My niece was at Oxford,' said Fraser. 'Few years back.'

'Oh yes?' I said. 'Which college?'

'Oxford Brookes.'

'Ah, well, that's not really Oxford, is it?'

'How d'ye mean?'

'It's a separate university. In fact it's just a jumped-up polytechnic, really. It's for people who can't get into the real Oxford.'

It was Fraser's turn to stare at me. 'Well thank you for putting me right on that,' he said.

A silence fell. Sidney lit a new cigarette, and coughed. Kenny, Fraser and Ramsay exchanged glances.

'Well, I ought to be getting along,' I said. 'I've got a few things to do.'

'Hey, ye cannae go yet, pal,' said Kenny. 'Ye havenae bought a round.'

'I think Miles can shoot off if he wants,' said Ramsay. 'I er, I think that'd be for the best.'

It was after this evening that the attitude of my colleagues towards me shifted – although I did not realise it – from curiosity, from regarding me merely as a weird loner, to active dislike, as Kenny Lornie, backed up by Fraser Muir, bore ready witness to the fact that my English standoffishness was not eccentric, but actively unpleasant. Mr Lornie, as I eventually realised, christened me Rupert, and the name stuck: Rupert I became throughout UKOCA, the arrogant academic from Oxford, devoid of all politeness and consideration for others, who thought the rest of the world beneath him. And just before Christmas, my unpopularity came to a climax.

I had given no thought to Christmas; I didn't care about it, and as for what it might be like for Lotte and my mother in Wimbledon, with my absence for the first time ever, I didn't care about that either. And Jenny – I chose not to think about Jenny. Jenny and her child – our child, who had been, and was no more.

What I cared about was the final chapter of the book, the chapter about humans, about infidelity in women: I couldn't make it work.

I became so frustrated that I began grappling with it in the office, an office now bedecked with decorations and Christmas cards, and lightly suffused with the beginnings of the yuletide spirit, all of which went over my head, and one afternoon after lunch with the holiday approaching, I shut my door, opened a new file on the computer, and began to wrestle with the heart of the argument.

Were all wives who strayed really looking for fitness benefits for their future children?

You would think so. Biologically. Must be the case.

But was Anna Karenina? Was Emma Bovary?

Well, perhaps unconsciously. Perhaps that was the biological origin of the urge to stray, even if they weren't aware of it.

But was Mrs Robinson in *The Graduate*? She was past child-bearing age, surely? She wasn't looking for fitness benefits. She was just looking for fun.

Where was the evolutionary advantage in that?

Damn.

It just doesn't fit.

Frustration, frustration, frustration!

But then, I was confusing something, wasn't I? I was confusing proximate causes with ultimate causes. Yes. Let's try it again. Let's see …

And a loud voice was suddenly singing outside my office:
'Hearts, Hearts, Glorious Hearts!
It's doon at Tynecastle they bide!'

I heard someone laugh and say: 'It's Kenny' and the voice sang
'The talk o' the toon are the boys in maroon,
An' Auld Reekie supports 'em with pride!'

'Kenny Lornie,' said another voice. 'Had a liquid lunch and he's three sheets in the wind.'

I opened my door. People were smiling. Kenny Lornie was standing in the middle of the floor.

'This is ma story!' he sang, now stretching wide his arms,
'This is ma song!
Follow the Hearts and
you can't go wrong!'

My frustration boiled over. 'D'you mind?' I called out. 'Some of us are trying to work.'

'Well there's some say that Celtic and Rangers are grand …'

'I say,' I called out again. 'D'you mind?'

'… But the boys in maroon are … what? What d'ye say?'

I said: 'D'you mind awfully keeping the noise level down? Trying to work here, OK?'

'What? You telling me tae shut it?'

A tenseness appeared on people's faces.

He looked around him and laughed. 'Ah dinnae believe it.' Then he strode towards me and pushed me hard in the chest so I staggered backwards. 'Nae cunt tells me tae fuckin' shut it, ye fuckin' English cunt ye,' he cried at me and pushed me further back, crying, 'Shut ya ane mouth Rupert, ye fuckin' wee cunt ye,' and he pushed me again shouting, 'Ah'll fuckin' sort ye oot, nae bother, eh?' till I had reached the wall and he had me pinned against it and his face was in mine and swamping me with drink fumes but by then a couple of guys had rushed over and taken his arms and Fraser Muir was one of them, pulling him off me urging, Kenny, Kenny, come on now son, easy now, come on.

'Fuckin' English cunt, I'll bend a fuckin' poker o'er ya heid!' shouted Kenny Lornie, still trying to get at me as he was pulled away.

I had hardly put up a fight. I'd been too completely taken aback to resist. And I was pretty shaken.

But nobody asked me how I was.

Nobody sympathised.

People turned away and got back to their work, glancing at me and whispering.

I tried to get back to mine, with little success, and ten minutes later Ramsay phoned me and asked me to come up and see him right away.

'What's all this with Kenny?' he said.

'He was singing outside my office, and I asked him to keep it down, and he just went for me.'

'Was that wise? Telling him to shut up? It's the run-up to Christmas, Miles. We tend to cut people a wee bit slack in the festive season.'

'I was trying to work, Ramsay.'

'Well ah'm telling ye, Miles, I think you made a mistake. And ye certainly picked the wrong person to make it with. He's from a very tough part of Edinburgh, is Kenny.'

'I don't think it justifies him going for me.'

'No it doesn't, and when he's sober enough to read it, he'll be getting a written warning. But you had a role in this too, ye know.'

I said nothing.

He looked at me and shook his head. He said: 'This is a bad business.' He bit a nail. 'Look Miles. Ye've been here six months now and to be quite frank you haven't endeared yourself to the staff, I have to tell ye that. Working in a place like this is not like being a university researcher, ye know. Ye can't just be a complete lone wolf. Ye've got to have some sort of human interchange with your colleagues and ye've hardly had any whatsoever. What's with you?'

'I've been trying to focus on my work,' I said, which was true, although it wasn't the work Ramsay assumed it was.

He started to speak and stopped. He breathed out and shook his head again. 'All right. All right. Anyway, there's something else. I want you to go to France.'

I am certain, now, that what Ramsay was doing was getting me out of the office, not least because the Christmas party was two days away and he did not want me in any situation where Kenny Lornie might have taken drink. He probably did have to send somebody to France that day, but it didn't have to be me, in fact, in normal circumstances it would almost certainly not have been me. But Ramsay was thinking on his feet and avoiding more trouble.

'Can ye go to France? More or less right now?'

'I suppose so,' I said, wanting to sound obliging after Ramsay's strictures. 'What for?'

'An oil tanker's gone down in the Bay of Biscay. Got the makings of a proper pollution disaster. Name of *Erika*. She's broken in two. Big cargo of heavy fuel oil, thousands of tonnes of it all pouring out, and the slick is starting to hit the beaches along the French Atlantic coast. That's a major wintering area for a lot of our seabirds, auks especially, you're a seabird specialist, you know that, don't ye?'

I nodded. I did.

'Ye got any experience of oiled birds?'

'Fraid not.'

'Ah thought the *Sea Empress* spill was down your way when you were in Wales?'

'It didn't quite get to Skarholm.'

'Well, ye're going to get some experience of it now, because this thing is certainly getting to the beaches in France, and oiled birds are being found, so what I want ye to go and do is a preliminary report for us on the whole situation, all right?'

I nodded again.

'If we go through the Foreign Office and the French government it'll take for ever, so I want ye to shortcut all that. I've got a mate over there who runs a little conservation NGO in Brittany, it's called Bretagne-Nature, based in Brest. He's a seabird specialist like me and you, a good guy, ah've known him for years on the circuit. His name's Hervé Kermarrec. These are his numbers, office, home and mobile.'

He passed me a paper.

'Ah want ye to go to Brest and link up with him because he's going to be doing a tour of the oiled beaches and he knows everyone, and he's happy to take you along. Ye can fly to Paris first thing in the morning and then get to Brest on the TGV, the high-speed train, we're sorting the tickets out now. Be there for as long as it takes to get a proper view of it all, all right? If ye can get any sort of feel for how it might actually be affecting UK birds, from any rings ye can pick up maybe, that'd be a big bonus. Can ye do that?'

'OK,' I said.

'Speak any French?'

'I did O-level, I was quite good at it. I can probably remember a fair bit.'

'All right. Hervé speaks English, anyway. After a fashion. Take ya time. Don't come back till it's sorted, and ye've got a proper overview of the whole thing.'

'All right.' I got up to go.

'And, Miles?'

'Yes, Ramsay?'

'Don't fuck this up.'

And it was with that chilly dismissal, that it began: the train of events that was to change everything.

He offends everyone by not socializing

11

Crude oil, the dark lifeblood of industrialised society, is at the heart of this story, most of all at its climax; and for me it has come to symbolise all that is ruinous in the human domination of the Earth. But when I went to France that December I was surprisingly ignorant of its direct polluting power, of the particular horror it can inflict on some of the natural world's most magnificent creatures, seabirds above all. I had never taken on board the appalling nature of the collision between feathered beings and unrefined petroleum: it's as if a particularly malign intelligence had set itself to devise the worst possible lingering suffering and death, out-topping crucifixion, for one particular life-form. When that life-form is the most inspiring symbol of flight and freedom, its transformation into a piece of sludge seems an offence against nature whose outrageousness cannot be measured. That was why Callum was angry with me, I came to realise, for shirking the rescue operation when the *Sea Empress* spilled its cargo off Milford Haven: I had skipped a lesson he thought important for me to learn.

Yet I felt none of that as I flew to Paris, boarded the TGV Atlantique at Gare Montparnasse and watched the grey winter daylight fade over the fields as we rushed westwards towards Brittany; I merely felt a dull resentment, that my writing routine was being interrupted, combined with a sort of half-formed unpleasant realisation that I had been unceremoniously shipped out of my workplace as an unwanted inconvenience.

It was not till the next day that the reality began to impose itself upon me. I had been met at the station in Brest by Hervé Kermarrec, who turned out to be a tall middle-aged man with long melancholy jowls like a bloodhound's, briefly lit up by a smile of welcome. He took me back to the offices of his charity, Bretagne-Nature, and the flat he occupied on the floor above – it was decorated with posters and pictures of seabirds and he seemed to be very much the bachelor bird man, living over the shop – and he cooked us a large plate of pasta while he outlined what was happening: the *Erika* was an oldish tanker chartered by the French oil company Total which had been bound for Italy carrying 30,000 tonnes of heavy fuel oil, but in the Bay of Biscay, or the Golfe de Gascogne as Hervé called it, she had run into a violent storm and foundered: she broke in two and began releasing her cargo.

The point was, Hervé said, that she was so far offshore – about 75 kilometres, nearly 50 miles – that the oil slick was likely to fan out and hit the beaches along a very extensive stretch of the French Atlantic coastline, and the seabird casualties were expected to be heavy. His English wasn't bad, if a little idiosyncratic, and in conversation with him I began to revive my own rusty French and pick up some specialised vocabulary: an oil spill was a *marée noire*, a black tide, while of the species most likely to be affected, a guillemot was simply a *guillemot*, easy enough, a razorbill was a *petit pingouin*, and a gannet was a *fou de bassan*.

We set out at six the next morning, Hervé providing waterproof overalls which we put on with rubber boots and gloves; and then we climbed into his battered Citroën van, whose seats he had covered with old sacks, and in the pre-dawn darkness we headed south to the Atlantic coast in search of the aforesaid black tide.

I can't remember now the name of the place where we met it, but I can never forget what it looked like. It was a small holiday beach somewhere west of Concarneau, which we found just as dawn was breaking; the sand was covered in a dark expanse, black and shiny in the half-light. The slick had come in during the night and the tide had left it behind and it was so perfectly smooth it was almost attractive in an abstract sort of way, but then I realised the smoothness was interrupted, near the edge, by a barely discernible bulge. We walked into the oil towards it, our boots starting to stick at once, and when we got to the bulge Hervé peered at it and said: '*Fou de bassan.*'

It was a gannet: the most spectacular of North Atlantic fishing birds, roaming the waters on its great white black-tipped wings, divebombing straight down from a hundred feet to the mackerel below, the apotheosis of free flight and aerial mastery and hunting skill. Now it was just a lump. It was as set in the crude as if it had been set in concrete. Hervé began to extract it, and I began to help him, trying to get a grip with gloved fingers to yank it out of the black goo, but the goo fought us grimly, until after maybe a whole minute, I managed to get free what I thought was a wing, and I pulled hard on that; with a sort of small ripping noise the wing came off in my hands and I fell fully backwards into the oil.

I couldn't move. Hervé came over to me and tried to pull me out and was unable to. He said: '*Roulez!*' I said: 'What?' He said: 'Roll! Roll!' gesturing with his hands. I managed to roll to one side, and then on to my knees, and as he helped me to my feet I began to heave with the stench of the crude that was now covering me. The gannet-lump was still where it had been, minus wing. Hervé said: 'Sit on the sand, I will return,' and I sat down, panting, holding my nose, trying not to retch, until in a few minutes he was back with a shovel and a bucket from the van, which we should have taken in the first place, and together we dug out the gannet, and scooped its wing up with it.

In the bucket, I remember, it was not just that it didn't look like a living thing – it didn't even look like an ex-living thing. It was just pieces of stuff. I tried to feel for the legs to see if it was carrying a ring; in vain. I couldn't locate them. You would in no way know that it was feathered, this object, or ever had been; you would in no way believe it had been capable of leaving the ground, never mind soaring to the heights and diving to the depths. Nothing could be more earthbound. It seemed to be made of mud. I wondered how long it had taken to die.

As the December dawn began to spread and lighten we walked along the beach and we saw there were more bulges in the smooth oil surface, perhaps one every ten or twenty yards; the slick was full of birds. We counted thirty-seven, and we dug out four more, all of which were guillemots, though none was ringed as far as I could tell, and then I started to vomit, so we went back to the van, and I at last took off the overalls and put on a fresh pair. Hervé took pity on me, and flashed his brief smile and said: 'I think we take breakfast now, hein?'

I vomited again.

All day, we worked our way down the coast of southern Brittany, trying to gauge the extent of the slick, and the numbers of affected birds, with me searching unsuccessfully for anything which might show an origin in the British Isles; and as time wore on we encountered numerous elements of the giant beach-clean-up which the French authorities were mobilising, as well as the equally expansive rescue operation being put in place by the LPO, the Ligue pour la Protection des Oiseaux, the French bird protection charity. In the latter, Hervé seemed to know many of the key people, and that evening we stayed in a *centre de soins*, one of the LPO emergency treatment centres. I forget where it was now. It might have been Lorient. I forget. What I remember is the smell as we entered the building, a weird combination of fuel oil, and fish soup, the latter being the *bouillie de poissons* which was being made in industrial quantities and used to feed the birds which had been brought in and were potentially saveable as they were more lightly oiled. They were nearly all guillemots. There were a few gannets and the odd razorbill and puffin, but guillemots seemed to make up the overwhelming majority of the victims: there were scores and scores of them just in this centre. The birds had to have their strength built up before they could be cleaned, as that involved being scrubbed for long periods by human hands and the stress of it would kill them, if they were weak – so, since they vomited back whole fish, they were being fed the *bouillie de poissons* directly into their stomachs with syringes by young volunteers, who were arriving all the time from all over France. With my French gradually coming back, I spoke to a young guy from Alsace and a young woman from Lyon; they had travelled these hundreds of miles just to offer their services. They were extraordinarily idealistic.

We slept at the centre and rose again before dawn, and while we drank our coffee Hervé told me that we had not seen the worst of it; that was beyond the Loire, the LPO people had told him, in the departments of Loire Atlantique and Vendée. So we headed south again in the camionette and found the black tide once more, engulfing the holiday beaches around Pornic; the LPO people had been right, and the oiling was severe. The worst of all was a long beach below low cliffs; Hervé reached the cliff edge a couple of seconds before me and I heard him exclaim '*Bordel!*' which is more or less the French for 'Fucking hell!'

I came up beside him and saw what he was looking at: the whole elegantly curving bay below, perhaps half a mile from end to end, was black. An army of clean-up workers in yellow overalls were starting to attack the oil slick with a bulldozer, and when we scrambled down to the beach we found that some of them were taking dead birds out of the oil and laying them on the sand above the high-tide mark in neat rows, prior to disposal; we saw at once there were more than a hundred. Just on this one stretch of beach. Hervé shook his head and murmured: '*C'est apocalyptique.*' I began examining the corpses for rings – they were virtually all guillemots – and at last I found a couple, and then a third, which appeared to be British; they were hopelessly stuck on the birds, but Hervé lent me his clasp knife, I remember it was a Laguiole knife he was very attached to and he asked me to keep it as clean as possible, and I hacked the ringed legs off to take back. Then I threw the corpses back on the sand, legless now as well as overwhelmed in crude.

It began to get to me, all this death.

I mean, I had never cared a fig if a guillemot lived or died, other than the loss of data which a death might represent, but holding the contorted bodies, you could not be unaware that the end these creatures had come to was horrific. I did not like it – which was an unfamiliar and strangely troubling feeling for me. And we kept seeing it that day and the next, as we moved south, until by the third afternoon of our trip we finally came to the end of it all.

We were on the outskirts of La Rochelle, in the LPO *centre de soins*; the first thing I saw on entering was a pen containing a dozen oiled but surviving gannets, staring at me with blue eyes which seemed almost human, and I chatted to the young guy looking after them whose name was Raoul and who came from Yvelines in the suburbs of Paris; he said he was a conscientious objector working for the LPO rather than doing military service. Hervé had gone off to talk to the people running the place, and a few minutes later he came back and said: 'It is nearly finished.'

'What is?' I said

'*La marée noire*,' he said. The oil slick.

'Where does it finish?'

'On the Île de Ré.'

It could have been anywhere, I suppose, or it could have been nowhere; but this is where it was. Three small words. Île de Ré. Three short sounds, around which my life pivots. Certainly, it was my Damascus road, this long narrow island of sandy beaches, salt marshes and oyster beds, this summer honeypot for holidaymakers; it was where my life began to change, with an accident, an astounding accident: a chance encounter of endless improbability. But it happened; and in a circumstance which of course was fortuitous, but which has since impressed itself upon me, it was actually the winter solstice, 21 December, when it took place, the very day when the dark ended its expansion, and the light began to grow.

Oil had come ashore, said Hervé, at the island's far end, thirty kilometres away, so we would go and have a look at it; but on the mainland further south, the LPO staffers had told him, there appeared to be nothing, so this was the limit of the beaches affected by the *Erika* spill. And we were more than 250 miles from Brest. It was gigantic.

When we drove over the arching road bridge to the island it was a mild afternoon of pale thin sunshine, and I saw at once that Ré was a pleasant and tranquil place with an obvious flavour of the south: there were pines and cedars and vineyards, and the low white houses were roofed with orange tiles, their shutters painted green. We were headed for the far north-west corner of the island and La Phare des Baleines, the Lighthouse of the Whales, and eventually we saw it marking the island tip, and parked the van, and walked through scrub to the shore.

There was a sort of slow-motion ballet going on: twenty ghostly figures in silver overalls were moving up and down the beach in the sunlit sea-mist, local volunteers cleaning up the oil. It was not as bad as many beaches we had seen. 'C'est des galettes,' said Hervé, meaning, it's pancakes, it was large dollops of the stuff scattered across the sand, but not a continuous, engulfing glutinous slick. We asked the volunteers about stranded seabirds and they said they had found a dozen, which had been tossed into a black rubbish sack; I got them out, and they were all guillemots, but none was ringed. I did my own scan of the beach while Hervé carried on chatting, but found nothing; and eventually we were ready to go.

But then on impulse I thought, if this is the last beach of all, have another look, and I told Hervé and he said he would look as well, and we shared a final scan of the tideline, going farther out, and this time I spotted something which I thought at first was just a clump of dark seaweed but which as I got closer I saw, with a small thrill of triumph, was a bird, which the volunteers had missed. 'Par ici,' I shouted over to Hervé. It looked like a guillemot; it was. It had been very badly oiled and it had one wing stretched out and seemingly dislocated and its beak was open, as if in the expression of a final agony. I picked it up and felt for the legs: even better! It was ringed!

'Hervé,' I shouted, 'Over here!'

And I realised then it didn't just have one ring, it had four, which meant it had been ringed for identification and study in a colony, and the thought crossed my mind that possibly, just possibly, it might even be one of ours, and I found a red ring, and then the BTO technical ring, R and T, and I scraped off the oil on the other leg and found one of the rings was blue … and a chill descended on my shoulders as I scraped the goo off the final ring and it too was blue and I held him in my hands, looking in sheer, absolute disbelief, gazing at him, gazing at what he had been transformed into, a foully polluted piece of death, an obscene lump, he who had been the supreme giver of life, *the supreme reproducer, the supreme shagger, Miles, that's what he is, he's a life force that boy, he's a life-force, Miles*, the voice was calling in my head, *he's a life-force, Miles* and suddenly some sort of wall inside me crumbled and collapsed with a roar and a cloud of dust and I cried out: 'Jenny!'

Hervé had come up and looked at me, astonished. 'Are you all right Miles?' he said.

I looked back at him, unable to speak. The wavelets were washing into the winter beach of La Phare des Baleines, in the misty sunshine. I was lost. I was completely lost. More lost than I had ever been in my life.

'*Ça va?* Are you OK?'

I stuttered at him, holding out the lump of tar that had been Arty Booboo: 'This guillemot – I know him.'

'What?'

'*Ce guillemot-ci – je le connais.*'

'*Vous le connaissez?*'

'I mean, personally. *Je le connais – personellement.*'

Hervé's eyes widened.

'Yes. You see the rings? *Vous voyez les bagues?*'

'*Oui?*'

'That is how I know him.'

'*Ah bon?*'

'He comes from my research station in Wales. He has a name. *Il a un nom.*'

'*Comment, un nom? Ce guillemot-ci a un nom? Quel nom?*'

'His name is Arty Booboo. *Il s'appelle* Ar-ty Boo-boo.'

'Aaaarrty Boooobooo?'

'*Oui*. He was the champion of the whole colony at sex, Hervé. You would admire him in France. *Il était le champion de sexe de toute la colonie.*'

'*Ah bon?*'

'He had more offspring than any other guillemot. He was a life-force. Do you say that in French? *Une force de vie?*'

'I understand what you mean, Miles.'

'I watched him for six years. I watched him make love, Hervé. I watched him make life. Every spring. Without fail. For six years. And look at him now,' I said, holding the blackened and agonised body out, with its gaping beak. 'It's not much of an end, is it, for a life-force? To become a lump, a fucking lump of fucking fuel oil.'

I found that tears were streaming down my face.

It was the first time I had ever felt pity.

Hervé didn't know what to say.

I didn't know what to say to him.

I felt almost immobilised with the shock. Here on this beach! ... After all the death we had seen ... he, to be part of it too! This unbelievable chance ... it was a gigantic jolt, a jolt to my whole system. Yet hovering about me too was another feeling, an inchoate sense that something else had also just happened.

I didn't know what it was.

I didn't understand it.

Hervé said: 'So what do you want to do, Miles? With your bird?'

I said: 'If it's OK with you, Hervé, I think I would like to bury him. I don't want him to be put in a rubbish bag like all the others. Can we get the spade from the camionette?'

'OK.'

So we did, and by the side of some gorse bushes above the beach I dug the hole for Arty Booboo, and I was about to lay him in it, when Hervé said: 'Do you want to keep his rings?'

'What?'

'The rings on his legs.'

'Christ yes. The rings.' I had forgotten, I looked at them. They were important. The evidence that this was a bird from Britain, from a precise location, in fact. There was no way I could slide the rings out of their enveloping oil; but there was no way I was going to hack off the legs which held them, either. Not that final indignity. I said to Hervé: 'May I ask you something?'

'*Bien sûr.*'

'Would you cut the legs off for me with your knife? So I can keep the rings? I don't want to do it myself.'

'OK.'

So Hervé Kermarrec took him from me, the supreme reproducer of Skarholm, the companion of my doctoral researches, the star of the front cover of *Nature* and the hero of *Everything Except Seahorses*, and without ceremony opened his Laguiole knife and hacked off his legs, and then I laid him as gently as I could in his hole, filthy and agonised and mutilated as he now was, and said goodbye to him and covered him with sand, and we left him and the beach of La Phare des Baleines and climbed into the Citroën van as the sun of the winter solstice began to set into the Bay of Biscay, and drove back along the Île de Ré to the mainland.

I was profoundly shaken. To have met with him here, so far from his home, and so vilely done to death! What were the chances of that? How many millions to one? It left me almost trembling, as if the oil had spilled onto Skarholm, had invaded my own world and covered me. And yet there was something more, besides the shock of it, which was deeply troubling. I couldn't put my finger on it. But eventually it was to manifest itself.

We had driven into La Rochelle with the blue-and-white Christmas lights shining in the trees around the Old Port. Hervé said, this evening is for us now and one is going to eat well and drink well, *on va bien manger et bien boire.* So we checked into a tourist hotel that was still open and enjoyed the luxury of a hot shower, and then we went out to a restaurant which we had virtually to ourselves, where Hervé insisted we drink the local aperitif, Pineau des Charentes, which was a bit like a fruity white sherry, served very cold, and after the first one we both took a second and then we greedily ate a great dinner, with a bottle of Muscadet.

We talked over the three days we had spent together, Hervé having witnessed a number of previous major oil spills, including the dreadful *Amoco Cadiz,* also off the coast of Brittany – he was one of the leading experts in Europe on oiled seabirds – but *Erika,* he said, was the worst he had seen in terms of extent (and in fact it turned out to be the worst oil spill that had ever happened in Europe in terms of seabird mortality, with the final death toll estimated at 300,000). He was much taken by the finding of Arty Booboo, so I told him about the Skarholm colony, and I explained how the birds were colour-ringed and that was how Arty had got his name, and how he had had more chicks than was normal, every year, and that was very significant, and he had even appeared on the front of *Nature.*

'He was the champion to reproduce?'

'He was.'

'I like that you have called him a … life-force. I like that.'

I suddenly found myself saying: 'It wasn't me, Hervé.'

'What?'

'It wasn't me who called him a life-force. It was a girl. I had a girlfriend. *Une amie.* She knew him. She … liked him. It was she who said he was a life-force.'

'And she would be sad? To hear of his death?'

'I suppose so. I suppose she would be, yes.'

'You will tell her?'

I shook my head. 'No.'

'Why not?'

'She's not my girlfriend any more. I ended it with her, Hervé. So I could write a book.'

'What is her name?'

'Jenny.'

After a moment he said: 'You have cried that name.'

'What?'

'At La Phare des Baleines. On the beach. When you have found him, Aaaarrty Booboo.'

'You mean I … shouted it out?'

'Shouted, yes. I remember you have shouted. And it was that. You have shouted: *Jenny!*'

'Did I?' I had no recollection.

'*Mais oui.*' He said: 'It makes me think to something.'

'What's that?

'There is a famous poem of my city. Of Brest. Where a man shouts the name of a woman.'

'Is there? What name is that?'

'Barbara'.

'Bahrburra?'

'Babbara!' cried Hervé loudly, taking me aback with the rat-tat-tat of flat French syllables. I hadn't suspected there was a showman in him. Maybe it was the Muscadet.

I said: 'Why does the man shout the name?'

'Because it rains.'

'What?'

'Because it is raining on Brest, without cease on that day, raining raining raining, and the woman is walking along the street in the rain, it is Rue de Siam which is the great street of Brest, she is a beautiful young woman and she is very wet, but even so she is smiling, she is so much smiling, and the man, he, *il s'abrite* … he …'

I tried to remember. 'He shelters? He is sheltering?'

'*Oui, sous un porche.* Under a porch?' I nodded. 'And the poet, he is watching, he is Jacques Prévert, do you know him?'

'I'm afraid not.'

'And while he watches, the man suddenly sees the woman and he cries BARBARA!'

Hervé shouted again, at the top of his voice, and stretching out his arms.

I jumped. The bored waitresses by the cash till turned to look at him in astonishment.

'And she runs to him, in the rain, and she throws herself in his arms. *Elle s'est jetée dans ses bras.* And they embrace themselves, the two. The one the other.'

I waited. I said: 'There is … no more, Hervé?'

'But it is magnificent, Miles.'

'How so?'

'Because one sees their love. And one hears their love. In the great shout of the man.'

I murmured the words to myself, *in the great shout of the man …* Herve smiled. 'As one sees your love. In the great shout of you.'

'What?' What d'you say?'

'C'est évident. It is evident, Miles.'

'What is?'

'Your love. For…the name. For the name you have shouted on the beach. For Jenny.' He took a sip of Muscadet. 'Do you not love her, Miles?'

I looked at him, open-mouthed. 'No, no. I told you, I ended it with her, Hervé.'

'It appears,' he said, 'that it is not ended.'

I shook my head. 'No. It's over. Really. It's over.' And I changed the subject back to major oil spills, and asked him to tell me more about *Amoco Cadiz*. But a surprise lay in store for me.

All the time I had been in Aberdeen, I had slept an undisturbed sleep and I had dreamed no dreams – truly, not one, or at least, not one I can remember, exaggerated though that might sound, from the time I first arrived in Scotland. It was as if some part of my brain had been placed into cold storage, the vault doors locked, the combination unknowable. But that night in La Rochelle, in the soft bed of the hotel room, when I had sunk down, down, down to it, to the abyss where the dreams are, the doors opened and I found myself back on the beach, and I was with Hervé: it was a beach that was covered in oil, an endless black slick of it, and we were walking along its edge. We were counting the lumps in the slick which were all guillemots, and we counted thirty-seven of them, one after another, and then Hervé pointed to a much larger one, and said: *'Fou de Bassan.'*

I looked and it was very big and I said, but that is too big even for a gannet, Hervé, far too big, and as we got closer I saw that it was Jenny.

My heartbeat rose.

She was lying in the oil on her back, trapped in it, and her eyes were fixed on me with an intense look I knew from somewhere but did not wish to see, and Hervé had got out his Laguiole knife and he said, do you want me to cut her legs off, Miles, so you can keep the rings, and I said no, no, and I tried to reach for her arm to pull her out of the oil but I couldn't get it loose and Hervé was opening his knife with a strange smile on his face and I started to panic and said to her, Roll! Roll! That is how you get out! And she simply looked at me with this expression which I knew from somewhere, which I could not bear, so I tried again with her arm and I prised it loose, first the fingers, then the whole arm, and I pulled really hard on her arm and with a long ripping sound it came away from her body in my hands and I screamed and woke up.

I sat on the edge of the bed.

I was breathing hard.

I went into the bathroom, and drank a glass of water. Then I came back and sat on the bed again.

It was a dream.

I mean, an awful dream. But just a dream.

People have dreams, don't they? Doesn't mean anything. So I put out the light, and I got back into bed, and drew up the sheet, and closed my eyes, and there was Jenny again, looking at me as she lay in the oil.

I had seen the look before, though I did not know where. It was piercing and intense. I could not bear it.

I looked at the time. It was 4.40 a.m. Two hours till morning. So I gave it one more try, I put out the light and got back into bed and closed my eyes and Jenny was there looking at me and I said *Fuck this* and I got up and threw my clothes on and went down to the lobby and I said to the night man, I'm going for a walk, and he looked at me with a bored shrug as if I were crazy. I walked out into La Rochelle's darkened streets and walked around the Old Port, looking at the shops and the restaurants and their menus wherever I could make them out for what must have been a couple of hours, until eventually I went back and showered and shaved and went down for breakfast. Hervé joined me almost at once, and asked me if I had slept well and I said, so-so, with a wobble of my hand. He asked me what I wanted to do now, as he was going to drive back to Brest rechecking the oiling sites on the way and I was welcome to accompany him; but as I had had enough of crude oil to last me a lifetime I said could I go back directly to Paris from here? And he said, sure, you can take the TGV direct.

So Hervé Kermarrec drove me to the station and I said goodbye to him, this man who I now realised, had more depths to him than I had imagined at our first meeting, and we shook hands, and the brief light lit up the melancholy jowls for a final time and he squeezed into his camionette and was gone, and I was left alone with my thoughts again. Which was something I really did not want, as I knew the image I did not wish to see was just on the edge of my consciousness.

When I had got my ticket, therefore, I went to the station bookstall and scanned the magazines for something in English and I spotted *The World in 2000*, the review of the coming year by The Economist and I bought it since I thought, that will keep at bay the image of Jenny in the oil, with that look on her face. And I began to read determinedly, and as we sped northwards over the wintry countryside at 300 kilometres an hour I tried to keep it at bay but I failed, because as we got closer to Paris I suddenly realised what Jenny's expression in the oil-dream was: it was the look on her face when I left her.

I sat up straight in my seat.

I saw her lying on the pavement where I had hurled her, with her face a mask of shock and hurt and stunned disbelief. It was my last sight of her. I had suppressed it entirely. But now it was as vivid in my mind as a neon sign and the feeling – the distress – was overwhelming … and everything in my mind seemed to come loose and be whirled around, whirling, whirling, I felt I was being torn up from my roots until a voice in my head barked No!

Come on, Miles, it commanded.

The book is nearly there. You're going back to finish it. Don't go all soppy this late in the day.

It was the man I had always been.

Don't lose your sense of purpose, the man shouted.

Get a grip for Christ's sake!

It was to be expected: the longstanding Miles Bonnici identity, with its primal project of father-outstripping, was deeply entrenched; and so as we sped onward I managed to calm myself, and think it through, and put my unexpected emotions back in some sort of box. But it was too late.

Goes to France. Oil spill. Finds his guillmot. Feels pity for 1st time

12

Something changed in me for ever, on the Île de Ré. I didn't understand it then, but I think I do now: when I stumbled upon Arty Booboo, twisted and deformed in his final agony, a crack was made deep down inside me, a crack in the the hardened carapace surrounding my soul, that allowed something in, something wholly new to me – pity, I suppose – which then paved the way for what followed. For the crack could not be repaired or sealed. I suppose I would have tried, I would have attempted to keep things the way they were, I would have returned to Aberdeen and maybe succeeded for a while, but in the end I could not have gone back to who I was, after what happened on the beach at La Phare des Baleines. Something would have triggered a crisis of identity. And the fact that this crisis was precipitated by the events which now immediately followed, is the most remarkable circumstance of my life, after the encounter with Arty Booboo itself.

When I left Aberdeen for France, I had left my mobile charger behind; when I got to Brest the battery had half run down, so I switched the phone off, stuck it in my bag and forgot about it. But as the train reached the outskirts of Paris my mind returned to Aberdeen and I realised it wouldn't look great if I'd been out of contact the whole time. So I fished the mobile out, switched it on and put it in my pocket, reckoning I would go to a café somewhere and try to call Ramsay. And at the Gare Montparnasse I got down and began to walk along the platform with the crowd of scurrying passengers when the phone began to ring.

'Miles?' said a female voice.

'Yeah?'

'It's Lotte. Can you hear me?'

'*Lotte?*'

'Yes it's Lotte. I've been trying to get you for two days. Can you hear me?'

'Yes I can.'

She said rapidly in a voice that seemed devoid of emotion: 'Listen to me, Miles. Mum is very ill. There's no point beating about the bush. She's got cancer. It was very advanced when they discovered it and she hasn't got long to live. You need to come home, right away.'

'I'm in France.'

'I know you are. Your office told me. But you need to come home. Now.'

'You mean, back to Wimbledon?'

'No, we're in hospital. It's the Royal Marsden in South Kensington. You've got to come, Miles.'

There was something in Lotte's forcefulness which brooked no rebuttal. I said: 'Oh. Right. OK. I'll come.'

'When will you come? Where are you now?'

'I'm in Paris. I've only just got here. But I could get a flight to Heathrow…'

'When would you get here?'

'Early evening, hopefully. Listen, Lotte...'

'Just get here, quick as you can.' And she rang off.

I stood on the now empty platform, stunned into immobility.

My mother.

Jesus.

I'd forgotten about my mother.

Like I had forgotten about Jenny.

She didn't have long to live, Lotte had said. That meant she was dying. My mother was dying.

I'd put her letters in the bin. I'd turned my back on her.

Like I had turned my back on Jenny.

But I didn't want her to *die*.

It wasn't my fault, though, if she had cancer, was it? That couldn't be laid at my door. There was no way Lotte was going to lay that one on me. And I was filled with a mood of defiance in which I sought to rebuff any guilt I might find myself feeling, by imagining it was Lotte who was wishing it upon me; and in this tangled state of mind I set off for the airport, and passed the whole journey back to London without actually visualising my mother, the real person, until I finally came to see her in her bed in the Royal Marsden Hospital where I walked in some time after nine o'clock in the evening and found Lotte sitting on a chair, in tears, outside what turned out to be my mother's room.

'Lotte,' I said.

She looked up at me: 'She's lost the power of speech,' she said. 'Just now. Just in the last hour or so.'

In such circumstances, of course, most siblings would have embraced.

I said: 'What … what has she got?'

'Cancer of the oesophagus. A tumour in her throat. She must have felt it for ages but she didn't tell me or anyone because she didn't want to make a fuss. She didn't even go to the doctor till she couldn't swallow any more. And now it's spread to her liver and her lungs.'

'Christ,' I said.

There was silence between us.

'Lotte, I should see her, yes?'

'They're changing her drip. I imagine they'll be done soon.'

I sat next to her, neither of us speaking, until two nurses came out of the room and one said: 'You can go back in for a minute, but she's very, very tired. Just for a brief minute, all right?'

My mother's appearance took me aback. She had lost so much weight as to be almost skeletal, her cheekbones and her nose seeming to stick sharply out of her face, while her skin had a weird waxy tone; her eyes were closed.

Lotte was whispering, 'Mum. Mum. Miles is here.'

She opened her eyes. She looked at Lotte – she did not switch her gaze to me – and nodded. Then she closed her eyes again.

I didn't know whether to try to speak to her, or what.

I had turned my back on her.

What was I to say?

Lotte was holding her hand. She sat with her for perhaps a minute, then she got up and said: 'I think we should leave her now.'

As we walked out, I said to Lotte: 'So, shall I come back to Wimbledon?' She nodded, but she said nothing, and she said nothing to me all the way home, either on the tube or on the walk from the station, until she put her key in the door, and then said, in the blankest of tones: 'There's some food in the fridge if you want. In the morning, could you go in and see her? I've had to let everything slide for the last week and I just have to catch up on some stuff. You can be there from half-eleven. I'll come in the afternoon.'

I said: 'Yes, of course.'

She turned and went up the stairs to bed, with not another word.

As I wandered into the house, the silent darkened house, the house I had grown up in – the house I had turned my back on – I felt strange. I felt like an intruder, as if I didn't belong here.

I drifted into the kitchen and sat down at the old pine dining table. I hadn't been great with her, my mother, had I? I mean, I had to do what I did. I had to leave Jenny, and go to Scotland, otherwise the book might never have been finished, and the book was the most important thing.

But when she had written to me, I hadn't replied.

I wondered if I might make things up with her.

Yeah, maybe that was it.

I suddenly felt hungry. I found some ham in the fridge and made myself a sandwich, which I ate mechanically, sitting at the table, wondering. Could I make things up with her? I could certainly try. She'd always been a good mother. She would always love me, I knew that. Unconditionally. So I suppose she would want it. I could say, look, I'm sorry about everything. It's just that I sort of panicked about getting my book done. I'm really sorry. I really am.

Yes. That's what I would do. I would go in and say sorry.

And I went to bed.

In the morning, I sat down and wrote a detailed email to Ramsay Wishart about the *Erika* spill, telling him of its extraordinary extent, and the fact that British seabirds had indeed been caught up in it, and apologising for being late but explaining the situation with my mother. Half an hour later he sent me a very decent reply, thanking me for the report and telling me to take all the time off that I needed. And then I went in to the Marsden.

When I got to her room, she was sitting up against a pillow, and her breathing was laboured.

I sat on the chair by her bed, and said: 'Hello Mum. It's Miles.' I was ready to take her hand, and I suppose I half-expected her to stretch out her hand to me, and perhaps smile faintly, but she didn't. Instead, my presence seemed to make her anxious. She began looking at me, then looking away, and looking at me again.

I said: 'What is it, Mum? Is there anything I can do? Anything I can get you?'

She pointed with her finger to her chest, and shook her head. She tapped her chest. She tapped it again.

I said: 'D'you have pain in your chest?'

She shook her head once more. Then she made a writing sign with her fingers.

I said: 'You want something to write with?'

She nodded. Her breathing seemed to be getting harsher. I went and asked a nurse for a piece of paper and a pen and brought them back and gave them to her; she wrote down a word.

I looked: it was *Me*. Then she pointed to her chest again, tapping her sternum and shaking her head.

'What, Mum?' I said. 'What's you?'

She took the pen again and this time she wrote three words: they were *All My Fault*

'What?' I said, completely mystified. 'What on earth is your fault, Mum? I don't understand.'

She took the pen again and slowly wrote three more words which mystified me even further.

I read: *I told Jenny.*

'What d'you mean?' I said. 'What did you tell Jenny?'

My mother seemed to be breathing in deeply, as if gathering her strength. At length she took up the pen and with a great and laborious endeavour she completed the sentence, and sank back on the pillow from the effort, and as she did so, the paper slipped from her hand down across the bed and on to the floor.

It drifted under the bedside table. I got down on my knees to reach for it. I grabbed it, stood back up, and looked at it. It was upside down. I turned it around and saw the words

I told Jenny you were good

Time stood still.

I looked directly into her agony and realised that it was not cancer that was the cause of it, but I myself.

And in a single moment, I saw everything.

I saw that there was Worth.

I saw clearly what it was. That it was eternal.

I saw that my mother had it. I saw that Lotte had it. I saw that Jenny had it. And in that seeing, in that instant, I loved them, all three of them, for all time.

Yet even more vividly I saw that I had not chosen it – that I had chosen the opposite.

I saw that I was a monster.

All of this, all of it, in one instant.

My head swam. I staggered back against the wall. And the horror of who I was overwhelmed me, but I could not … I could not … for my mother was there in bed in front of me, breathing heavily, and I understood instantly that if there was anything left to me, it was to focus on her and not on myself, and I bent over and said: 'Mum. Mum. Listen. I'll make it right. I will. I swear to you, Mum. I will make it right with Jenny. I will find her and make it right. I promise.'

She stared at me wild-eyed, as if it had exhausted her, the effort of writing, or even more, the effort of saying what she had said. It was as if it had done something to her, damaged her even further in some awful way – I mean, admitting her despair of me. And I suddenly knew that that was the worst, and I did not want her to despair. It wasn't for me that I wanted it. I wanted it for her. Not to die, without hope.

I put my lips to her ear and whispered urgently, 'Listen, Mum. I'll make it right. I will do. Whatever it takes, however long it takes, if it takes me all my life, I will do it. I will make it right with Jenny. I promise you.'

She seemed to nod.

Did she nod?

I wasn't sure.

She seemed to be staring straight ahead.

Then she closed her eyes.

I said: 'Mum. Mum. Can you hear me? Mum?'

But at that moment a nurse came in and said, 'We have things to do now, Mr Bonnici, I'm afraid you're going to have to pop out for a wee while,' and I said 'But I'm talking to her, I have to talk to her,' and the nurse insisted, hanging over me in anticipation so I turned to leave and as I got to the door I called out: 'Mum! I will make it right! I promise!'

And then I ran. I managed to walk along the landing from the ward to the stairs, but on the stairwell my steps picked up speed and when I got outside into the Fulham Road I began to run properly, I ran down the pavement and into the roadway to dodge the Christmas shoppers who stared at me in astonishment and then I turned off into an empty side street and began to run at full pelt, running and running through the streets of South Kensington with my arms pumping, running as fast as I could and as far as I could to get away from it, to get away from who I was. I could not stand it. I would have just run and run, I think, until I lost consciousness, had not a shoelace worked loose and caused me to trip and to tumble head over heels, and I lay sprawled on the pavement panting, with the skin ripped off my palms where I had broken my fall, and my life an abomination.

13

What happened at my mother's hospital bedside is something I think about to this day, because in some ways it is still a mystery to me. It defeats me as a scientist, and with my intellect, I don't understand it; but I do with my emotions. It was a sudden revelation, that there was worth, which is the best word I've been able to come up with: that my mother had worth, that Lotte had worth, and that Jenny had worth, but more than that, there was a greater Worth, with a capital W if you like, which their individual worths were all part of.

But what was it? I don't know. I suppose some might say it was God. My answer to that is No it wasn't, because I don't believe God exists. So what, then? I've no idea. But since this account is written just for myself, I am not labouring under the necessity of providing a convincing explanation of it, so I will simply leave it there. I only know that I saw it and it changed me; it changed my old life, for one that was new, which began when I opened my eyes, for after I fell, I lay on the pavement with them closed for long seconds: I did not want to open them on a world where I knew the truth about myself. Then a nervous voice said: 'Are you all right, young man?'

I opened my eyes. I saw black court shoes with gold buckles. I looked up. It was a woman in late middle age in a camel coat, with a pearl necklace and a Harrods bag of Christmas shopping. I said: 'Not really, no.'

Concern crossed her face. 'Shall I call an ambulance?' she said. 'You took the most frightful tumble.'

'It's OK,' I said, and I got to my knees. 'It's all right, really.' I stood up. I was unsteady. She said: 'You should come and sit down. On the wall here. Do, do sit down.' And I let her guide me to the nearby low wall of a front garden. I looked at my hands: they were bleeding and trembling. As was all of me.

'Are you sure I can't call somebody for you?' said the woman, but I thanked her, and said I'd be fine, and at my insistence she rather hesitantly left me, looking back over her shoulder a couple of times; and I was alone with who I was.

I felt as if my whole being was ill. It was under a weight, a great weight, forcing me down.

I had destroyed Jenny Pittaway.

She who had given me only love, and who in giving me love had told me plainly she could not survive if she was broken again.

I had broken her again.

I had destroyed her life, and in doing so I had destroyed my mother's life. I had destroyed my mother's optimism, the greatest of all her qualities.

It was like white noise in my ears, it was not bearable, and what I thought about, was oblivion.

How I could find it.

What came into my mind was a train. I could stand on the line, and wait for the train. An express train would be good. Wait for the rush of it, straight into me. That would be oblivion. That would be good.

Or, I could stand on a station platform, and fall in front of it, just as it arrived. That would end it. That would end me. The me that was not bearable.

I wondered where the nearest train was. And a voice in my head said: *But you have to go back.*

And I thought, maybe the tube. Where was the nearest tube station? South Kensington. I could go there. And the voice, it was not the voice of the man I had been, it was a new voice, it said, *no, you have to go back to them.*

I could go to South Ken right now. Train every few minutes. Soon be over. And the voice said, *You cannot turn your back on what you have seen. Your fate is not to die. Your fate is harder. Your fate is to live with it.*

And I said out loud, 'Yes, I know.'

'Where have you been?' Lotte cried, 'Where have you *been?*' She was outside the room again, once more in tears. Nurses were coming and going through the door, hurrying.

'They threw me out,' I said, 'so they could do stuff. What's happening?'

'She's had a stroke,' said Lotte.

'A *stroke?*'

'Can you believe it? On top of cancer, she gets a stroke? Thank you, God.'

I wondered if it had happened just as I was leaving; if in any way the stress of the writing episode might have triggered it. I wondered if she had heard what I had said, if she had taken any of it in.

'We need to see the doctor,' Lotte was saying. 'The consultant. We need to talk to him. Will you go and find him?'

'Of course,' I said.

He was a burly middle-aged oncologist with a broad Geordie accent, a kind man, direct with us, but in the gentlest way. He took us into a side room and said: 'Yes, we think that unfortunately your poor mother's had a stroke. We think she's probably had a brain metastasis, the tumour has now spread to her brain, and there's been a bleed into it, a haemorrhage, but we are going to do a CT scan to confirm it.'

'What does that mean?' Lotte said.

'Well, what it really means is that she could die now at any time. She could die today. Although she could linger on for a few days more. But we're in the end zone now, that's what you have to face.'

Lotte bit her finger.

'With the tumour, the tumour in her throat, could you not operate on that?' I asked him.

'Things are too far gone for that.'

'In what way?'

'An operation will not cure your mother. We can only offer her palliative care, and try and make her as comfortable as possible.'

'Is she conscious?'

'Not at the moment.'

'Will she be?'

'She may not be. Actually, that may not be a bad thing.'

'Why is that?'

'The final stages of oesophageal cancer are not good.'

'Is she in pain?' said Lotte.

'I don't believe so, no. But we will monitor her very closely. We're going to put a stent in her airway to ease her breathing. But look, there's another issue we have to address now. We can't avoid it. It's about resuscitating your mother. In fact, about not resuscitating her.'

'What d'you mean?'

'Let's be brutally clear about the situation. Your mum has an advanced oesophageal tumour that was compressing her airway and it's now paralysed her laryngeal nerve so she can't speak, and she has liver and lung metastases and now a further metastasis in her brain into which she has had a bleed ...'

'And ...?'

'There is no possibility of being able to cure her. And if any other acute event occurs, like she has another stroke, or she stops breathing or her heart stops, we're not going to try and resuscitate her. It would just prolong her suffering.'

Lotte looked at him.

'But we need you to agree to that. We need you to sign a form.'

'To sign a form … to let her die?'

'Yes.'

Lotte began to cry. 'I don't want to do it.'

The consultant looked at me.

I said: 'I think I'll be guided by my sister.'

He said: 'This is very hard, isn't it? Very hard. But you know, all we can do now is minimise her suffering. I think it's very unlikely she will regain consciousness. Think about what you want for her. Think hard about that. Do you really want to keep it all going when her quality of life will be non-existent?'

Lotte was still crying. She said: 'I suppose not, no.'

The doctor looked at me again. I nodded.

So we signed it, the pair of us, the Do Not Resuscitate order, the grim paper which felt like a warrant for her execution; and while we were waiting for it to arrive, the distance between Lotte and me hung heavy in the air, her distress so intense yet twisted into something more bitter still by her hatred of me; while for myself, even worse than the self-loathing which had become my whole existence, was the inability to do for my sister what I now wanted to do more than anything in the world, which was to comfort her.

That afternoon, we began our death watch over our mother, and it was a non-speaking vigil; although Lotte was on one side of the bed and I was on the other, there might have been an ocean between us. And in those long hours of silence when I burned with guilt and shame, I also began to think about everything: I saw with clear eyes, for the first time, these three women whose own lives I had so harmed. My mother first of all: I gazed on her skeletal, stricken face which had repulsed me the day before and now I loved it with all my heart, and I realised fully what a wonderful mother she had been, and how complete and unconditional had been her own love for me and her belief in me, and how I had managed to extinguish even that. I could well understand why Lotte despised me – I despised myself for it even more. Lotte who was honest and honourable and brave. I looked at her across the bed. Lotte who was everything I was not.

And most of all, I thought of Jenny.

For the first time I took on board, objectively and with no reference to my own need, how exceptional she was, Jenny Pittaway; in those hours, I saw with a sort of astonishment what she had given me and how unstinting had been her giving, Jenny who had said in the dark of our embrace on Ithaca that she would love me all her life, Jenny the madcap drinker and teaser, Jenny the island-collector, Jenny who danced through the bluebells, Jenny the bird-hide seductress, Jenny the latter-day Penelope, Jenny who saw instantly the worth of my mother and of Lotte, in a way I never did, and maybe even saw worth in me, misguided though she was – and my heart opened to her properly, I loved her fully, and I knew that I would never love anyone else in the same way, and my fate was bound up in her.

And in realising that, I saw the impossibility of mending things. I thought, simply and without self-pity, if there is a Hell, this is what it is like. There is no redemption to be had. I had vowed to my mother that I would find her and 'put it right', but I saw that 'putting it right' would very probably never be possible. Maybe my mother knew that. Maybe it was the cause of her despair. Certainly, Lotte knew it. Oh yes. And as the wordless afternoon wore on and we watched our mother in vain for any flicker of returning consciousness, I began to feel that I had to try to tell my sister what had happened with me, even if she were incredulous at my presumption and scorned the whole notion.

And she did.

In the evening we went back together, again in total silence; and on opening the door of the Wimbledon house Lotte simply headed for the stairs without a word, but when she was half-way up I said: 'Lotte.'

She turned: 'What?'

I was very nervous. I had no idea what to say. I blurted out: 'I know what I've done.'

'*What?*'

'I know what I've done.'

She looked at me in astonishment.

I found it hard to speak but I said: 'I know what I've done to Jenny. I know what I've done to Mum. And to you. I told Mum I would put it right. This morning, before she had the stroke. I told her I would find Jenny and put it right. Wherever she is. I told her today. I promised her.'

Lotte's eyes widened. She cried: 'You bastard. You absolute piece of scum. Saying that is meant to absolve you in some way, is it?'

'No no.'

'You total piece of shit.'

I was taken aback.

'I didn't think you could sink any lower. But you have, you absolute, unbelievable shit.'

I said: 'I just thought—'

'You thought what? That that makes everything fine? Miles knows what he's done? He fucking knows what he's fucking done? Three fucking cheers, eh?'

I shook my head. 'No, no—'

'I've only got one thing to say to you: fuck off. Right? Fuck off now and fuck off for ever. You broke Jenny's heart, you unbelievable, cruel bastard, and you broke Mum's heart, God knows she had a hard enough life with Dad, and now her end is terrible but you've managed to make it worse than anyone could ever have imagined, she's had six months of unhappiness and stress every single day, every single sodding day because of you and the only thing that's ending it is cancer of the fucking throat, and as for Jenny, have you got any idea what it was like for her? Have you? With your dumping her just like that, she was in bits, and then what she felt driven to, the abortion, have you got any idea in your miserable mean-minded screwed-up little soul what that did to her? Well have you? The woman who loved you? You couldn't fucking care less, you don't give a shit about anything but yourself and I hate the very sight of you, Miles, I hate having to look at you, I hate you being in this house, I hate the very floor you walk on and the air that you breathe and most of all I hate you being around Mum and the sooner that she dies, yes, the sooner that she dies and I don't have to have a single thing to do with you ever again and you can just fuck off, fuck right off out of my life, the better it will be, you total, filthy, fucking bastard.'

And she turned and ran up the stairs, slamming her bedroom door. I could hear her weeping.

I went into the kitchen and sat down. I was trembling. I felt like I had been hit by a truck. But in spite of it all, my intelligence was still functioning, and I knew two facts: that everything Lotte had said was right and just, and that what I had to do, was simply see things through as best I could.

Had my mother died soon after her stroke, that day or the next, I think Lotte would have severed all contact with me very quickly; but unusually, she lingered on, Muriel Bonnici, suspended unconscious between life and death, for more than a week, and in that never-ending time, or so it seemed, my sister and I were thrown together into a sort of intimate if unwilling partnership. In the morning after her tirade at me, which was Christmas Eve, I caught her coming down the stairs and I said, 'Lotte look, I know you don't want to have anything to do with me and I understand that, but I am going in to see Mum just like you are and it's the holiday season and it might be difficult to get transport with the tubes and stuff, so why don't I just organise it? Makes sense. You don't have to talk to me.' She looked at me in anger and defiance but then her face sagged with the weariness of it all and she said: 'All right.' So that day we went in and came back in a taxi, and on Christmas Day too, and then on Boxing Day and the days which followed, expecting her to die on every visit but instead spending hour after hour sitting on either side of her bed, watching her for any sign of reviving consciousness or discomfort; and imperceptibly, I began to look after my sister, bringing her glasses of water and the occasional coffee, and taking over the lead role in the caring, liaising with the consultant and the staff while Lotte herself was focused on our mother entirely, holding her hand without a pause until the tendons in her own wrist became strained.

When we got home in the evenings I cooked for us both, pizzas and ready meals which we consumed in silence, in a strange reversal of the companionship of eating together; but it was together, that we ate. And we breakfasted together, and we travelled to the hospital together, we made our daily pilgrimage together to the deathbed, silent always, yet I know that for all the unspeakable damage I had done, Lotte started to sense that something in me had shifted and began to accept, in spite of herself, that in the infinitely sad journey with our mother towards her end, I was part of it just as she was.

It was a time when I thought even more deeply about my life and the form it had taken, and this was when I began to understand, as I never had before, how twisted it had been by my father – how the hatred which Andrew Bonnici had sparked in me had yanked everything out of shape. And I thought about the marriage he had made with my mother, and how if I had been unlucky in one parent, I had been so lucky in the other without ever appreciating it, and how the price I would pay for what I had done was to lose her now when at last I loved her – a loss which came closer, slowly but surely, as she steadily shrank back towards the skeleton inside her until on the evening on December 30 her breathing became harsh and strident once more, in spite of the stent in her airway. We decided we wouldn't go home; we thought she might die in the night. The nursing staff found us a room to sleep in, although sleep barely came; in the morning we resumed our bedside watch as she fought for breath with the tumour invading her windpipe and pneumonia now attacking her lungs, and it went on all day, the desperate sound, *heergh-heergh*, it was the most distressing thing you can imagine with Lotte clinging fiercely to her hand as if she might hold Muriel Bonnici in this world by main force until finally, late in the evening the gasping slowed; and then it stopped.

We bent over her.

'Mum!' said Lotte. 'Mum! Mum!'

I called the nurses. They ran in.

'Mum!' Lotte was whispering.

One of the nurses felt for her pulse. Then she said, in the gentlest voice: 'She's gone.'

Lotte dissolved into tears, it was as if her whole being was made of tears.

I could not comfort her. How could I comfort her?

Yet after a minute or two I went over to her and said: 'I think we have to go home now.' She looked up at me and she nodded, and I helped her to her feet, and brought her out of the room with my arm partly around her – the first time I had touched her since I returned. She paused at the door – we both did – and we bade our mother farewell.

I wished … I wished and wished … but it was too late for wishing.

It was nearly midnight when we got back to Wimbledon: we had a long wait for the taxi as it was New Year's Eve, and more than that, it was the eve of the Millennium, it was 31 December 1999, and we passed the blurred faces of revellers on the streets. Lotte kept her usual silence on the way, but it seemed a different silence now, one of grief and exhaustion rather than hatred, and as we went in through the door I said: 'Will you let me make you a cup of tea?' and she nodded.

She appeared profoundly shocked. She sat at the kitchen table and seemed to shiver. When I had given her the tea, I sat to drink my own on the far side of the kitchen to her, obliquely, so she didn't have to look at me. But after a few minutes I glanced across and I saw that although she was making no sound, the tears were running down her cheeks, catching the kitchen light; and our eyes met.

She said: 'Why did it have to be two?'

'I'm sorry?'

'She was so good. She was so wonderful. And as if she didn't have enough to put up with Dad, she had you as well. Why not just one bastard in her family, why did she have to have two?'

I said: 'Well ... if you want me to tell you, Lotte, I can tell you.'

'Why then, you bastard? Why?'

'Because I was obsessed with Dad. All my life.'

'What does that mean?'

'I've been obsessed with *beating* him. That's what the books were about, and my career, everything. I've had no other real feeling in my life.'

'I don't follow.'

'You fought him, Lotte, you were stronger than me. I just wanted him to like me, so I was clever, to win his approval, and when he wouldn't like me even then, the only thing I had, to prove to myself I was worth something, was to be *better* than him. I've been obsessed with that. Since, since I was about fourteen. I've had no other real feeling in my life.'

'It's no excuse, Miles! It's no fucking excuse!'

'I didn't say it was. I'm just telling you, the way things were. Why I've been like I've been, a, a useless son. A useless lover. A useless brother, if you like. And the only thing I've got left, Lotte, which is of any worth at all, is the truth, it's to admit the truth and say, this is how I was – this is what I did, to the people who loved me.'

'It's no excuse.'

'Of course it's not an excuse. There can never be an excuse. It's only *me* that's *to blame*. I'm just saying, I was like that, because of Dad. You asked me, and I'm telling you.'

Lotte looked into space, shaking her head. She said: 'He was so hard on her. He was such a nasty cruel sod.'

I said: 'He was more than that. He was weird. There was something weird about his self-regard. It didn't allow anybody else to be considered, even those who were closest to him. He was twisted. And that's what has twisted me.'

Lotte looked at me. She started to say something and stopped. She breathed out. She said: 'Do you want to drink something stronger?'

'You want some wine?'

She nodded.

I opened a bottle of red from the kitchen rack and poured us two glasses. Lotte sat staring into hers. At length she looked up at me and said: 'You know, Miles, Mum might have had a difficult marriage but she coped with it, she handled it. But it was the last six months were the unhappiest. Of her whole life. What you did to Jenny, and what that did to her. And the way you turned your back on her. You caused her such unbelievable fucking misery. And all she'd ever given you, was love.'

I nodded.

'And as for Jenny herself, you just, you just finished her. You totally fucking destroyed her life. And when you wouldn't come down to see her, when she was in such terrible distress after what she went and did, she regretted it terribly as soon as she did it, when you just ignored her ... She was truly in bits about it all. I don't think I can ever forgive you for that.'

I nodded again. It hung in the air. I said: 'Do you know how she is?'

She looked at me and I suppose she was weighing up whether or not to tell me. At length she said: 'She's OK, considering.'

'She in New Zealand?'

She nodded. 'I had a Christmas note from her. She's trying to rebuild. But I would say ... I would say she is permanently damaged.'

'What if ...'

'What if what?'

'What if I wrote to her?'

Lotte gave a harsh laugh. 'What, to say you're *sorry*? Eh? *Sorry about that, destroying your life*? So now you're going to add being patronising to everything else, are you?'

I nodded for a third time. And from outside came a rippling series of explosions, and flashes in the dark sky showed through the blinds.

'What's that?' said Lotte. I think she had lost all sense of time.

'It must be the fireworks,' I said. I glanced at my watch: it was midnight. 'For the New Year. For the new Millennium.'

'A new age,' said Lotte. 'Without Mum. Well, they can keep it.'

Over the next few days I did most of the organising of the funeral, partly because my sister seemed to be laid low by the trauma of our mother's end and spent much of the day in bed. I still felt like I had flu, I felt a sense of worthlessness and self-hatred which made me physically sick. But I knew I had to get on with it, and two days before the funeral I said to Lotte we ought to talk through the arrangements and she reluctantly got up and we sat at the kitchen table and I went over everything with her, the service, the burial, the hotel reception, and she said it all seemed OK although to be honest she didn't give a flying fuck about any of it. The life seemed to have been drained out of her, leaving only a sort of dull residual bitterness. She said: 'All very efficient, Miles. No doubt you'd make the railways run on time. You'd have done well with the Nazis.'

I said I had settled everything so she didn't need to worry about bills, I had been through what household utility bills I could find and taken care of them, although at some stage we would probably need to talk about what was going to happen with the house.

Lotte said: 'Whatever you want.'

The funeral was scheduled for Thursday and I said I would stay on for a couple of days to sort out the loose ends and I was planning to go back to Aberdeen on the Sunday, unless she wanted me to stay longer, in which case I would.

She said: 'You're going back to Scotland?'

I nodded.

'What you gonna do up there? Find redemption?'

I said: 'There is no redemption for me, Lotte.' I suddenly felt tired. I said: 'I'm going for a walk now,' and I went out.

She was looking at me curiously as I left.

When I got back, something in her attitude had shifted. She was detached and quiet but the bitterness seemed to have gone. She said: 'Listen, Miles. Thanks for organising everything. I appreciate it.' And that evening when we ate a curry together she began to talk of some of the relatives who would be coming, and she said did I realise that Aunt Harriet and Aunt Marjorie hated each other and should be kept apart if possible and Uncle Dan from Dorking would get completely paralytic on sherry if we let him. The next day she took up the arrangements and went through them and made a couple of changes; and on the day of the funeral she had become the hostess, reserved and grave but competent and in charge.

At the graveside we stood together and we each threw a handful of soil on the coffin lid and Lotte dissolved into tears once more but this time she turned to me and buried her head in my shoulder and – if hesitantly – I put my arms around her. When we finally got home in the early evening she said she felt exhausted by it all and just wanted to sleep it off and did I mind if she went to bed right away and I said sure; but the next morning she said: 'We could go for a pizza tonight if you want.'

I said sure, once again.

We shared a bottle of Chianti. We chatted in a perfunctory way and then, sitting back in her chair, Lotte said: 'Tell me again about you and Dad. I didn't really get it. You said you ... wanted to be *better* than him? To *beat* him, you said?'

I told her. I told her the whole thing, from smashing my fist into the window of the garden shed to whispering *Fuck you* in his ear when he lay dying, I told her how obsessed I was with it and how it took pride of place over everything else, which was why I had done everything I had done.

Lotte sat thinking about it.

She said: 'So what's happened, Miles? With you. What's changed?'

I said: 'You really want to know?'

'I do, yes.'

I said: 'It started with a bird. A dead bird on a beach.' And I told her the improbable story of being sent to France to report on the oil spill and finding Arty Booboo on the Île de Ré, and how because of that something had changed inside me and I had started to feel for Jenny, and how at our mother's hospital bedside everything had come together and how I had suddenly seen who I was.

Lotte listened, all the way through.

I said: 'I saw what I had done. All of it, sort of, in a flash. Like, a revelation. I never dreamed it would happen. It just did. I saw who I was.'

Lotte thought about it. She took it all in. Then she said: 'So what now?'

I said: 'Well, there are only some things I can do, aren't there? I can't make it up with Mum. I can't make it up with Jenny, though I would if I could, I would do that more than anything in the world. But I can see that I can't. And that's the price I'm going to pay, Lotte, for what I did.'

She nodded. 'So what can you do?'

'Try and live a different life.'

'What sort of life?'

'One where I don't hurt people.'

Lotte looked at me.

She said: 'In Scotland?'

'Well, yeah, for the moment, anyway. I'm on a year's contract up there and it's got another six months to run, and if I just gave it up I would be letting down a very nice guy who helped me get it.'

'And you'll finish your new book, in that time, I suppose?'

'No.'

'No?'

'That I am giving up. I've done with the fucking thing. It's what caused all the trouble. I destroyed Jenny for it, Lotte. I hate it now.'

Lotte nodded. She sipped her wine. She looked at me. She said: 'It's a funny world, isn't it, Miles?'

'Is it?'

'You know what I thought, the instant I set eyes on you at the Marsden? Well, I suppose you do know, 'cos I told you. I thought, Mum'll die and there'll be the funeral and that's it, and from that moment, from the fucking moment the fucking soil hits the fucking coffin lid I'll never have to see the evil bastard fucker again, or say a single fucking word to him, ever again.'

'Yes. Sure.'

'But like I said, it's a strange world. Doesn't run in grooves, it doesn't run straight, the way you think it will.'

'In what way?'

'Well, here we are.'

'How d'you mean?'

'We're talking.'

'And … what?'

'Maybe we should continue to talk.'

'You mean – you would want to see me again?'

'I think so.' She drank her wine. 'What do you think?'

'I can't believe that … you would ever not hate me.'

She said: 'I've got a feeling, Miles, that there's a part of you, that hates you, even more than I might.'

'That is true, Lotte. That is the truth.'

'So there don't need to be two haters of you, do there? Be a sort of waste of energy, that, wouldn't it?'

'So you mean …' – it started to dawn on me, I had never for a second considered the idea – 'we might be brother and sister? I mean, like, properly? We might be friends?'

'Yeah, well maybe we might.'

'I would like that very much, Lotte.'

'But it's not simple, Miles. There's something you've got to do first.'

'What's that?'

'You've got to join the human race.'

My face fell. But she saw it and she said: 'Don't worry. I think you might get in. I'll sign your application form.'

And for the first time since I had returned home, she smiled.

The next morning she told me she had had an offer to take her act on a world cruise, so she would be away for at least eight weeks. 'Singing to rich wrinklies,' she said. 'They're just gonna sit there, straight-faced. My stuff'll all go over their heads. But sod it, I think I could do with the sun. It's come at the right time.'

In the afternoon we went for a walk on Wimbledon Common, and we paused at the spot where our mother had painted the winter sunset so well. She filled our minds.

Lotte said: 'Miles, are you … are you going to cope with things?'

'I think so, yeah. Thanks for asking. What about you?'

'Yeah, I'll be OK.'

When we turned to start walking back she said: 'You know, I thought a lot about you, last night, and this morning.'

'What about?'

'About the fact that, I've never really known who you were. All that stuff about being obsessed with Dad, being obsessed with beating him – I just didn't know that.'

'Well it's true.'

'I'm sure it is. But it's the … the obsessed thing, I didn't realise. Lasted a very long time, didn't it?'

'Years and years.'

'And you said yourself, to the exclusion of everything else?'

'I suppose it did.'

'Would you say you were an obsessive type of person?'

'Maybe I am.'

'See, something that occurred to me is, if you've had one huge long obsession in the past, maybe you're just going to get another one, in the future.'

'Such as what?'

'About Jenny, say.'

'Wouldn't that be entirely natural? Considering everything?'

'Yes, of course, Miles. Yes. But also, no.'

'How no?'

'You know what I said about joining the human race?'

'Yeah?'

'What d'you think I meant by that?'

'Well, obviously, be a nice guy, and stuff. Don't hurt people.'

'It does mean that, yes. But it means more.'

'In what way?'

Lotte said: 'Look, we're quite enjoying each other's company, aren't we? Maybe it doesn't just have to be here, maybe I could come and see you in Scotland.'

'I would love that.'

'OK. Say I do. Say I come up to Aberdeen. What would you show me?'

'What would I show you?'

'Yes.'

'Jesus. I dunno. I s'pose my flat's quite nice. I mean, it's all right. And there's a beach where I run, that's quite nice.'

'But what would you show me about the city itself? Or the countryside around it? What are the sights? That I might be interested in?'

I stopped. I turned and looked at her. I said: 'I haven't got a fucking clue.'

She laughed. She said: 'See Miles, I think that one of the things that goes with somebody being obsessive, is that they tend to be not really interested in things, or in people, outside themselves.'

'Maybe that's true. You think it's true of me?'

'Well isn't the reason that everything went the way it did, that you were more interested in yourself, and in trying to surpass Dad, than in Jenny? Or in Mum. Or in me, for that matter?'

'Yes, Lotte. It is.'

'So I would hazard a guess, that if you're not interested in Aberdeen, you're probably not interested in your work colleagues, either.'

I smiled a weak smile. 'You got me there.'

'And I imagine you don't have many friends.'

'Not a one.'

'See, you had this experience you told me about, starting with your bird on the beach and finishing up at Mum's bedside, and I've thought a lot about that and it seems to me that it was remarkable, it really was, and what it did was open you up, at last, to Jenny, and to Mum, and I suppose, to me.'

'It did. It did.'

'But that's not enough, Miles.'

'How?'

'If it's to be truly worth something, it has to open you up to everybody.'

A light began to dawn, deep down in my soul.

'When you go back I know you'll be 'obsessed', if you like, with Jenny and everything, of course you will, you couldn't not be, but if it's just an obsession like it was with Dad, which shuts out everything and everyone else, it isn't right. It's a self-indulgence.' She stopped and turned to face me. 'That's what I mean by joining the human race.'

I said: 'But I don't feel I'm entitled to … I feel the only thing I'm allowed to do is hate myself.'

'I know you'll always punish yourself over Jenny. And over Mum. All your life. But I think you're allowed to live again. And if you're going to live, live fully. If you want to pay something back, you can't just retreat into obsession. You've got to engage with things outside yourself now, Miles.'

I nodded. I saw it.

'And with other people.'

'Yes,' I said.

'That most of all.'

Mother dies.
He realizes he's been total shit.
Sister comes round a bit.

14

When I got back to Aberdeen, late on the Sunday evening, I sat down and wrote two emails.

The first was to Callum McSorley in Aberfair. It said: 'Dear Callum, You have supported me so much that I owe it you to tell you this and offer some sort of attempt at an explanation. I am giving up the book. I mean, I am abandoning it completely and will not be finishing it. I am telling OUP. The reason is, my obsessive desire to do it has led me down a pretty dark path morally. You may remember when I came to see you I told you my girlfriend Jenny Pittway was being obstructive about it and I had to get away from her. Well, that was a lie – she couldn't have been more helpful, and in leaving her I hurt her very badly, so coming to Scotland was on a false and dishonest basis from the outset. Now I just want to try and rebuild my life in an honest way. Thank you very much for helping me to get here – I will finish the research project to the very best of my ability, and not let you down. And thanks for everything, Callum. You've been brilliant. I hope we can still be friends.'

The second was to my editor at OUP, whose name was Barnaby Atherton. He had been helpful and enthusiastic and I felt a pang in writing it.

It was headed: '*Doing It for Themselves: Female Infidelity in Animals and People.*'

I wrote: 'Dear Barnaby, I am afraid I have decided for personal reasons not to continue with DIFT. My decision is irreversible. I am putting a cheque in the post to repay the advance in full. I am sorry if this is a disappointment, but there it is.'

When I had sent the emails I opened up the files for the book, and I methodically deleted every one and deleted all the backups, until none of it was recoverable. And I said out loud, when I had finished: 'Good riddance.'

The next morning Callum sent me a very supportive reply, saying of course we could still be friends, and wishing me well;

Barnaby sent me an anguished reply marked URGENT, begging me to reconsider; and I declined.

All that was the easy bit. It was the essential bit, that's why it was easy. Everything else about living, was hard.

For the purpose with which I had gone to Scotland had ceased to exist: all there was in my mental life now, was what I had done. I had been kept so busy by my mother's final days and their aftermath with Lotte that there hadn't been a lot of time actually to dwell on things, but now there was all the time in the world, and it pressed in upon me: I felt full of self-loathing and weighed down with guilt and with remorse. The worst thing was the impossibility of even making a move in Jenny's direction, since I recognised that to try to contact her in any way would, as Lotte had said, be contemptible; I could see it stretching away into the future, a wrong that couldn't be righted, that would last for ever, as if that was all that life would now ever be. It was like the air that I breathed: it presented itself to me at every turn, when I opened my eyes in the morning, and then all through the day in my work at UKOCA, where the staff were gripped – weren't they just – by the reappearance of Rupert, the appalling Rupert, last seen slammed up against a wall and about to be marmalised by Kenny Lornie in his drunken rage: was ever a person subject to so many whispers and shifty glances? They got a final taste of tittle-tattle when Ramsay Wishart called us both into his office and told us to apologise to each other and shake hands, which we did, and Ramsay quietly let it be known that I had done a good job on the oil spill in France and then suffered a major bereavement, which perhaps drew from the glances some of their sting. I don't know. At least work took my mind off things. There was no such relief when I went back to my flat in the evening where there was no more writing to be done. I found it hard to listen to music, and I even lost interest in cooking. There was only sitting and thinking, and I longed for someone to talk to, but who was there except Lotte? And Lotte was off in the Caribbean somewhere, singing her saucy songs to wealthy pensioners. I missed her keenly. It was the first time I had ever missed anyone.

It was the first time I had ever been lonely.

Yet I did not seek refuge in drink, as I had when Jenny dumped me in Oxford; I avoided alcohol completely. I was not wholly lost. There was something positive at the bottom of me, made up of what I had seen at my mother's bedside, and also, of Lotte's saying to me explicitly that I was allowed to live again – that was worth everything, it was almost the sanction for me

to exist. I knew who I was now and I would not lose sight of it.
I coped with the dark feelings, they were what I merited, and
in spite of them I began to try to build something, and I will
always love Aberdeen, severest of cities, because it was there, in
that late winter and early spring of the Millennium year, that I
opened my eyes to the world.

I started by looking at the townscape for the first time – thinking
of what I would show Lotte if she ever came on a visit – and initially
I saw what everybody sees, such as the fact that the granite was
cold and grey, but after rain the mica grains in it sparkled and
transformed the stone into something almost jewel-like. Then I
began to vary the way I walked to work and I found the expansive
Georgian elegance of Golden Square and of Bon Accord, as well
as the tight and curious intimacy of the ancient lanes and wynds,
and then I discovered (on a run) the medieval university village of
Old Aberdeen and was drawn back there again and again – it was
exquisite, it was a mini-Oxford – and the more I saw, the more I
wanted to see, and I started to notice subtler things. For example, I
realised that from Union Terrace, I could distinguish twenty-nine
separate spires and pinnacles, while in Rosemount where I lived,
I began to register quirks and oddities, like how the barber did a
roaring trade on a Sunday, or what was advertised in the butcher's
window:
> Beef skirt
> Boiling hens
> Natural skin haggis
I even started to hear the Aberdeen dialect, the Doric, and to
pick it up:
> Fit like?
> Nae bad. Foos yasel?
> Ach, chavvin' awa'.
And in my second week back, I stumbled upon a further way
forward.

One of my walks to work took me past a peculiar building
which in appearance was somewhere half-way between a church
and a small castle (later I learned it had been a school.) I noticed
that at the door was a queue – it was just before 9 a.m. – of what I
perceived as scruffily dressed men, underneath a sign proclaiming
The Magdalenians. Passing it again the next day I observed a smaller
sign which said *Helping the Homeless,* and I looked at the guys
queuing up and saw who they were, and over the next couple of

days I thought about it, and when Saturday came I went and I rang the bell myself, and a girl came to the door and I said is this a place for the homeless and she said it's a day centre, aye, and I said well I wondered if you wanted any help, like maybe on Saturday night, I could do Saturday nights and she said are ye experienced in social work or anything and I said afraid not, and she said well what can ye do and in a sudden flash of inspiration I said well I can cook and she shouted over her shoulder *Shona!* And Shona shouted *What?* And the girl shouted *Guy here wants to help* and Shona shouted *Oh yeah?* And she shouted *Guy says he can cook* and Shona came to the door and looked at me and exclaimed Invite the man in for God's sake, Theresa.

She was imposing, Shona McAfee, well-built psychologically as well as physically, about my age but sort of, battle-hardened: she was deputy head of The Magdalenians, which was a small, long-established charity for the homeless. They had four shelters across the city where men could sleep – other groups looked after women – plus this their day centre, which offered midday and evening meals. Shona looked me up and down, and said, you say ye wanna help, then?

'If I can.'

'And you are?'

'Miles. Miles Bonnici. Italian name.' I spelled it out.

'What d'ye do?'

'I just work in an office.'

'Why d'ye wanna help us?'

'Well I've got some free time, I'm free on Saturday nights, and I thought it would be something worthwhile.'

'You could do Saturday nights?'

'I could, yes.'

'And you say ye can cook?'

'I can cook a bit, yes.'

'Jesus, Mary and Joseph.'

'I'm sorry?'

'Mister, you are the answer to my *prayers.*'

'Why's that?'

'Cos Saturday nights here is mince an' tatties night, it's a tradition and the clients really like it, but Vincent, the feller who cooked it for the last two years moved over to Inverness before Christmas and ah've been doing it maself for the last month and ah really should be doing other things. You think you could do it? Mince an' tatties?'

'I don't know what that is.'

'Minced meat with mashed potatoes. It's not rocket science.'

'I think I probably could.'

'It's the Saturday supper. The guys look forward to it. We serve it with skirlie. Ye know what skirlie is?'

I shook my head.

'It's like a Scottish stuffing. Made of oatmeal and onions. I could show ye how to do it.'

'OK,' I said.

'It's usually for about forty guys.'

'OK.'

'Quite a lot of work. Lot of spuds to be peeled.'

'That's OK.'

'Well when could ye start?'

'How about tonight?'

So Shona gave me a tour of the centre, with its pool table and its TV and video recorder and its newspapers and bookshelves and board games and dartboard, and its clients who seemed to be of all ages but predominantly men, middle-aged and fairly battered by life and mostly wreathed in cigarette smoke, and then its big kitchen with its four hefty industrial fridges and its food cupboards packed with tins of baked beans and chopped tomatoes, and she told me that 80 per cent of the food was donated by local shops and what the rough quantities were for mince an' tatties for forty guys. Then she introduced me to the rest of the staff and I came back when the centre closed for an hour at 5 p.m. and made what I thought was a respectable stab at the dinner – including the skirlie – which was served from seven. The guys cleaned their plates, anyway. Shona thanked me fulsomely and was keen for me to come back the following week and I did, but this time I brought a rucksack with a few private ingredients of my own: I had a bottle of olive oil which I secretly added to the mash, and a bottle of red wine which I covertly added to the mince, and a packet of thyme which I slyly added to the skirlie, all with the intention of producing lusciousness and depth of flavour, and two of the guys came to the kitchen after dinner and said how tasty it was. The next weekend they talked among themselves about it, more of them, and told Shona, and she came into the kitchen and said to me: 'Ye've got a fan club out there.'

I smiled. 'Really?'

'They love it. Where'd ye learn to cook?'

'I just picked it up. I'm interested in it.'

She looked at me. 'Who are you?' she said.

'I'm just a guy,' I said.

'Yeah, but why are ye here?'

I said: 'Well. I've led a fairly privileged life, and I, I just thought it was time to give something back.'

She thought about it. 'Fair enough,' she said.

I said: 'I've been looking at the er, at the chaps. I mean, I haven't spoken to them. But some of them look like they've had a pretty hard time.'

'Aye they have,' said Shona. 'They all have, or they wouldnae be with us.'

'And why are they?'

'Different reasons. Alcohol and hard drugs is a lot of it.' She sat down and lit a cigarette. 'We get quite a few roughnecks.'

'What are roughnecks?'

'The guys who work on the oil rigs. They go out on the helicopter and they do two weeks on and two weeks off, it's very high wages and they come back with their pockets stuffed with cash and a lot of it goes straight down their necks. There's a big drinking culture. It can put a real strain on families and relationships. Eventually for some guys the drink takes over, they get NRB'd, and it's all downhill from there. '

'They get what?

'NRB is Not Required Back. They're fired. But by then they're already on the slippery slope, and they can end up on the street.' She blew out smoke. 'We get quite a lot of ex-servicemen too. Gordon Highlanders. That's the local regiment. Some are lost without the discipline of the army. Some have had bad experiences. And we get guys with mental problems, schizophrenia, and quite a few druggies, heroin, mainly.'

'Are they the hardest to deal with? The heroin addicts?'

'No. People with alcohol problems are worse. Guys on heroin are usually quite chilled. Alcohol brings with it an element of violence. If you invented alcohol today, it wouldnae get a licence.'

'And you deal with them, if they get violent?' I looked at Shona. I could see the strength in her.

'They don't get violent in here. We have a strict no-alcohol, no-drugs rule.'

I made a mental note to keep quiet about the red wine in the mince. I said: 'But if there ever is a problem?'

'There's always ways of dealing with it. They key thing is to show respect. Be firm, but show respect. If ye don't, it's a challenge.'

I said: 'So they sleep in your hostels?'

'Aye, we have forty beds. The city council provides more.'

'Are you ever full, and have to turn people away?'

'On occasions. But we have a great big cupboard out there fulla sleeping bags and winter clothes, and if somebody's gotta sleep on the street, we make sure they're equipped.'

'That must be hard,' I said.

Thinking about it.

For the first time in my life.

'Sure. I mean, not just cold and wet. Ye get beaten up. Ye get humiliated. Go to sleep in a shop doorway on a Saturday night and ye can be woken at 2am by four guys pissing on ye. They've just come out of a club and they're all pissing all over ye and laughing. Imagine that? The older, more experienced ones avoid the city centre complete. We had one guy slept in the cemetery, down by Duthie Park. Name of Snuffy. Dunno what his real name was. He's dead now.' She puffed on her cigarette. 'We found him there one Christmas when he didn't turn up for Christmas dinner. We asked the guys and we tracked him down, me and Vincent, the feller who did the mince an' tatties before you. He was lying on a pile of soaking wet duvets. On Christmas Day. He was badly depressed. We persuaded him to come in for a shower and his dinner, and I remember, Vincent told me, when he peeled his socks off, Snuffy's socks, all the skin on his feet came off with them. Ye wanna maybe talk to some of these guys?'

I said: 'Well, sure, if it happens naturally. I'm sort of trying to get to know myself, and I know I haven't got much of a social talent, to put people at their ease. I think at the moment that if I can just do something here that helps, and do it well, then that's worth doing, isn't it?'

'Aye Miles,' Shona said. 'Aye, it is.'

My talk with Shona McAfee was the first real human contact I had had since I came back to Scotland. It was even, perhaps, the first proper human contact of my adult life, in that I was neither despising nor seeking anything from my interlocutor, merely having an interested equable exchange. It gave me a glimpse what being normal was like, of how it would be, as Lotte had said, to join the human race. Yet it was a trick I found myself unable to repeat in the offices of the United Kingdom Offshore Conservation Agency, as my isolation from my work colleagues seemed to be more complete than ever, almost as if, beyond disliking me, now in some weird way they were scared of me, or at least very wary. I think it was because of the violence that had been suddenly made manifest in my clash with Kenny, something wholly foreign to the lives of these well-minded conservationists which had deeply disturbed them. I sensed this pretty quickly and I made sure I had something to read when I went to the canteen; and from one day to the next, in terms of the proper human relationships I now was more than ready for, there was nobody. So the weeks went by, and I worked hard on my report on the fishing industry and the damage it was doing to the life of the ocean – I began to see the point of it – and in the evening I walked back to Rosemount and cooked my dinner and tried to read or listen to music, then went to sleep to dream of Jenny, unfailingly, night after night, in a sort of riot of imaginings which in the darkness took over my mind completely, all of them strange visions without resolution, without meaning, without hope.

And then Lotte returned, and brought hope with her.

My sister had been away on her world cruise for fully three months and I had missed her keenly. She came back in early April and I flew down to London on a Friday night for the first weekend after her return, for once apologetically crying off from my Saturday stint with the mince an' tatties at the Magdalenians. She met me at Heathrow and we embraced, somewhat nervously: it had been a long gap after the start of our new relationship. But a bottle of Beaujolais relaxed us and she began to tell me about her odyssey; it had not been uniformly pleasurable.

'It's the whole cruising thing, Miles,' she said. 'Lots of well-off, basically old people, or at least middle-aged. Probably all Tory voters. And my stuff, I mean my songs, they're kind of on the subversive side, you know? I ended up doing a lot of standards, just to keep'em happy.'

I asked her what her favourite place had been and she said, San Francisco. 'I really liked the bars. Part of the city called the Castro.' She said: 'You know it?'

I shook my head. I said: 'I am very, very happy that you're back.'

She smiled a warm smile. 'Me too, brother.'

In the morning we had a solemn duty to perform: we visited our mother's grave. She had been buried with our father and the headstone referred only to him; we made plans to change it, and we tidied up the grave itself, which was scruffy and overgrown. In the afternoon we went over the house checking what maintenance was needed, and after a long talk we decided we would sell it, although not immediately: Lotte was happy to go on living there for the time being. And in the evening we went into the West End to see a movie.

It was *American Beauty*, that haunting depiction of the tensions underlying aspirational suburban life. We went to eat in Chinatown afterwards and discussed it and I said I wasn't quite sure who had mysteriously shot Lester, the central character, at the end: was it his wife? Of course not, said Lotte, it was the neighbour, the ex-Marine Corps colonel who was secretly gay. Why did he shoot him, I said, because Lester knew his secret, she said, the secret about himself the colonel couldn't face. That was the colonel's problem. He was denying who he was. She said: 'I don't think people should deny who they are. What do you think, Miles?'

I said: 'I agree. Yes. I think you've got to be honest about yourself.'

'And you're trying to be, aren't you Miles? I know you are.'

'Trying to, yes.'

'But … what about me, Miles?'

'What about you?'

'Do you think I should be honest about who I am?'

'Sure. You are, aren't you?'

'All right. What if I told you that, while I was away, I fell in love?'

'Well, I'd be thrilled for you. Absolutely thrilled.' I squeezed her hand. 'Can you … can you tell me his name?'

A pause. Then Lotte said: 'It's not a he, Miles.'

'What?'

'It's not a he.'

'Oh,' I said. 'Right.' It dawned on me. 'It's a she?'

'Yes it is.'

We looked at each other.

'I … I had no idea.'

'Why would you, Miles? What do you know of me? When did we ever speak? Before – before Mum died.'

I said: 'Did Mum know?'

'No, I never told her.'

'Why not?'

'It might have been hard for her. She was pretty old-fashioned, wasn't she? I thought she might … mind.'

'Yeah, maybe. Maybe. But, listen, Lotte … I don't mind. That's not a problem for me in any way whatsoever. In case you think it might be. I just want you to be happy and I will want that all my life.'

'Really?'

'Well of course.'

There were tears in her eyes. 'It would mean the world to me if I can be myself with you, Miles.'

'Of course you can, you silly sod.'

'You know, part of me wishes so much I had told Mum. I think I'll always be sorry I didn't. It'll be my biggest regret.'

'But you were thinking of her, weren't you?'

'I suppose I was.'

'Don't regret it then. Make it up with me.'

And she did, she confided in me, and talked with slowly growing assurance for the rest of the weekend about her love affairs and how whenever she fell in love she seemed to get knocked back because she thought she set her aim too high, including with the last one, a brown-eyed Italian passenger liaison officer on the cruise ship called Lucia. I entered Lotte's world of light and dark, of happiness and unhappiness, of which I had been ignorant all my adult years, and when we said goodbye it was with a warmth of a new intensity, and an agreement for her to come up to Aberdeen in her turn three weeks later.

I planned the weekend: I had things I could show her now. On the Friday evening I picked her up at the airport and drove her around the city to get a feel for the grey granite townscape; we had dinner in an Italian place off Union Street. On Saturday morning we drove to Stonehaven and walked along the cliffs to Dunnottar Castle and came back for lunch in Stonehaven itself, the fishing village, in a restaurant overlooking the harbour, and in the evening she helped me cook the mince an' tatties at the Magdalenians. Early on the Sunday we set out for Deeside, which I had reconnoitred the weekend before. It was a soft spring day with the birches in pale green leaf and the geans, the wild cherries, in white flower all along the road; we drove to Braemar and then on up above the valley to Linn o'Dee, and from there we walked into the Cairngorm foothills, through Glen Lui and the exquisite pinewoods to Derry Lodge, with willow warblers singing all around, silvery descending cascades; while we were eating our picnic, a golden eagle floated over us.

Lotte was an urban soul, really, and this was all new for her; the novelty added to the loveliness of the landscape and she adored it. She was particularly happy all day, and when we finally got back to the airport terminal and were about to say goodbye, she said: 'By the way. I forget to tell you. It's been accepted.'

'What?'

'Your application. It was formally accepted this weekend, in fact.'

'What application? What are you talking about?'

'Don't you remember?'

'Uh-uh.'

'To join the human race.'

It dawned on me. The delight spread through my being. 'You mean, I'm in?'

'You're in.'

I beamed at her. I marvelled at her. I squeezed her hand and said: 'So long, Sis. See you very soon.'

'So long, Bro.'

We hugged, and she kissed me on the cheek and set off wheeling her case towards Departures, with me waving, but after a few yards she stopped, and turned on her heel, and walked back towards me.

I said: 'What's the matter?'

She seemed to be hesitating.

'What's up, Lot? You OK?'

She said: 'She's come back.'

'What? Who? Who's come back?'

'Who d'you think?'

My heart rate shot up. 'Jenny?'

She nodded.

'You mean, she's come back to England?'

She nodded again.

My heart rate went crazy.

Lotte said: 'I think she feels, what happened, isn't going to beat her. She is one tough girl.'

'Where is she? She in Oxford? In London? Where?'

'I don't think I can tell you that.'

'Can I contact her?'

'I don't think you can, Miles. Come on.'

'Then why'd you tell me?'

'I dunno.' She looked down and shook her head. 'I don't know why I told you. Maybe I shouldn't have done.'

'No. You should. It's right that you did.'

'Well, there you are then.'

We had not mentioned Jenny in either of the weekends. It had been a sort of unspoken agreement. But of course she had been in the background all the time.

Now I said: 'You know, Lot, at some stage I will have to try … I will have to try to put it right with Jenny. I will have to.

D'you understand that? I will not be able to live, if I don't. D'you understand?'

'I do, Miles, yes.'

'And a moment will come … there will be a moment … when I have to do it. And when it does come, I will ask for your help.'

'I suppose so. But the moment is not now. And it may not be for a long time.'

'All right. Maybe not. Maybe not.'

I smiled, to reassure her, and she smiled back at me, and we embraced again, and off she went to catch her plane to London.

But the moment came sooner than either of us expected.

He's lonely for just time
Thinks about homelessness.
Sister - gay
J back in Uk

15

It was a morning in late May. I had gone upstairs to see Sidney Jeffries, the white-haired Yorkshireman I had met that night in The Grill, who ran the UKOCA seabirds section, and his deputy, Roddy Baird, a Scot about my own age. In spite of everything, I had managed to make my first human contacts in the agency with these two gentlemen, because I had begun researching the effects of commercial fishing for sandeels, those pencil-like small fish which make up a huge proportion of the diet of birds such as terns and puffins, and Sidney and Roddy had been very helpful when I consulted them. They explained to me how big boats, especially from Denmark, were hoovering up the sandeel population off the Scottish coast and putting the breeding success of numerous puffin and tern colonies at risk – while the sandeels were just going to be made into fertiliser. I went back to see them to get more detail and they were very obliging again – I think they started to realise I was actually human – and then when I went up on a third visit to their office, on this May morning, I was greeted effusively.

'Here's someone who knows all about Kenny and his funny little ways!' cried Roddy Baird, grinning, as I knocked on their door and walked in.

'You're not wrong there,' grunted Sidney Jeffries.

'I'm sorry?' I said.

'Kenny Lornie,' said Roddy. 'He's not only had a fight with you, he's had a fight with the warden on Lanna.'

'What?'

'He's been kicked off the island. Can ye believe it? Although I daresay, you can.'

'I'm afraid I don't follow,' I said. 'Kenny's been kicked off … where?'

'Lanna.'

'That's an island?' I had never registered the name before.

'Aye,' said Roddy. 'Way out beyond the Hebrides. Where we're doing the seabird census, to stop the oil drilling.'

'Or at least, we were,' growled Sidney. 'That twat has put the whole thing at risk.'

'I'm sorry,' I said. 'Can you explain a bit more?'

'Lanna's a seabird colony,' said Roddy. 'Probably the best in the British Isles after St Kilda. And now the government wants to license oil drilling right next to it.'

'Why?'

'Because of the Atlantic Frontier.'

'What's that?'

'The new oil province?'

I shook my head.

'North Sea oil's beginning to run out, OK? So the government and the oil companies have started looking for fresh offshore fields on the other side of Britain. The western side, in the Atlantic. And they're finding them. There's already three or four in operation. Foinaven, Schiehallion, Macdui. And now they want to prospect for another one right next to Lanna.'

'But that's outrageous, isn't it?' The oil-clogged corpses of the *Erika* started to float back into my mind.

'Well, we kind of think it's a try-on, but it's certainly outrageous, aye. So we're objecting, and the basis of the objection is a proper survey of Lanna's seabirds. A census. Which Kenny Lornie had gone out to do.'

'And what's happened, again?'

'He's had a fight with the warden Kintyre keeps there.'

'Who's Kintyre?'

'Lord Kintyre. The owner of Lanna. The Tiger Laird.'

'The *what*?'

'The Tiger Laird. He keeps tigers at his castle. Balnay, over in Argyll. And he goes in the cages with them, and plays with them, and so do his keepers, except his keepers keep getting killed.'

'Really?'

'Three of them, so far. Couple of years back the local council tried to stop him. There was a court case. But he won it, so he still goes in with his beasties. You no' read about that? He's a big story up here.'

'I'm afraid I didn't.'

'Aye well, Kintyre's the owner of Lanna too, and he keeps the island closed, the public cannae get on it, and he also keeps this guy there to stop anybody trying. Name of Fergus. Meant to be a very big guy, isn't he, Sidney?'

'Bloody giant,' said Sidney.

'And Kenny's had a fight with him. What's more, he's come off worse. He's been hurt. And he's been kicked off the island, he's been expelled, and the boat's bringing him back to Oban just now and Ramsay and Fraser have gone over there to pick him up. They're freaking out. We're all freaking out. Are we not, Sidney? Are we not freaking out?'

Kenny Lornie. My nemesis. Built like a young bull. He'd had a fight and come off *worse*? Wow. This guy on the island must be big, all right. I said: 'What did they have the fight about?'

'Well he's provoked it, hasn't he, Kenny?' Sidney Jeffries said. 'I don't doubt that for one minute. It's his daft Scottish nationalist nonsense. He tried it on with Kintyre himself when he went to see him over at his castle, to get permission to go on the island, they had an argument and he nearly blew the whole thing there and then. And I just know that's what he's gone and done, he's done the same with Fergus the warden on the island itself, and now he's screwed up everything. Ramsay should never have sent him. I warned him. But he wouldn't listen.'

'D'you know what exactly happened?'

Roddy said: 'Apparently Kenny was told by Fergus he couldn't go somewhere on the island, and Kenny said oh yes he could, and one thing led to another and then they came to blows.'

'It's his mad nationalist agenda,' said Sidney. 'The laird-bashing. You know? I'm Scottish and I'm not going to be told by a laird who is basically English – or his representative – where I can go in me own country. It's the Who Owns Scotland argument. The lairds own all the land, and the way Kenny sees it, most of them are really English. English intruders. Exploiters. That's what he thinks of Kintyre, even though Kintyre's a chief of the Macdonalds and he's probably far more Scottish than Kenny is.'

'So – what happens now?'

'Worst case is, the end of the survey. The end of the objection. The end of the defence of Lanna. The twat.'

'Can't you just object anyway? Why do you need a survey?'

'Because proper objections have to be science-based. If we want to say, you can't put an oilfield *there*, you bunch of benighted tossers, because the seabirds are too important, you've got to say scientifically what the seabirds there *are*. And the particular problem we've got here is, that Lanna is the only major UK seabird station that's never been properly surveyed.'

'Is it?'

'Remarkable anomaly. Quite remarkable. Look. The seabirds of the British Isles are probably the best observed on Earth, right? Every island, every stack, every sodding cliff ... they've all been scientifically surveyed two or three times at least. And here we've got Lanna. Wonderful place. Completely untouched, uninhabited, sizeable island, right out on the edge of the continental shelf, big nutrient upwelling, so the bird numbers are sensational. Huge gannetry on two offshore stacks, could be fifty thousand pairs, plus there's a whacking great fulmar colony, as you'd expect, and enormous numbers of the auks, gillies and puffins especially, as well as thousands of kittiwakes. Probably big numbers of Manxies and of things like stormies and Leach's petrels, maybe even things we don't know about, things we don't even realise are breeding north of the equator, like Swinhoe's petrel, or something. Priceless. I've seen it, I've sailed around it, it's absolutely amazing, it's clearly one of the best seabird stations in the whole bloody Atlantic Ocean, but we can't say that scientifically, because the birds *have never been damn well counted.*'

'Never?'

'Not properly. People have had a go, looking at it on boat trips, but the weather's too treacherous to linger. To survey it properly you would need at least a week or two or even more, based on the island, and that's never been possible because, by the time people got round to doing things like that systematically, after the war, the Kintyres had closed it.'

'How can you close an island?'

'It's very rocky, right? And there's only one way you can get on it. There's a cove, a natural harbour, and the way into it is through a narrow gap in the cliffs, and they put chains across the gap.'

'But Lord Kintyre's allowing a survey now?'

'Well he was, until Mr Kenny sodding Lornie got his hot little hands on it. At least, in a manner of speaking, he was.'

'How d'you mean?'

'It was weird. Wan't it, Roddy?' Roddy Baird nodded. 'They laid down all these really tight conditions. Kintyre said that we could send one person, not a team like we normally would, just the one, who would be shown the island and the birds by your man Fergus, for a maximum of three days. He would be supervised by Fergus at all times and the deal was, he had to do exactly what Fergus told him. To the letter. And get this. He wasn't allowed any cameras. What's that about? Eh? Why can't we take a camera? Right peculiar. And our chap could write a report, based on what Fergus had shown him, and that was it, that's your lot, and we could use that as the basis of our oil-drilling objection, take it or leave it.'

'If it was that restricted, it seems surprising they let you go at all.'

'Ah well. There's a history there. 'Cos two years ago, right, there was another series of seabed blocks where oil drilling was proposed, forty-five miles further north. And we asked Kintyre if we could survey Lanna *then*, so we could object, 'cos we thought even these blocks were far too close to the island and its seabirds for comfort. But Kintyre says no we can't. Won't give a reason. Just says, afraid it's not convenient. So we had no basis for objection and the licences were duly granted, and the next thing you know, they've only struck oil in one of the blocks. American operator called Taft. Subsidiary of BP. And now they're developing a field there, it's called Macdui, there's an offshore oilfield less than fifty miles from one of world's prime seabird colonies.'

I said: 'So what's happening now?'

'Three months ago, the latest oil licensing round comes up, and we could scarcely credit it: this time the bloody government want to license exploration in Lanna's *own sector*, in the very seabed block that contains the island, block 13 of quadrant 132, if you want chapter and verse, can you credit it?

I thought again of the *Erika*. 'I think that's appalling.'

'So we write to Kintyre once again and we say, look, your Kintyreship, this is getting crazy, you're going to have another oilfield right on top of your precious island this time, right up your bum, mate, unless you allow us to survey the birds and mount a proper science-led defence of it. And he writes back by return saying, once again, No way. Absolutely not.'

He looked at me.

'Sweet baby Jesus, what possible objection can the bloke have to us trying to save his island from a major threat of oil pollution? I mean, what?'

'I've no idea, Sidney.'

'But then, a month ago, he changes his mind. Just like that. Sees sense, I suppose. He says we can do it, but it has to be with all these wacky conditions, just one person, no cameras, one guy shooting around in an inflatable with your man Fergus. Who unfortunately turns out to be Kenny.'

'Why Kenny, and not you guys?'

'Kenny's acting head of marine industry, but he would probably say himself, the real reason he should go is that he's got the best birding skills in UKOCA. And maybe he has. But he's a liability, with his opinions and his inability to control his bloody tongue. And now he's screwed everything up. Kintyre was on the blower to Ramsay this morning about it, shouting blue murder. I told Ramsay not to send him, after the row at the castle. But he's got a soft spot for the lad, 'cos he comes from an underprivileged background or some such bloody nonsense. Well, you know all about that, don't you,' he said to Roddy Baird. 'You're his mate.'

'Ye've gotta say, Kenny's story is remarkable,' Roddy said.

'Why's that?'

'Cos he's a lad from the schemes.'

'The *what*?'

'The big post-war public housing schemes around Edinburgh. Big, rough, council estates. Kenny's from one of the roughest. He's from Sighthill. And he's a scientist! From Sighthill! And he's not just a scientist, he's an executive in a government agency! It's unbelievable.'

I said, because I thought I ought to: 'I'm very sorry I fell out with him, before Christmas. I think I was in the wrong.'

'Well, that's what he's like,' said Sidney. 'Though in your case, it probably didn't help that you told him to get stuffed when he offered to take you birding.'

'What?' I said.

'That night you had a drink with us in The Grill. He offered to show you the guillemot colony at Fowlsheugh. You more or less told him to go and stuff himself.'

'Christ, did I really?' I had no recollection.

'Aye lad, you did.'

'That's awful,' I said.

'Wasn't very gracious.'

I sat there, thinking about it. I was mortified. And just to fill the silence, I said to Sidney: 'So, who is this Fergus character, anyway?'

'Fergus? Ha. Comes with the territory. Been there years. Outlandish-looking guy. Very big. Like, a giant? Six-foot-eight, six-nine, more? With red hair and a big red beard. Looks like a pirate or something, almost like something from a cartoon, somebody you'd scare your kids with. Fergus The Bogeyman.'

'He's there all the year round?'

'Not in the winter, I don't think. He's there for the seabird breeding season, certainly.'

'Just by himself, on this remote island?'

'Just by himself.'

'Isn't that unusual?'

'Certainly is. Dangerous, too, to be there alone. You're running all sorts of risks. Fall in the sea, you're dead. The estate boat goes out once a week or so, but what if you have an accident in the meantime? Mad, really.'

'Why is he there?'

'I think Kintyre has him there to keep people off. To make sure Lanna stays closed.'

'Why on earth *is* it closed?'

'It goes back to just before the war,' Sidney said. 'Strange story. Nineteen thirty-nine, it was. A rumour got around that there was treasure from the Spanish Armada buried on Lanna and that summer, a pile of people went over there to dig for it until Lord Kintyre – this'll be the present one's grandfather – he threw them all off. And that's when they closed it, and it's been closed ever since. In case anybody tries it again, I suppose.'

'How did the rumour start?'

'Bloke called Crinan published a book about it. History of the island. I've got a copy of it at home, it's quite hard to get hold of, but you can borrow it if you're really interested. I can bring it in this afternoon.'

'Thanks a lot,' I said. 'I will.'

The news about Kenny Lornie caught and held my full attention. It was one of the few things that had done so in weeks, since I learned of the return of Jenny: she had filled my mind, I had thought of virtually nothing else. It was the fact that she was no longer in unreachable exile eleven thousand miles away, which seemed to open the gates of possibility. Now she was in Britain there had to be a way of … not just getting her back, but of … making it right. Or at least, of making the attempt.

Every day, I ran through it in my mind. As Lotte had pointed out, I couldn't just approach her, and say, *Sorry for destroying your life.* Could I? There had to be something special, something uniquely fitted to the circumstances and I didn't know what, yet I felt it would emerge, and when it emerged I would know it; and in the meantime I lived with the longing in the daylight hours, and when the night came she flickered more vividly than ever on the screen of my dreams.

But in spite of all that, the story of Kenny Lornie and his clash on this island left me riveted, for Kenny had also come to loom large in my mind, as a sort of symbol of how awful I'd been before I changed; and Sidney's reminding me that he'd actually offered me friendship, and I'd thrown it back in his face, greatly reinforced the feeling. I was deeply ashamed of the way I'd behaved towards him, so I was gripped by this news about him being involved in another violent encounter and I wondered what on earth it could have been about, his fight with this warden character.

Fergus, he's called.

Hardly likely Fergus told him to shut up, like I did, was it? Must be something about the island itself.

All afternoon my imagination wandered over it, and eventually I turned to the internet, more or less in its infancy then – Google and Wikipedia were still in the future. To my regret, on Lanna, there was very little, other than how remote it was, sixty miles west of the Hebrides, and how in the Middle Ages it held a monastery. But there was quite a lot about the Earl of Kintyre, who was a real celebrity in Scotland, I began to realise, not just because he was a prominent nobleman, head of one of the oldest Scottish families, the Kintyre Macdonalds, the southerly branch of the Clan Donald, and a friend of the royals – all that was trumpeted in a gushing *Daily Telegraph* profile of him and his beautiful American second wife – but also because of his views, and most of all, his zoo.

In the extensive grounds of Balnay, his ancestral castle in Argyll, he had built up a large menagerie where he indulged his passion for keeping the big beasts, the great cats in particular. In the cause of conservation – something he was at pains to stress – he successfully bred Siberian tigers, as well as other charismatic and endangered species such as gorillas and Asian elephants. Balnay wildlife park had become both a conservation success story, certainly in terms of captive breeding, and one of the biggest tourist attractions in Scotland; but what really drew the crowds, and had kept Lord Kintyre in the headlines for several years, was what one might term his zoo-keeper's philosophy.

The gulf between people and the great wild animals, his lordship held, was man-made, artificial and to be done away with. They were not our inferiors but our brethren. To this end, those at Balnay were treated as honoured guests rather than craven captives; the park was for them, not for the public, who were merely admitted upon sufferance; and most of all, intimate bonds were to be forged between animal and keeper. This meant stepping boldly and unprotected through the bars and into the enclosures, to become friends, to get on tummy-tickling terms, with such as adult male gorillas and adult Siberian tigers. Lord Kintyre led the way himself, and the photos of him romping with his tigers, as if they were golden retrievers, had gone round the world – I gazed on them, fascinated – but over a decade, his original take on animal husbandry had cost two keepers their lives. They were bloody and shocking deaths, by tigers both, yet the mounting criticism had left the Earl unrepentant and undeterred; they were caused by two rogue beasts, he said, two out of more than two dozen, and these exceptions merely proved the rule that the vast majority of tigers were trustworthy, emotionally predictable and 'honourable'; in a much-repeated quote, he said that they were 'gentlemen'. But when a third keeper was killed, crushed to death by an elephant, his local authority, Argyll and Bute, decided that enough was enough, and issued an order under the Health and Safety at Work Act to make him toe the conventional line, and stay this side of the bars.

His resultant appeal to an industrial tribunal had been an enormous news story in Scotland and a pretty big story in the rest of Britain (although it had passed me by.) Christened the Tiger Laird by the Scottish press, Kintyre had revelled in the publicity, not least because it gave him a platform for his singular views on conservation and population growth, centring on the proposition that there were far too many humans in the world for the good of animals, and a substantial reduction in their number – the number of humans – was devoutly to be wished, whether by war, disease or famine, he did not care.

People were the problem, he repeatedly proclaimed; that was even the title of a book he had written. Interviewers flocked to him, to gather up his remarks like exotic fruit; he was regretful but entirely unrepentant about the deaths of his keepers, saying they were good men who had known the risks and had accepted them when they took on their jobs, and contended that Balnay Wildlife Park enjoyed massive support among the local population, which, as it had become a significant local employer, it probably did; and he gave more than a broad hint that were he banned from intimate personal contact with his animals, by what he termed the boobies of Lochgilphead – where the council was based – he might well close his enterprise down. It was an extraordinary case, and its most extraordinary aspect was, that he won.

It was a complete vindication of his approach, he declared outside the tribunal; it was a victory for the cause of the great beasts, which were nature's most perfect and inspiring creations and were being driven to extinction by the greed and selfishness of humanity; to save a single tiger, he proclaimed, he would gladly sacrifice a million people. And people were duly scandalised; or in some cases, moved to agreement; but everybody took note of what he said. As did I.

Unusual man, I thought. Huge ego, clearly. Must be quite something to see him romping with his tigers, Yet my mind came back to what had just happened. Never mind his zoo. What about his island?

Why does he not want people on this island of his?

Lanna.

It's really remote. It's the remotest island in the British Isles.

If it's so remote and hard to get to, why does he go to the lengths of keeping a man on it, to keep people off it?

A giant, it is said.

Who came to blows with Kenny Lornie.

Why? Over what? They were supposed to be surveying the seabirds together. *Helping* each other.

What had Kenny done?

He must have done something, surely?

What, though?

I couldn't imagine.

I went back to the Net but could find nothing more in the way of a clue; yet just as I was about to log off, the search threw up something wholly unexpected: his lordship had reviewed *Everything Except Seahorses*. It was more than two years earlier, in an obscure journal called *The Freedom Review*, and the name of the reviewer was given merely as <u>Rollo Kintyre</u>, but I checked and Rollo was the Earl's Christian name; I was pretty sure it was him. His <u>review</u> was not very long but he praised the book as 'a <u>triumphant flying</u> <u>of the flag for biological determinism</u>' and said it was 'another nail in the coffin of the standard social science model'.

Well, well. That was fascinating too. Yet it was the island where Kenny Lornie had met his Waterloo that I was really interested in, and at the end of the day I went back up to Sidney's office and he gave me the book as he had promised, and I strolled back to Rosemount in the evening sunshine, wondering if it would give me any ideas about what might have set things off on this faraway lump of rock in the sea.

Instead, it led me somewhere else entirely.

Tiger Lawd-Aspurall

16

The dustwrapper had long gone. Cloth-bound, battered and worn, it was a slim volume, and the title page read: *LANNA: THE LOST ISLAND*, by Melrose Crinan, WS. Underneath it said: *Published by Royal Mile Press, Edinburgh, 1939.* It was dedicated to Godfrey, 8th Earl of Kintyre, KT, GCVO, MC, and it began: *The voyager to America who fares forth, not from Liverpool or Southampton but from the port of Glasgow, may, should his vessel take the northerly course around Ireland and he taking a stroll on deck on the starboard side after half a day's sailing, glimpse on the horizon – in the best visibility – an unmistakable speck.*

I've always remembered that. I can recite it from memory.

Mr Crinan continued: *This is the most the world now sees of an island wholly exceptional in its story, which long ago was famed as Canterbury and Compostela still are famed today, but which, being swept by the irresistible tide of history into precipitous decline, has languished these near four hundred years past in a most unmerited oblivion.*

It was Mr Crinan's mission to bring it out of its obscurity back into the light, and he set about telling, in a vigorous if rather florid style, a story which held my interest, as it was full of incident and went back fifteen hundred years.

Lanna, I read, was the remotest of all the Western Isles, and at 56°44'N, 09°29'W, the most distant part of the United Kingdom apart from Rockall. But Mr Crinan was at pains to stress that in spite of its great remoteness, Lanna's physical blessings were a wonder, headed by Acarsaid Mor, its great anchorage, which was, he said, the most perfect natural harbour in all the Hebrides, entered through a narrow turning defile in the eastern cliffs and thus completely sheltered. Yet there was even more: the island possessed a green heart where crops could be grown and livestock pastured, with a freshwater spring on either side. Considering its location, it was miraculous, and *no doubt*, wrote Mr Crinan, *but that the first holy man who set eyes upon it must have been convinced, that the island had been created expressly by the Almighty, for the sole purpose of worshipping Him.*

That was Columba, who brought Christianity to Scotland in the year 563, when he sailed over from Ireland and on Iona, founded his abbey. Lanna was a daughter house of Iona, Mr Crinan said, founded by the saint himself or by one of his followers in about 574, not as an abbey at first, merely a priory, housing a prior and eight monks, and it existed and worshipped in parallel with its mother house, and in peace in that great age of the Celtic saints, for more than two hundred years, *until the devils came out of the North.*

The Vikings struck the island in 796, two years after Iona was sacked; they put the monks to the sword, but for their Prior, Corman, the Norsemen reserved a special fate: they tried to make him defile the cross, and when he resolutely refused, they dragged him up to the island's peak, and there, on two longship oars lashed together, they crucified him.

It was the only known Viking crucifixion. Mr Crinan wrote: *Corman was left hanging, to rot and be consumed by the ravens; and so it would have fallen out, but one monk the Norsemen had missed. His name was Finbarr, and when they stormed ashore he had been gathering the eggs of sea-fowl at the other end of the island; he secreted himself away, and when the raiders at last departed, he took his prior's body down and gave him decent burial, along with his brethren. But what must he do? He was alone with no means of escape, since the sea-devils had burned the monastery boats. The Lord provided. A whale came into the great anchorage, called out to Finbarr, and told him to return to Corman's grave and cut off from his body the right hand, with the marks of the nails which had fixed him to the Viking cross to bear eloquent witness to his martyrdom; he did so, and then the whale carried him on its back, clutching his sacred relic, eastwards over the sea to Iona, the grieving mother house, where he told his tragic tale.*

It was only the first of many miracles attributed to Saint Corman, as he became, and as Lanna eventually became his shrine, with its treasured relic of his pierced hand, and its high peak forever named after his agony as Cnoc na Croise, the Hill of the Cross. This was the beginning of Lanna's great story, this was the second reason the island was remarkable besides its geography: for the power of its legend, which drew people to it from afar, in even the frailest of craft over the most tempestuous of oceans. But not immediately; for with the advent of the Norsemen, darkness descended on the Celtic church of the west for three centuries, and Lanna did not re-emerge into history until the advent of the Lords of the Isles.

I had never heard of the Lords of the Isles. Now I learned to my fascination of this long-lost kingdom of the sea, this Gaelic-speaking state of the Clan Donald which at its medieval apogee ruled all of Scotland's western seaboard; there was something thrilling about its story, something almost dreamlike, for it was a principality of the Atlantic, it was grounded on the jagged coastline and the countless sea lochs and the islands without number, and its great stone castles were castles of the water, the thirty castles which enforced its writ all the way from Borve on Benbecula down to Dunaverty on the Mull of Kintyre – Tioram and Mingary, Sween and Ardtornish, Dunollie, Dunstaffnage, Dunyveg and the rest, all of them opening to the sea and linked with ease and speed by their birlinns, their square-sailed Highland galleys.

Mr Crinan told of the new empire's origin in the expulsion of the Norsemen from the Hebrides, led by the first of the island lords, the great warrior Somerled, whose descendants became the Macdonalds. It was they who put together the kingdom of the sea, he said, and it was Somerled's son Ranald who gave the realm a formidable spiritual dimension at the outset in the creation of two great monasteries – the Abbey of Iona, and the Abbey of Lanna. Ranald began them again, as modern religious houses looking ultimately to Rome, and run by the most established of the monastic orders, the Benedictines: Iona was refounded in 1203, and Lanna two years later. Yet while the first is known and loved still for its holiness, the second is lost to us, Mr Crinan said. Lanna is the lost island, though its story is just as memorable; for now Lanna Abbey became the great pilgrimage destination of Scotland.

The great attraction was of course the shrine of its patron saint: St Corman seemed to catch the imaginations of the medieval faithful, more than St Andrew, more than St Mungo, St Margaret or any other Scottish holy figure, and indeed far beyond Scotland's borders. For could any relic be more worthy of visitation than what the Abbey claimed – *and who*, Mr Crinan said, *was to disbelieve it?* – was the hand of the crucified martyr, with Jesus's very same wound in the palm, carried miraculously over the sea by St Finbarr on the back of his whale? The cloth at Canterbury stained with Thomas à Becket's blood, even the Virgin's own milk in its glass vial at Walsingham, did not compare. *It seemed to devout souls,* he wrote, *that one who had shared the same fate as Our Saviour must occupy in Heaven a most favoured place, and so be in an ideal position to intercede with the Lord one behalf of those who petitioned him.* And countless pilgrims did. For more than four centuries they came, the

Donalds, the Anguses, the Mairis, the Eilidhs, piously imploring him for favours, for fortune, for cures from disease, for marriage or for children, while many more beseeched him to seek forgiveness for their trespasses – Corman was thought to be notably influential with the Lord in the bestowal of His mercy.

I read of their perilous journeys across the turbulent ocean: *their numbers were not small*, said Mr Crinan, *who came to grief*. But for those who succeeded, there was the joyous sight of the great Celtic cross which the Abbey had erected on the island peak to mark the martyrdom of its saint; the heartfelt relief of the entry into the harbour and the welcome from the monks their hosts; the ceremony in the church where St Corman's hand was taken from its golden reliquary and displayed, to the adoring congregation; and finally there was the procession to the top of Cnoc na Croise, to hear mass at the very spot where the saint had met his fate.

That the pilgrims were able to do this, Crinan wrote, was the joint achievement of two formidable institutions, the Order of St Benedict and the Clan Donald, and it could not be stressed enough what a significant achievement it was to have established a working monastery on this very extremity of Europe. Never, he wrote, was the Rule of St Benedict followed in such testing conditions as in the Abbey of the Seals, as it came to be called for the wonder of its remoteness. Only the most robust of monks, carefully chosen by their Benedictine superiors, were able to cope with its rigours.

But of course, with the Reformation, it all came to an end; and with its ending came the strangest episode of all in the island's story. The author explained that the monasteries of Scotland were not all suddenly extinguished after Protestantism became the religion of the land in 1560, in the way their English counterparts had been twenty-five years earlier; not a few of the communities belonging to the Scottish religious houses remained in place and were simply allowed to die out. Some monks left and became secularised; some embraced the reformed religion; but others knew no other life and clung on to what they had, and in some cases, that was for decades, with Lanna being one such example.

The sources are few and obscure, Crinan said, but it does appear that by August 1588 there were a handful of elderly men still eking out an existence on the island when Lanna was embraced by history for a final time, in the shape of the Spanish Armada. Its commander, the Duke of Medina Sidonia, had taken the fateful decision, after the battles against the English fleet in the channel, to return to Spain by the long route around the north of Scotland, with dire consequences for many of his galleons, shot up, short of fresh water and provisions, struggling with navigation, and their crews increasingly diseased.

A third did not make it, many of them wrecked on the west coast of Ireland; and one was very probably wrecked on Lanna. The two likeliest candidates, said Mr Crinan, were the *San Maria del Junca* of the Squadron of Andalusia, a ship of 730 tones carrying 20 cannon, which had started out from Spain with a crew of 66, and the *Santa Barbara*, of the Squadron of the Hulks, a much smaller vessel of 370 tons with 10 cannon and a crew of 24, both of which disappeared without trace. Lanna is a very likely last resting place for one of them.

What happened, we only know from a testament, and we do not even have the testament itself: we have merely a report of it. In October 1588 a senior minister of the new reformed Church of Scotland by the name of Archibald Hopetoun sailed to Lanna to check what the situation was with the former monastery and its dwindling community, and made, he said, an astonishing discovery: there was no one there, but there was a message.

It was written in Latin on parchment from the Abbey's former scriptorium and he said he found it in the empty refectory, where the last inhabitants had eaten together; it was short, but it told a dramatic story. It was allegedly dated to the August – nobody but Hopetoun ever saw it – and it said (adapted from Hopetoun's Scots):

From the great ship wrecked on our island a sailor swam ashore bearing gold pieces but died. This gold we fought over, I and my companions; now only I am alive, but am sorely wounded and soon will die myself. I curse this gold for it has been the end of me. I curse myself for I will burn in hell. I curse the island of Lanna that was my home. May those who seek it never find it. May voyagers to the island be forever lost.
Walter that was the monk wrote this.

There was no sign of the author. There was no sign of human life whatsoever. Nor, for that matter, was there any sign of the gold pieces. Nobody ever elucidated further what had happened. But it was enough.

For so began, Mr Crinan wrote, the final stage of the Lanna's story, and the most unfortunate one: that a place which so inspired its pilgrims, which had aroused great devotion and love and courage, should sink to its final incarnation as *An t-Eilean Air Chall*, The Lost Island. Such it soon became, as the curse of Walter the Monk was bruited abroad and the vivid and superstitious imagination of the Hebridean mind went to work on it: in the Western Isles it became generally accepted that if you sailed for Lanna you very likely would not reach it, you would be lost as Walter had wished, and that if you did manage to get close, the island would disappear on you – it would miraculously vanish. And vanish it did, from history certainly; no one ever went to live on it again, no one wrote about it, no one was interested, all down the centuries, until at last in 1928 Godfrey, Eighth Earl of Kinytre and First World War hero, who was its Macdonald laird, turned his attention to his forgotten domain.

Mr Crinan was an intimate – the Earl's family solicitor – and His Lordship was inspired, he said, by a visit to Iona, where he saw the restoration which had been carried out under the aegis of the Eighth Duke of Argyll; what could be done for the one great monastery of the Isles, Lord Kintyre realised, could be done for the other. And so he instituted a programme of works, which were continuing, to clear and restore the crumbling buildings of the abbey and the castle, to improve access at the anchorage, and most visibly, to refix the great stone Celtic cross on Cnoc na Croise, which had long since tumbled down.

I had just finished that sentence when a piece of paper fell out of the back of the book: it was a yellowing press cutting, a full-page feature from the *Daily Express* of July 1989 headed: *The Island and the Spanish Armada Gold Rush* with a strapline above which said: *Fifty Years Ago This Month, Remote Hebridean Isle Was Invaded By Gold-Diggers*. It told how, when Melrose Crinan's account was published, the Scottish press had picked up on the story of Walter the Monk and his gold and his curse, and one piece in particular had speculated that the Armada bullion must still be there on Lanna, probably buried and waiting to be dug up; and how the island had subsequently been assailed by a torrent of treasure hunters, until Lord Kintyre and his retainers threw them off, and closed the island, and closed it for good.

Poor Melrose, I thought. The aim of his book was to bring Lanna out of obscurity, but he sent it right back in.

The irony!

He must have felt it keenly, for he was not only enthused by the restoration works, but he had been attempting a parallel restoration of his own, one for people's minds, which now was similarly closed off. It was clear that the island and its fate had captured the heart of the Edinburgh solicitor. *Lanna the lost island stands for so much else which is gone*, he wrote. *It stands for the Lords of the Isles and their vanished kingdom of the sea; it stands for the worth of pilgrimage, one of the noblest impulses of the human soul; indeed it stands for the lost glory of the Celtic Church.* But it was the disappearance of the island itself from people's consciousness which exercised him most. *That Lanna should today be forgotten is an offence against history and geography*, he said, *for it is extraordinary, a corner of the earth as blessed as it is remote: the devotion of its monks and the pious courage of its pilgrims hang about it still, mingling with the roar of its waves and the cries of its sea-fowl.* Most regrettable of all, Mr Crinan wrote, was that its very beauty was hidden from the world. *Those, and there are many, who are stirred by the loveliness of the Hebrides*, he said in his final sentence, *may understand the essence of this island so long hidden from us, if I say with the conviction of one who has come to know it well, that of all the Western Isles, sprinkled in their wild beauty over the sea, Lanna is the jewel supreme.*

That was it.

I snapped the book shut. I had been reading for three hours.

I sat there, thinking.

Then I got up and went into the kitchen and poured myself a glass of wine. I opened a window: it was late evening with light still flooding the sky.

I sipped the wine.

I had an island filling my mind, for the first time.

I suppose it was because over the previous months my eyes had been opened to so much of life which I had previously ignored, and now I was curiously receptive to this singular story, with its saints as heroes and its Viking villains and its Gaelic lords and its pilgrims taking on the Atlantic in their open boats … I realised I knew nothing of the Hebrides and the loveliness of which Melrose Crinan spoke, and I found that, for the first time, I dearly wanted to see the Western Isles for myself; and I wished to see Lanna most of all.

At last I can grasp the allure of an island, I thought.

I could see what Jenny saw, what did she say when we first met, *most islands have a special feel*, and I pooh-poohed it, but I was wrong and she was right, and it was then that the idea was born.

It began deep down in me, it was a tiny spark; but really, even in its initial incarnation it was fully formed, it needed no developing, I was completely sure of it, even before her other words floated into my mind, the words she spoke outside the pub that evening in Wytham village, *islands are the way to me* and *you'll have to win me with an island.*

I did not need them.

I knew that Lanna was the way back to Jenny, however ridiculously far-fetched the idea might seem.

I knew with the heart, not the head, so I did not doubt.

I barely slept that night; I lay thinking it through, forming the plan, the plan that was very likely impossible because it could break down at any link in its chain.

Impossible, rationally, that is.

But I was not rational.

I did not have reason on my side. I had faith.

I left the flat at 7.15 to go and see Ramsay Wishart in his office as he always got in early, before anyone else. It was a glorious, crystal May morning in Aberdeen, the gulls seemed to be crying everywhere, and when I got to the UKOCA building, I met with a surprise. Going in, I bumped into Kenny Lornie coming out.

He had obviously had the same idea as myself about an early visit to the Director. I stared at him. The left-hand side of his face was covered in the biggest bruise I had ever seen, a great smear of yellow and blue. He caught my eye.

'Aye, have a look at that, Rupert,' he called out. 'Have a good look. The fuckin' English lackey of a fuckin' English laird did that. One a yours. But he didnae stop me! He didnae stop me frae findin' oot! Ah know now! Ah know what's there!' And he pushed past me, and was gone.

I briefly wondered what he meant.

What's there?

What would be there?

But I dismissed him from my mind as I climbed the stairs to the fourth floor: I was sure Kenny Lornie wasn't going back to Lanna.

No. Kenny was history. It was I who would be going.

When I knocked on Ramsay's door he was testy. 'Yes, Miles, what is it?'

'It's about Lanna, Ramsay.'

'Yes, what about it?'

'I've heard what happened and I thought, er, I might be able to help.'

'And just how would *you* be able to help, Miles?' Tapping his pen on his desk.

what does Kenny know about Laura?

'Well, if you were looking for somebody else to go out there in place of Kenny Lornie, I thought I might fit the bill. I know how to count seabirds on cliffs. I did it for six years.'

'Yeah well, that's fine, thank you Miles for your kind offer, but that's not the problem, there are at least a dozen people in this agency who can accurately count breeding seabirds, the problem I have is with Lord Kintyre because after this fiasco, he's not going to let us back on his fucking island. So now if you'll excuse me—'

'That's the other thing, Ramsay.'

'What is?'

'I thought I might be able to swing it with him. To go back.'

'You?'

'Yes.'

'Why you?'

'I think I might be able to, er, get on his wavelength.'

Ramsay looked at me with a mixture of surprise and contempt. 'Is that because you're a posh English public schoolboy, Miles?'

I winced. 'No,' I said. 'It's something else entirely. Something specific. He reviewed a book I wrote. He gave it a very favourable review. He'll know who I am.'

Ramsay Wishart was a decent man. He looked at me and saw the wound. 'I'm sorry,' he said. 'I'm sorry, Miles. Sit down.' He ran his hand through his hair. 'But this is a bad business. We were there, we were nearly there, we'd actually got on the island, and then – well, you've got cause to know what Kenny Lornie can be like, haven't ye?'

I nodded.

'The boy's a brilliant ornithologist. And he's from a very deprived background and he's pulled himself up by his bootstraps. All to his credit. But – he cannae keep his fucking feelings to himself. Unfortunately. And because of it, it looks like it's screwed up our plans to save Lanna, well and truly.'

'I bumped into him just now, on the way in.'

'He say anything to ye?'

'Only some minor insults. He caught me staring at his bruise …'

'It's some bruise. He's got a hairline fracture of the cheekbone.'

'Has he really? Are you getting the police involved?'

'Kenny doesn't want to. He's insistent that we don't, says he's not going to talk to them, even though in legal terms he's obviously been the victim of a serious assault.'

'So what's he doing now?'

'He's gone off on sick leave. I told him to take as long as he wants. Guy's had a bad experience, for Christ's sake. After the fight, this Fergus character kept him locked up in a hut for a full day till the boat arrived to take him back. Virtually imprisoned him.'

He looked at me and shook his head.

'Ye know, the thing that gets me, the thing that irritates me most, is that Kenny is not really showing any contrition for this, this total fucking shambles, and he normally would, he's basically decent. But he's not. He's talking about the English lackey of an English laird trying to keep the island all for himself, but when I say, yeah OK, but what are we gonna *do* now about Lanna and the oil, for Christ's sake, he says: 'What's on Lanna will save it, wait and see.' No it won't. What on earth's he talking about?'

It wasn't a question that expected an answer. I said: 'So can I ask you, Ramsay, what's the position now?'

'The position, Miles, is that the Earl of Kintyre says we can get lost, we had our chance and we blew it, we can't go back on his island. And he's threatening to make a formal complaint to the Scottish Office about us.'

I said: 'D'you not think it might just be worth putting to him, that there is somebody else we could send in Kenny's place, somebody who is not only professionally qualified to do the job, but it's somebody the Earl is personally acquainted with? In so far as, he reviewed my book?'

Ramsay looked at me. He pondered. He said: 'Och, what's there to lose? I've got to call him anyway this afternoon.' He looked at me. 'In the extremely unlikely event of him agreeing, you really think you could do the survey? If we gave ye proper briefings and everything?'

'I used to think I was Britain's Mister Guillemot, Ramsay.'

'All right. I'll let you know what he says. But don't hold your breath.'

All day, I held my breath.
All day, I thought, this is my way back to Jenny.
It will happen.
Jenny, Jenny, Jenny.
I had an unshakeable feeling I would do it. I had faith.
Finally, at 3.45, Ramsay called me up to his office.
He said: 'Well I'll be damned. Kintyre says ye can go and see him and make a case. He's not promising anything, but he'll see ye. Monday at 4pm.'

It was Friday. 'Where?'

'At Balnay. His castle, over in Argyll. Long way. More than 200 miles. Got a car, haven't ye?'

'Yes.'

'Then ye'd better get over there.'

Long history of Lenna.
He thinks getting on to Lenna
will bring J back.

17

I gunned the Mini Cooper down the side of Loch Nay, along the switchback shore road edged with the oakwoods of mid-Argyll; I had spent five hours, as I urged the car across the breadth of Scotland through Dundee and Perth and Crianlarich and finally to the west coast, thinking only of the plan, the crucial plan, and what the holes in it might be, and what I would tell the man who had the power to agree to me going to Lanna, the island that was closed, when the most recent visit of a UKOCA scientist had ended so calamitously.

If I were him, would I agree to my going? No way, I thought, I definitely would not.

And then with what I was going to specify, as my condition? Even less of a chance. None whatsoever.

Yet I was sustained by a deep faith that it would work, which seemed all the stronger for being wholly unreasonable, and which filled me with optimism, and purpose, and good spirits, until I got stuck behind a lorry. It was a big grey truck, a concrete mixer, which seemed out of place in the Western Highlands, and I was trapped behind its lumbering progress, cursing, for maybe fifteen minutes, until it slowed for a sign pointing off the road which read: BALNAY WILDLIFE PARK: CONSTRUCTION TRAFFIC ONLY. As it turned in, it was passed by another big lorry coming out, filled with rubble, and in the distance I could see a large crane, and I realised I had arrived at Lord Kintyre's zoo, where they were obviously building something significant; in a few hundred yards the main gates appeared which were shut and bore the legend: *Closed on Mondays.* I had a quick gawp for a tiger or two: I could see nothing.

The castle itself was nearly a mile further on, the entrance large, open, and unwelcoming:

CASTLE BALNAY. STRICTLY PRIVATE.
NO ADMITTANCE EXCEPT ON BUSINESS.
By order. Balnay Estate.

I drove in and found myself rising up through the oakwoods into a formal parkland: there were sheep grazing, a glimpse of thoroughbred horses in a paddock, and the castle itself could be seen intermittently through the trees as I approached it in what seemed like a circle, until finally I came out on to an open gravel plateau and there it was before me, with its six pointed turrets atop the most steeply pitched of roofs. I sat behind the wheel, absorbing it all, then I opened my briefcase and took out the photocopied sheet of paper I had been studying intently. It read:

KINTYRE, 10th Earl of, cr 1762, Rollo Alexander Somerled Macdonald LVO; Lord Macdonald of Islay before 1493; Lord Balnay, 1615; Viscount Balnay, 1694; Hereditary Cupbearer to the Lord of the Isles; Laird of Lanna. b 28 March 1955, yr s of 9th Earl of Kintyre KT GCVO FRSE MC and Sally, d of Mrs and Mrs Emmett Mossbacher of Middleburg, Virginia; S father, 1982. (S brother as Viscount Balnay, 1982.) m 1st, 1990, Lady Angela Wykeham-Winter, yr d of the Earl and Countess of Galloway, two s (marr. diss. 1998); 2nd, 1998, Dr Nancy Cipriano, d of Dr and Mrs Henry Cipriano of Cincinnati, Ohio. Educ: Eton Coll; Christ Church, Oxford. Page to the Lord Lyon, 1965. Founder and president, Balnay Conservation Trust; Board member, National Trust for Scotland. Member, the Queen's Bodyguard for Scotland (Royal Company of Archers), 1988. Publications: Balnay, Captive Bred But Living Free, 1993; People Are The Problem, 1997. Heir: s Viscount Balnay, qv. Address: Castle Balnay, Argyllshire, PA31 8PV. Recreations: entering and belonging to the animal kingdom. Clubs: Turf, New (Edinburgh).

I scanned it a final time, looking for clues, for the weakness, for the thing which would overcome all his objections: if it was there, I couldn't spot it. He had reviewed *Seahorses* favourably, which seemed to have got me this far, but other than that, there appeared to be nothing I could home in on, and I tossed the paper into the well of the passenger seat and opened the car door. The air was exhilaratingly fresh, which seemed a good omen. In the sunshine the loch was blue below me, with a stirring panorama across to the hills on its far side, and above me the 10th Earl of Kintyre's home rose, dark grey and immense behind its dry moat. Four green bronze cannon guarded the moat bridge; two stone greyhounds guarded the main door. There was a bell-pull. A distant bell sounded. I waited and waited. Then, an elderly woman.

'Dr Bonnici,' I said. 'To see Lord Kintyre. I'm expected.'

'You'd best wait there,' she said, closing the door.

I glanced at my watch; it was OK, I was nicely on time, somewhat early, in fact, but it was five minutes before the woman was back, telling me I had best see Mr Crinan. She led me up steps into an echoing hall, big as a gymnasium, that was wallpapered with weapons: there were blade weapons and firearms, scores of them, short swords and claymores, pikes and halberds, muskets and pistols arranged in rows and circles on the whitewashed walls, their polished steel catching the sunlight from the high windows. I gazed at it all; I lingered, and when I looked up the woman had disappeared.

'Hello,' I called out. 'Er, hello?'

She reappeared from a passageway, a blank look on her face; I followed her past a suit of armour and down a corridor lined with stags' heads, and then she was knocking on the half-open door of what I could see was a small, wood-panelled room.

'Mr Crinan,' she said, 'This is doctor …'

'Bonnici.'

A bespectacled slim young man about my age with short, curly blond hair, and a dark green tartan cravat under a fawn waistcoat, rose from behind a desk and held out his hand. 'Dr Bonnici, how do you do, Gervase Crinan, I'm so sorry you've been kept waiting, thank you Mairi, that will be all, yes, thank you, thank you… yes?'

I was looking intently at him. I said: 'You were at Oxford.'

He put his head on one side and regarded me with a quizzical smile I was to come to know well.

'You knocked on my door once. At Pembroke.'

He raised his eyebrows as the quizzical smile continued.

'And you were wearing a hat, a funny red and white hat …'

'Ah,' said Gervase.

'That had bells on it.'

'My jester's cap,' said Gervase.

'And you were wearing a bright red … blazer …'

'My Loretto jacket,' said Gervase.

'And you asked for someone. With a double-barrelled name.'

'Hughie. Hughie McPherson-Davies. He was the year behind me at school, he had just come up. Super chap. He was on another staircase. I vaguely remember. I was going to surprise him. One was more inclined to play the fool in those days.'

He had the softest Scots accent I had ever heard. Barely detectable, like a faint breeze on your cheek. But it was there.

I said: 'The reason *I* remember is that when I said, no, he doesn't live here, you said, are you absolutely one hundred per cent certain?'

Gervase smiled.

'So I looked at you closely and I took in your hair and your glasses. Not to mention your … cap.'

'Oh, the follies of youth.'

'Although I'm afraid I can't have offered much in the way of a civilised response. I wasn't the friendliest of souls back then. I was pretty obsessive about my work. I'm trying to become more civilised now.'

'What were you reading?'

'Zoology. I'm a scientist.'

'Of course. That's why you've come. You want to go to Lanna. Well, good luck with that.'

'Where were you?'

'Christ Church. Reading History. Like his lordship. I'm his lordship's secretary, by the way. I'm afraid your appointment is running a little late.' He checked his watch. 'Half an hour or so. Not much more. Anyway. What a jolly surprise to find a contemporary, here at the very edge of the known world. I think it calls for a drink. Sun's over the yardarm. Glass of sherry?'

'Er – yes, all right,' I said.

He poured two glasses from a small decanter. 'Shall we dispense with the formalities? Do call me Gervase.'

'I'm Miles,' I said.

'I have to say, Miles,' he said, handing me my glass, 'I think you may not find his lordship in the most obliging of moods.' I sat in a chair across the desk from him and he sipped his sherry and said: 'This affair on the island, most unfortunate, and well, it's put Rollo, that's his lordship, into the most frightful bate. Never seen him in such a mood. Raging, almost. I think the chances of him letting you go back out there are remote and to be honest, I'm surprised he's even agreed to see you. You do accept it's a quite extraordinary state of affairs?'

'Absolutely.'

'What d'you make of it yourself?'

'Only what I've heard. That they had some sort of row about where our man could go, and they ended up in a fight, and your man, er, Fergus, got the better of it and locked our man in a hut until your boat brought him back.'

'What does your man say?'

'Well the funny thing is, he's not saying much at all. He's got a massive bruise down one side of his face, and he has clearly been the victim of a serious assault. You'd think he'd be telling his tale to the police as fast as he could get it out, but, nope. Doesn't want to talk to them. He's merely gone off on sick leave. People are nonplussed. Though I should say at once, the agency is mortally embarrassed by what has happened. Very anxious about the possible repercussions. But I think, most of all, still very concerned to defend Lanna from the threat of oil pollution, if this can be done.'

Gervase said: 'From our point of view, what makes the matter worse is that it was on the cards, with your Mr Lornie. You could see it coming, from the moment he left here. You know he came to Balnay, to discuss the trip?'

'I had heard, yes.'

'Not a happy visit. He got off on the wrong foot with Rollo from the word go. Tried to lay down the law to him about the reform of land ownership, which is one of his lordship's *bêtes noires*, like it is for all the Scottish aristocracy. They're very apprehensive about the proposals going through the new Parliament. They feel under assault. This was not a good time to put the matter to Rollo, not that there ever would be a good time. It verged on the unpleasant.'

'You were there?'

'I was.'

'What did Kenny say?'

'He was told by Rollo that he would be permitted to go to Lanna only under strict conditions, he must obey to the letter everything Fergus told him, and in particular, he was absolutely forbidden from setting foot anywhere on the island where Fergus said he could not go. He objected to this at once, saying that if he were to carry out a scientifically accurate census of the seabirds of Lanna he had to have free access to all of it, and Rollo told him this was not possible, and he said he could not see why. Rollo said he did not need to know why, merely that the island was private property and he could not have access to it as and when he chose, and Mr Lornie said that that was all very well but it was a state of affairs likely to be changed by the Scottish Parliament and Rollo said the *Scottish Parliament*? as if he were naming some particularly unspeakable disease, that collection of superannuated sociology lecturers sitting on their arses on The Mound? They are a laughing stock and their opinions are of consequence to no-one but themselves and Mr Lornie said yet the land reforms and the right of access they are bringing in will be real and Rollo said no-one but a few mad Marxists wants such measures and your man said, raising his voice, it is right that the Scottish people should have access to all of Scotland, I'm surprised he didn't call his lordship Citizen Macdonald, and I thought Rollo was going to explode. I did.' Gervase sipped his sherry. 'But he kept his temper, just, and he said, well now, Mr Lornie, you claim to speak for the Scottish people, may I ask you something and Lornie said, you may, and Rollo said to him, *A bheil Gaidhlig aghaibh?* meaning, do you have the Gallic? And Mr Lornie looked at him blankly and Rollo pursued, *Nan e Albannach a th'annaibh, ma ha?* meaning, are you not a Scotsman then? And with Mr Lornie still looking blank, Rollo said, I fail to see how you can speak for the Scottish people if you are unable to speak your own language and Mr Lornie went a shade of puce with anger.'

He sipped some more sherry.

'What… were the things Lord Kintyre was saying?'

'It was the Gallic.'

'Scottish Gaelic?'

Gervase nodded.

Lord Kintyre speaks it?'

'Fluently. He and Jamie, that's his elder brother who was killed, they had Gallic-speaking nursemaids from the isles. It's a family tradition. They had the Gallic before they had English.'

'And you speak it too, do you?'

'I'm having a go. I don't find it easy. Doesn't often sound like it's written and some of the grammar is jolly involved. The prepositional pronouns, in particular, are the very devil. But Lord Kintyre is fluent, and he said to Mr Lornie, your claim to speak for the Scottish people is contemptible nonsense and I am minded to bid you good day here and now, but for the fact that we are dealing with a wondrous place which is gravely threatened. He said, Lanna is closed, it is closed for a good reason, which is so that its purity may be maintained and it will not be polluted by human presence, but I am prepared to allow you on it briefly for the purposes of your agency preparing a defence against oil exploration in its vicinity, as long as you adhere strictly to the conditions I lay down. If you do not agree to these conditions, you will not go. Is that clear? There is no argument or discussion to be had, none whatsoever, so the matter is simple – do you agree to my conditions? And after a pause Mr Lornie, looking like he had swallowed a wasp I might say, said Yes, and Rollo said you will do exactly as you are told by Fergus and go only where he indicates you are permitted and nowhere else? And Mr Lornie said Yes again and Rollo said I have your word on that? And Mr Lornie said Yes once more, at which point Rollo got up and said then I bid you good day and left him to my tender loving care, to show him out. He did not deign to talk to me on the way to the front door and when I said goodbye he just glared at me and I thought, when this bugger gets on the island, there may be trouble. And so it has come to pass.'

'Well, well,' I said. And I wondered once again – why on earth had Kenny actually *come to blows* with the man he was supposed to be co-operating with? Why would he put the whole project at risk? When he obviously cared about it, himself?

I said: 'What about Fergus? What does he say about what happened?'

'Fergus? Tush. I fear I am not privy to the thoughts of Fergus Pryng.'

'Is that his name?'

'It is. And where Lanna is concerned, Fergus speaks only to Rollo, and Rollo speaks only to God.'

'D'you not know him?'

'I have met him just the once, here, quite recently. About five weeks ago. He came to see Rollo about something. Remarkable-looking cove.'

'So I've heard.'

'Huge man. Could have been a berserker in a Viking army, yet almost wholly taciturn and self-absorbed. Made no response whatsoever to my attempts at small talk. But the meeting – into which I was not allowed –was a different story. There were raised voices. I was in the adjoining room and couldn't help hearing them, they were actually shouting at each other, and let me say Miles, in the twenty months I have been working for the tenth Earl of Kintyre, I have heard him shout at a few people but I have never, ever, heard anyone shout back.'

'What were they arguing about?'

'It was to do with Lanna. I heard the word Lanna shouted, but I couldn't make out anything else. I think it may have been about arranging the trip by your agency because the correspondence started shortly thereafter. But I don't know for sure. Lanna is a mystery to me.'

'You haven't been yourself?'

'No, I have not, and it's a sore point.'

'Why's that?'

'I badly need to go for a book I'm trying to write. It's a history of the Kintyre Macdonalds. Rollo's branch of the clan. Ending with a portrait of the man himself. I'm sure there'll be a market for that, the Tiger Laird stuff is pretty sexy in publishing terms. But Rollo is the Laird of Lanna as well as everything else and the island means a lot to him, so I have to write something about it, and more than that, I have made a discovery in the library here which I like to think is in its own small way rather sensational in historical terms, and Lanna's at the heart of it.'

'What about?'

'You've heard of the Bruce? Robert the Bruce? Bannockburn and a' that?'

I nodded.

'Remember the story of the spider?'

'Remind me.'

'Robert the Bruce is sitting in a cave with his fortunes at their lowest ebb, thinking more or less, sod this for a game of soldiers, and he watches a spider struggling to weave its web.'

'Yes,' I said. 'Yes, I remember. And the spider keeps falling down but manages to do it in the end and Robert the Bruce sees that as a sort of er, symbol or whatever, of not giving up.'

'Exactly so. Bruce inspired. Scotland reanimated. English oppressor sent packing. Know where the cave was?'

'No idea.'

'Nobody does. See,' said Gervase, leaning back, steepling his fingertips together and becoming expansive, 'in the winter of 1306 The Bruce disappears from history. Only for a few months, but he does disappear. Beaten in two successive battles, first by the English, then by the Macdougalls, though he paid them back with interest at the Pass of Brander. Anyway. In 1306 Bruce had to take to the heather, as they say. Rather like the Mafia taking to the mattresses. Only damper. And he fled here to Argyll and threw himself on the mercy of Clan Donald and Angus Og, who was then their chief. Not boring you, am I?'

'Not in the slightest.'

'The Macdonalds hid him somewhere in the Isles, and he saw his spider and the rest is history.' He smiled. 'Now. Nobody knows his exact whereabouts, that winter. The best candidate for his hideout is Rathlin Island, off the Ulster coast. That's what John Barbour says in his poem. That's the tradition. But I don't think he was on Rathlin.' He looked pointedly at me.

I obliged him. 'No?'

'I think your man was on Lanna.'

'Really?'

'There's a medieval book called The Lanna Chronicle, the chronicle that the monks wrote on the island, and there's a copy here in the library. It's in Latin but I've been going through it with the help of a Victorian translation, and there is this entry for 1306.'

He passed me a piece of paper he had on his desk. On it was written: *Hoc anno ad insulam advenit dominus magnus, qui per totam hiemem mansit.*

'Shall I translate?'

'If you would.'

'In this year a great lord came to the island, who remained throughout the winter. What d'you make of that?'

'I couldn't really say.'

'It's obvious. It must be The Bruce. The great lord who remained throughout the winter. It's exactly the right time, and he's not named, because they're keeping his identity a secret. All makes perfect sense. Lanna was the remotest spot in all the Western Isles, inaccessible, safe, and the story of a cave is probably just to throw people off the scent. A monastery would be much nearer the truth. It's sensational. It fills in one of the last empty pages of Scottish history. But to write all this properly I've got to go to the blasted island, can you see that?'

'Yes I can,' I said truthfully.

'I need to go there, I need to look at it, wander over the ruins and get a feel for it, and Rollo won't bloody well let me. Why on earth not?'

I shook my head.

'Just gives me a flat No. *Sorry Gervase, Lanna's out of bounds.* Why, for God's sake? Why to me? What's he think I'm going to do there, steal seabirds' eggs? Dig for Spanish gold?'

'Have you told him about your Robert The Bruce theory?'

'Of course I've told him. Something that would redound vastly to the credit of the Kintyre Macdonalds. People who saved Scotland's greatest national hero. Take a bow, Rollo. I've even shown him the entry from the chronicle, I took him into the library to show him the actual manuscript. Makes not a blind bit of difference. *Sorry Gervase, No can do. Jolly interesting theory. But Lanna's off limits.* I say, but Rollo, I'm your family historian. One likes to think one is a trusted retainer. Just smiles and shakes his head. Why keep me off and let Fergus Prying on? And especially, when my great-uncle wrote the book on the blasted place.'

'Was that ... *Lanna: The Lost Island?*'

'It was. Melrose Crinan. Great-uncle Melrose. My grandfather's brother. You know it?'

'I read it just a few days ago.'

'Did you really? Jolly good. Quite hard to get hold of these days. Style's a little on the flowery side, don't you think, though historically it's pretty solid. But old Melrose, God bless him, missed the Bruce reference completely. I've got it all to myself. This is a genuinely significant historical discovery and all I need is a day or so on the island to flesh it out and Rollo won't let me on. He won't let me on. He won't let me on.'

Gervase's frustration seemed to be verging on distress.

'It's not right. I don't understand it. The estate boat goes out every week or so to resupply Fergus and I could hop aboard that, easiest thing in the world, but Rollo says no. Why? What earthly reason can he have to refuse? Is he hiding something there? Does he have a secret? Does he have a mistress on the island?'

'Beats me,' I said.

'It beats me too. But here am I, and there is Fergus in his splendid isolation. Fergus The Solitary, King of Lanna! Monarch of all he surveys, with the run of the place, and all he does is keep the trippers off and write a report every year about the seabirds. I would be making a contribution to history. It's not fair. It jolly well isn't fair. Anyway.' He gave a wry smile. 'I'm forgetting myself. I've allowed myself to run on. I'm so sorry.'

'Not at all.'

'It's just that, one is quite isolated here, not surrounded by chums, so I suppose when a like-minded soul turns up out of the blue like you have done, one is perhaps tempted to unburden oneself a little too freely. My sincere apologies, Miles.'

'Not at all, Gervase.'

He checked his watch again. 'They should be winding up soon. We can wander down there if you like. It's quite a spectacle.'

'What is?'

'Chaps playing with tigers.'

Gervase was naturally loquacious, and with his loquacity boosted by a like-minded soul turning up out of the blue, as he put it, and his own tendency to gossip, he went on to tell me various things, including some he shouldn't have done.

Walking through a long, walled formal garden, lined with lavender beds not yet in flower, he said: 'The present Earl of Kintyre's by no means a typical Scottish peer, you do realise that?'

'Why?

'The Scottish aristocracy don't open zoos.'

'No?'

'Let alone get on friendly terms with fearsome beasts. They do the opposite. They hunt things. They run sporting estates. They charge people to come and fish for salmon and shoot grouse and stalk the stag on the hill. Balnay was a renowned sporting estate, one of the most illustrious in Argyll. The ninth Earl, Rollo's father, brought off a celebrated Macnab here in 1967.'

'A what?'

'A Macnab. When one kills a salmon, stalks a stag and shoots a brace of grouse, all in one day.'

'Right.'

'But when Rollo inherited, he got rid of it all, the fishing, the stalking, the shooting, he stopped the lot and started his zoo instead.' Gervase picked a sprig of lavender to sniff. 'Sorry. Mustn't call it a zoo. Try to remember. Wildlife park. Captive breeding centre.'

'Why did he do that?'

'Well, this explains it all.'

Before us, at the end of the walled garden, was an arbour, a rose bower set back from the path, and at its centre appeared to be a statue: it was a bust on a stone plinth. I approached it and peered and saw the bronze head of a young man. Underneath was a carved inscription. It said:

Captain The Viscount Balnay   September 6, 1953 – June 14, 1982
He was a verray parfit gentil knight

And below that was carved, in smaller lettering:

Chan eil aoibhneas gun Chlann Domhnaill

'That's Jamie,' said Gervase. 'His lordship's elder brother. The one who should have inherited.'

I saw an austere, unsmiling young face.

'Viscount Balnay,' Gervase explained, 'is the courtesy title for the heir to the earldom.'

'And he died?'

'Killed in the Falklands war.'

'Was he now?'

'Captain in the Scots Guards. When they stormed Mount Tumbledown. His father and grandfather had each won Military

Crosses with the regiment in the two world wars and Jamie was out to win an MC for himself. He stopped an Argy bullet instead.'

I peered again at the inscription.

Gervase said: 'The Chaucer is appropriate, of course, but I find the Gallic more moving.'

'The phrase beneath it?'

'Yes.'

'What does it mean?'

'There is no joy without Clan Donald.'

I stood musing on it, looking at the young face, set and determined.

'Broke his father's heart, they say. The old boy died the same year.'

'So Rollo…became the heir? And then, succeeded to the title?'

'Certainly did,' Gervase said. 'The second son succeeded. Which explains everything.'

'Does it? How come?'

'Because Jamie was brought up from his earliest years knowing he would inherit, and Rollo from his earliest years knew that he would not. So you have two completely different mindsets. One is a mindset of awesome responsibility and seriousness. You are destined to be a great figure, not only a nobleman, but to be a clan chief, to be the father of your people – that's what clann means in the Gallic, it means children – whereas your younger sibling is not destined to be anything in particular, and must scrabble about for an identity. Not great. You get jealously. You get a divide. With Jamie and Rollo the divide was widened because they took against each other. It was partly because Rollo was very fond of animals from an early age and kept wild creatures as pets, and Jamie was much fonder of shooting them and thought his brother was not manly enough, and it worsened when their mother died.'

I thought back to the biography I had been studying.

'Wasn't she an American?'

'Sally Mossbacher. Heir to the Mossbacher brewery fortune. The belle of the Virginia hunt country. Rollo was much closer to her than he was to his father, and when she died, he was only 18 and he was inconsolable. I got all this from him one night, sitting around drinking his Glenfiddich. Eventually the old man and Jamie told him he had grieved long enough and to pull his socks up and he told them to do something unrepeatable. It was a real rift and Rollo went off, he went his own way, pursued his path trying to help the great beasts, working for various wildlife and conservation charities with not a lot of money to his name, then suddenly when he's 27, bingo! An Argentinian bullet hands him the earldom. And he finds he is in a position to start a zoo and put his er, rather recherché ideas about tickling tigers' tummies into practice. If either Jamie or his father could see what he's done with the estate, they'd be horrified. They would turn in their graves. Shall we peruse it?'

We left the garden and walked out into its park itself, a rolling landscape of low hills and forest with extensive enclosures scattered about it: in one of them I could see a herd of deer, or perhaps they were antelopes, and in another, something that looked like a tapir. And not far away to my right was the tall crane I had glimpsed from the road, lowering over a substantial construction site which seemed to be full of men busily working: I could hear clankings and grindings issuing from it. There was a substantial low-rise building going up, covered in scaffolding.

'Tell me what all that is,' I said, pointing, as Gervase led the way down a path. 'I got stuck behind one of the lorries going into that. Huge great truck.'

'That,' said Gervase, 'is Kintyre's Folly. At least, that is how I privately refer to it.'

'Why's it a folly?'

'It is a building with the all the characteristics of an eighteenth-century Gentleman's Folly, such as extravagance and impracticability, yet it is more foolish than any of those.'

'What is it?'

'It is officially an aquarium. That is what it said on the planning permission. That's what the staff have been told. That's how it's been reported in *The Oban Times*.'

'Well that's all right, isn't it? Wouldn't that be quite a tourist draw, quite an addition to the wildlife park?'

'Were it truly an aquarium, perhaps so.'

'But it isn't?'

'It is not.'

'What is it?'

'You will not guess what it really is. In secret, mind.'

'You'll have to tell me.'

'A penguin pool.'

'*A penguin pool?*'

'And not just any penguin pool. The best, most luxurious penguin pool in the whole world. It seats 400 people, on two levels for viewing, one above and one below the surface of the water. There has never been anything like it.'

'So why's it a secret? Why the aquarium story?'

'You will have to ask Rollo. Its true purpose is known only to a tiny handful of people. I would guess that he wants to announce it with éclat, so it may burst upon an astonished world, as it were.'

'Why's he doing it?'

'To restore the fortunes of Balnay. Look, Miles,' said Gervase. 'I shouldn't really tell you this, but Rollo is broke. He's in debt up to his eyeballs. His problem is that feeding all these blasted animals – there are more than four hundred of them – costs an unbelievable amount of dosh, week in, week out, never mind the staff costs and everything else, and he simply hasn't got it any more. The admission charges don't nearly cover it. It swallowed up his income years ago and now he's used up his capital, he's gone through the Mossbacher brewery millions which came with his mother, and this is some sort of desperate last throw. He thinks thousands of punters are going to flock to it.'

'Flock to his penguin pool?'

'That's what he thinks.'

'What do you think?'

'I think it's crackers,' said Gervase. 'Penguins are fine by me, but I do rather have the feeling that when you've seen one penguin, you've seen 'em all. I do not think folk will head here from the four corners of the land as Rollo presumes. I do not think it is *vaut le détour*, never mind *vaut le voyage*, despite the fact that he's spending twenty-three million pounds on it.'

'Jesus. I thought you said he needed money?'

'He's been selling off his paintings to finance it. Old Masters which have hung on the castle walls. In some cases, for centuries.'

'Really?'

'He's sold a Tintoretto, a Guido Reni, a Poussin and two Canalettos. Or should that be Canaletti? Plus a lovely Allan Ramsay. He's tried to do it anonymously, in different sale rooms, to avoid attention, but people know, of course. I've been involved with a lot of it. I think it's a sad business.'

I said: 'And when's it all going to be finished? The … supposed aquarium?'

'Ah. Well. There's been a problem there. It's taken more than a year and it was due to be completed on the first of April. That date was set in stone. But some time in February they discovered a crack opening up in the floor of the pool and they found they'd buggered up the foundations – I think they might have used the wrong sort of cement or something – and they realised they'd have to do it all again. Rollo was incandescent. He wanted it open in time for the start of the tourist season at Easter. Now they have another unmissable target for the handover, which is the first of June.'

'But … that's in three days' time. Will they make it?'

'They're very close. The men are working round the clock, working through the night under floodlights, on double pay. Rollo is on the site and on the phone to the builders every single day. I have to say, he is consumed with it. With his Folly.'

'Are there any penguins here yet?'

'If there are, I haven't seen them, though Rollo is employing two South African chaps as consultants. Marine biologists from the Cape. Penguin wranglers, so to speak. Sinister-looking fellows, I have to say. They're here.'

I said: 'So Gervase, tell me, if it *doesn't* work, if people don't come in their thousands to see his new penguin pool, what happens to Lord Kintyre then?'

'Then, I think the truth is, his lordship goes under. Like penguins do, in fact. But penguins come back up, don't they?'

'Indeed they do.'

'I doubt if Rollo will.'

18

Knowing what I now knew about the Laird of Lanna made the sight
of him a few minutes later even more riveting, but it was someone
else I glimpsed first: I saw a woman being chased by a tiger.

She was running away in the middle of a high-fenced enclosure,
a young woman in a royal blue tracksuit with long black hair tied
at the back, and the tiger, a tiger that seemed to me absolutely
enormous, an immense striped mass of rippling muscle, was
cantering at her heels; it reared up in its hind legs, towering over
her from behind, and brought its front paws down on her shoulders
on either side of her neck. The woman opened her mouth to scream.
But what came out was a laugh, in fact a peal of laughter as she
tottered around with the great beast on her shoulders.

I was dumbstruck.

'That's the new Countess,' Gervase whispered. 'Nancy Cipriano,
as was. Tiger expert from San Diego Zoo.'

She turned and managed to wriggle out from under the tiger's
grasp and as it came back down on to all fours she caught its ears and
ruffled them vigorously like one would do with a well-loved retriever.
She was face on to me then; she was slim and remarkably pretty.

'Quite a looker, isn't she?' I whispered back to Gervase.

'His lordship is besotted.'

Then two men came into sight, both smiling; they came up to
the animal and ruffled its fur themselves. One of them, tall and
well-built with a stiff bearing, wore the same blue tracksuit and I
watched in disbelief as the animal reared up to his face and began
to lick him, vigorously, again like the family pet dog.

'That's Rollo in the blue tracksuit,' Gervase murmured.

'Who's the other guy?'

'Tony Barlow, the head tiger keeper.'

In the middle of the enclosure was a tall wooden ramp and
the three of them moved towards it with the tiger following, and

they took it in turns to run up the ramp with the great cat running alongside them and then grabbing them around the waist in what was clearly a familiar game.

'That is a quite amazing animal,' I said.

'We have nineteen of them. This must be Shura. The new Siberian tigress whose measure they are taking. Though, might *tigress* be politically incorrect now, like actress? Should one just say tiger, whatever the sex? What d'you think?'

I was too busy thinking what an extraordinary man this was, he who had power over my fate; and in that moment he caught sight of us and waved to Gervase and called: 'Another fifteen minutes. See you in the library.'

The library of Castle Balnay was a sumptuous room of grand proportions, although I noticed, now that Gervase had told me about the Old Masters, that there were two rather obvious empty spaces on the walls. We sat on a sofa and I drank it all in and I said: 'Tell me Gervase, how did you come to work for Lord Kintyre?'

It was through his father, he said, who was a prominent Edinburgh solicitor and the Earl's personal lawyer. 'And he's head of the firm, Sandy Crinan is senior partner of Crinan and Crinan of Melville Street, and I'm his only son and he's desperate for me to carry it on, and the long and the short of it is, I don't want to. Ever heard of a thing called the Signet?'

I shook my head.

'It's the old royal seal that was appended to legal documents in Scotland, and senior lawyers in Edinburgh became known as Writers to the Signet. And there's still a Society of Writers to Her Majesty's Signet, ceremonial thing largely, and the members are the crème de la crème of Edinburgh law and they put WS after their names. And my old pa is a big noise in it, Sandy Crinan was Deputy Keeper of the Signet, which is as high as you can go, and I just know he will not die happy unless he sees me become Gervase Crinan, WS. But I just can't face it.'

'Why not?'

'Och, I can't face the life of an Edinburgh lawyer. You know? With the perfect Georgian office in the New Town. The perfect scalloped fanlight over the door. And lunch at the New Club. Tea with the other partners. Weekend golf at Muirfield. The same social round, the Holyrood garden party, the summer ball at the Signet library, the annual dinner in Highland dress, all with the same people from the same social group who all went to Fettes or Loretto or the Academy, God, it would drive me completely crazy, it's just so stultifying. It wasn't for me.'

'What was for you?'

Gervase hesitated for the first time since our meeting, just ever so slightly. He said: 'I've always wanted to write.' To write creatively, he said, but he hadn't managed it – and a couple of years earlier he had come home from a long period abroad rather at a loss, and his father suggested to Rollo that he had an idle young writer on his hands, and what if he were to write a history of the Earl's branch of the clan? And Rollo agreed. I think he fancied the idea of having his own amanuensis, his own Boswell, and my old pa no doubt thought, this will make the son and heir settle down and see sense at last and become a lawyer after all. Gervase Crinan, WS. Though I fear I won't, even if I hate the idea of my dear old dad dying unhappy.'

'And he's Kintyre's lawyer still?'

'Yes, although they had a row a few weeks ago. Curious business. Rollo asked him for an opinion on whether he owned the seabirds of Lanna.'

'Whether he *owned* them?'

'That's right. And my pa said he probably did, although there might be some doubt, and Rollo hit the roof, he said he didn't want an opinion with doubt in it, he just wanted a piece of paper from a lawyer saying all the seabirds of Lanna were his and he could legally do what he damn well pleased with them and if my pa couldn't give it, he would find someone else who would, which my pa found insulting and he told Rollo so. Rollo apologised. They came to some agreement. But it was unfortunate. My old pa was quite upset.'

I was about to ask him why on earth the Earl of Kintyre would want to be sure he could do whatever he wanted with the seabirds of his island when the door opened and the man himself walked in.

We got up. Gervase said: 'Rollo, allow me to introduce Dr Miles Bonnici. We were contemporaries at the university.'

'Really?' said Kintyre. 'The House?'

'I was across the road.'

'Pembroke?'

'Yes.'

'Were you now?' he said, offering his hand. 'We used to call Pembroke the Christ Church stables.' He laughed briefly: a white flash. 'And before Oxford, pray?'

I told him.

'Hmph,' he said. 'Hotbed of lefties, that place. But at least you appear to be a properly educated young man. In contrast to the violent vulgarian your agency initially saw fit to wish upon us. Do sit down. Gervase, can we sort out some tea? Tea all right?'

'Absolutely.'

Gervase glided out. His lordship sat down opposite me, and I realised what was striking about him: his teeth, perfect brilliant white teeth which flashed every time he opened his mouth, so that he always seemed to be smiling. But his mood was in the eyes. They were not smiling at all.

'Do you know this execrable man Lornie?' he was saying. 'The most perfect shit, in every way. Ill-mannered, arrogant, aggressive, more or less a Marxist.'

'Not really,' I said. 'He's a colleague of course, but a distant one. We're in different departments.'

'Remarkable. Came here first and tried to lay down the law to us. I sent him away with a flea in his ear, but I should have insisted on him being replaced then and there. My own bloody fault. And *then* he goes to the island and attacks my warden. Outrageous. Well, he bit off more than he could chew with Fergus, and serve him right. Why on earth did you send him in the first place?'

'I believe his main qualification was that he is said to have the best bird identification skills of anyone in UKOCA.'

'Is he now?' said Kintyre. 'Hmmm. The best bird identification skills, you say?'

'Apparently.'

'Tell me, er, Doctor, is it Doctor Bonnici?'

'Yes but it doesn't matter.'

'Tell me, what *exactly* did Lornie say about what, what had happened on Lanna?'

'As far as I am aware he merely told Ramsay Wishart, the UKOCA director, that he had an altercation with your warden which turned violent.'

'But did he say *why* he had the altercation?'

'Some sort of argument about where he could and could not go. I think that he admits that he struck the first blow.'

'And that was it?'

'As far as I'm aware.'

'Nothing else about the island itself?'

'Such as?'

'Well, about, ah, what he might have ah, seen there, for example?'

'Not that I know of.'

'You haven't spoken to him yourself?'

'I had the briefest of encounters with him. Which in fact was unpleasant.'

'And he said nothing specific?'

'Not that I remember.'

What I remember now, in fact, is that Kenny had said, *I know what's there*. But I did not remember it then.

Gervase glided back in and sat down. 'Tea on the way,' he said.

'So where is Lornie now?' said Kintyre. 'What is happening with him?'

'He's gone off on what might be called sick leave. He has a fracture of the cheekbone.'

'Excellent! Hear that, Gervase?'

'Yes indeed, Rollo.'

'Serve the bastard right. Hope it hurts. And before going off, did he make an official statement about what happened?'

'I think he was going to, but if he did, I haven't seen it.'

Kintyre drummed his fingers on the table. He looked me in the eyes. I held his gaze. He said: 'And so, when your agency has made such a comprehensive bloody cock-up of this business, you come here now, Dr Bonnici, expecting me to agree to your going to Lanna, in his place?'

'I have come, Lord Kintyre, to argue the case for the seabird survey on Lanna to be finished, in spite of what has happened, about which the agency is greatly embarrassed and profusely apologetic, and to argue that I am capable of carrying it out, without any further mishaps.'

'And what would the thrust of your argument?'

'First, that the seabirds of Lanna are worth saving, something which I myself of course can only take on hearsay.'

'Oh they are, Dr Bonnici, they are.' He seemed to be weighing me up. He said: 'Lanna is a jewel of the natural world, a quite astounding phenomenon. It is overflowing with life. The seabird numbers are scarce to be believed: Fergus estimates well over a quarter of a million. But that is by no means all. The principal point about Lanna is that it is untouched, and by that I mean, that it is untouched by people, in a world which people are polluting and destroying ever more, every day.'

There was a knock on the door and a middle-aged woman came in with a large tray. 'Thank you Agnes,' said Kintyre, as Gervase took the tray from her, set out the cups and began pouring.

'The point about Lanna,' Kintyre said, 'is that it is the one small part of the world where I have direct power to exclude human beings and their contamination, and thus keep it in its unpolluted state, and it is a power I will continue to exercise. It is why I sent Fergus Pryng there, soon after I came into my inheritance. My grandfather had good practical reasons for closing the island, which my father followed, but I keep it closed for what I beg to think is a profounder reason: that in a world which is ever more despoiled, it is one small, remote and exquisite place, where the writ of human contamination does not run.'

He sipped his tea. Then he looked at me and said: 'You will understand therefore, Dr Bonnici, that I see permission for any outsider to go to Lanna as a wholly exceptional privilege.'

I nodded.

'Even Gervase here, who has one might say, good reason to go, has been denied.' He turned to him. 'Be patient, Gervase. Your time will come, soon enough.'

'Thank you Rollo,' said Gervase, surprised.

'So why, Dr Bonnici, I ask you – why, when the privilege which was granted so exceptionally to your colleague Lornie was so foully abused, with all the undertakings he gave shown to be utterly worthless, should I make the same mistake again?'

Gervase was watching me keenly.

I said: 'Might I reply by asking you a question in return?'

'Go ahead.'

'Have you ever seen an oiled seabird, Lord Kintyre?'

Kintyre paused. He thought. He said: 'I ... don't think so. Not personally. No.'

I said: 'I think it would be fair to say that if you see an oiled seabird close up, there are few sights in nature which are more appalling. Because seabirds are masters of flight, or masters of swimming, they're all masters of movement in one way or another, and crude oil renders them helpless, and in the most gruesome, filthy way. It just destroys them, but slowly, it is the most terrible lingering death. Oil's not something they've evolved alongside so they have no way of coping with it, they're completely defenceless, and with a major oil spill thousands of birds can be affected – I witnessed such a one six months ago, it was the *Erika*, the tanker which went down in the Bay of Biscay and I saw countless, countless birds which were barely recognisable even as having been living creatures. You know what they'd become? They were just lumps of sludge, hideous lumps of agonised sludge, and I tell you, Lord Kintyre, I will never forget it.'

Arty Booboo had come into my mind.

Kintyre was looking fixedly at me.

I said: 'If an oil well is sited in the vicinity of Lanna it will present an enormous danger to its seabirds, either from a blow-out with the well itself or from a tanker accident. My agency finds it scarcely believable that the Government's energy people are even willing to contemplate the idea, but presumably that is partly because Lanna's birds have never been formally surveyed and so remain officially an unknown quantity. It is an anomaly we are all aware of, and I know you have had your reasons for keeping the island out of bounds, but now this anomaly is putting Lanna and its seabird populations at risk. But the risk can be avoided, Lord Kintyre. In UKOCA we are convinced that the inclusion of the Lanna block in the bidding round is a 'try-on', and a well-founded objection, such as we are preparing, will scupper it. But to make it, we have to have a formal scientific survey of the island's birds, even a minimal one. We are of course only too aware of how … of how lamentably the recent business ended, yet we still believe that we should carry through and finish the survey, and that with it, we can end the threat to Lanna, once and for all.'

Kintyre looked at me for long seconds. He said: 'You are certainly articulate, Dr Bonnici.'

'I'm merely stating the facts of the case.'

'Then tell me: what guarantee do we have that you yourself will co-operate fully with Fergus? For if I do allow you to go, you must be bound by him in everything. In your movements above all.'

'I can't see why I wouldn't, Lord Kintyre. I can't answer for Kenny Lornie. I've no idea what made him behave the way he did, other than the fact that I personally know him to be a volatile character. But I can't see why I wouldn't go along with Fergus in everything he wants. And you can take your own view of me, can't you? Here I am, sitting before you. And may I say' – and I smiled – 'you have already passed favourable judgement on something of mine.'

'Ah yes, your book on promiscuity. The seahorses book. I reviewed it, didn't I? Your director reminded me, and I looked it up. Yes, it was well done.'

I didn't have anything more to say.

Kintyre was weighing it in his mind. He turned and said: 'What do you think, Gervase?'

'Well, Rollo, I have to say, as someone who has several times tried to make a case for going to Lanna without success, the case that Miles has just made seems to me unassailable. The oil danger is clearly real.'

'Yes,' said Kinytre. 'Yes. Yes. Hmmm. Very well. Very well, Dr Bonnici, you have indeed made your case, and I am minded to let you go. But listen to me now. You must do exactly as Fergus Pryng says, and in particular with regard to your movements. There are areas of Lanna which are out of bounds to everyone. If Fergus says you are not to go somewhere, you are absolutely not to go there. Do I have your solemn assurance on that point?'

'Certainly.'

'Furthermore, there is another condition: you are not to take a camera to Lanna. Do you agree to that?'

'I do.'

'If you take a camera and Fergus discovers it, your stay will be terminated instantly. Do you understand?'

'I do, yes.'

I was nearly there.

'Very well,' his lordship was saying, and about to get to his feet, and I half-interrupted him. 'Lord Kintyre, there is one more matter.'

'Yes?'

'I daresay you will find this tiresome. I hope you will not think it is presumptuous. But it is necessary. There is a condition, on my side.'

'I beg your pardon?' said the earl, his eyes hardening.

'What happened on the island between Fergus and Kenny Lornie was dreadful, and one of the difficult aspects of it is that there were no independent witnesses. It is clear to me that your warden, who may have the best intentions, is nevertheless a man capable of violence, and I feel it would be very unwise now if I were to go back there alone.'

'So what are you saying?'

'I am saying I would like to take a companion with me. As a precaution. As a witness. I think the situation is unprecedented, and it calls for that.'

'No. No. Not at all. We have said all along, only one person from UKOCA. That's the deal. Take it or leave it, Dr Bonnici.'

'I have anticipated you. I'm not proposing anyone from UKOCA.'

'Then whom are you proposing?'

'A woman. An old friend. Her name is Jenny Pittaway. She's a New Zealander. She's slightly younger than me, a good swimmer and she can handle boats.'

'And is this woman an ornithologist?' said Kintyre.

'She is not, unfortunately. But she's full of common sense.'

'No,' said the earl again, shaking his head. 'No.'

'Then I'm afraid I will be unable to go. I'm very sorry.' And as my plan began to fall apart, at that very moment the door opened, and in walked the woman I had seen being chased by a tiger, half an hour earlier. She must have showered: she looked wonderfully fresh in a white blouse and cream slacks, with her long black hair falling around her shoulders; I noticed the huge diamond ring on her wedding finger. We all got to our feet. 'Darling, this is Dr Bonnici, from the offshore conservation people and we are just discussing Lanna,' said Kintyre. 'Dr Bonnici, my wife.'

She held out a hand. 'Hi,' she said. 'Nancy Kintyre. You talking about his silly old island? He gets so damn worked up about it. I've been having to calm him down.'

'Well, it's a difficult situation,' I said.

'What is?'

'Lord Kintyre has agreed to me going out to finish off the seabird survey so we can object to the government plans for oil drilling, but I'm afraid that I've insisted on taking a companion with me, because of the, er, the unfortunate … you heard about the, er … the fight? Between Fergus and my colleague?'

'Yeah,' she said. 'Kinda crazy. And you wanna take somebody with you?'

'Just as a witness, really. In case there's any more trouble. A woman friend who is very level-headed.'

'Sounds good to me. What's the problem?'

'Lord Kintyre's not keen on the idea.'

'What's not to like, Rollo?' said the countess.

His lordship was actually put on the spot. I wouldn't have believed it if I hadn't seen it. He seemed to be tongue-tied.

'Come on, Rollo, what's so terrible about this? Not keen to have a woman on your precious island, that it?' She turned to me: 'I sometimes think it's like his man-cave.'

'Of course it isn't,' said Kintyre, greatly irritated.

'Then why don't you let her go?'

Kintyre snorted. 'Very well,' he said. 'Very well, Dr Bonnici. You win. You may take your friend with you to Lanna. But she will be subject to exactly the same restrictions as you, you understand that?'

'Of course. Thank you.'

'And now if you will excuse me, we have other matters to discuss. Gervase, show Dr Bonnici out, would you? Good day to you, sir.'

I was there.

Well. Nearly there.

M comes to ask Lord Kintyre if he can do seabird survey.
No camera wants to take J

19

It was midnight when I got back to Aberdeen and fell into bed exhausted, but I went in to see Ramsay first thing the next morning and found him awaiting my return with anxiety.

'Well?' he said. 'Well?'

'It's a Yes.'

'Great. Fantastic, Miles. Well done.'

'But with a condition.'

'What's that?'

'I said to Kintyre that I would only go if I could go with someone else. Because clearly this Fergus character is in some way unstable and may be prone to violence. And after some to-ing and fro-ing, he saw the point of that, and agreed.'

'He agreed to somebody else going?'

'He did.'

'Well done. Bloody well done. Very sensible. Before, he was totally insistent we could only send one person. Who d'ye want to take? Roddy Baird in Seabirds would be the best choice. Or even Sidney himself if Roddy can't manage it.'

'Ah well, there's a bit of a problem there.'

'What's that?'

'They won't agree to anyone else from the agency.'

'Eh?'

'Only me, from UKOCA, on the island.'

'So who … who's going to be the second person?'

'We compromised. I suggested this old friend, a woman, a friend from way back, science degree, good swimmer, knows how to handle boats. Very suitable in every way. I'm going to ask her. If she'll come I'm happy to go, but otherwise, Ramsay, I think the whole enterprise is just too risky.'

Ramsay bit a nail. He said: 'Christ, this is very irregular, Miles. It really is. But then' – he shook his head – 'the whole thing is becoming a very bad business. Know what's happened now? Kenny's disappeared. Ye believe it?'

'Disappeared?'

'He cannae be found anywhere. None of the staff can locate him. He's not at his home. And I need to talk to him urgently, I need him to put his formal account of what happened on Lanna in writing, between him and Fergus. It's damn serious situation. Where the hell's he gone? And now you come along and say ye want to go out there with some old girlfriend like it was a romantic weekend. Very irregular indeed.'

I was about to protest at Ramsay's perfectly accurate portrayal of the situation when he continued: 'But ye know what? I'm past caring. I'm past playing it by the book. All I care about is saving Lanna from having a fucking oil field next to it. And if you can bring back a seabirds report that'll let us do that, I don't care how ye get it.'

I went back to my office immediately, locked the door, and phoned Lotte at home in Wimbledon. There was no answer. I tried her every hour and at one o'clock she picked up.

'Lot?' I said.

'Milo! Lovely boy! How the devil are you?'

'I'm fine,' I said. 'Fine. Look, er, something's come up.'

'What's come up? Nothing bad I hope?'

'No, nothing bad. I don't really know how to put this other than to say, the time has come.'

'What time?'

'The time for me to contact Jenny.'

'Ah,' said Lotte. 'That time. I've been wondering when that time was coming.'

'Will you help me? Will you put me in touch with her?'

Lotte was clearly pained. 'Why now, Miles? It's still very soon after everything. She's trying to recover. She's trying to rebuild.'

'Please.'

'I really don't think the contact would help her.'

'Lotte, look. You accept, don't you, that sooner or later I have to try to put things right?'

'Yes. I do accept that.'

'Well one of the things I'm certain of, is that I will only get one shot at it.'

'That's probably a reasonable assumption.'

'So I have to do it the right way. And something has come up, that sort of offers me the best chance I think I will ever have, of … beginning to mend things.'

'What is it?'

'I – I don't really want to go into it. But it's a proposition. It's a proposition I want to put to her, which is a very special one. It's unique, really, and I think it's now or never.'

'Hmmm.'

'Will you help me, Lotte? Please?'

She was torn.

'Will you?'

She said: 'I'll have to think about it.'

'Why?'

'I can't just say yes on the spot. I'm going to have to think very hard about this, Miles.'

I said: 'The way this works, Lot, I would sort of need to know by this evening.'

She sighed. 'All right. Call me here at seven. But listen. The answer may well be No. All right?'

'OK,' I said, crossing my fingers. And once again, all afternoon, I held my breath. But when I called back, the answer was Yes.

She said: 'My main thought is, I suppose if not now, then when?'

'Absolutely,' I said.

'So, OK, I will put you in touch with her. But there's a strict condition.'

'What is it?'

'If she turns you down, you will let it go at that. Right? For ever. You won't bother her ever again. Not once. And you won't do anything like stalking her, God forbid, because if you do, Miles, it is finished between you and me. For good.'

'Lotte,' I said, I swear to you, I swear on, on – on Mum's goodness – that if she says No to me, I will never trouble her again. Not for a second.'

'Very well,' she said. 'Got a pen?' And she read out a telephone number.

It was a London number.

I said: 'When could I try her?'

'You could try her maybe in about an hour.'

'OK. Lot?'

'What?'

'I'll never be able to thank you enough.'

'Just remember what I said to you, brother.'

I had an hour to prepare myself, so all through those long, long minutes I psyched myself up, I marshalled my arguments, I thought about my words, I thought about my tone. And then it was time.

I had never been more nervous.

I dialled Jenny's number with a trembling hand.

She answered immediately.

I said: 'Jenny?'

'Yes?'

'It's Miles. Miles Bonnici.'

There was a gasp, a little explosion of breath – 'Oh!' – and she slammed the phone down.

I was at a loss.

I phoned Lotte.

Lotte's phone was engaged.

I tried her every few seconds for fully five minutes and eventually she answered and I blurted out: 'She hung up on me as soon as she heard my voice.'

'I know. I've just been speaking to her. What d'you expect? She's very upset.'

'God. What can I do? Have I blown it?'

'It was a terrible shock to her. And she realised I must have given you her number, and she was very upset with me. But I asked her, I said I knew it was an enormous ask, but would she listen to what you had to say? Just hear you out. And in the end, she was very reluctant, but she said she would.'

'Really?'

'Yes.'

'Can I ring her again?'

'You can, but give it fifteen minutes or so, to let her get her breath back, so to speak. It was a very big shock. You can try her then, and I think she will speak to you. I think.'

'Oh Lot, thanks a million.'

'Be calm, Miles. Just take it very easy.'

'I will.'

I waited the fifteen minutes then dialled her number again.

She answered. She said in a level tone: 'Hello.'

'Jenny? It's Miles.'

'Yes Miles, I realise it is, because I've just been speaking to Lotte and cursing her for giving you my number, she was way out of order because you must surely realise I want nothing whatsoever to do with you now or at any future moment of my life, I can't *tell* you how much I want nothing to do with you, but she informs me you have a little proposition to put to me and she has asked me if I would listen to it, so only out of the regard I have for your sister I went against all my better judgement and said I would. So why don't you put it to me? Eh? Miles? Your little proposition? I'm all ears.'

I know what I should have said, calmly and deliberately: that unlikely as it might seem, a lot of things had changed in my life and I had come to realise that I had behaved appallingly towards people, and to her, Jenny, above all, and I wanted to make a very tentative approach to see if I could go any way to begin to make amends; but what I actually said was well there's this island see it's called Lanna and it's way out beyond the Hebrides it's the remotest island in Britain and no one can get on it although you can get on it physically but I mean you're not actually allowed on it 'cos it's closed by the owners that's Lord Kintyre who keeps the tigers at his castle and it's called the lost island and it's the hardest island to get on to in all of Britain maybe even in the world and I'm going out there to survey the seabirds and I, I wondered ...

'Yes?'

'I wondered ...'

'Wondered what?'

'If you'd like to come with me.'

There was a pause, in which I could hear my own heart beating. Then Jenny said: 'Has somebody just dumped you, Miles?'

'No Jenny, it's not like that.'

'Some piece of tartan totty?' Some Aberdonian babe?'

'No.'

'Has she just cut your balls off with a nice sharp pair of Scottish shears?'

'No, no, no.'

'You feeling *particularly* down tonight? At a *particularly* low ebb?'

'It's not like that.'

'Then what is it like, Miles?'

I was terrified of inarticulacy; I knew I had but a few moments and if I got it wrong, bye-bye, that would be the end of everything, but all I could say was: 'It's just, it's that I know what I am, Jenny. I know what I've been.'

'And what is that?'

'A shit. Awful. Terrible. A shit to everybody but most of all a shit to you.'

'Really? And how did you come by that conclusion?'

'I, I just saw it one day. I just understood.'

'What, like in a vision? Did you have a little vision? A little vision of shittiness?'

'Well – sort of, I suppose.' It wasn't going well. I was starting to feel stupid.

'And when was this, Miles?'

'Quite some time ago. Months ago.'

'So why are you contacting me now?'

'Because … I've waited to approach you for, for a way that would show you that I am … serious.'

'As opposed to what? Frivolous?'

'No no, just, serious.'

'And what d'you mean by that?'

'I understand how terribly I've behaved to you. I want you to know that, first and foremost. I know what I've done. I've known for quite some time. It might seem very unlikely to you, but a lot of things have changed in my life and I've come to see how awful I've been, but I've waited, I've waited to try to contact you, until, until I could show you I was serious, which is why I wondered if you'd like to come to Lanna.'

'I still don't get it, Miles.'

'Well look, Jenny, look. When men try to make up to women, to show them that they've behaved very badly, appallingly, and they recognise that, and they want to make amends, what they do is, traditionally, they make offerings, don't they? D'you know what I mean? As a sort of, symbol. But after, after what I did, what I did to you, what could I ever offer you? A bunch of flowers? A box of chocolates? A bottle of champagne? Or even, I dunno, even a diamond necklace or whatever, you'd throw them all right back in my face, wouldn't you?'

'Too fucking right I would, Miles. Too fucking right.'

'I'm offering you an island.'

There was another pause then, a long deep silence in which I began to dare to hope. At length she said: 'And it's where, this island?'

'Off the west coast of Scotland, but way, way out. Out beyond the Hebrides, sixty miles out in the Atlantic. It's the remotest island in Britain. And it's closed, you can't get on it. It's called Lanna. It's known as The Lost Island. It's meant to have Spanish gold on it and it's meant to be cursed.'

'And you're going out there?'

'To survey the seabirds, yes. It's a unique chance to see it.'

'And you're going when?'

'In about five days' time.'

'For how long?'

'About three to four days.'

'And you're inviting me to go with you?'

'I am, yes.'

'But why would I, Miles? Why in God's fucking name would I want to spend even a single second in your company?'

'I can see why you wouldn't, of course I can, and if you tell me to fuck off you'll be completely justified, of course you will. But I feel that, I have to do it. I have to ask you.'

'Why?'

'To try to ... to begin to ... to repair what I did to you. To atone. Maybe I can never atone. But I think I have to try.'

'Why do you have to try?'

'Because, because in spite of everything, I feel it's the right thing to do.' I said: 'I haven't got any other reason.'

I didn't. That was it.

She did not reply. After about ten seconds I said: 'Jenny?'

'I'm thinking.'

There was another long silence.

She said: 'You know what I feel right now? Violated.'

'I'm so sorry.'

'I feel violated that you've had the unbelievable, the unbelievable presumption, the unbelievable *gall*, to contact me.'

'I can understand that. I am so sorry. But I thought I had to do it.'

I could hear her breathing.

She said: 'And when is this trip again?'

'Five days' time.'

'And how long for?'

'Three or four days.'

'Going from where?'

'From Scotland. Probably Oban, on the west coast.'

Silence fell again. Eventually I had to break it. I said: 'Do you think you might consider it, Jenny?'

She said: 'You know what? I'm tired and I'm really upset. I just want to go to bed now. Why don't you phone me back tomorrow night and I'll tell you.'

'Tomorrow night?'

'Yeah.'

'What, like this sort of time?'

'Yeah, that's OK.'

'And you'll let me know?'

'Yes I will let you know.'

'All right. Goodnight, Jenny.'

'Yeah.' And she rang off.

Another day of waiting, a day of agony this time, an anguish of suspense. I told Lotte. She said: 'I'll pray for you, Miles. Well, I would if I had someone to pray to. I'll just do some big hoping.'

I told Ramsay. He said: 'She's making up her mind?'

'If she can do it, yeah. Like, if she can fit it in, get away from work.'

'And when will you find out?'

'Tonight.'

'Christ. All right. Ye know, there's still no sign of Kenny. It's like he's disappeared off the face of the earth.'

'Really?'

'What's happened to him? Where's he gone?'

'I wouldn't have a clue, Ramsay.'

I told no one else. I had no one else to tell, although in my mind, I did try to tell my mother. I said, *look, Mum, I'm trying to put it right. I said I would, didn't I? I swore to you I would. Well, now I'm trying to.*

And then at last the evening came, and I picked up the telephone to learn my fate.

Again, she answered at once.

'Jenny?'

'Yeah, hello Miles.' She had a strange sort of grey tone, as if all emotion had been drained from her.

'I, er, wondered if you'd thought about … things.'

'I have, Miles.'

'And have you come to a conclusion?'

'Yes I have.'

'And … may I ask … what it is?'

'I will come with you to your island.'

'You will?' I could scarcely believe it. 'You'll come to Lanna with me?'

'Yes.'

'That's wonderful, Jenny.'

'Before you say how wonderful it is, you should ask me the reason why I'll come. Go on. Ask me the reason. Ask me.'

'OK. Er, what's the reason … why you'll come?'

She said: 'The reason is, Miles, that it won't make any difference. To show you that. That's the reason I'll come.'

I didn't really understand. I was too elated. I said: 'OK. But you will come?'

'Yes, I will come.'

I had never felt like I felt: I was at a peak of joy. I could barely contain myself, I wanted to shout out, to whoop, and it was with difficulty that I was able to give her a sober account of what she needed to bring, and when she needed to meet me, and the fact that it would be in Oban in the Western Highlands, and she could get a train there directly from Glasgow, and oh yes, there was this curious condition from Lord Kintyre, that's the island's owner – you couldn't bring a camera. No cameras allowed on Lanna.

'Why not?'

'I dunno. But that's the condition.'

'OK.'

And with that we agreed on the rendezvous and said goodbye, calmly and civilly; and I put down the phone and punched the air; and I rang Lotte and she said, 'Oh Miles, all my thoughts will go with you'; and I rang Ramsay and he said: 'Well, at least that's something. Let's get on with it. There's still no sign of Kenny'; and for the next five days, as I made ready and worked out what I needed and got my briefings from the agency – Sidney Jeffries insisted in particular that I should keep a lookout for any sign of a bird called Swinhoe's petrel, a bird I had never heard of – I moved about in a sort of exultant daze; and on the duly appointed date I went to Oban to meet Jenny Pittaway, and as I drove the long route over the Highlands, from the east coast of Scotland to the west, my hopes had never been higher.

Kenny's disappeared.
I agrees to go to Lanna.

PART TWO

20

And so it began, that summer of the Millennium, the extraordinary set of events which changed the lives of everyone who was involved, and I look back at it now with incredulity, still finding it hard to believe it took place, the climax most of all – but it took place all right, though not of course as I had anticipated, for when at last I sailed to Lanna, my hopes had been comprehensively shot to pieces. Jenny's demolition of my mounting expectations with a few words in Hamish's Kitchen was as heavy a blow as I am ever likely to experience: I stared at my dream, and saw that it was finished. I felt that life was over. I felt like a dead man. And yet I agreed to the trip, a trip whose purpose was merely to prove I wasn't wanted.

Was that irrational? Maybe. But it seemed to me it was right, for I felt that if there was a price to be paid for what I'd done, I had to pay it. When we met in Oban I saw at first hand the depth of Jenny's hatred for me, and somehow I didn't think I could run away from that, as I had fled from Jenny herself in such a cowardly fashion when I finished with her in Oxford. So I would go with her, I decided as she impatiently stirred her coffee, not with any vestige of hope that she might change her mind – I knew she wouldn't – but in a different way altogether: as a penance. It seemed to me, there in the café, that this was the act of contrition I'd been looking for, and in thinking of Lanna, the pilgrims suddenly came into my mind, and I thought, I will be one of them. Yes. This journey will be hard, yet it will be serious, as those pilgrimages were, and it is righteous. Hitherto, I thought, I have escaped any consequences of what I did to Jenny. Now that they are here, I must embrace them.

Call it weird, but that's what I felt, that's why I went with Jenny Pittaway to Lanna, even though I thought, this is going to be the most painful and miserable time of my whole life, as I watched her come down the deck and engage Murdo the skipper in a conversation about the *Katie Colleen*, and then about the Hebrides, of which she knew nothing. Although I have to say that when Murdo began to point out all the islands we could see in the immense seascape opening out in front of us as we passed the tip of Kerrera, islands scattered across the silver waters like grey-blue shadows in the evening sunlight, I felt a jolt of excitement in spite of everything, as I suddenly realised what I was looking at – it was the realm of the Lords of the Isles. It was the lost kingdom of the sea.

Yet in all that talk about Mull, and Seil and Luing the slate islands, and Lunga and Scarba and Jura, and the Garvellachs and Colonsay, all of which were visible and which Murdo knew intimately, Jenny addressed not one word to me; and nothing when Murdo began to talk about the Western Isles and his own home of Harris, and Iona which was his favourite (which he told Jenny was a *thin* place, meaning that the curtain between the material world and the spiritual world was very thin there and you could easily pass through it – leading me to think he was not your normal gruff trawler skipper); and nothing when Donald the young deckhand, who had been gazing at Jenny open-mouthed, began to tell her about Lord Kintyre and his tigers, and then to tease her about Lanna being cursed, and Fergus being a monster man – in all that conversation, which must have lasted half an hour, Jenny addressed to me not a syllable, so eventually I said I would go below to check through my gear.

Murdo said: 'Donald here'll be cooking our tea just now, ye could give him a hand, if ye like,' and he threw me a glance which said, *can you keep an eye on the lad …*

'Sure,' I said, and in the *Katie Colleen's* cramped little galley I helped the young man fry the sausages and bacon, and heat the baked beans, and butter the bread and make the coffee, and as there were only two seats at the small table, I suggested he take the first sitting with Jenny, which pleased him no end as I could see he was very taken with her, and so, while they enjoyed their dinner date, I found myself back in the wheelhouse with Murdo.

I said: 'Tell me about Lanna, Murdo.'

'Well, Dr Bonnici …' he began.

'It's Miles,' I said. 'Miles.'

He nodded his acknowledgement. 'Well, Miles. It *is* a very special island, no doubt about that, I mean, just physically or geographically or however you want to put it, because of Akkersatch.'

'Because of *what*?'

'The harbour. *Akkersatch Mor*, in the Gallic. The big anchorage.'

It dawned on me. That was how you pronounced *Acarsaid*, which I had seen on the map.

'You'll see. It's completely sheltered, and ye can get in it more or less at any time. Whereas, somewhere like St Kilda, which is quite a lot like Lanna, really, you can have a problem, 'cos ye can't get into Village Bay, that's the landing place, in an east wind. You know St Kilda?'

'Afraid I don't.'

'Well, it's beautiful, sure, but for me the army base spoils it a wee bit. Whereas Lanna is completely unspoiled.'

'You sound like you love it.'

'Ha! Not sure ah'd say that. Ah'd say my feelings for it were complex. Ah mean, I knew of it, I knew of the legends and stuff, from growing up in a fishing family on Harris, and it was just called The Lost Island. *An t-Eilean Air Chall*. Nobody ever went there. Not that there was any need to. We had enough on our plates with the Minch.'

'The what?'

'The sea between the Western Isles and Skye. Can be very tricky.'

'Right.'

'So when ah got this job for the Balnay Estate, I suppose I had mixed feelings at first. Just a ... you know ... there was like a wee twinge of ... superstition. But it's never been anything other than straightforward. I enjoy seeing the island now. It's a bonny place. It really is. It has a very strong feel of the past about it, the monastery is still right there, and I ...' – he shot me a sideways glance – 'I can feel the people there sometimes. The people of the past. But it isnae a sinister feel, curse or no curse.'

'How long you been doing it?'

'This is my fourth summer.'

'And how often d'you go out?'

'We take Fergus out there in mid-April, then we go more or less on a weekly basis, weather permitting, to keep him supplied and check he's OK, until he leaves in early July.'

'What's he do the rest of the year?'

'No idea. After he leaves, he goes back down south somewhere.' He looked at me. 'He's English, ye do realise that?'

'I didn't, no.' Then I vaguely remembered, hadn't Kenny Lornie said something when I met him coming out of the UKOCA building ... *the fuckin' English lackey of a fuckin' English laird* ...?

'Oh aye,' said Murdo. 'Very English. Talks like ... well, you'll see. And he goes back down south, and then Lord Kintyre tends to go out to the island with his family, we take them for a sort of mini-holiday, and they have guests. Including some of the royals sometimes. We had ... though I'm no supposed to talk about that.'

I said: 'Isn't it dangerous for Fergus, being there all by himself?'

'I would certainly say so. But if that's what they want, that's what they want. He has good communications. He has VHF radio for boats near the island and Single Sideband for long distance, run off a petrol generator, and he's got a safety comms schedule.'

'A what?'

'He checks in with Stornoway Coastguard at the same time every morning and evening without fail, so if he missed a call they would know something was wrong.'

'Right,' I said. 'But why is the guy there? I still don't really understand.'

'He's a sort of warden. That's why Kintyre employs him. Ah think he's a trained biologist. From various things ah've heard him say, I would think he has a degree. He does a report on the seabirds and other wildlife for Kintyre each year but mainly, ah get the feeling he's there to keep other people off the place. See, the estate closed it before the war, 'cos of the treasure hunters … you know about all that?'

'I do, yes.'

'And it's still closed, and they've gone to the trouble of installing these chains across the entrance to Akkersatch, they're operated by a winch, and ye might just get past them in a small inflatable, say, but they will keep a boat like this out, right enough. So ye don't get ya yachts coming across from Barra and places and spending the weekend on the island, the people running all over it and picnicking and camping and starting fires and everything. And Kintyre keeps his island private.'

'Are you and Fergus close?'

Murdo didn't reply. I looked at him. He was screwing up his face in concentration. 'Well – no,' he said. 'We're not. I respect him. And ah think he respects me. And ah see him at least a dozen times every spring and summer, and ah come ashore, and he gives me ma breakfast or ma dinner, and a cuppa tea, and he's perfectly … he's perfectly …'

'What?'

'Ah was gonna say, friendly. But he's not friendly.'

'No?'

'He's … what is he? He's civil. Perfectly civil, perfectly polite and considerate. But he isnae … friendly. With me, at any rate. There's a distance. Ah feel like he's holding something back, all the time. Though I've no idea what.'

'But you said you respected him?'

'Ah do, aye.'

'In what way?'

'Well – there is something about him that is ... that is, honest. And ... upright. That's the word ah would use.'

'That's a striking judgement, Murdo.'

'Maybe. But you can just sense it. Like the guy wouldnae ... cheat ye. In any way. It's like he's very *moral*. Almost like a minister.'

'A minister?'

'Of the church.'

'Really?'

Murdo said: 'The thing is, though, what ah still don't get is, what's he about? Guy's out there on Lanna for three months every year. By himself. No friends. No family. Sees me and whoever else is crewing the boat for an hour once a week, if we can get out with the weather, and that's basically his human contact. How the hell's he stick it?'

He looked at me.

'If he was religious, if he was out there worshipping the Lord, that would explain it, I suppose he'd have a purpose, but ah cannae see that he is.' He shook his head. 'Ah dinnae ken what it is.'

I said: 'But you say he's OK to deal with?'

'Well he always has been ...'

'You mean ... till the fight?'

'Aye,' said Murdo. 'Aye.'

I realised he was concerned. I said: 'Tell me about it.'

Murdo reflected. He said: 'Well ya colleague Mr Lornie was difficult from the start, right? Ye know he's got a thing about the lairds?'

'I do.'

'And Alastair, the estate factor, warned us he'd had words with Lord Kintyre at the castle and we should be careful with him. And when he turned up ah think he just saw us, the estate boat and a' that, just as Kintyre's lackeys. Barely had any conversation wi' us, on the way out. Barely a word. On a thirteen-hour trip.'

'Really?'

'That's OK, if that's the way he wants it. So we left him with Fergus and came back, and then the next day at six in the morning ah get a call from Alastair telling me to drop whatever ah'm doing and get back out to Lanna right away, cos it appeared there'd been a been a fight on the island between them and I said a *fight* and he said aye a fight and I said what about and he said he'd no idea but to get out quick there cos Lornie'd been hurt and he had to come off. Wasn't till late evening that we got there, in the twilight and the moon was up, and the first thing I saw as we swung into Akkersatch was Fergus on the quay pacing up and down, which ah thought was strange cos normally he stands there still as a stone statue while we tie up, and his breathing was heavy and he was sweating and his eyes were sort of flashing and he said *there has been, ah, an incident, Mr Lornie and I have had a violent disagreement* and I said what happened? and he said *he attempted to assault me and I was obliged to defend myself. He will need medical treatment* and I said where he is now? and he said *He is in his hut, where I have detained him.* I said well is he in bad shape, or what, can he walk? and Fergus said *I believe so* and I said *I'd better come with you, hadn't I?* so we go over to the hut which I see Fergus has locked from the outside, with the key still in, and I call through, *Mr Lornie it's Murdo the boat skipper here, we're going to take you back to Oban, OK?* And he calls back, *Aye, OK,* sort of subdued, and Fergus undoes the lock, and he's breathing heavily, sort of tensed, I felt like he was waiting to spring, so I said, *I'll do this, Fergus* and I open the door, and there is the guy with this massive bruise and black eye all down the left-hand side of his face and I said *how are you feeling* and he said, *I'm all right* and I said *can you walk* and he says *ah think so,* but he's a bit unsteady and I said *give me your bag, and we will go to the boat right now.* So I grab his bag in one hand and I take his arm with the other with Fergus hovering about us and we get to the boat where Donald is waiting and we get him aboard and offer him a lie-down in a bunk and he says, *ah'll stay on deck.* And I nip back to unmoor while Donald is starting the engine and I say to Fergus, *what was all this all about for God's sake?* and Fergus says *he attempted to go to a forbidden area despite my clear instructions to the contrary and then he set about me when I attempted to stop him* and ah'm thinking yeah, OK, ah realise he's an awkward customer but you've battered half his face in, man, for what, setting foot in the wrong place? And I said, w*hat's happening with the seabird survey now then*, and Fergus said he didn't know, so I said, *we'll see you soon ah suppose,* and we shook hands and I got on board and we're off, and then, then it was the strangest thing of all.'

'What?'

'As we make our turn to head out, Fergus is still standing on the quay watching us, in the moonlight, I remember, the moon was reflected in the water and suddenly Lornie gets to his feet and he shouts at him, *Ye know what, Fergus? Ye know what ye shoulda done, if ye wanted to keep ya wee secret? Ye shoulda thrown me off a cliff. Your mistake, pal.'*

'Keep his secret? What secret?'

'No idea.'

'And that's all he said?'

'Well, then he points to his bruised face and he shouts *This winnae do it, Fergus. No way. Ye shoulda thrown me off a cliff when ye had ya chance, pal. Too late now.* And that was it. Though I could see Fergus, on the quay, he looked distressed, he seemed to be biting his knuckles.'

'What d'you think he meant?'

'No idea.'

'Is Lanna meant to have a secret?'

'Not that I know of.'

'About the gold, perhaps? D'you think Fergus might have found the Spanish gold?'

'Who knows? Ah think Lord Kintyre'd be taking an interest if he had. But my advice, Miles, would be, er, not to mention Lornie and all this, when ye get to the island. Just get on with ya survey, all right? Don't do or say anything to upset him about this.' He gave me a fixed stare. 'That would be my advice to you.'

I felt a tiny tremor of incredulity. 'Are you saying you think Fergus might be … dangerous?'

'No … but, look. Just in general, I've watched him for quite a time now, right? And there is a part of me that thinks, this great big guy goes to this remote island for three months every year all by himself doing nothing very much other than looking at the seabirds and occasionally warning visitors off with virtually no other human contact and no real reason for him to want to do it, to want to be there, that I can see, and there's a small part of me which thinks, *maybe this guy is simply crazy.*'

He turned to me again.

'Ye know? Like a homeless man in the street, muttering to himself? Except, he's on an island. He hasnae ended up sleeping in a shop doorway, he's ended up sleeping on Lanna.'

'And do you think he's crazy?'

Murdo weighed his words. 'No,' he said finally. 'I do not. Somehow he acts like he does have some purpose being there, some moral purpose. I just sense it, though ah cannae figure it out. But what ah do think is, he might be quite unpredictable, especially now after the incident. He seemed very, very upset by it. And you'll see, he's a truly massive guy, and your man Lornie, he's no seven-stone weakling, is he?'

'He is not.'

'And Fergus battered him senseless. Just for setting foot in the wrong place. So, be careful, Miles. You and ya colleague Miss Pittaway there... Go along with him, do as he says. And also, he's got something wrong with him, which might be upsetting him. Ah've only noticed it this year. He's got difficulty moving. Ah think he might have arthritis or something. It's not making him any more relaxed.'

There was a peal of laughter from the small galley below.

'Somebody's enjoying themselves,' said Murdo. 'Our turn for dinner, wouldn't ye say?'

When I look back at the conversation I had with Murdo McLeod as we sailed down the Firth of Lorn, I am struck by how perceptive he was about Fergus, and how close he got to the truth about him, whereas another boatman, it seems to me, another tough trawler skipper from the shores of the Minch, might have dismissed Fergus merely as a freak. From my UKOCA research project I had formed a generally unfavourable view of fishermen, based on the damage they were doing to the marine environment, but I had not met any, and the only things I could see in Murdo were positive ones. The fact that now, understanding everything, I cannot explain it to him, is a great regret.

The day was winding down when we came back up on deck; Jenny and young Donald at the wheel seemed the best of friends; on the port side Colonsay was a fading shadow on the horizon and Murdo explained that the Ross of Mull, the 20-mile long peninsula on the south of the island, was keeping us company to starboard as we headed due west or nearly so, at a steady eight knots; when we got to the end of it, he said, we might get a glimpse of Iona. The sky above us was still blue, though deepening now, and the sea was choppy, not rough; but on the western horizon was a growing bank of dark cloud.

'There's a low coming in, isn't there?' I said to Murdo.

'Aye there is, but then it's going to pass. Ye seen the forecast?'

'I have. I think we're in luck.'

'That you are. Low will have gone through about the time we get to the island, and then ye've got a weather window that looks great.'

'Yeah, three days of high pressure. Should be ideal for the survey.'

And I started to think about it – the seabirds survey – for the first time, I realised, since I had caught sight of Jenny on the station platform at Oban; and I was suddenly filled with ... not hope, but a sense of something positive. The survey mattered, and I was privileged to be doing it, it was the true reason for this voyage after all, it was a contribution I might make to the betterment of the world: to help save the seabirds of Lanna from the dangers of crude oil would be a truly worthwhile enterprise, would it not? This voyage was not a disaster, even if my love had run aground. My thoughts came together: it was in oiled seabirds that I had found my epiphany, there on the Île de Ré, and maybe, I started to think, maybe it was in something like this, in looking after the natural world, in helping to save it from ruin and degradation that I might ultimately find a purpose … for at the back of my mind was the great overarching question, which had replaced all others: *what will I do now with my life?*

I looked at Jenny who until a few hours earlier had filled so fully my vision of the future, Jenny just a few feet away on the other side of the wheelhouse yet wholly beyond my reach, still chatting to Donald and occasionally to Murdo: she had not directed a single word to me since we left the harbour. It hurt so much I almost laughed. Could she keep it up throughout the whole trip, I wondered? She certainly did on that first day, for as the June evening lengthened – 'at this latitude it doesn't really get dark,' said Murdo – and a few tiny lights appeared on the Ross of Mull, though the surging cloud bank in the west and north shut out any chance of a sunset or even a view of other islands, she said she would turn in, and went down into the cabin without even a glance in my direction. It felt like a stinging slap in the face. But it was what I'd signed up for, was it not? She'd been straight with me, she'd offered me the choice. It was my penitential pilgrimage.

When I went down into the cabin myself Jenny had drawn the curtain across her bunk and to all intents and purposes was asleep, but somehow I didn't think she was sleeping yet: I sensed that she would be listening to me come in, she would be thinking of me, and nursing her hatred. Keeping it hot. Part of me didn't believe that she could do that, the Jenny Pittaway I knew, but another part of me accepted, maybe she could, because that was the size of what I had done, of the hurt I had caused. I got into my own bunk and lay there listening to the continuous purring clatter of the engine and the knock and slap of the swell against the hull and I thought only of her as I fell asleep, she rocking with the ocean as I was, less than ten feet away from me, but she might have been on Mars: the beloved, the entirely beloved, and now the entirely lost.

I was awoken by Murdo saying: 'Lanna, Lanna, this is *Katie Colleen,* come in Lanna,' repeating it every thirty seconds or so. I rolled out of my bunk and looked at my watch – it was twenty past six – and pulled on my boots and went up to the wheelhouse. 'Morning,' Murdo said. 'Sleep OK?'

I grunted affirmatively.

'Not long now,' he said. 'We're in VHF range and I'm just trying to raise Fergus. He must be out.'

I looked about me and found that the whole world was grey: the sea was grey and the sky was grey and there seemed no boundary between them, the air was filled with rain and wind and the waves were capped with foam, though the boat was ploughing through them steadily enough. There was no sign of the island, only a grey wall in front of us. 'How far off are we?' I asked.

'Have a look,' said Murdo, and he pointed to the radar, and I saw on the screen, with a kick of excitement, the outline of the island in glowing green lines, dead ahead. I thought: Curse or no curse, I don't think it's going to vanish from the radar, is it? 'About seven miles now,' said Murdo. 'Less than an hour. D'ye fancy making the coffee? Make four mugs,' and while I was in the galley Murdo kept on calling the island and eventually the radio squawked back at him: '*Katie Colleen*, Lanna.'

'Good morning Fergus over,' said Murdo.

'Morning Murdo over,' crackled the radio.

'About seven miles out, less than an hour now over,' said Murdo.

'Yes OK, over and out,' the radio squawked.

So that was Fergus. He wasn't just a legend. He really existed. And he didn't have a lot of small talk.

Young Donald showed his sleepy face then, and I gave him two mugs of coffee and suggested he rouse Jenny with one of them, which had the effect of making him instantly wide awake, and I took the other two mugs up to the wheelhouse and gave Murdo his.

'Lousy weather,' I said.

'Och man, it's a wee bit dreich, but this is nothing. It's barely Force Four. Ye want to see these seas when it's really bad.'

'Would that stop you going to the island?'

'We'll go in a Force Six, even Seven, maybe even Eight in an emergency, but we probably won't need to any more because Kintyre had a helipad put in last year. Don't think your man Fergus was very pleased. Kintyre did it after he'd left for the summer.'

'Why wasn't he pleased?'

'He thinks it lessens the isolation of the island, which he says is its most valuable quality.'

'It'll be a lot less isolated if they put an oil platform next to it.' I had taken on board my mission; I was going to put regrets behind me; I had something to do that was important.

'You're not wrong there,' said Murdo, shaking his head. 'The idea's outrageous.'

The grey world around us looked interminable, it looked as if it would never shift, and there seemed to be no seabirds, everything was empty and chill, and Jenny shivered when she clambered up on deck clutching her coffee mug, followed by Donald. She nodded at Murdo and me, which I suppose allowed her to greet us both without actually uttering any words in my direction, and she took up her position of the night before on the far side of the wheelhouse, and we all stood in silence as the *Katie Colleen* shouldered her way through the greyness, for half an hour and more, until Murdo said: 'Squall up ahead. Might just find the good weather on the far side.' I gazed at it, the curtain of darker grey hanging across what had to be the invisible sea-sky border, and the wind rose as we approached and we tightened our grips, and the rain came down, and soon we were in it and the wind howled and the rain beat upon us and drenched us, and then, in one of the most memorable moments of my life, the wind dropped and the rain ceased and the greyness began to thin and light flowed to us from behind it and the sky became blue and the sea became bluer and the light became golden and in front of us appeared Lanna, the Lost Island, rising out of the Atlantic as if it had been created freshly by the Lord but a few seconds before.

I was astonished at how green it was. The waves breaking on its fringing dark rocks were bright white, the sea of its setting was deepest ultramarine, and the form of the whole island was noble, like the nave of a church rising to a peak where I saw, with a leaping heart, the great Celtic cross.

I was lost for words.

But Jenny found words.

'Jesus Christ,' she said. 'Will you look at that.'

Skipper Murdo talks about Fergus

21

My first sight of Lanna will never fade from my mind. I suppose we were especially blessed because it was so sudden, and we were so close when it finally appeared – less than a mile away – that the spectacle of it struck us with all the more force, but for me there was something beyond that: it was as if I had been given a great reward. I was instantly at one with the pilgrims, I knew precisely what they felt when they finally saw the island and its great cross from their open birlinns, and no hot coffee for them, remember, no dry bunks and no radar, either, I was privileged and protected beyond what they could dream of; and yet I was somehow of their number, because I too had gone there with a moral purpose, with a seriousness of the heart, and I felt, as they must have done, that in return, what was at the end of the journey was special.

Jenny was somehow similarly affected, in a way I think she couldn't quite understand. She knew nothing of the pilgrims, she couldn't identify with them as I did, but this connoisseur of islands, this island-collector whose lifelong passion I had tried to play upon and who had greeted my scheme with contempt, found herself moved. It was entirely unexpected; it temporarily overcame her simmering anger. Part of me wants to believe she was touched by some deep power that the island possessed to reach out to those who approached it – the very opposite of the curse it was meant to carry – for could so many devoted souls travel there with such intense emotions for so many hundreds of years and not leave something of themselves behind? But maybe Jenny was just affected by the sheer beauty of what we saw, for Lanna was beautiful anyway, but to an almost dream-like degree with the magnificent weather which had now descended on us. We were wrapped in a high-pressure system halting the Atlantic westerlies and drawing warm air up from the south – a blocking anticyclone, as the Met people call it – and apart from the retreating low on the eastern horizon, the sky was cloudless; there was hardly any wind and the sea was moved only by a slight swell. 'This is the Azores High,' said Murdo, smiling. 'Not often like this. Ye're very lucky.' The sunshine was so strong that after the greyness of the previous hours the colours of the island seemed overpowering in their brightness and we could see every detail in sailing towards it, every shadow of every rock, every indentation of the cliffs, and as I got over my shock at the initial vision, I began to take in what I had officially come for: the seabirds.

Their numbers were extraordinary. We were entering a colossal, buzzing seabird city, dwarfing anything I'd seen on Skarholm, and the air was crammed with them. It was like being in the middle of a major railway station filled with commuters, it was like being in Waterloo at rush hour, with thousands of individuals hurrying on their own separate ways: winged creatures without number making their own patterns above us, criss-crossing each other, each with a purpose of its own and keeping just enough distance from the next bird somehow to avoid colliding, while all about our ears was their hullabaloo, the squawking of the guillemots and the low throaty growls of the gannets and the cackling of the fulmars all combining into one endless, harsh chorus which the sharp calls of the prettiest gull cut through: *kittiwaak! kittiwaak!* The noise blanketed us, as did the smell, the sour aroma of the guano: the whole mile-long range of cliffs was speckled throughout with nests and the numberless nesters coming and going, while in the distance, beyond the peak of the cross, we could see the two stacks, Stac Mor and Stac Beag, the two great sea rocks holding the gannet colony, which were snow-white on top with the birds and their droppings.

As we got closer in there were legions more of birds on the sea surface, mainly auks – guillemots, razorbills and puffins – and in the perfect sunlight the puffins in particular seemed handsome beyond words, with their dazzling bills and their bright red feet which we saw as we approached them, as some simply dived to get out of our way but others ran along the water to take off, and I stole a glance at Jenny, and she seemed to be spellbound.

We were headed for the southern end of the island where I could see clearly there was a castle on top of a high promontory which formed the island's southern tip – I came to know it as Castle Point – and from it, the eastern cliffs flowed northwards and upwards until at the far end they reached the height of the cross, three hundred feet above the sea. As we got closer I started to perceive that in the low cliffs along from the castle was a gap, and we nosed our way gently into it: it was a dark defile and at one point it was no more than thirty feet wide and it curved around clockwise until it suddenly opened out into a broad stretch of sunlit still water, perhaps seventy yards across, with on the left hand, western side, a stone quay carved out of the rock, and on its inward, northern end a broad natural sandy beach which shelved up into the island; a grey inflatable was parked in the middle of it. It was the most remarkable natural harbour I'd ever seen – the most perfect shelter, screened from the sea. For a second time in ten minutes I was amazed, as I imagined the pilgrims must have been when they first set eyes on it, and stealing another glance at Jenny I could see that she too was wide-eyed with astonishment – although that was about to turn abruptly into something else.

'Welcome to Akkersatch Mor,' murmured Murdo. 'And there's your man.'

The solitary figure standing on the quay, I realized as we glided in, was striking to a degree. He really was a huge man. His clothes seemed entirely shapeless and colourless, as if all his garments were all one garment, but there was colour at the top: he had long, wispy, thinning red hair around a bald pate and an overgrown, long red beard, both with traces of grey – he struck me as a sort of oversized ginger version of Santa Claus. I reckoned he was about fifty. He watched impassive as young Donald leapt from the bows on to the quay with the fore mooring rope and slipped it through one of the quayside rings (which were level with us precisely, I realised, explaining the timing of our trip: we had arrived at high tide). Donald did the same with the aft rope, adjusted it as the *Katie Colleen* backed a little, and Murdo cut the engine.

Fergus Pryng stood facing us. The sunlight caught his forehead: he appeared to be sweating. He held a notebook in his hand. He glanced at it and said: 'Good morning to you.'

I wasn't sure I had heard correctly: he seemed to have the caricature of a deep, old-fashioned upper-class English accent, of speaking with a plum in his mouth, as they say.

He spoke again, and I realised that he did.

He said: 'Please to tell me, which is Doctor Bonnici.'

'That's me,' I said.

He stared at me. He stared at me intensely as if I were a picture in an exhibition and he were trying to work out how the painter had captured the light.

Then he said, glancing at his notebook: 'And Miss Pittaway?'

For God's sake, there's only one woman here, I thought.

'That's me,' said Jenny.

Fergus repeated his stare. I could hear the distant seabird chorus and the tiny slop of the remnant swell on the quay wall. Then he said in his deep plummy voice: 'Before you disembark, it is imperative that you understand the principle on which you will be allowed to set foot on Lanna. The principle is this: you are not free to go where you choose. Do you understand?'

'Yes,' I said.

'Sure,' said Jenny.

'You must go only where I tell you, and nowhere else. This is an absolute rule. If you break it, even in the slightest degree, you will be detained ...'

Detained? I thought. What's that mean?

'... and removed from the island at the earliest possible opportunity. Do you understand?'

Jenny and I both voiced our assent.

'You will already have been notified of the prohibition on cameras. No cameras of any shape or form are allowed on Lanna. I take it neither of you has a camera?'

'No,' I said.

'No,' said Jenny.

'Though just to be absolutely straight with you,' I said, 'I didn't properly make it clear to my colleague Miss Pittaway here about the no-cameras rule and she inadvertently brought one with her. But we handed it over to Murdo in Oban, as soon as we boarded.'

'A camera has been brought here?' said Fergus, his voice rising.

'Yes, but in the custody of Murdo.'

'Do you have it, Murdo?'

'I do, Fergus.'

'Let me see it.'

Murdo rooted around inside the wheelhouse and found Jenny's camera in its case. He held it up.

Fergus reached out his arm. 'Let me see it.'

Murdo reached over the side of the boat and handed it to Fergus. Fergus opened the case and took out the camera.

I could see it was a Canon.

Fergus's eyes were flickering. He said: 'This should not have been brought here!'

'It was gonna stay on the boat, Fergus.'

'It should have remained in Oban! The prohibition on cameras is absolute!' and with that, with a swing of his arm and a sort of awkward twist of his body, he tossed it into the water.

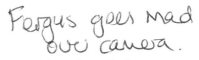

Fergus goes mad over camera.

I remember the parabola of the camera curling through the air with the sunlight flashing on it, as we watched open-mouthed, then the *pel-loop* as it hit the surface and went under, and the light catching it again as it tumbled down through the dark green water and vanished; and for a long second everyone on the boat was too astonished to speak. Then we all sounded off at once.

'Fergus, steady on now,' said Murdo.

'Hey, there's need for that,' said I.

'What the fuck you doing, mate?' cried Jenny.

Young Donald was open-mouthed.

'Do you think this is all a joke?' cried Fergus, almost shouting. 'A game? Do you take this island for a holiday resort, where you can snap away at anything that takes your fancy? Lanna is not a tourist attraction!'

'Fergus, Fergus, come on now, it wasnae gonna leave the boat,' said Murdo.

'It should never have been brought here, Murdo. It should have remained in Oban. The prohibition on cameras is absolute. You know that.'

'It's my fault, then,' said Murdo. 'They handed it over as soon as they got on board. There was no intention whatsoever of bringing it ashore.' He was trying to calm him down. 'I apologise. But it's sorted now, isn't it? It's sorted out ...'

Fergus was breathing heavily. His nostrils were flared and his eyes were glaring.

'They've got the message, Fergus, right enough. But ah think we should get them off now, with their gear, don't you? Ye've got something very important to do, have ye not?'

'Yes,' said Fergus. 'Yes. Yes we have. Very well, then.' He was coming down. 'Yes. Will you see them into the guest accommodation, Murdo? Then perhaps you might join me for a cup of tea.' He said to me: 'Dr Bonnici. Please to come over for a briefing in half an hour.'

'OK,' I said.

And with that he ... I was going to say walked, but he didn't walk, he hobbled, he hobbled away along the quay as if every bone in his body were aching.

'Arthritis, ah think,' murmured the skipper. 'It's got worse in just a fortnight.' He turned to Jenny. 'Christ, ah'm really sorry about that, about ya camera. Ah had no idea he was gonna do that.'

'What kind of crazy nutter is this fucking guy?' said Jenny.

'Look, basically, he's OK,' said Murdo. 'He's basically a decent man. Ah'd tell ye if he wasnae. But he's still upset at what

275

happened with your predecessor, ah can see that, about the fight they had, he's still keyed up about it. So just do exactly what he says, all right?' He looked at us both. 'Just don't try going anywhere he says ye can't, and it'll all be fine.'

I was very glad of Murdo's stable presence and I began to think with just a tinge of apprehension that he was about to sail away and leave us alone with this … unpredictable giant. This camera-sinker. With the guy who stove in Kenny Lornie's face.

'Tell me again, when are you back for us?' I said.

'Friday lunchtime.'

'Can't come soon enough,' Jenny murmured.

Murdo said: 'It'll be fine. He's very keen on doing the survey. Just go along with what he says, that's all. Now we'd better get ya gear off and get ye settled in.'

He and Donald helped us with our bags and offloaded another big holdall full of provisions for our stay, and as we moved off the quay to the beach and the rising ground that led up into the island, I looked about me. On either side of the sand there was a tiny stream, a burn, as they say, not more than a few inches wide, flowing into the anchorage and I noticed with astonishment that alongside both of them there were yellow flag irises in flower – how in God's holy name did they ever get out here, I wondered – and close to each watercourse was a fairly substantial olive-green hut. 'That's you over there,' said Murdo, pointing to the hut on the far side of the beach. 'That's the guest accommodation. This is Fergus here,' and I looked at the hut we were passing, which had several aerials on its roof, and saw there was another, larger hut beyond it – 'That's the stores,' said Murdo – and that behind them both, the ground climbed directly to the old castle, which loomed above the anchorage as a whole. Then, as we got to the top of the beach, the heart of Lanna spread before us, just as Melrose Crinan had described it – a bright green bowl of tussocked grass rising to the hill of the cross half a mile away and delineated by the burns on each side, with in the level foreground, the monastery.

'There ye go,' said Murdo. 'Abaid nan Ròn. *Abatch nan Ron.* The Abbey of the Seals.'

For the third time that morning I was astonished. I was half-expecting a ruin. Instead I saw a complex of fully-formed, clearly ancient buildings in grey and brown stone, several with pitched roofs; I was taken aback at the extent of it all, here on this remotest of islands, but there was something else, something I did not know how to describe, a sudden intense sentiment resembling fascination, but stronger still … I did not know what it was. I had never experienced anything like it before. I gazed at the abbey. I felt an enormous pull.

'Can ye see now what an incredible place this is?' Murdo said. 'Sheltered harbour, fresh water in the burns, land for growing or grazing … when ye think about it, is it any wonder they put a monastery here?'

'Yes indeed,' I said. 'I can see what St Columba saw in it.'

Jenny said nothing.

Our hut was large, and secured, I noticed, with cable stays, with wire hawsers stretching from each corner to stakes in the ground, while two rock pipits, small and brown, the sparrows of remote islands, were flitting about it. It was exceptionally well-appointed: four bedrooms with double bunks; a central living space with two small sofas and a coffee table; a kitchen with a sink, a water heater, a four-burner stove and a fridge-freezer all powered by calor gas, as well as a dining table and chairs; and a bathroom which featured a chemical loo which flushed, and even a shower. The water came from the burn, said Murdo, and it was fine to drink. Even more notable were the small details. The linen, the duvet covers on the bunks and the towels were all luxurious, as were the glassware and the china in the kitchen, even the curtains in the windows.

'This is all pretty smart.'

'Nothing but the best for the guests of his lordship,' said Murdo, and he showed us how everything worked, and then he said he would leave us to it, and he and Donald shook hands with Jenny and me, and wished us luck with everything, and said they'd see us on Friday, and were gone.

It was a difficult moment.

'Jenny,' I said.

She came out of her bedroom. 'Yeah, what?'

There was an angry look on her face – the ugly hardness was back and I realised that any good feelings she might have formed about the island from her initial view of it had been thoroughly dissipated by what Fergus had done with her camera.

'I know this is awkward, but we have to talk because of what's happening here, that we haven't talked about before.'

'OK.'

'I'm going to be doing a census of the seabirds, counting them, probably from a boat, and if you could give me a hand with it, that would be the most enormous help.'

'What d'you want me to do?'

'Not quite sure till we've spoken with Fergus, but I'm probably going to ask you to write things down as I say them, numbers and lists.'

'OK. I can do that.'

'Maybe even drive the boat at some stage. I told them you had a lot of experience with inflatables.'

'That's OK.'

I said: 'We will have to talk on some occasions. Just for business.'

'That's all right.'

'Good.'

'I just don't want any social intercourse with you.'

'Sure.'

'None whatsoever.'

'Sure. That's fine.'

'So I don't want to fucking chat with you, or stroll around with you, or go swimming with you, or anything. And I don't want to eat with you. I don't want to have breakfast, or lunch, or dinner with you. I'll eat by myself. And I'll make my own fucking coffee.'

I thought I'd grown hardened to it, but it still felt like a punch in the guts. I managed to say: 'Sure.' And I added, because I thought I ought to: 'I'm really, really sorry about your camera. The agency will replace it. And if UKOCA won't, I'll replace it myself.'

Jenny said: 'Whatever.'

The *Katie Colleen* was churring out of the anchorage when we walked over to Fergus's hut, twenty minutes later. The hut's interior was a mess: the radio table with two transmitters was obvious, but everything else was a jumble, maps, books, binoculars, plates, mugs, clothes, although what also stood out was a shelf of framed photographs, half a dozen of them, of what all looked like a man and woman with a young child. Fergus was sitting at the dining table and on it was what I recognized as an enlarged version of the Ordnance Survey map of Lanna (it was a small inset on the map of Barra and South Uist). We sat opposite him. He still appeared to be sweating. He looked at us closely; he seemed to glare at us. Then he said: 'I repeat my earlier admonition: this is not a place where you are free to wander. You understand that?'

We said we did.

'Then let us begin by denoting clearly where is out of bounds to you,' he said. 'In essence, it is the whole of the western side of the island. Here.' He drew his finger down the west coast. 'This is all low cliffs, in places only thirty to forty feet high, and continually struck by the waves, which not infrequently come over the top. It can be very dangerous. And because of the waves, which would wash away nests, it is quite devoid of ornithological interest. There is nothing. Nothing at all. You will see that along *here*, there is a fence, a simple fence, more of a boundary marker, really, along the western slope of Cnoc na Croise, that is the hill with the cross, which prevents access to the western coastline. You may not pass that fence under any circumstances whatsoever. Is that clear?'

We nodded.

'Should you do so, you will be detained ...'

There it was again. *Detained*. And just for a second I thought: *This guy is crazy.*

'... and removed from the island at the earliest opportunity. You understand?'

We said we did.

'The other principal exclusion zone is the castle above us. It is crumbling and dangerous and wholly out of bounds. You are not to set foot upon it, even upon the lower slopes. Is that clear?'

We nodded once more.

'Do I have your agreement?'

'Yes,' we said.

'Finally, if by any unexpected chance, you should find yourselves in a boat without me, you are not to proceed, under any circumstances, to the western side of the island. There are offshore reefs which are extremely dangerous. Do I have your word that you will abide by this restriction?'

'Yes,' we said.

'Good,' said Fergus. 'So we understand each other.'

Then Jenny said: 'So where *can* we go?'

'Madam?' said Fergus.

'I mean, I'd quite like a swim, like, this evening, maybe, and we obviously can't swim in the sea, so could I have a swim in the harbour?'

Fergus reflected. It suddenly struck me that the idea of someone swimming in the anchorage had simply never occurred to him before. He thought about it hard. He tried to see an objection. He couldn't. He said: 'You may.'

'Thanks.'

I said: 'And can we walk up to the cross?'

Fergus thought about it again. He said: 'Yes, so long as you remember what I told you about not crossing the fence on the western side of the slope.'

'Thanks.'

'And also,' he said, 'you are not to take binoculars up to the cross. Unless I am with you.'

I was about to say *Why on earth not?* but I held my tongue. I said: 'OK. And what about the monastery?'

'You are at liberty to examine the buildings. They are very well preserved and remarkably atmospheric. The grave slabs in particular repay close inspection.'

I nodded.

'Then let us turn to what concerns us directly, the eastern side of the island. The eastern cliffs are the principal seabird habitat, and it is the cliff-nesting birds which are the easiest to census in the short time we have available, I'm sure you understand that, Dr Bonnici?'

'Absolutely,' I said.

'The burrow-nesters, the puffins and the Manx shearwaters, as well as the petrels, present much thornier problems of enumeration.'

'Of course.'

'But the cliff-nesters readily admit of surveying, which we shall do from the sea. We are exceptionally fortunate with the weather. It is rarely so clement.' He turned to Jenny. 'Now Madam. I understand you are familiar with the workings of inflatable boats and their outboard engines.'

'Pretty much,' she said.

'Would you be willing to drive the inflatable, so that Dr Bonnici and I could both count and thus cross-check each other's results?'

'Sure.'

'It would make for a count which is that much more robust, do you see?'

'OK.'

'Excellent.' He turned back to me. 'I suggest we concentrate on the most numerous species, which are the fulmars, the guillemots, and the kittiwakes. I understand you are a guillemot expert?'

'More or less.'

'Good. We will count the guillemots as individuals, and the fulmars and kittiwakes by apparently occupied nests, and so as pairs. And I suggest we count by dividing the cliffs up into sections, using landmarks which I shall point out.'

'That was exactly my idea.'

'Excellent. I think that will be enough to get a proper scientific estimate, even if a very basic one, for the significance of Lanna as a seabird station. To attempt anything serious with the razorbills

or the other gulls would require I think too much time. We will
need today and tomorrow for the cliffs. On Thursday we will look
at the gannetries on the offshore stacks.'

'But the gannets are on the tops, aren't they? We can't count
them from the sea, surely?'

'No indeed. But we are fortunate in that the peak, Cnoc na
Croise, overlooks both the stacks directly, and we are able to look
down upon them.'

'Does it now? So you will have already made an estimate?'

'In very general terms. But, yes.'

'And what is it?'

'In excess of 50,000 pairs.'

I whistled. 'That's up with St Kilda, isn't it?'

'St Kilda is 60,000 pairs, the largest colony in the world. But
Lanna is substantially in excess of both the Bass Rock and Ailsa
Craig. We may be the world's second biggest gannet colony.'

'And do you have a feel for the other species?'

'Only very roughly. Fulmars are the most numerous – I would
guess well in excess of 20,000 pairs. Kittiwakes perhaps 3,000
pairs. Guillemots perhaps 20,000 individuals.'

'What about the burrow-nesters?'

'Hopeless to attempt anything serious in the time that we have.
But the puffins are certainly here in thousands, the shearwaters
probably in lower but still substantial numbers. Their rafts are very
visible offshore in the evenings.'

'You mentioned the petrels. Is that stormies and Leach's?'

'It is.'

'Where do they nest?'

'The storm petrels nest in the monastery buildings, in the cracks
and hollows of the walls. The Leach's petrels nest on a scree slope
below the summit of Cnoc na Croise. They both come ashore
during the small hours. We could look at them tonight if you wish?'

'I'd love to,' I said.

'Perhaps we could observe the storm petrels tonight, and the
Leach's the night after?'

'Sure. Great.'

'The storm petrels flitting about the monastery in the half-light,
in particular, is a most arresting sight.'

'I'd love to see it.'

'Precise counting will not be practicable, but you will see that
there are significant colonies of both species.'

'That's great.'

Fergus said: 'Do you have any other questions?'

I said: 'What about the predators?'

'Predators?'

'What about the bonxies? The ravens? The crows? Greater black-backed gulls? What sort of numbers?'

'There are none.'

'None?'

'None.'

'There can't be *none*.'

'There are none.'

'But this is a paradise for seabird predators. It's like a living larder.'

'There are none.'

'There have to be *some*.'

'There are none.'

I gazed at Fergus. He was sitting upright, entirely impassive. Speaking what I knew to be nonsense. But I remembered what Murdo had said about not upsetting him.

'Right then,' I said. 'OK.'

'Do you have any further questions?'

I said: 'And as for the west coast of the island?'

'Yes?' His tone had instantly hardened and his eyes flashed.

'I mean, on the whole of the west side … there is nothing of significance there … in seabird terms … at all? Not even a few tysties? Black guillemots? Low cliffs, sort of place they might nest …'

'Nothing whatsoever.'

We needed survival suits, plus lifejackets, which we donned in the big store hut – there was a rack of them, bright orange in different sizes, presumably to accommodate guests – and had Jenny and I been on good terms it would have been fun to try them on and help each other squeeze into them, but now it was a merely mechanical process, and anyway, I was preoccupied with what Fergus had said about there being no predators. I was muttering to myself about it and I said out loud: 'Says there's no bonxies. In a colony this size. Talking nonsense,' and Jenny said: 'What?'

'Says there's no bonxies. Have to be.'

'No fucking idea what you're on about, mate.'

'Bonxies. Bonxies are great skuas. Like a cross between a gull and a buzzard. Big, piratical things, they chase other birds like gannets, make 'em drop the fish they've caught. In a massive seabird colony like this they'd flourish. They'd have to be here. So would

282

ravens. So would the big gulls. But he says there's none of them. That's just patent nonsense. Why's he say that?'

'Search me. You're the bird man.'

I was still perplexed as we walked down to the beach above the anchorage where the rib, the grey four-metre inflatable, was moored to a metal ring fixed in a large rock several yards above the tideline. Fergus limped down to join us, and I marvelled again at his size, and noted his obvious pain in moving, and he untied the painter, the mooring rope, and together we pushed the boat into the water on its wheeled cradle; with some difficulty he clambered in and we followed, and he pulled up the wheels and pushed down the engine and started it, and showed Jenny how it worked, and she sat in the stern and gently opened the throttle, and my survey of the seabirds of Lanna at last got under way.

It turned out to be harder than I'd anticipated. At first we slowly ran through the bustling, caterwauling seabird city, along the length of the cliffs with Fergus pointing out different landmarks – big ledges, overhangs, fissures – and me making notes, and then on a second run we agreed on the delineation of the whole mass into sections: there eventually were fourteen of them. I wished to goodness I had a camera to make sure there were no mistakes as some of the landmarks were fairly faint, but no cameras were allowed, were they? And rather than just accepting this as a bizarre rule of the Balnay estate, as I previously had, for the first time I thought: Why, though?

Why no cameras on Lanna?

What doesn't he want photographed?

I looked at Fergus opposite me as I thought it. But he wasn't going to answer that, for at that moment he was scanning the sea, with his eyes and with his binoculars, and he seemed to be anxious about something, though I had no idea what.

When we started the actual count I was very grateful for the fact that we were on the sheltered side of the island, and for the calmness of the water – in the lovely weather it was exceptionally smooth for the Atlantic, it was almost millpond flat – as I quickly found that looking upwards through binoculars from a boat made me feel nauseous if there was much noticeable motion, and I asked Jenny if she could keep it as level as she possibly could and she nodded, and she did – she was clearly very used to driving inflatables; but counting was still a difficult trick to pull off and you had to focus really hard to make sure you didn't count the same spot twice. Right away I saw the point of Fergus's suggestion that two of us should do it and compare notes, because we started with the kittiwakes, the loveliest and daintiest of the gulls, which made the most obvious nests on the cliff face, and in the first section I made it 231 nests and Fergus made it 248 so we did it again and we agreed on round figure of 240. Then we did the fulmars, those stiff-winged petrels which seem to glide their way through life, which were harder to count because they barely made a nest at all and just sat on the cliff ledge with their single egg; picking them out needed intense concentration and was very tiring for the eyes, but we managed to arrive at a figure of 1,125 nest sites for the section as a whole. And finally we got to the guillemots, much more obvious as they stood upright on their ledges in long lines with their dark backs to the sea, and I was more in my element now, and I could estimate by the hundred, and Fergus and I agreed that in the first cliff section there were approximately 1,600 guillemot individuals, all or most likely to be sitting on eggs, and I felt a huge sense of achievement, until I looked at my watch, and registered that we had been out for two hours, and we had completed one section of Lanna's seabird cliffs, out of fourteen.

If I'd been a smoker, this was the moment when I'd have had a cigarette. Instead I was grateful for the water bottle Fergus proffered, passing it to Jenny first.

She took it and drank and handed it back without a word.

We counted another section of the cliffs then, which took a further hour. At the end of it I felt exhausted, and I could see that Fergus was in discomfort: he was sweating profusely and at moments his face seemed clenched. He was clearly in pain with his arthritis, if that's what it was, and I wondered if he was taking painkillers.

He said: 'We shall return now for lunch and to rest. One can only do so much.'

It was not a convivial lunch for me. I thanked Jenny for driving the inflatable and she just nodded. I said: 'Do you want to use the kitchen first?' and she said all right, and made herself a sandwich, and took it over to the monastery to eat without so much as another syllable to me. I ate my own bread and cheese by the harbour. We were an hour and a half onshore before we went out again – Fergus clearly needed a substantial breather – and Jenny was as good as her word about no social contact: she said nothing to me in all that time. I used it to write up some of my notes, but I still found it painful in the extreme. It was what I had agreed to, though, and I consoled myself with the worth of what I was doing.

In the afternoon Fergus and I sort of got into a rhythm with our counting and we worked long and hard, and by evening we had completed six of the fourteen cliff sections – we had counted 1,935 kittiwake nests, 13,500 fulmar nest sites and 10,350 individual guillemots – and as we purred back into the anchorage and beached the boat I felt satisfied, as I could see we would complete the count the following day. And then it was Jenny time again. ➤

I said: 'Would you like the kitchen first? You're very welcome.'

She said: 'No, I'm gonna go for a swim.'

That was it.

I said OK, and I started to make my solitary dinner: I cooked a bowl of pasta. I wondered about the water temperature for swimming – even with all the sunshine the Atlantic in June at fifty-eight degrees north would be very cold – and then I heard Jenny go out behind me, and looking through the kitchen window I saw she was wearing a wet suit. She had thought to bring one. Problem solved, I supposed. So I sat outside to eat, in the evening light, and watched her swim back and forth across the anchorage, with her goggles on; I'd forgotten what a natural water baby she was, this Kiwi daughter of the sea, and I watched her dive down, for quite long periods, for twenty seconds and more, the wet suit protecting her from the chill, and I remembered what a good diver she was too, I remembered her finding sea urchins on the seabed off Ithaca, I remembered I had actually dreamt about that …

Her finding things … On the seabed …

Something stirred in my mind.

I finished my pasta and walked down the beach past the inflatable, to the water's edge, and I called out: 'Jenny!'

I called a couple of times and she heard me, and swam to shallower water, and stood up. She was about fifteen yards away.

I said: 'You got a minute?'

'Yeah, what?'

I said: 'Have you got a minute *here?*' Beckoning her in.

She waded towards me. 'What?'

I beckoned her in again. She raised her eyebrows and gave an exaggerated sigh, and waded in until she was just in front of me, where she stood with her hands on her hips. 'What'd you want?'

I dropped my voice. I said: 'Jenny, are you trying by any chance to recover your camera?'

A sort of guilty grin crossed her face. 'I might be.'

I closed my eyes. I said: 'Jenny, please, please can I ask you to stop.'

285

'Why? That big fucking nutter had no right to do what he did.'

'I know he didn't. But if you get it back and he sees it, you will put everything at risk here.'

'But what's the big deal with cameras anyway? Why no cameras on the island?'

'I do not know. I wonder myself. But it's their rule. And if you break the rules here, there will be drastic consequences.'

'Hmmph,' she said.

'I can see your camera was valuable and it probably had personal stuff on it and I've already said, if the agency won't replace it, I will, but if you find it and bring it up from the bottom now and Fergus sees it, he will go apeshit. Honestly. He will just explode. We will be kicked off the island in short order just like my predecessor was, that's the guy whose face he smashed in, remember? And the whole purpose of why I've been sent here will be destroyed.'

'He wasn't gonna see it. I was gonna make sure of that.'

'The risk is just too great.'

Jenny said: 'Hmm.'

I said: 'Look. I know you came out here with very little notice and the thing for you as well as for me was, it was about – well, you know what it was about. We didn't really have time to talk about the background. But there is a very serious reason why I am here doing this survey. You can see how amazing the place is, as a seabird colony, can't you?'

'Yeah?'

'Well, the British government wants to develop an oilfield right next to it.'

'An oilfield?'

'Yep. Right here. And let me explain it, will you? Will you come in and I'll explain to you exactly what the position is, and exactly why it matters, why it matters an awful lot. Will you? Please?'

Jenny deliberated. She said: 'All right then. But I'm gonna have another swim first, *if* you don't mind.'

'OK but please don't find your camera.'

She came in five minutes later, camera-less, thank God, and changed out of her wet suit. She had a shower. Then she got herself a plate of ham and some bread for her dinner and ate it in the kitchen, and eventually sat down on the sofa opposite me.

She said: 'All right. You can explain.'

I told her. I told her about crude oil which was what our whole civilization ran on but which was such terrible stuff for wildlife in general and for seabirds in particular, if there was a spill. I told her how Lanna was one of the most important seabird colonies in the UK and probably in the whole Atlantic Ocean and how the British government was now auctioning off to oil companies the very seabed area it was situated in, to prospect for oil reserves beneath it. I told her that an oilfield was already being developed 50 miles to the north, which was a pretty big risk anyway to these birds, but that to have one developed on top of Lanna itself would just be catastrophic.

She said: 'Why are they doing it, if everybody knows how great the birds are?'

'Because, it's a weird anomaly, because the birds here have never been properly surveyed, scientifically. 'Cos the island has always been closed, OK? Really, the whole thing's a try-on by the government, and UKOCA, my agency, we're confident we can stop it if we mount a proper objection, but that has to include a scientific survey of the seabird numbers, which is what I've come to do. What my predecessor Kenny Lornie came to do, till he fell out with Fergus. It really, really matters, Jenny. Honestly. I can't tell you how disastrous crude oil is for wildlife.'

Jenny said: 'I seem to remember you were never bothered about it before. If my memory serves me, you had a row about it, with – what was his name? On the island, Skarholm. Your former boss.'

'Callum McSorley. That's true. We did have a row. I was wrong. He was right. He was absolutely right. Oil spills are the most terrible thing.'

'So why d'you think they're terrible now if you never did before?'

'I saw one for myself at, first hand. In December.'

She looked at me.

'There was a tanker broke up in the Bay of Biscay, it was carrying thousands of tons of crude and it spilled all along the French coast for 250 miles and the seabird mortality was enormous. I was sent by my office to report on it so I saw it all close up. Oil is a terrible death for seabirds, Jenny. It fucks them up like you cannot believe. When I saw it I thought it the worst form of torture you could inflict on another living thing. It was a vast, vast wildlife disaster.'

And then before I could stop myself, I said: 'Arty Booboo was killed by it.'

'What?'

I instantly regretted saying it. I was desperate not to make use of the past. I stayed silent.

Jenny said: 'Miles?'

I said nothing.

'*Miles*. What did you say?'

I felt I had to answer her. 'I said that Arty Booboo ... was killed by it.'

'Arty Booboo?'

'Yeah.'

I saw the memory slowly flood back into her face ... . the champion shagger, whose prowess she had challenged me with, the night we first came together ... the legendary being who had gone on to grace the wall of our loo, who she felt was watching her, every time she took a pee ... the handsome seabird she'd eventually seen in the flesh, in the telescope on his home cliff, and admired, and even been aroused by ... the creature she had christened *a life-force* ...

'He was killed? How?'

'Like all the others. By the oil. He was completely covered in it. Smothered in it. Snuffed out.'

'But this was in France, he was killed?'

'It was.'

'How do you know?'

'I found him.'

'You *found* him?'

'I came across him on a beach. I picked him up just by chance but I could see who he was from the rings on his legs. Must have been a billion to one against. I mean, finding him. It was on the Île de Ré, that's off the west coast. Near La Rochelle.'

Jenny looked at me, her mouth open.

I said: 'I buried him. The other dead birds were being tossed into rubbish sacks, but I gave him a burial.'

She was quiet for long moments. She said: 'That must have been a shock.'

I said: 'It was, yeah.'

And again before I could stop myself, I said: 'It was where I started to change.'

She looked at me again.

'To see who I was. To see the ... appalling person I was. To see what I had done. What I had done to you.'

Jenny's eyes were fixed on me.

I said: 'It started there, when I found him on the beach. It sort of unlocked something inside me which ... in the end let me see it all. Which was why I asked you to come here. To try to put it right. Even if it's not possible.' I held up my hand, I said, 'It's OK, it's OK, I know it's not possible, Jenny, I understand that, I'm not trying to persuade you or anything. But I promised my mother on her deathbed, I would try to put it right with you, if it took me all my life. There, that's it, that's my spiel. Don't worry, I'm not going to talk any more about it.'

Jenny stared into space.

I doodled on my pad. I didn't know what else to say.

Moments passed.

Jenny got up and went to the kitchen and poured herself a glass of water.

She came back and sat down.

Then she spoke.

'All right, Miles. All right. I can see that maybe you have changed, maybe you really have, and *if* you have, that's a good thing. It's a big thing. And I welcome it. It might make the world a better place. And maybe if it was just me, I might even be able to say, I forgive you, I forgive you for ruining my life. I mean, probably not, actually. But I might. In principle. If it was just me. But it isn't.'

She drank her water. She said: 'I have a date in my life, now, a date in the calendar. You want to know what it is?'

'Yes, if you wish, yes.'

'It's March 17th.'

'OK.'

'It's actually St Patrick's Day, but that's not why it matters to me.'

'Why does it matter to you?'

'It's my due date.'

'Your *what*?'

'It's the date I would have given birth. If I hadn't had the abortion.'

'Oh.'

'It's what I worked out.'

'OK.'

'It's his birthday. The boy.'

'The boy?'

'He was a boy. I just know he was.'

'OK.'

'See, I had the abortion 'cos you didn't just break my heart, you fucked up my head. I was lost, I was completely confused, I didn't think I could bring into the world a child to have a father like the man you were, when I found I was pregnant and no, I didn't tell you, but I appealed to you, I sent a letter *and* another letter *and you didn't even reply*. But then, as soon as I had done it, I knew it was the biggest mistake of my life. And not just a one-off mistake. I realised it was going to follow me. 'Cos I'd worked out pretty much when I must have conceived, and so I began to think, back home in Auckland, this would be two months now, then this would be three, and I was looking up pregnancy symptoms on the Net and everything and I thought, I'd be having morning sickness now, and then at six months, at Christmas, I was thinking, my belly would be swelling now and people would be able to see it, our relatives would be visiting and they'd be patting me on the tummy and saying, how's it going Jen and I'd say fine, and it got closer and closer to the due date and on 17 March … that was the low point of my life. When I would have held him in my arms. I thought about taking a bottle of pills. For the only time. I thought, either go, or stay. In the world, I mean. Stay in this world or leave it. It was a near-run thing, but I chose to stay. Though I realised the only way I could survive would be to stamp out any good feelings I had, but if I did that I could probably survive anywhere, so I decided to go back to Britain and not be beaten by a bastard like you.

'And I came back, and I found a job, and I found a relationship, the ideal relationship, with a man who doesn't give a shit about anything. It's simply sex. I fuck him hard. He likes that. I think he thinks I like it too. He's good-looking but he's brainless. I don't like him. I don't like anything. All I can think about is how he would be three months old now, and I would be holding him in my arms and he would be looking up at me and recognising me, by three months they recognise your face and he'd be recognising me and smiling. And next year, on 17 March, will be his first birthday. He would have been one. My child. The child I destroyed. And so on and so on each year for the rest of my life, when he would have started talking, when he would have started school and started riding a bike, his second birthday, his third birthday, his fourth birthday, so can you see Miles, that is what will follow me to the end of my days and it doesn't matter how much you've changed, how much of a good guy you are now, I'm thinking about the boy who never was and I'm not realistically gonna say to you, am I, *ah fuck him, let's get back together?*'

I didn't have any words.

Jenny said: 'I'll go to bed now, I think.'

Hanna - beautiful, big seabird colony
Fergus - posh. Go where told. No
camera. Don't boat to Western coast
or cross fence ~ No binocs near Cross

No predators

22

In all the months since I had begun to think about her once more, I
had never truly understood what Jenny was feeling, I realised; and
now that I did, it left me stunned, it left me almost stupefied with
a wholly new level of guilt. I could not sleep; I lay in bed tormented
by my new knowledge and the fact that there was nothing I could
do to put things right, to relieve the distress I had created, even
to lessen its intensity. At 1 a.m. I got up and left the hut and went
over and knocked on Fergus's door, as we had arranged, and he
brought out a big lamp and we walked over to the monastery and
in the midsummer gloaming, against a sky still pale, I could see
small dark shapes fluttering in the air around the stone walls and
arches and gothic window frames; I thought at first they were bats,
but then Fergus shone his powerful torch and in the beam I saw
the long narrow wings and the white rumps and I recognised they
were the storm petrels which nested in the cracks in the buildings,
the Mother Carey's Chickens, the ship-followers, the small birds
of the open ocean, coming ashore at night to escape predators after
their long days far out over the waves. I knew objectively that to
see them up close like this in the half-light was magical, it was a
rare and wondrous experience, yet I could barely take it in; all I
could think of was Jenny and her distress.

I started to think also of the boy who never was, in the way
that Jenny was thinking: I had been his father. We would have
been his parents; we would have been united in a child. And for
the first time in my life I saw a child as something positive, I who
had thought of children merely as ghastly encumbrances, I who had
told her after our anniversary dinner that I would sooner have a pet
rat than have a child, and I understood that the loss was my loss
as well as Jenny's, although the pain, let it be said at once, was all
hers. All, all hers. It made me want to be infinitely gentle with her,
infinitely tender, I don't mean in touching her, I mean simply in
being about her, in being in her presence or in how I spoke to her,

I wanted to be infinitely considerate, if such a thing were possible; and I vowed that I would give her every atom of space she needed until the moment came, which would not be long now, for us to part for ever – for parting was all we could do.

That was never more clear.

And yet in the morning ... something was different. I was up first and after a few minutes I heard her come into the kitchen behind me and before I knew it I had I said: 'Would you like a coffee?' and she said, yes please. The tone of voice was new. It wasn't friendly; but it wasn't unfriendly. I could sense it in her body language too, in how she moved: the ugly hardness seemed to have gone, the confrontational aspect to the way she carried herself, and in its place was ... a solemnity. There was a sort of grave intensity about her, which filled me with admiration and love for her, alongside the sorrow, the sorrow which was underneath everything and which somehow, now, embraced me too; and I sensed she knew that, and although nothing was possible, nothing could be done, nothing could even be said, in our remaining time we would be together, perhaps, in a different way.

And so I began to talk to her, in a manner wholly dispassionate, and she was able to respond in kind. In tiny things. On the beach waiting for Fergus by the inflatable I asked her if she had her suncream and she said damn I've forgotten it and I said it's all right you can use mine and she said OK thanks and then I said *I'd* forgotten the water and she said I'll go back up and get it and I said thanks in my turn. The small inconsequential exchanges which lubricate life and which she had previously refused to engage in. It made the hard day's counting easier. She began to be part of it, she began to take on board, as I had myself the previous day, just how special was the vast seabird city we were at the heart of; I remember, one of the kittiwake nesting sites was at the mouth of a large cave at the foot of the cliffs and I could see that as she nosed the inflatable in for us, she was affected by the spectacle and the close proximity of these most beautiful of creatures with the soft grey of their backs and the purity of their white heads and their heartstopping aerial grace. And the birds on the sea surface began to animate her as well, I could feel her starting to take pleasure in the puffins and their cousins all about us, for she asked me a question, she said, apart from the puffins, it's the guillemots, is it? and the razorbills? how d'you tell 'em apart? and I said, look at the bills, one's thin and one's thick, the guillemot is smoking a cigarette but the razorbill is smoking a cigar, and she nodded in acknowledgement almost with a smile.

When we came in for lunch I made myself scarce with a quick excuse, to give her space; I know she appreciated it. Fergus, for his part, again looked desperately tired and seemed to be fighting hard against the pain in his joints, yet he said determinedly, we will finish it today; we had four more sections to do, but these were the biggest, at the northern end of the cliffs where they rose to their peak, three hundred feet above the sea. We did it, though, counting until the evening, with two or three welcome distractions, the first being announced by Jenny's cry, which escaped from her in spite of herself: 'Look! Dolphins!' Fergus and I turned and saw a pod of them, curving through the water a hundred yards away with their polish and panache, their pale flank stripe clearly visible. 'Common dolphins,' said Fergus. '*Delphinus delphis.* A heartening sight, is it not, Madam?'

'It is,' said Jenny.

'One might say they bring their blessing to our endeavours,' Fergus said.

'Yes,' said Jenny. 'Yes, they do.'

The second distraction was even more memorable for as we began to count the final part of the cliffs, the section nearest to the stacks and their gannet colonies, the gannets themselves found a shoal of fish in our vicinity and began to divebomb it. We stopped to watch. There was no alternative: it was like being caught in an artillery barrage, with big birds plunging straight down into the water from a hundred feet up, turning themselves into weapons and firing themselves, wheeling into the dive and tucking their wings in to make themselves rockets – scores of white rockets shooting down instead of up, a great salvo of rockets exploding in the sea all around us. We were awestruck. I know I was, anyway; and when it was over Fergus said: 'We are blessed again. That is one of the greatest of the spectacles of the Earth,' and Jenny nodded vigorously.

But there was a third incident which was more curious. We had actually just finished the fourteenth and final cliff section – wc had totals for the whole island now and I can still reel off the numbers, 3,166 pairs of kittiwakes, 22,715 pairs of fulmars and 19,701 individual guillemots – and we were sharing the water bottle in relief and self-congratulation, when Fergus looked up and seemed to notice something on the sea surface, in the distance. He brought up his binoculars and then threw them down and snapped at Jenny: 'Madam! Please to change places with me – immediately!' So Jenny shifted to the side and Fergus plonked himself by the outboard and at once opened the throttle to full and we shot over

the surface scattering birds in a high-speed curve back towards
the anchorage, with Jenny and me exchanging quizzical looks as
we held on to the grab handles. What on earth was Fergus doing?

Not that it mattered. For the count was completed, and I knew
that the figures, when added to those of the gannets which we
were going to do the next day from the Hill of the Cross, would
form the centre of the case against oil exploration around Lanna;
they might save this wonderful island, and I would have played
a part. I felt that after a life which had been so self-regarding I
would at last have done something worthwhile, even if the worst
of my sins – I glanced at Jenny – was beyond repair. I had come
on my pilgrimage to Lanna seeking redemption, I thought, and
I had gained understanding. But redemption ... redemption had
proved a step too far. And that was the price I would pay. For
the rest of life.

As we sped over the water I thought about what I would say
to Lotte.

It just didn't work, Lot.

It was just ... impossible.

The damage was too great.

The damage I had inflicted.

There was nothing that could be done about it.

She would be so upset.

We could go on holiday together, though. Yes. That's what we'd
do. We'd go to Paris, maybe, and eat ourselves silly. Lose ourselves
in food. Or go to Venice, and lose ourselves in art. Or something.
And then I would enter upon my new life. Whatever it was going
to be. With the ache that would last until I died.

And yet Jenny was doing what she could, in the face of
impossibility.

When we got in she said: 'I'm gonna go for a swim.'

I just said: 'OK sure.'

She said: 'Miles?'

'Yeah?'

'I'm not gonna look for my camera.' Again there was the hint
of a smile.

I smiled back at her. I said: 'Thanks.' I loved her even more
for that, for her making the effort in a hopeless situation; and
watching her carve her way elegantly around the anchorage on
what was another lovely evening, I thought about what I could
give her, on the same terms. So when she had come back and

showered and changed and made her dinner, I said: 'Jenny, I was wondering something.'

'Yeah?'

'Neither you nor I will ever return here, I suppose, and the island is a remarkable place, and I know quite a lot about it 'cos I read the one book that's been written about it before I came, and it's got an amazing history – and I wondered if you'd like me to tell you about it, and maybe we could have a look around. Because we'll both be gone soon and it might be a shame to leave it, without ... you know. Understanding it a bit. Knowing something about it.'

Jenny thought in her turn.

It didn't matter if she said No.

But she nodded, and said: 'Yeah, OK.'

So we went out into the soft evening light, and we sat on the beach by the inflatable and I told her about the priory founded by St Columba and how eventually the Vikings had come in their longships, no doubt grounding them right here where we were sitting now, and slaughtered the monks and dragged Corman the prior up to the top of the hill and crucified him on their oars, and I told her the story of Finbarr the survivor and his whale, and how the legend of the saint and his miraculous relic began, and how the Benedictine abbey was founded around it by the Clan Donald and the Lords of the Isles; and I told her how the monastery flourished all through the Middle Ages, and how it all came to an end, with the legend of the wrecked Armada galleon, and the treasure, and the curse, and eventually, the gold rush in 1939, which was why the island was closed.

She was interested: some small gate had been opened inside her. We spoke in the new language we had learned, called neutral, distinguished by the fact that it only had one tone, which was level. It worked fine.

She said: 'D'you think Fergus has had a look for it?'

'For what?'

'The gold.'

I half-laughed. 'That's never occurred to me,' I said. 'I think he concentrates on the birds.'

'Wouldn't you look for it though, if you were stuck out here? For long periods of time? Just, poke around?'

'Dunno.'

'I know I would.'

'I suppose I might,' I said. 'Fergus, I dunno.'

She said: 'What is it with this guy?'

'I wish I could tell you.'

But the question was rapidly to become acute.

We walked up from the beach then and over to the abbey, which was the first time I had approached it in daylight. We stopped and gazed on the ensemble of stone buildings, empty but in no way ruined, or at least, very well restored by the Earls of Kintyre; they sat serene in the evening sun.

Jenny said: 'So this was a monastery? With a full complement of – monks, and stuff? Like, living here?'

'For hundreds of years.'

'But – it's so remote, here! It's like – on the edge of the world!'

'It is, yes.'

'How did they stick it?'

'Only some of them could. That's what the guy says, who wrote the book. But they were worshipping God, I suppose. Being here was part of the deal.'

'Must have been so hard for them.'

We moved through the gate of the outer wall into the abbey precincts and Jenny stopped.

She held out her hand for me to stop too.

She was silent for a few moments.

Then she said: 'This place has very strong feelings.'

I was about to say, what d'you mean?

But I realised I knew what she meant. I felt a prickle in the skin on the back of my neck.

'But I don't feel afraid,' she said. 'Shall we go in?'

So we entered the Abbey of the Seals, this … this lost city, almost, this long-lost community of men trying to find the path to heaven from a lump of rock on the edge of existence, men in gowns with the tops of their heads shaved and their everyday emotions banished, striving so hard and so seriously to get to God – here were their community's perfectly-preserved walls, its Gothic window frames, its doorways and its stone staircases and only the men themselves were missing… yet they were not, they were still here, we both sensed as we wandered through arches and found what had to be the cloister, the central square space with buildings on all four sides, one of them being the small but elegant abbey church. Inside, leaning in the shadows against its walls were what seemed to be tall, intricately carved gravestones; grave slabs, I think Fergus had said. The dark choir was perfectly still and quiet. But the stillness resonated with – presences. I had an overpowering sense of being amongst others, of being in a company. I had never felt anything like it in my life before.

'They're all around us,' Jenny whispered. 'Watching and listening.'

I nodded.

I was less the sceptical scientist than I had been. And I remembered what Melrose Crinan had written, that they sang their divine offices here day after day, worshipping the Creator with all their being, for more than three hundred and fifty years – how could they not leave something of themselves behind? Their intensity remained.

'It's like Murdo said on the boat, about Iona, isn't it?' Jenny murmured.

'What?'

'The curtain here is very thin.'

'Yes,' I said.

Then she raised her voice: 'We're going now,' she said. 'Thank you for having us.'

We walked back out of the dark church into the evening sunlight. 'This is quite some place,' said Jenny, and I nodded up at the great Celtic cross on the hilltop and said, shall we complete the tour, and she said, sure. So we began to plod our way up Cnoc na Croise, and as we climbed the long green slope I paused and turned to look back down on the abbey and the anchorage and blow me but there was Fergus, outside his hut, watching us through his binoculars. I said: 'Hey, look, we're being spied on. Look. He's making sure we keep on the straight and narrow.'

Jenny said: 'What *is* it with this guy?'

I said: 'There's a part of me which thinks he might be mad. I don't think he is. But I really don't know.'

It was the next bit I never saw coming. When we reached the top and the enormous stone cross – it was about fifteen feet high – a panorama of almost theatrical splendour opened up before us, with the setting sun painting the sea below the colour of beaten copper and lighting up the two stacks with their gannet colony, which we were looking down on, just as Fergus had said. We were duly staggered; and we started back then, with the shadows lengthening, we descended the slope nearer the western side of the island and we had gone about two hundred yards when it happened: Jenny behind me suddenly screamed.

She shouted *Aargh!* and there was a *whoosh* by my ears and a speeding shape in the air and she cried: 'What in God's name was that?' as the shape became a big brown bird, banking away from us and around for a second attack as there was another cry from her and another rush of air and a second shape sped past my head and I shouted: 'It's bonxies!'

'What?'

'Bonxies! Great skuas! The birds!'

'What the fuck are they doing?'

'They're attacking us.' I laughed. 'We're getting bonxied!'

The first one swooped down again on its bombing run and we both ducked as it sped just over us. I said: 'They're trying to hit our heads. Make a fist and hold it above you. Use your fist to deflect it.'

'What they doing this for?'

'We've trespassed on their territory! Look out!' Another attack came in and this time I followed its swoop, the dark, stocky bruiser of a bird, like a plump brown gull: it just missed my head. 'It's a pair of them and they must be nesting nearby,' I called to Jenny who was ducking as the second bird descended on her. *Whoosh.* 'I knew they had to be here. Fergus said there weren't any but I knew he was talking nonsense. Here it comes again!'

Whoosh!

It became almost a ballet, the skuas attacking us as we stumbled down the hill and Jenny and I ducking and crouching to avoid them; and then, to our amazement, Fergus appeared.

He was coming up the slope towards us, he was hurrying, in so far he was going as fast as he could hobble, and he was carrying something.

He got closer.

I said: 'Christ he's got a gun.'

I saw it was a rifle. It was a .22. I recognised it. Aled the warden on Skarholm had one to shoot rabbits.

He levelled it and fired.

I shouted: 'Jenny come here, come here right now, stand behind me.'

The skuas were still swooping upon us.

Fergus was about fifty yards away; he raised his rifle and fired again and this time one of the skuas crumpled in the air and tumbled down and landed right at our feet.

Jenny picked it up: it was strikingly handsome, with white flashes on its chocolate-brown wings – and a bloody bullet hole in the centre of its chest. It seemed too beautiful to die, but dead it was, its head slumping, and she looked at it with incredulity. She picked it up, and she shouted: 'What've you done this for?' She ran to Fergus holding the bird. She cried: 'Why've you done this? It was only protecting its nest. It wasn't gonna kill us.'

'I have been remiss,' said Fergus. 'I should have seen them before. They must have arrived in the last two days whilst we were doing the survey.'

'Yeah but why are you shooting them? You're meant to be the warden, aren't you? You're meant to look after the birds, not shoot them, you cruel bastard.'

'Madam,' said Fergus, 'you are meddling with matters of which you know nothing.'

The other skua was circling above us, giving a harsh call.

Jenny said: 'Well you're not shooting that one, mate.'

'Dr Bonnici!' called Fergus.

'I'll stop you,' said Jenny. 'I'll get in your way. You'll have to fucking shoot me first.'

'Dr Bonnici!' called Fergus. He was getting agitated. 'You must return to your hut at once, with Miss Pittaway. At once, sir.'

I wouldn't say he was actually threatening us, with his rifle, but he was holding it and it was loaded and he was upset and I thought he might be crazy and now I was really afraid of what might happen, so I took Jenny by the arm. 'Come on, Jen,' I said.

'I shall accompany you,' said Fergus.

'He's not shooting that second fucking bird,' said Jenny, trying to shake me off.

'He's not, he's coming down with us,' I said. 'Come on, Jenny, come on. We have to go down. We have to.'

So Jenny allowed me to lead her down the slope, continually looking back at Fergus who was following us, past the monastery to our hut, where Fergus said: 'Dr Bonnici, you must now remain in your hut. Both of you. You must remain there, sir.'

'OK,' I said. 'OK, Fergus. Let's keep it all calm, eh?'

Jenny and I went in and sat on the sofas. I saw she was trembling. 'The bastard,' she said. 'The crazy fucking cruel bastard. That bird was so beautiful. What'd he have to shoot it for? He's meant to be the warden, isn't he?'

'I just don't know,' I said.

'They were only protecting their nest, weren't they? Doing what comes naturally? So why's he want to kill them?'

I shook my head.

'What reason can he have?'

There was a noise at the door, at sort of rattle and a click. I moved to it. I said: 'Fergus …?'

The voice was muffled. 'We shall meet in the morning, Dr Bonnici. At eight o'clock. Good night to you.'

I tried the door handle. It moved, but the door wouldn't open. I said: 'Christ, he's locked us in.'

'He's going back to shoot the other bird,' said Jenny. 'The bloodthirsty fucking swine.'

Our windows looked mainly over the anchorage and we could not see the slope up to Cnoc na Croise; but we sat listening and sure enough, after three or four minutes we heard the sharp crack of the rifle, and a few seconds later, a second shot, and then silence.

Jenny said: 'Why?'

The word hung in the air.

'Well, it's his island, isn't it?' I said. 'He can do what he wants here. He's the King of Lanna. Fergus the Terrible.'

Jenny snorted. 'You're not answering the question.'

'What exactly is the question?'

'What the fuck *is* it with this guy, Miles? I mean, what? There's something very strange about him and I don't think you've registered it, you been too busy counting seagulls. I don't just mean the way he looks and talks. There's something weird going on here.'

She stood up and started walking up and down the hut.

'Think about it. He throws my camera in the harbour. He says we can't go to half the places on his island. He goes mad in the boat, turns it around and tears off like a lunatic for no reason. Now he's shooting the birds he's meant to be protecting. Can't you see? It's all gotta add up to something. Something very strange.'

'You may well be right.'

'So what is it?'

'I couldn't say.'

'OK. Take it stage by stage. Why no cameras on the island? Haven't you asked yourself? You're doing this survey, wouldn't it help to have some photos to go with it?'

'Certainly would.'

'Fergus wants to help the survey, doesn't he? So why's he say no cameras?'

'It's not just him. Kintyre himself told me no cameras were allowed. I think they just don't want any publicity for the island. They just want to keep it completely private.'

'Maybe. But he got *so* upset, didn't he, when he thought there was one here? He finds one and he actually goes and *destroys* it? Like, *right away*? I think it's more than just, no publicity for Lanna.'

'Such as what?'

'I think there's something here, right now, that he doesn't want photographed. Something particular.'

'Possible, I suppose.'

'So what might it be?'

'I dunno.' I thought about it. I said: 'You are right, though, Jenny, I have been completely preoccupied with the survey' – I'd been completely preoccupied with Jenny too, of course – 'and I've had no time to consider it, but now that I remember, there was something that Murdo the boat skipper told me. I'd completely forgotten it. He told me Fergus had a secret.'

'What sort of secret?'

'No idea. But Murdo told me that when they were taking Kenny Lornie back, when they were sailing out of the anchorage, he shouted it out. He taunted him with it, Murdo said. And Kenny sort of implied he'd found out what it was, and Fergus seemed very upset.'

'So what d'you think it might be?'

'Haven't a clue. Neither had Murdo, and he's been coming here for years. Something else I remember now. He said he thought Fergus was an upright man, a very moral man, but he felt he was holding something back. There was something he was keeping from him. All the time he'd been coming here.'

'What do *you* think it might be?'

'Well. For anyone familiar with the legend of Lanna, you'd think it'd have to be the Spanish gold, wouldn't you? Pieces of Eight, and all that. What the treasure hunters came over looking for in the thirties.'

'That'd be a pretty good secret.'

'Yes,' I said. 'Though on the other hand, if you *found* the Spanish gold, you wouldn't just keep it here hidden, for ages and ages.'

'You'd do something about it.'

'You'd remove it from the island, at least. Wouldn't you?'

'You would,' said Jenny. 'I don't think it can be the Spanish gold.'

We both sat and thought about it.

'OK,' I said. 'Here's a crazy idea. What if – what if it's *another person*? This would be a great place to hide out, don't you think? Guy called Gervase, who is Lord Kintyre's secretary, he told me he thought Lanna had been the hideout for Robert the Bruce, in the Middle Ages.'

'But who for now?'

'Let's think. Somebody Fergus doesn't want known about would have to be … a fugitive of some sort. Lord Lucan? Some gangster, or something? They usually hide out on the Spanish Costas. But they're watched there, aren't they? Interpol, and stuff. Here, you'd be beyond the sight of the law.'

'You think Fergus might have links with organised crime?'

'I suppose anything's possible.'

'But if Fergus is the employee of Lord Kintyre,' said Jenny, 'and he doesn't own the island himself, isn't it actually more likely he'd be hiding someone to do with his boss?'

'You're right. It is.'

'And who might that be?'

'Some friend of Kintyre's? Or some member of his family he doesn't want people to know about? Aristocratic families can be pretty weird.' Another bizarre thought occurred to me. I said: 'You ever heard of the Monster of Glamis?'

'The monster of what?'

'Glamis. It's an old Scottish castle. Where the Queen Mother grew up. And in the nineteenth century, it was meant to have a secret room, where the heir to the family fortune was imprisoned for life, 'cos he was monstrously deformed.'

'You mean like, there might be a monster of Lanna?'

We looked at each other.

'This is getting kind of far-fetched,' I said.

'I think it is,' she said.

'But … I do think there must be something, if Kenny Lornie taunted Fergus about it.'

'Well then just look at what is definite,' said Jenny. 'Two things you absolutely can't do here, right? First is, you can't have a camera. You have a camera, he destroys it. Second thing is, you can't go to the west side of the island. Under any circumstances. So what's that tell you?'

'What?'

'Stands to reason. The secret has gotta be whatever it is on the west side that Fergus doesn't want photographed.'

'That would appear to make sense.'

Jenny got up and walked over to the door, and rattled its handle. Then she walked back to one of the two rear windows of the hut. She felt round the frame, examined its screws. 'Know what, Miles,' she said. 'I think I'm gonna take a little look.'

'A look where?'

'At the west side.'

'You can't do that.'

'Why not?'

'Well – when are you going to do it?'

'First light. Before Fergus is awake. Gotta sleep, hasn't he?'

'But we're locked in.'

'This window will unscrew.'

My heartbeat went up. 'Jenny, come on now, this guy is potentially dangerous. Part of me thinks he's actually crazy. He beat up my predecessor just for going to the wrong place and now he's got a gun. We have to be careful here. We're kind of exposed. We're a very long way from the forces of the law.'

'You don't have to come, Miles.'

'So why do you have to go?'

'Cos that bastard threw my camera in the harbour. And he's out there killing the wildlife he's meant to protect. Some warden he is. I'll do an exchange with him.'

'What exchange?'

'He took my camera. I'll take his secret.'

'Jenny, please.'

'I'm gonna have a look, Miles. You're welcome to join me. But I'm gonna go.'

'But it could fuck up the survey.'

'Haven't you done most of it now?'

'I've done the best part of it, yeah, but—'

'So even if Fergus calls off the rest of it tomorrow, you could still write a report on the seabirds?'

'I suppose so, but—'

'Then I'm going.'

I knew there was no arguing with her, and the idea of trying to restrain her physically, given everything that had passed between us, was unthinkable. I looked at the window with her and I saw that the tilting pane could indeed be taken out of the frame; so wholly against my better judgement, and filled with trepidation about what Fergus might do if he found us, I gave in and agreed to accompany her, if only so I could watch over her and make sure she came to no harm in her loopy scheme. I got out my own map of the island and we pored over it: the main feature of the west side seemed to be a group of offshore rocks about half-way along, which was labelled Sgeir Dubh, *skayr doo*; I remembered Fergus had warned us against the west side offshore reefs which were extremely dangerous. But the real danger, I thought, might well be Fergus Pryng himself.

For a second night running, I could barely sleep; I lay awake with a weird mixture of emotions until at 4 a.m. I rose and made coffee for us both, and at 4.10, just before sunrise, we unscrewed and removed the window, using a knife from the well-supplied cutlery drawer and climbed out. Everything was very still and quiet in the pre-dawn half-light. It was obvious that if we went straight across the top of the beach we risked being seen if Fergus was by any chance awake, so we ran up along the burn to the edge of the monastery then crept through the buildings and ran low towards the boundary fence on the west side of the island, and crawled underneath it. In front of us was a green ridge; when we crested it we found a small valley with an obvious path in the middle, coming from Fergus's hut, and we could see the sea; we followed the path and came to the clifftop, with a drop to the water of only about 30 or 40 feet. Here we were, on the forbidden west side, yet there was no obvious secret, no sign of any other habitation, say, where a fugitive might be hiding, where the Monster of Lanna might be detained; all we could see was the Sgeir Dubh reef offshore. We continued to follow the path and after about a hundred yards it dipped under a large boulder and came to a halt, in a sort of natural shelter, a half-cave.

'What's this?' I said.

'Let's have a look,' said Jenny.

We scrambled into it. There were signs of habitation: a tarpaulin on the earth with a couple of blankets, and a sort of low bench made out of pine, not very big. I glanced around and said to Jenny, nodding seawards with my head: 'This is some sort of observation post. Look.'

We were now directly opposite Sgeir Dubh, a long group of black rocks, almost an islet, about a hundred yards out, just as the map had indicated: a perfect view of them, from slightly above.

'What is he looking at there,' Jenny said, 'that he doesn't want anybody to know about?'

The sea was still calm, with no waves and little discernible swell; I put my binoculars on the rocks and started to study them. I realised Sgeir Dubh was a sort of double reef parallel to the coastline, maybe a hundred yards long and higher on the western, seaward side, with a brief glimpses of what appeared to be more or less sheltered water in between its two arms, a sort of lagoon, perhaps twenty yards across; the rocks sloped up to their highest point, where the two arms seemed to join, at the northern end, about seventy feet above the sea, I reckoned, and I was seeing it, I realised, at high tide; at low tide it would be more. There were many smaller rocks scattered around the central complex, some just breaking the surface and some which had clearly become invisible as the tide rose, and I realised what a dangerous place it must indeed be for any boat to approach.

Jenny said: 'I'm lying on something hard.'

She fumbled under the blanket and pulled out a small copper tube.

'What's this?'

'Cartridge case,' I said. 'He's been shooting from here. What's the crazy bastard been shooting?'

'More er, what were they called, bonxies?'

'Christ only knows,' I said. I started scanning the rocks again, closely this time, foot by foot, inch by inch, then in one of the places where the enclosed water was visible, I thought I glimpsed something. 'Hang on a minute,' I said. 'What's that?'

'GET OUT!' exploded a voice beside us. 'GET OUT OF THERE AT ONCE!'

Fergus was standing on the path peering into the shelter. 'Come along, get out!' he roared.

We had no choice and crawled out to face him: his eyes were glaring, there was sweat on his brow, and a fleck of spittle on the edge of his mouth. 'Bloody people!' he shouted. 'Give me those!' He indicated my binoculars. I took them off my neck but only defensively, so I could hold them away from him. 'What's your problem, Fergus!' I shouted back at him. 'What are you so defensive about? What's your big secret? We don't want to harm anything. We're here to protect things.'

'Give them to me!' shouted Fergus. 'Give them to me now!' He lunged at me stiffly, half-caught my bins and I pulled them away, and he lunged at me again and I dodged him and in his stiffness he stumbled past me, and went over the edge of the cliff.

I seem to see it all in slow motion now, him tumbling forward with his arms waving in circles and the second's pause before the colossal splash and Jenny screaming Oh My God! and this great beast of a man flailing in the water trying to support himself thirty feet below us, crippled by his arthritis, weighed down by his clothes and his great size. Incredulity froze the frame. But only for a second. I remembered the training Callum had instilled in me on Skarholm for something like this. For people falling into the sea.

'Christ, Miles, what do we do?' cried Jenny.

'We do this first,' I said, and I reached into the shelter for the small pine bench and I heaved it into the water near Fergus and shouted, 'Fergus, grab the bench, grab it if you can.'

He seemed to be floundering.

'Can you grab the bench, Fergus?'

He couldn't. I gave him ten seconds. Maybe fifteen. Then I said to Jenny: 'I'll have to go in for him.'

'What, jump in yourself?'

I was tearing at my laces to get my boots off. 'He's going to drown if I don't. Can you get the inflatable? Can you run down there? He leaves the keys on a hook in his office.'

'Get the inflatable?' said Jenny.

'And bring it up here. Come out of the defile and go right, go round Castle Point at the bottom of the island and bring it up to us. I'll try and keep him afloat. Can you do that?'

'Yes.'

'Right away?'

She nodded. We looked at each other, we looked into each other's eyes, but there was no time.

'Quick as you can then,' I said.

What else was there to do? Fergus was drowning. I jumped.

That it was still so calm that day was our great fortune, as even a moderate swell would have made breathing without taking in water infinitely harder – that, and the Gulf Stream making the Atlantic at 58 degrees North a lot warmer than it would have been across the pond, on the coast of Labrador. But its cold still whooshed the breath right out of my body when I hit it and went under, and came up to see Fergus flailing hopelessly a few yards away from me, with the wooden bench a couple of yards beyond him. I swam over and pushed it to him and I shouted Fergus, grab the bench, grateful beyond words for its presence, as had it not been available the only thing for Fergus to grab hold of would have been me, and he would have taken me down with him. He got hold of it; it floated him. I grabbed the other end. I shouted: 'Hang on. Jenny has gone for the inflatable.' I prayed then, I prayed that his door was unlocked and she could find the keys and could get the thing into the water by herself and get it started and as the minutes went by the cold crept through me, almost to paralyse me and Fergus as well and I began to think, we might not survive this, as I could feel the pounding of my heart and my teeth were chattering and there was a buzzing in my ears which got worse and worse and worse and then I realised with a leap of joy that it was the sound of the inflatable's outboard as Jenny tore across the water. She came up to us and eased it down but I realised at once we would never in a million years get Fergus into the boat: you would need an industrial crane.

'Quick,' I called out. 'We've got to secure him. Gimme the mooring rope.' She threw it to me and in spite of my hands feeling dead, as if they did not belong to me, I somehow managed to pass it under his arms and round his chest and she reached down and grabbed the free end and tied it tight round one of the grab handles on the boat's side. Fergus was now attached, backwards; I swam round to the other side and tried to haul myself on board but despite all Jenny's efforts to help I just couldn't do it; my strength was nearly gone. I had enough sense to stop before it went completely and I hooked my arm through another of the grab handles and I said to Jenny, 'Go, go, tow us back.' She opened up, as fast as she dared, round the Castle Point, and through the defile and into the anchorage – it seemed like an hour but it probably only took about four to five minutes – and she carefully ran up the beach as far as she could, with her bizarre cargo.

Fergus lay poleaxed at the water's edge. I managed to stand up and Jenny and I went over to him and we each took an arm but he was just too heavy. I thought he might be unconscious but I saw his eyes flicker. I shouted in his ear: 'Fergus! Fergus! C'mon man, you have to help us, we can't lift you by ourselves.'

With a weird noise in the back of his throat signalling a tremendous effort, and with us helping, he struggled to his feet, and we walked four steps up the sand, then he collapsed and we fell down with him. Twice more he fell, before we got him to the open door of his hut, and lowered him on to his bunk, and pulled the sodden clothes off him till he was naked and put the duvet on top of him then found two blankets and put them on top of the duvet. He seemed half-conscious but I said: 'I think he'll be OK.' We turned and we went outside and I immediately fell over. I felt exhausted and almost unbearably cold. Jenny helped me to my feet and helped me across the top of the beach to our own hut which was locked, of course, but thank God Fergus had left the key in and we opened it and the first thing I did was ask Jenny to push one of the sofas behind the door to block it from a rampaging Fergus who might come back for us and I started to strip off my wet clothes and I said, 'I'll just get under the duvet' and I did.

Jenny tucked the duvet under my body.

I was shivering uncontrollably.

Then she brought her own duvet and put that on top of me.

Two duvets.

She stood for a second.

Lives turn on such a second.

Then she stripped to her underwear and got in alongside me and wrapped her arms around me and put her body next to mine, using it to warm me. Skin to skin.

Her eyes were tightly closed.

And slowly my shivering calmed as I warmed with her, long minutes, and eventually, when I had become still, I stretched out my own arm and I brought her towards me, ever so slightly.

Her eyes opened and she looked into my face.

I looked back at her.

And she began to weep.

She wept and wept and wept. It was unending, like a baby crying, minute after minute after minute, a great unrelenting outpouring, as if a dam had burst of all the grief and the heartache and the unhappiness, and I was part of it, I was carried away with the flood like she was, the flood of her tears, it carried us both to wherever it would, we were given over to it completely, until eventually it let us down somewhere and the weeping quietened, as if the crying baby had finally dropped off.

But she was not asleep.

Her head was on my shoulder.

I could hear the distant calls of the seabirds and even the thin *tseep* of the rock pipits around the hut.

I said: 'You know … the boy who never was?'

She moved her head and looked at me.

'He was mine too.'

She was silent for long moments. Then she said: 'He was. Yes.'

'And maybe you don't have to be alone, with that any more.'

I could feel her heart beating.

I said: 'Some things can never be repaired. But maybe some other things … might be built?'

She bit her lip.

I said: 'I did change. And I've known since I changed that I can never love another person. Even if we part now, I will love you all my life. Like you said to me, in Ithaca, and I threw that away. And I know I don't deserve to have it back, but even if I can't have it back, it won't alter, Jenny, even if we leave here and go our separate ways, I will never stop loving you. I want you to know that.'

Jenny gazed at me. It was a gaze that seemed to go on for ever. And then she brought her mouth to my mouth, and she dissolved into me.

308

23

In how many lives can it come, the sentiment of being new-born? It is surely the rarest and greatest of all blessings, and I wish I had a religion or something to provide a ceremony or a metaphor adequate to enshrine it; but since I am a mere godless scientist, I will simply say that for me, in my years on this earth, I know it will never be surpassed.

Yet fate can take curious turns; fate can take us wholly by surprise. Or why else now, when I had attained the climax of my life, would another climax overtake it almost at once? For I had indeed reached a culminating point of joy when Jenny and I finally reunited in the hut on Lanna, just as I had dreamed that we would, as lost love was won back, as my promise to my mother on her deathbed was fulfilled and the mending could tentatively begin after all the hurt and the heartbreak I had caused – it was the peak and pinnacle of my experience and there should have been time for it to be savoured, you would think that life would allow the ending of such a story to have its own resplendent space, would you not? And I suppose it did, for a while, as we fell asleep in each other's arms, for an hour maybe, or maybe it was two.

But we did not know that there was a second saga in which we were unwittingly involved, a second train of events which had also been moving inexorably towards a culmination of its own and which was to take over our lives, which burst upon us, there in our reunited sleep, with a sudden irruption, like the bump-bump-bump-BUMP at the start of the Fifth Symphony.

Beethoven said: *thus fate knocks at the door.*

Bump-bump-bump-BUMP.

It woke us.

'Christ, it's Fergus. If he's gone mad, we might have to fight him off. Come on, get ready.'

We got out of bed and I threw a towel around my waist and we moved to the door, tensed. I called out: 'Yes, Fergus, what d'you want?'

Fergus said, his deep plummy voice now sounding hoarse: 'I am come to thank you.'

The tone was not hostile. Jenny and I looked at each other. We moved back the sofa and I opened the door and saw a colossal, bedraggled figure. He looked exhausted.

Jenny said: 'Come in, Fergus. Come in and have a cup of coffee, for God's sake.'

'No, it is just that I ... I am to thank you for what you did. Most sincerely. I recognise it as a truly courageous and worthy act. It would be unconscionable not to. And it has ... precipitated things. It has brought certain considerations to a climax.'

The tension and aggression had gone and there was a weariness in his face. As if something had shifted. Or, given way.

He said: 'I have felt I am ceasing to be human. I am denying everything for one purpose. And no one can do that for ever. My powers are failing. And what happens when I am gone?' He seemed to be agonising over something. He said: 'I am starting to think it has all been a mistake. Which is a dreadful prospect to contemplate. But anyway, it will be known now.'

We were mystified. I said: 'Would you ... would you like to explain?'

He said: 'I have something to show you. I will come for you at four o'clock.'

'What about the gannets? Aren't we going to count the gannets?'

'We will no longer need the gannets.'

It may be understood that we were so much involved with each other that we did not at first pay excessive attention to what Fergus had promised.

Jenny said: 'What d'you think that means then? This the secret of Lanna he's gonna show us?'

I shook my head. 'Dunno. Don't really care.' I took her hands in my hands and I brought them to my lips and kissed each one. I could still barely believe what had happened, and I feared greatly for its fragility, for we had not yet spoken about it, we had sealed nothing with words and the overwhelming fear I had was that Jenny might yet change her mind again. I knew only too well now how damaged she was and how deep was the wound; I was going to presume nothing, I most assuredly was going to take no liberties, and she could have all the space she wanted in the world. But I looked straight at her, and she held my gaze, and we came together, lips to lips; and I started to have faith.

Although I still couldn't quite … even understand it.

I said: 'Jenny, I want so much to believe, in us, and in now, but this is the problem. For what I did … there is no forgiveness. I will carry it with me till the day I die. It's about redemption, do you see?'

'Redemption?'

'There is no redemption for me. You can't forgive me and of course I understand that. But I can't forgive me either, and I will go to my grave with what I did to you. It is who I am, now.'

Jenny was silent, thinking, it seemed for an age. Then she said: 'It's true, Miles, that I can't forgive you, any more than I can forgive me, because that would be to lose sight of the boy who never was, and I don't ever want to do that.'

'Yes of course.'

'But something has altered.'

'What?'

'It's something to do with when you jumped into the water. And I have to say to you, that if it hadn't happened, even though I could see you had changed and I respected you for it, I would have gone my own way without you, yes I would.'

I could hear the rock pipits *tseeping* outside.

'But it did happen.'

'And … what?'

'It lets me love you. I don't quite understand how or why, but it does. It lets me love you again.'

'Does it?'

'Yes Miles. And I do.'

They were the best words I will ever hear in my life.

We talked then, for more than two hours. We spoke of everything that happened with our break-up, or rather, my desertion – with me concerned above all to tell her the unvarnished truth, yet aware of just how brutal and painful that truth might be, the truth of my malevolence and duplicity – as it was, for example, when I told her about Jasper Bakker beating me to my research conclusion, and how it was the first failure I'd ever known and it felt like my world had fallen apart and how I blamed her for it …

'You *blamed me*? What on earth had I done?'

'You'd done nothing whatsoever. You'd only ever helped me. But what my brain told me was, I'd spent all that time chasing after you, that I should've been spending on my research, and if I hadn't, I would have beaten the Dutch guy.'

'That's nonsense. Just the most awful nonsense.'

'Of course it is.'

'And for *that*, you ...'

'Yes.'

'But Miles, you *destroyed* us.'

I said: 'I did, Jenny. And I destroyed my mother as well.'

Tears came into her eyes. 'Ah, Muriel,' she said. 'God rest her soul.'

And I told her properly how the jolt of finding Arty Booboo had unlocked something deep inside me, how I had thought of her in that very instant and called out her name, and how it was in that frame of mind that the next day I had learned of my mother's illness and returned to London to find her dying, and how what she had written on the piece of paper, in her despair of me, finally let me see everything.

Jenny thought about it.

She said: 'She did say that.'

Remembering.

She said: 'It was at your front door. At the end of my first visit. That day we drove down there, when she gave me the picture of the sunset. When we were leaving.'

'Yes?'

'She suddenly whispered it in my ear. Then she was embarrassed.'

I said: 'She didn't want to lose you.'

She nodded.

And she told me eventually what it was like for her, when I left her, and it was very hard to hear – about the scale of her distress and her sheer bewilderment above all, her not understanding why I had gone, and then discovering she was pregnant and not knowing what to do and eventually deciding on the abortion and how afterwards she came back to the house – our house in Jericho – and she was more distressed than ever and in fact she was bleeding and in pain and Lotte came up to Oxford and found her, and Lotte looked after her, she stayed with her continually until she went back to New Zealand – apart from the day she flew to Scotland to try to make me change my mind.

'God bless your sister,' she said.

'Yes,' I said. 'God bless her and save her.'

It wasn't a happy talk. But it wasn't really an unhappy talk. It was just, the truth.

It was a sort of surgery, the excision of a huge malignant tumour, a procedure that involved pain and trauma, but when it was over, though we were both shocked by the process and aware that there would be deep and lasting scars, we knew that the tumour had gone, and we could heal; we could begin again. And we did, we cooked together, we cooked a brunch of bacon and eggs and toast; I was never more grateful for that great human institution, breaking bread. It could not be an innocently joyous meal like our dinners on Ithaca, for we were not in the green fields of new love, we were somewhere very different, on the far side of a terrible hurt; but there was a calmness about it, a solemnity, and we knew that a bond had begun that would last until our deaths.

It was when we went for a walk that we began to think more about Fergus and what he was going to show us.

First, though, Jenny had a mission.

She led me by the hand to the abbey, and paused at the entrance. 'We are going to come in,' she said, to no one in particular; then I realised she was addressing the inhabitants. We stepped through the gap in the outer wall, then into the cloister and on into the darkened empty church with its grave slabs leaning against each side; and once again I had the most powerful sense of being in a company, of being amongst others, as, clearly, did Jenny, for she said out loud: 'Will you bless us?'

Her voiced echoed in the shadows.

She said: 'Will you bless our coming back together here, so it may be for always, and so we may take your blessing away from here with us?'

She stood with her eyes closed. I felt once more the skin prickle on the back of my neck.

Then at length Jenny said: 'Thank you.' And she took my hand, and she turned and led me back out into the sunshine and into what seemed like a new world: it seemed like a world full of peace, as we walked up the slope towards the cross, with the beauty of Lanna belonging now to us both together (though I noticed the weather seemed to be changing: the blue sky was coated with a milky-white haze). When we got to the top and once again beheld the astounding view over the stacks, Jenny remarked that the lovelinesss of the place might at least be some consolation for living here by yourself, as Fergus did.

'What's his name again?' she said. 'Fergus ... Pryng?'

'Yeah. With a y.'

'Funny name.'

'I think it's actually quite posh.'

'The only Pryng I've ever heard of is the woman who does the cruelty-free cosmetics, Bronwen. You know? Bronwen Pryng?'

'Fraid not.'

'She does all the big environmental campaigns. Saving the rainforest, and everything. She's really cool and trendy. Very stylish, and very ethical. You think they're related?'

'No idea.'

Jenny said: 'So what d'you think, Miles? D'you think he's gonna show us his secret? D'you still think it might be another person?'

I said: 'It could be. But then, what about the lookout post, opposite the rocks, where he came and found us? That's got to have something to do with it, surely?'

'I suppose so.'

I said: 'I have an idea, though. A new one.'

'What?'

'I think it might be a bird.'

'What bird?'

I said: 'Have you by any chance ever heard of Swinhoe's petrel?'

She looked at me blankly and shook her head.

I said: 'It's a small seabird that breeds in the Pacific, on islands off Japan and Korea, OK? But in the last few years birds have been turning up in the North Atlantic and a few have actually been trapped in Britain. The guy in charge of seabirds in my agency says it's just possible it might be breeding on a North Atlantic island, and Lanna would be a prime candidate. He asked me specifically to look out for any mention of it by Fergus.'

'OK.'

'And that'd be a huge story, in conservation terms. It'd be a sensation in birding circles, anyway.'

'Would it?'

'You bet. The wildlife story of the year. Swinhoe's petrel! Breeding on Lanna! Headlines!'

'Would Fergus want to keep that a secret?'

'Almost certainly. Because if the bird was here, the birders, the twitchers, they'd all try to get here to see it, and Kintyre and the Balnay estate wouldn't want that at any price. It'd be like the 1939 gold rush all over again. I think Fergus would definitely keep that a secret.'

'Well, we'll see,' said Jenny.

And the moment came when we saw.

Fergus arrived on the dot of four. He had recovered somewhat; he was stiffer than ever, but at least he seemed to have dried out. He said: 'You will need your suits and lifejackets. We are going in the boat.'

As we clambered into the inflatable and Fergus purred us out through the defile, I had a strong feeling that because of everything that had happened, we would be heading for the west side of the island, and perhaps for Sgeir Dubh, and so it proved; but when we rounded Castle Point, we found a change in the water. The slap of a swell hit us side on. 'The scend of the sea,' said Fergus. 'That has come from America. The end of the good weather approaches. A storm is on the way.'

Watching the rocks come closer I felt a mounting sense of excitement: I was more and more convinced my new hunch was right, and I would bet a month's pay that Swinhoe's petrel, a bird hardly recorded in the North Atlantic, was breeding here. There'd probably be a colony, a small colony of them. Imagine! I could imagine writing up the scientific paper. It would be an ornithological sensation! And it would almost certainly help to stop any new oil field.

Although, could we see them in daylight? Didn't most petrels come back to their nest sites in the dark? Like the stormies in the monastery?

So why was Fergus taking us now?

I said: 'Are you protecting something, Fergus?'

'You will be shown.'

'Is it a bird?'

'I shall show you.'

'Not Swinhoe's petrel by any chance, is it?'

'You will see.'

As we approached the rocks we veered to the seaward side; Fergus slowed right down and ran towards the point where the reef began to slope up to its peak and at the base of the slope, I saw, was a gap, a narrow gap which presumably only existed at high tide. He edged up to it, then brought us through it gingerly and into the enclosed water between the outer reef and the inner. We were now shut off from the open sea, in a sort of a walled lagoon. He idled the motor and let us drift for moment.

Then he said: 'There.'

I looked past him, and saw it, twenty-five yards ahead; for a second I could not take it in, as if the connection between my eyes and my brain had failed. But as I registered what I was looking at, in an intense moment of incredulity that suddenly felt like a series of locks flying open all at once, I understood: I understood everything, I understood Lanna's incredible secret, I understood what Fergus was protecting.

Jenny said later that my mouth was open. She had said to me: 'What? What is it?' and I couldn't speak. She pulled at my lifejacket. She said: 'What is it, Miles?'

'The bird on the water,' I said.

She looked. 'What is it?'

I said slowly, not taking my eyes off it: 'It's beyond belief.'

She said: 'But what is it?'

'It's a great auk.'

She had to think for a second. 'You mean – the bird that, er, Callum – Callum told us about?'

'Yes.'

'The bird that's extinct?'

'Yes.'

Jenny gaped in her turn.

'The bird that's been extinct,' I said, still not looking away, 'for a hundred and fifty years.'

'He's the oldest male,' Fergus said. 'He'll dive in a second. He's not used to you.'

The bird was watching us intently. He was magnificent, big as a goose, dark with white underparts and a big white patch on either side of his dark head, and suddenly with a swift and supple jump forward, he dived. Fergus pointed below the boat and I glimpsed him, a blur in the green water, shooting beneath us at astonishing speed. Then he was gone.

I was lost for words.

Fergus engaged the inflatable drive, very slightly, and purred us further into what I realised was a big enclosed area, entirely sheltered from the waves. Even at high tide the seaward rocks were about seventy feet above the sea, and at the end they formed an overhang: underneath it was a sort of wide flat rock shelf that sloped down to the water.

Fergus pointed.

With a thrill of astounded excitement I realised there was a group of birds on the shelf, all quite close together. They were tall and upright, like slimmer versions of king penguins, their short stubby wings seeming like withered arms. I counted: ten.

I dropped my voice to a whisper. 'How many are there?'

'Some are away feeding. But, six breeding pairs. At least four non-breeders, possibly five or six. Sixteen birds at least, possibly seventeen or even eighteen.'

'And that's it?'

'I believe so.'

'God Almighty,' I said.

Fergus murmured: 'D'you see the ring in the rock by your shoulder? Please to tie us in.'

There was a metal ring fixed into the rock surface. Jenny passed me the mooring rope and I secured it.

The birds were twenty-five yards away on their flat rock shelf, all watching us now, clearly agitated, shifting on their feet and moving their heads up and down.

'Be very quiet and very still,' Fergus said. 'They're sitting on eggs. We mustn't drive them off.'

Jenny murmured: 'This is unbelievable.'

It was indeed hard to believe: it felt like a dream, watching these creatures that had come back from the dead, these creatures that the world had written off for a hundred and fifty years, yet here on Lanna, here they survived. How, I thought, how, how, how? How were they here, living and breeding still? I had a million questions I wanted to ask. But I simply said: 'When will the eggs hatch?'

'In about two weeks.'

'How long does the chick stay on the ledge?'

'Two days.'

'Is that all? That's amazing.' I realised at once this was new to science. I said: 'There's nothing like that in the Atlantic auks. Razorbill chicks are seventeen days. Guillemots, twenty-one.'

'There is in the Pacific ones, some of the American auks,' said Fergus. 'The ancient murrelet chick is gone in two days.'

'So two days and then – they stay here, in amongst the rocks?'

'No, they go to sea. Close by their parents, of course.'

'Out to sea straight away?'

'Yes. They're big chicks.'

'Then what?'

'Away for the whole winter.'

'Where?'

'The Bay of Biscay, perhaps? Greenland? Who knows? I do not.'

I continued to marvel at the situation. 'And they've never been spotted? No one's ever caught sight of one?'

Fergus paused. He said: 'Actually, a man saw one off the Butt of Lewis five years ago. A competent birdwatcher. He saw it from the shore and he ran into the sea to try and get closer, and told people. The rumour has reached me. But no one believed him. He was ridiculed. Thank God.'

'When do they come back here?'

'About the end of April.'

'And when do they lay?'

'About mid-May.'

'Do they synchronise it?'

'They would seem to, yes. More or less.'

'So they all lay at once?'

'As far as one can tell, yes.'

'And so they hatch together, and fledge together?'

'They're all gone in one day.'

'To minimise the risk of predation?'

'One would imagine so.'

I thought about it. 'After all, they're pretty immobile, aren't they?' I said. 'Chicks would be easy targets for predators, for greater black-backs, or ravens, or bonxies, say.'

'Not any more.'

'How d'you mean?'

'I've shot them all,' said Fergus. 'We must leave now. We've disturbed them long enough.'

24

The shock; the sense of wonder; the disbelief, almost, at what we had seen; but most of all the shivering excitement I felt, as we bumped back over the increasingly choppy sea to the anchorage on that day, June 8, 2000, they are all emotions which have never left me, and never will. For I grasped it instantly, I saw all the implications, and I trembled with the knowledge; and all the way the key question built up inside me, larger and larger, until at last, when we had brought the inflatable up the beach and got out and secured it and the three of us stood facing each other, it burst from me: '*Who knows?*'

'Kintyre,' said Fergus.

'Right,' I said. 'And that's it?'

'Not exactly.'

'How d'you mean?'

'Your colleague Lornie saw them.'

'*What?* You showed then to Kenny Lornie?'

'By no means. He discovered them himself.'

'Jesus Christ.'

Kenny knew. That's what he was shouting about from the *Katie Colleen*, as he sailed away.

That's what he meant when we met outside Ramsay's office and he said to me *I know what's there.*

'How on earth did he find out?'

'He chafed at my restrictions on going to the west side of the island and he left his hut, just as you did, in the early morning—'

'He found the shelter?'

'I do not know if he found the shelter exactly, but he certainly must have looked out over Sgeir Dubh and he must have seen at least two of the birds in his binoculars, probably with the light of the rising sun directly upon them.'

And Fergus proceeded to relate how Kenny had come running back down to the anchorage shouting *Fergus!* at the top of his voice, *Fergus! Fergus! Ye've got something amazing offshore there* and Fergus saying what is amazing and Kenny saying *ye've got fuckin great auks there, Fergus, great auks, man, they're extinct and you've fuckin got them, right there* and Fergus, suppressing his panic, saying don't be so bloody ridiculous, you've been looking at great northern divers, because they did look similar at a distance, he told us, and Kenny saying, *great northern divers my fuckin arse, these had loral spots man, big white loral spots* and Fergus saying you are imagining things and Kenny saying *bollocks ah know what ah was looking at, so c'mon let's get there now in the inflatable and ah'll show ye maself* and Fergus saying they weren't going anywhere and Kenny shouting *nae bother I am if you're not* and diving into Fergus's hut and grabbing the inflatable's keys and running down and starting to unmoor it and Fergus hobbling after him as fast as his arthritis would let him and shouting to him to stop, stop, and trying to grab him and Kenny throwing a punch at him which hit him on the shoulder and half knocked him down and Fergus picking himself up and moving towards Kenny and smiting him, that was the only way I could imagine it or describe it, smiting him on the side of his face with his great fist powered by that immense bodily frame with all its force, and knocking him senseless. And he dragged him back up to the stores hut, and locked him in, and radioed the Balnay estate to send the boat right away; and the rest we knew.

'Christ,' I said, shaking my head. It was almost beyond imagining. But it was real. And then an even stranger question presented itself. I said: 'But Kenny hasn't *told* anybody. Since he got back. Why hasn't he told anybody about it?'

'It is possible he may be uncertain. He presumably did not see the birds close up, and he has no photographs.'

Of course. *No cameras on Lanna.*

I said: 'He might just have told Ramsay, that's our boss, in confidence. But I think I'd know, from Ramsay's attitude.'

'One would suppose you might.'

'So why hasn't he said anything?'

'It matters not,' said Fergus. 'You are now the official representative of UKOCA on Lanna, is that not so?'

'I am, yes.'

'Then what Lornie thinks he saw or perhaps did not see is immaterial. I have shown the birds to you, in your capacity as the representative of your agency, with the intention of formally handing over to UKOCA responsibility for their conservation. It is for you to make it known to your superiors.' He seemed to sag, as if he were weary. 'It is your time now,' he said. 'These are the rarest organisms on earth. They are critically endangered. The great responsibility of their protection passes to you. I can do it no more. But we need to talk about it. We must talk about it at length, about how we deal with Kintyre ...'

'God yes, I'd forgotten Kintyre,' I said.

'... and about the birds' conservation and their future, so that we may minimise the chances of failure, once their existence becomes known to the world at large. Which I fear, may be very great.'

He looked utterly drained.

Jenny has always had far more instinctive common humanity than me. She said: 'Fergus. Come and eat with us, why don't you? We'll be having dinner in an hour or so. Come and join us.'

He hesitated. Then he said: 'I should like that. We shall talk about it then. Thank you.'

So Fergus Pryng hobbled off to his hut and we watched him go in wonder, this man and the staggering knowledge he had held in his bosom for God knows how long. I shook my head and cried out: 'Jesus!' And as we walked up to our own hut Jenny said: 'So that's the secret of Lanna?'

'Well, I reckon, don't you?'

'No Spanish gold? No fugitive hiding out? No monster?'

I shook my head.

'Am I right in thinking this is even bigger?'

'Do you understand,' I said, opening the door, 'have you even got any idea, of how just how big it is?'

'Well. Pretty big, I should think.'

'Jen, this is the biggest story there's ever been, in terms of wildlife, or nature or the environment or whatever you want to call it. The most incredible story in the world.'

'It's that big?'

'Can't you see?' I said. 'This is like, like finding the ivory-billed woodpecker. But it's bigger than that. It's ... it's up there with the Loch Ness Monster.'

'Ah come on, Miles. Really?'

'In terms of impact, yeah it is. It'll be featured on every national newspaper front page and every national TV station. These birds will be instant celebrities. Global celebrities. They'll be like movie stars. The first pictures of them will be the most remarkable images of the natural world that have ever been published.'

'Wow.'

'Jenny, humanity will be spellbound. The great auks of Lanna will become the great icons of nature. They'll replace the giant panda. Overnight.'

'How d'you mean?'

'As the key emblems of ... rarity, but more than that, of ... of ...'

'Survival?'

'Yes, exactly. They're meant to have been extinct for 150 years.'

'Yeah, I suppose so. Like, back from the dead?'

'Absolutely. And their story is such a sad tale, isn't it? The way they were wiped out in their thousands, don't you remember, the way Callum told us on Skarholm?'

'I do. So they'll be symbols, won't they? Of surviving against all the odds.'

'Of surviving human greed, Jenny. Human cruelty. Human destruction of the natural world. Miraculous symbols of survival, in a world that's under terrible assault from human activities. And human activities which are now actually threatening *them*.'

'How?'

'With the oil exploration. But the auks will save Lanna, now, no doubt about that. There'll be no oilfield here. That's why Fergus said this morning we wouldn't need the gannets. He'd decided to spill the beans.'

'Why d'you think he did?'

'I'm not sure. I daresay we'll find out.'

We cooked dinner. We made a hearty stew out of cans of steak and potatoes and peas and carrots, and when it was nearly ready I went over and knocked on Fergus's door. The wind was rising and the sky was clouding over. When he came out, he appeared to my surprise to have combed his hair and perhaps even to have combed his beard, and to have put on a clean shirt. Or at least, a different shirt. He was limping more than ever and he hobbled with me back to our hut and squeezed in and sat down. He was so big he took up one side of the kitchen table all by himself.

Jenny was finishing off the stew. It was a pity we didn't have any wine to offer him, but he sipped a glass of water. And I said straightaway: 'We were wondering, Fergus, how does Lord Kintyre fit into all this.'

Fergus said: 'He will be incandescent with rage.'

'Why?'

'Because he fears a new gold rush, as it were. You know about the gold rush of 1939?'

'I do. I've read the Crinan book.'

'Rollo fears that if the existence of the auks is made known, there will be a similar scramble to see them. Or very possibly, worse. A crazy stampede.'

'I suppose he may be right.'

'And that it will not just be a passing fad, like the gold was, but it will be a permanent blight on the island, on its remoteness and freedom from what he would call human pollution.'

'But he must have known, surely, Fergus, that it would get out sooner or later? I mean, how long has he known about the birds?'

'Two years.'

That brought me up short. 'What? Kintyre's only known about the birds for two years?'

'Yes. Since I was obliged to tell him. To show them to him, as I have shown them to you.'

'You knew about them before he did?'

'That is so.'

'So why were you 'obliged' to tell him?'

'To prevent the seabird survey of Lanna proposed at that time by your agency.'

'You mean, the original plan, two years ago?'

'Yes.'

'It was *you* who scuppered that?'

'Yes.'

'Why?'

'I thought the risk of discovery of the auks too great.'

I was astounded. I remembered Sidney Jeffries telling me how surprised the agency was, that Kintyre had refused the initial survey, without giving a reason.

'But ... that was intended to prevent the original oil drilling, wasn't it? Which became the new field – Macdui?'

'Yes.'

'But Fergus ... now they're pumping oil less than fifty miles away. It's only a couple of hours' flying time, for a seabird. Isn't that a terrible risk? To all the birds on the island? To all the hundreds of thousands of seabirds here?'

'Most assuredly.'

'I don't understand.'

'I consider,' he said, in a very solemn voice, 'that I was wrong. That I made a grave mistake.'

'Well well,' I said.

We served the stew in bowls with spoons, and chunks of hot bread. Fergus ate enthusiastically, making slurping noises.

I said: 'So let me understand. You prevented the original UKOCA survey which might have stopped the Macdui oilfield?'

'To my eternal regret.'

'And you did it by showing the great auks to Kintyre.'

'Yes.'

'And what was his reaction?'

'He was duly amazed. As anyone must be. And most powerfully moved, as you may well imagine for someone with a consuming interest in wildlife and its conservation. He saw absolutely the unique nature of their survival.'

'So he agreed to block the survey?'

'He did. He regarded the risk of discovery – as I myself did then – as too great.'

'But hang on … this year's survey … he did agree to it?'

'Only under pressure from me. He was most reluctant.'

'What sort of pressure?'

'I threatened to make the existence of the birds publicly known.'

'Did you, by God?'

'I considered I had made such a cardinal error, in failing to stop the development of Macdui, when that might have been possible. But at least Macdui is fifty miles off. Drilling in the near vicinity of Lanna, on the other hand, was to be prevented at all costs, and the UKOCA seabird survey seemed the only way to stop it.'

'So – you changed your mind?'

'Yes. It was still a risk, but not to carry it out was now the greater risk. The oil development is now the major threat. It is a monumental threat. It is growing and growing. You know they call it the Atlantic Frontier?'

'I do, yes.'

'I never dreamed it would happen here. And yet, they are coming. I cannot adequately express my hatred and contempt for them.'

'Who?'

'The oil people. Their greed is endless. They want to turn this beautiful ocean into a factory. And the danger is not just from the production, I have begun to realise. It is from the transportation as well. We are on a major tanker route here, from Sullom Voe. You know Sullom Voe?'

We shook our heads.

'The big North Sea oil terminal in Shetland. The tankers heading south take a route round the west of Ireland and they pass within twenty, even ten miles of us. They can sometimes be seen on the western horizon. I have even watched them with Kintyre. You realise that just in the last eight years, there have been four major tanker disasters off the coasts of western Europe? Four major oil spills with catastrophic consequences for wildlife, and for seabirds especially.'

'Four?'

Fergus rattled them off. 'The *Aegean Sea* off Galicia in 1992. The *Braer* off Shetland in '93. The *Sea Empress* off the coast of Wales in '96, and the *Erika* in the Bay of Biscay last December.' He was clearly very familiar with them.

'I went to report on the *Erika* for the agency,' I said.

'Did you now?' said Fergus.

'It was terrible.'

'I can well believe it. They all are. They keep happening. When they struck oil in the Macdui field two years ago, it focused my mind. I realised how dreadfully short-sighted I had been.' Fergus looked mournfully into his bowl. 'I suppose I never expected them to succeed.'

I said: 'But ... Kintyre didn't want to do the survey this year ... even with the direct oil danger to Lanna itself?'

'That is so. He insisted that confidentiality remained the paramount objective. There were raised voices.'

I remembered what Gervase had said to me about the shouting match he overheard at the castle.

I said: 'Isn't that a bit ... strange?'

Fergus said: 'I found it remarkable, and I still do, that Rollo seemed impervious to the risk of an oilfield right on Lanna's doorstep. I accept that he is a singular man, and not to everyone's taste. Yet I have always seen eye to eye with him, on matters of wildlife and conservation. We both concur that the principal danger to the planet is the human one. But how could he not see that oil is now the greatest risk to Lanna, even greater than public knowledge of the presence of *Pinguinus impennis*?'

'I wouldn't know, Fergus.'

'I suppose it is because the island has an almost mystical significance for him, as his own piece of the Earth which is unpolluted by humans.'

'He went on about that when I saw him at Balnay.'

'Well, I suppose cannot blame him. But I think he is greatly misguided. Why would he be willing to risk an oilfield next to it?'

It was now, really, that I should have seen it – what Kintyre was doing, his outrageous plot, his incredible scheme; but I still didn't put two and two together. I merely said: 'But your wishes prevailed?'

'He had no choice, when I threatened that to stop the new drilling, I would take any action necessary, including revealing the existence of *Pinguinus*. He was most unhappy. I attempted to reassure him. I argued that the survey could be safely carried out, with the restrictions we insisted upon.'

You reckoned without Kenny, I thought.

I said: 'So when Kenny Lornie discovered the auks – two weeks ago – did you inform Kintyre of that?'

'Of course.'

'What was his reaction?'

'He was incensed. He was almost speechless with anger. *I told you so*, and all that, *I told you this would happen*. I told him that the matter was not open and shut, Lornie could not be sure of what he had seen, and he had no proof. Rollo said that whatever the case, the survey was off. I supposed it was.'

'Right.'

'We then waited with bated breath to hear back from your director but in the event he made no reference to any unusual birds. He merely apologised, and offered to do the survey again with another UKOCA scientist. Rollo relayed this to me, and said that naturally, he had refused. I, on the other hand, insisted that the offer be taken up.'

'You threatened him again?'

'Yes. He was forced to comply.'

I said: 'So it wasn't just my eloquence that got us here?'

'Rollo had no choice.'

Thinking about it all, and trying to weigh everything up, I realised we had to talk practicalities. 'Well then, Fergus,' I said. 'What do we do now?'

'We must do two things. We must act quickly, and we must bypass Kintyre.'

'Explain.'

'If your agency is to look after the birds, you must have a conservation plan in place for next spring, when they return from the sea to breed. You understand?'

'Yes, I can see that.'

'But for your agency to draw up such a plan, indeed to agree to it in the first place, the senior officials must know the auks are here on the island, must they not?'

'We'll tell them the instant we get back, never fear.'

'You will not be believed,' said Fergus.

'Ah.'

'You have no photographs. What you say will seem ridiculous. Great auks, forsooth! Have you been drinking?'

'So what are we to do?'

'You must persuade them to come out here and see for themselves. In the utmost secrecy. A small group. Your director, and perhaps one or two others.'

'OK.'

'But there are two problems. The first one is time. In two weeks' time, the eggs will hatch, and the chicks will be on the breeding ledge for no more than two days, and then they will be gone. Out to sea. We know not where. The Bay of Biscay? Greenland? But there will be no sign of them here, for another nine months. So if your colleagues get here after that point, their suspicions that you are a mere fantasist, will be confirmed.'

'I think I can persuade them to act quickly.'

'Let us hope so. But then we encounter our second problem, which resides in Castle Balnay. Your senior colleagues are government officials, civil servants. They follow the rules, do they not? When you tell them that there are great auks on Lanna, when you tell your director that, and say that he should go out to the island as a matter of urgency to see for himself, what will he do?'

I thought about it. 'Ramsay ... well, he'll go through the proper channels. I suppose he'll pick up the phone to Lord Kintyre.'

'Precisely. And what will he say to Kintyre?'

'That he thinks there may be ... great auks on Lanna?'

'And what will be Kintyre's response?'

'That ... there aren't any?'

'Indeed. That this is arrant nonsense. He will say to your director, I have bent over backwards to help you, I have waived the rule that no outsiders are allowed on Lanna, and the first man you send me attacks my warden, and the second has hallucinations. He will say, it will all add meat to my complaint about you and your incompetent agency, to the Scottish Office.'

'Hmm,' I said.

'And if your director is still robust enough after that, to go on to say, then Lord Kintyre, may I go out to your island to see for myself, what will be Kintyre's response?'

'You may not?'

'Quite.'

'Hmm,' I said again.

'Whatever happens, I am certain that Kintyre will be able to delay another trip by UKOCA officials until after the birds have left for the winter, so there would be no sign of them when your team arrives.'

'So what do we do?'

'We must bypass Kintyre completely. Your people must break the rules. They must come out here in secrecy, without him knowing, even if they feel they are trespassing. Either by boat or indeed by helicopter. We have a helicopter pad here now. And they must come in the next two weeks. Sooner. As soon as humanly possible.'

I said: 'Could they bring cameras?'

Fergus thought about it. He was torn.

I said: 'I think they'd have to, wouldn't they? Otherwise, they wouldn't come.'

'Very well.'

'So it'll be my job to persuade them?'

'Yes. Perhaps your Mr Lornie might back you up? Two of you might do it.'

'But he seems to have disappeared, Fergus. Nobody knows where he is. I can't explain it. No one can.'

'Then perhaps I might speak to your director, directly. By radio.'

'That might be an idea. Yes, that might do it.'

Jenny had been taking all this on board and now she said: 'Fergus, should a future conservation strategy be to protect the birds *in situ*? To keep them here?'

'Yes,' he said. 'No one has successfully bred auks in captivity. A woman in the West Country tried it for a long time with guillemots. She got them to mate and lay eggs and sometimes the eggs hatched but the chicks always, always died. I fear that to take the birds away from Sgeir Dubh would be a disaster. It would doom them to extinction.'

'A *second* extinction,' I said.

'Yes, Dr Bonnici.' Fergus nodded his head gravely. 'A second extinction indeed. It is only *in situ* that they will be preserved. So you must design a conservation strategy to do that.'

'What should the essence of it be?'

'Discretion. Absolute discretion. At the outset, certainly. Keep the knowledge confidential, amongst as small a group as you can make it, for as long as humanly possible, certainly at least until your strategy is put into place.'

'Why is that?' said Jenny.

'Because of the frenzy that will ensue, the instant their existence is known. The scramble to see them.'

I nodded. 'He's right. The first pictures will be worth a fortune. Literally. Millions of pounds.'

'*Millions?*'

'Of course. News organisations will bid against each other for first use. They'll go right round the world. But the journalists and photographers are not the half of it. The twitchers will be just as bad, if not worse.'

'Twitchers?' said Jenny.

'The birdwatchers who specialise in rarities,' I said. 'They tick off rare birds. They chase down 'ticks'.'

'Madam,' said Fergus, 'do you have any idea what they are like, how obsessive, how ruthlessly determined? This is the greatest tick, the greatest twitch, there has ever been, or ever will be. Once they know of it, they will do anything to get on Sgeir Dubh. Anything. They will not only hire boats, they will hire planes. They will certainly hire helicopters. It would not surprise me, not in the least, were they to hire a submarine, or to come in by parachute. They will stop at absolutely nothing, and the photographers and TV crews will be the same, and let me say, there may be even greater danger, from the eggers.'

'Eggers?'

'There are still a very small number of full-time egg collectors in Britain. They too specialise in rarities, the more difficult of access, the better. A nest at the top of a Scots pine, or half-way down a sheer cliff, is meat and drink to them. They too are ruthlessly determined, and this is the greatest challenge they will ever face; to obtain an egg of *Pinguinus impennis* the greatest coup they could ever dream of. They will come. Believe me.'

I said: 'So how do we go forward? What will be the basis of everything?'

'You will have to establish an exclusion zone for boats, with a permanent watch on the birds in the breeding season. Twenty-four hours a day, seven days a week. Thankfully the shelter on the clifftop opposite Sgeir Dubh provides an ideal site. And the castle is even better. It has a direct view of the breeding ledge.'

'I thought it was unsafe.'

'That was to keep you off it.'

I think it would be true to say that I was more interested in the wondrous birds on their breeding ledge, and Jenny was more interested in their protector.

'Fergus,' she said, as I got up to put the kettle on, 'you said you had told Lord Kintyre about the auks two years ago?'

'That is correct.'

'How long had you known about them yourself?'

Fergus hesitated. He said: 'For some time.'

'Did anybody else know about them?'

Fergus said: 'The former estate boatman, Hughie McAllister. Big Hughie, as he was known. The late earl's batman in the war. But he did not understand what they were. He thought they were geese, and of no importance.'

'Did anyone know about them apart from him?'

'Not that I am aware.'

'So you've kept it ... a secret?'

Fergus said: 'I suppose one might say that.'

'Why?'

The question sounded a little brutal. Jenny said: 'I mean, I'm just wondering.'

He seemed reluctant to expand. I didn't want us to press him on the point. Coming back to the table I said: 'Look, whatever your reasons for keeping it quiet before, I think one thing perhaps we do need to understand is, why exactly are you telling us now?'

Fergus hesitated. He said: 'I have been ... reluctant to accept what the situation is. But the ah, the incident this morning put things into sharper focus.'

'What things?'

He hesitated again. Then he said: 'For one thing I have a substantial and growing problem with my health. I have contracted rheumatoid arthritis, and the prognosis is that it will only get worse. Movement will become very difficult. I will effectively be crippled. I am obliged to accept that I will not be able to protect the birds, as I have done. And even more so, of course, because the principal threat to them now is not the world finding out about them, but oil. I cannot protect them against the development of this accursed Atlantic Frontier. Only an organisation such as your own can do that.'

Jenny said, very gently: 'How have you protected them, Fergus?'

'I have watched over them during the breeding season.'

'Every day?'

'Yes.'

I said: 'That's what, from late April to early July?'

'The chicks generally hatch in about the third week of June and as I told you, are gone almost at once. But I spend another couple of weeks here, just in case.'

'When you're, as it were, wardening them, what does that involve?'

'I spend a lot of time on the castle, because it has an excellent view of Sgeir Dubh. It is end-on, but in the telescope on high magnification one can actually see the breeding ledge perfectly well. In addition, its elevated viewpoint at the end of the island also enables one to see any boats which approach, from either side and from a considerable distance, and make sure they are not admitted to the anchorage, or allowed to go near Sgeir Dubh.'

'And what about the shelter? Where you found us?'

'I have used it for a closer watch on the birds, especially when the chicks hatch, to control potential predators.'

'You've shot them from there?'

'Anything that was a risk, yes.'

'Which was why you shot the bonxies last night?'

'Yes. Some years ago I saw a bonxie swoop down onto Sgeir Dubh and take an auk chick.' He seemed uncomfortable. He said: 'I hate shooting them. And the ravens, and the greater black-backed gulls. I detest it. I think it makes me a lesser person. But the risk is simply too great.'

Jenny said: 'You're by yourself doing all this?'

'Yes. Apart from the odd short visit from Kintyre, yes.'

'Doesn't it get – well, pretty lonely?'

Fergus said 'There is a price to be paid for the privilege of watching over them.'

Jenny said: 'Can I ask you, Fergus …'

'Madam?'

'Have you done it for quite some time? I mean, for like, quite a number of years?'

'I suppose one might say that.'

'Have you sort of, devoted your life to it?'

Fergus did not reply at once.

The kettle whistled. I said: 'Hang on, I'll just make the coffee.'

Fergus was reflecting. He said: 'Leaving this behind will seem very strange. Very … hard. Abandoning the birds, in effect.'

'Yes?'

'And yet … I admit to a curious sense of liberation.'

'In what way?' said Jenny.

'I will be able to see my daughter on her birthday.'

He paused.

He said: 'But it is too late for Bronwen.' He looked up. 'My wife. My ex-wife.'

Jenny's eyes widened. 'Bronwen Pryng?'

'Yes.'

'The woman who does the ethical cosmetics? And all the environmental campaigns?'

'Yes.'

'She's your *wife?*'

'She was. We are divorced. Because of … this. Alas.'

I made the coffee. We sipped our mugs and I said: 'Jen, I don't think we need to press Fergus too much on the personal side. I think what we need to focus on is the birds. Now Fergus, I take it you've been making systematic observations of them?'

Fergus said: 'Yes and no.'

'What's the No?'

'I have had to resist the temptation to get too close. For example, to colour-ring them for individual identification purposes, or to weigh them or take measurements.'

'So you haven't physically touched them?'

'No. Great though the temptation has been. The risk of driving them off their eggs is too great. So I have not ventured on to the ledge when the birds are there, although I have placed several mooring rings in the rocks to observe them more closely when the sea is calm. They were very anxious at first but they have slowly got used to me. Though you will have noticed that your presence alarmed them.'

'Can you identify individuals?'

'Only with long observation. And then, with difficulty.'

'But the first bird we saw, you said was 'the oldest male'. How did you identify him?'

'By the grooves on the bill. They form a pattern which can exhibit slight differences between birds. This bird is the most recognisable. From the pattern on the upper mandible.'

'But how d'you know he's a male? Because I take it the males and females look the same? Like guillemots and razorbills?'

'They are indeed, like the other Atlantic alcids, sexually monomorphic.'

'So how do you know it's a him?'

'I have observed him copulate,' said Fergus.

Then Jenny said: 'Know what? Thing I can't get over is their similarity to penguins. When I was seventeen I went with my family on this fantastic wildlife cruise, this is back home in New Zealand, we sailed out of Invercargill down to the sub-Antarctic islands, it's like the Galapagos of the Southern Ocean? I saw a lot of penguins quite close up, and I can't get over how similar the great auks are.'

'But they were the original penguins, Jen,' I said. 'Don't you remember Callum telling us on Skarholm? *Pen gwyn?*'

'Hard to believe they're not related.'

'Madam,' said Fergus, 'they have merely co-evolved. The alcid auks of the northern hemisphere and the spheniscid penguins of the southern are separate families entirely. In the case of the great auk of the north and the penguins of the south, they have both exchanged flight for swimming and diving ability.'

'But they look so alike.'

'I grant you they are not dissimilar.'

'They could be penguins' first cousins. I mean, they could almost be a penguin species, couldn't they?'

And that was when I finally saw it. It struck me now with a sort of fascinated shock.

'Fergus?' I said.

'Yes?'

'Lord Kintyre is building ... a penguin pool.'

'A what?'

'A *penguin ... pool*. At the castle. In the wildlife park at Balnay.'

Fergus fixed me with his hard gaze.

'It's state of the art, really big, it seats 400 people and it's costing twenty-three million pounds. He's had to sell his paintings to finance it.'

Fergus's eyes started to widen.

It tumbled out of me.

'It's virtually finished. It should have been finished by now but it's been delayed. It's a secret. He's told everybody it's an aquarium, but his secretary told me what it really was – a *penguin pool* that he thinks will attract thousands of visitors. He's in huge debt. He's facing bankruptcy. And he thinks this will restore his fortunes.'

Fergus's eyes had almost become saucers and his mouth was open and with an eruption the like of which I had never witnessed he brought his great fist down upon the table with a crash that sent a plate flying on to the floor where it shattered into pieces. 'The baastard!' he cried. 'He wants them for himself! The baastard!' And he staggered to his feet, knocking over his chair, and paced about the room wild-eyed, biting the back of his hand.

Jenny began to see it. She said to me: 'Kintyre wants the great auks?'

'That's what it looks like.' I was stunned myself.

'The baastard!' cried Fergus. He hit his fist against the wooden wall of the hut. It shuddered.

'Like, for his zoo?' said Jenny. 'So he's gonna kidnap them, or something?'

The implications were dawning on me. 'It would be the greatest zoo attraction on earth, wouldn't it? Extinct birds? People'd come from all over the world. They really would. Make him millions. Pay off his debts.'

'God,' said Jenny.

'The bastard!' cried Fergus. 'He will have to kill me first! Kintyre will have to kill me before he gets his hands on them!'

It occurred to me that perhaps his lordship had been planning precisely that. For as Fergus paced up and down our hut I saw, in a flash, what an obstacle he was; Kintyre wanted to bring the great auks of Lanna back to his zoo, but he must know that his warden, this huge, formidable strong-willed man, who was permanently on the island while the birds were there, would never agree, and indeed, would resist.

How would he get round that?

I remembered Gervase mentioning a couple of 'penguin-wranglers' at Balnay; he said they were 'sinister-looking'. Was it their job to be Fergus-wranglers as well? To ensure that, in the difficult and dangerous operation to catch the great auks on their Sgeir Dubh breeding ledge, Fergus Pryng, who was taking part, tragically fell overboard and was drowned?

Was it mad to think that?

I didn't think it was. It seemed to me that Kintyre was capable of it, if his whole future depended upon his plan working.

'The bastard!' cried Fergus, hitting the side of the hut once more. His face was purple. 'The fucking bastard!'

I didn't know swearing was in his nature; and he was sweating as well as swearing. I got up and touched his arm. I said: 'Fergus, Fergus, come on now. Come and sit down. Let's all be calm. We have to discuss this.' I guided him back to his chair. Jenny fetched him a glass of water. He took it and drank half.

I said: 'We can stop him, Fergus. We will.'

His chest was heaving up and down. Jenny and I waited for him to calm. He drank the rest of the water. At length he said: 'Very well. Doctor Bonnici. Please to tell me again, what you know.'

So I told him at length about meeting Gervase and how he had said to me in confidence that Kintyre was badly in debt and even facing ruin, but was trying to restore his fortunes, by building a super-sized 'penguin pool' at the wildlife park, which was costing millions and which was nearly finished.

'How nearly?' said Fergus.

'They're going to be filling the pool any day now.' And I suddenly remembered something else Gervase hold told me, that Kintyre had asked Gervase's father, his family solicitor, for a legal opinion saying that the seabirds of Lanna were his own property, to do with as he liked, and been infuriated when some doubt about the proposition was expressed.

Fergus made a growling noise at that last bit. But he had regained his composure, although his eyes were flashing.

'He must have conceived the scheme at once. Two years ago. As soon as I had shown him the birds.' He bit a finger. 'It was clearly a mistake to show them to him. Another mistake, along with stopping the original seabird survey. But at the time I thought I had no choice.' He looked at us. 'He has deceived me royally. He has taken me for a perfect fool. Though that matters not a jot, it is the fate of the birds that matters.' He bit a finger again. He said: 'If he takes them to Balnay, they will not survive. These are the most miraculous survivors of all living things, and Rollo Kintyre will extinguish them. But why should we be surprised? This is the human character. Man the destroyer.'

I said: 'We can stop him, though, surely? It'll be illegal, won't it? Under the Wildlife and Countryside Act and everything? Interfering with a wild bird or its nest?'

'Yes it will, but if he gets his hands on the birds, possession may well be ten points of the law.'

'How?'

'He will present his pool as a perfectly-equipped captive breeding centre. Captive breeding is what he is known for. Don't you see? It will be for the great auks of Lanna that he has gone to all this trouble, not for himself. You say his financial troubles are not publicly known?'

'Apparently not.'

'Then he will say this is simply the best conservation option, and he is going out of his way to do the right thing. It will be a bold government minister who will order the birds to be taken back out to sea, with all the disturbance which that will involve, and all the risk to them, once they are known about by the world at large, with the accompanying sensational publicity.'

I saw it. I nodded.

Fergus said: 'If Kintyre's pool is everything you say it is, many people will think the birds are best at Balnay. To be gawped at by the public. With their freedom gone. Their dignity gone. And their future extinction, their *second* extinction, assured.'

'Then what are we to do?'

'I shall confront him.'

'When?'

'Now.'

Risk - egg collectors
Lord Kintyre - wants them
for penguin pool.

25

Jenny and I were swept along by what was happening as Fergus led us out into two gathering storms – one, the tempest from above, starting now to lash us with wind and rain, and the other, the storm shortly to break about the head of Rollo Macdonald, Tenth Earl of Kinytre, clan chief, controversial celebrity, zoo-keeper extraordinaire, friend of the great beasts and now debtor who had staked his all, to fend off financial ruin, on a desperate last throw with the rarest creatures on the planet.

We helped Fergus stumble across the head of the beach to his own hut and we stood by him as he began to call Castle Balnay on the radio; after a minute or so he was answered by a Scottish voice who turned out to be Alastair Stewart the estate factor; Fergus told him he needed to speak to his lordship as a matter of urgency and Alastair promised to page him.

We stood waiting.

We said nothing, as the wind whipped round the hut, although Jenny and I exchanged glances.

And then after several minutes we heard the unmistakable smooth tones of Lord Kintyre: 'Lanna, Lanna, this is Balnay, come in Lanna.'

Fergus took the mike and said: 'Balnay this is Lanna, go ahead, over.'

'Yes, Fergus, what is the matter, over.'

Fergus said: 'I know what you are planning Rollo and I will not let you do it.'

There was a pause.

Kintyre said: 'Say again Fergus, over.'

Fergus said, slowly and deliberately: 'I know what you are planning, and I will not let you do it. Over.'

'What are you talking about?'

'I know about your pool, Rollo.'

'What pool?'

'The so-called penguin pool you are building. Your secret scheme.'

'You must mean the aquarium, Fergus. There is nothing secret about it. It is all perfectly open. It has even been in the *Oban Times*.'

'Its true purpose is the secret, Rollo. You are building it for *Pinguinus impennis*.'

'Fergus, this is complete rubbish, where have you got this idea from?'

'There is no use denying it because it is obvious. You wish to take the birds for your own personal profit and selfish ends and if you do so, you will destroy them. I do not care if you deny it. It does not matter if you deny it. What matters is that you understand what I am saying to you now, and I am saying to you, that I will not let you do it. I wish that to be as clear as I can make it. I – will – not – let –you – do – it.'

There was another pause.

I imagined Kintyre in the castle, and what was racing through his mind.

Then he came back on. 'Fergus, listen to me. Listen to me now. What do you think the future is for the birds on Sgeir Dubh?'

'Their future is to remain in the only place where they will survive.'

Kintyre said: 'Do you not think that the dangers besetting them on the island are increasing by the day? Look at the risk from oil. Look at the Atlantic Frontier. We have discussed it together. You have impressed upon me yourself, what a real and growing danger to Lanna and its wildlife, the oil development is. Think about the long term. Do you really suppose that the safest option for the birds in the long term is merely to stay where they are?'

Fergus said: 'I do think that, Rollo, and as long as there is breath in my body, I will ensure that that remains the case.'

'But what if there is an oilfield put in near Lanna? Or what if – what if one of those tankers we have watched together, in the distance, were to run aground on the island and spill its oil? That would be a catastrophe.'

'Yes, I think that is possible, but the greater danger to the birds, and what concerns me now, is your wish to remove them.'

Kintyre said: 'Fergus, listen. I care as much as you about the welfare and future of the birds. It is my highest priority. And I have devoted my life to the safeguarding of threatened species. You must acknowledge that.'

'I do acknowledge that, but what you are planning for *Pinguinus* now is about you, not about them.'

'No, Fergus. The opposite is the case. I will give them a future, and let me tell you, I would want you to be the key part of it. I would want you to be in charge of them, with your vast experience and understanding. Join with me in it, Fergus. Let us do it together. Let us take these wonderful survivors, these unique survivors, into the twenty-first century, and watch them astonish the world. It will be the most noble of all conservation projects. Join with me in it. Over to you.'

Fergus said: 'But you will exhibit them, Rollo. For money, over.'

'Would you have me deprive the world of them, once they are known about, over?'

'It is no use. I am not calling to be persuaded. I am calling simply to warn you, that if you attempt it, I shall stop you.'

There was another pause.

Kintyre said then, and his tone had hardened: 'And just how will you do that?'

'I will stop you with my person and with any means at my disposal.'

'Does that include firearms, Fergus? I know you have a gun there.'

'It includes everything.'

Kintyre said: 'Then I think I will have to talk to the police. I shall do so at once. You have just threatened me with a deadly weapon. You are clearly unstable and a danger to others. You will have to be removed from my island as soon as possible, as a matter of public safety.'

I saw it. Christ, it was clever. He didn't have to murder Fergus to get him out of the way – he could say he was armed and dangerous and get the police to do the job for him.

But Fergus was unfazed. He said: 'I think you should know, you will not only have to deal with me, you will have to deal with the government, in the shape of the Offshore Conservation agency.'

'What do you mean?'

Fergus said: 'Stand by.' He turned to me. 'Talk to him and tell him what the score is. Concisely. OK? You key the mike.'

I nodded. I took the microphone. I said: 'Lord Kintyre, this is Miles Bonnici of UKOCA.'

Kintyre said: 'Yes?'

'We have seen the birds.'

'What?'

'Fergus has shown us the birds on Sgeir Dubh.'

'You have seen the birds?' His voice had risen several tones.

'Yes, and Fergus has asked us to take over responsibility for their conservation.'

'He said that?'

'He did, and I feel obliged to tell you, on behalf of the agency, that any attempt on your part to interfere with them at their nests would be treated under the Wildlife and Countryside Act as a criminal offence.'

Kintyre cried: 'Put him on! Put him on!'

I handed Fergus the mike. He said: 'Yes, Rollo.'

'How dare you!' screamed Kintyre, and it was a true scream. 'How dare you speak of my birds to others! You have betrayed your trust as a servant of my estate, the trust I placed in you as a nobody, a jumped-up nothing, and this is how you repay me! You piece of shit! My ancestors would have known how to deal with you, they would have hung you alive from the walls of Balnay for the corbies to pick out your eyes!'

And then there was silence.

Fergus took up the mike. He said: 'Balnay, this is Lanna, come in, over.'

Nothing.

'Balnay, Balnay, this is Lanna, over.'

The wind rattled the hut.

Fergus turned to us. 'He's gone.'

I said: 'What happens now?'

'I fancy he may attempt some sort of *coup de main*. Some sort of raid on the island, to seize the birds. If he were not planning it already. But I think he may well attempt it now.'

'So what do we do?'

'It is for you to mobilise your agency with all possible speed. Let us hope that your return goes ahead as planned. If not, we will have to think again.'

'What will you do?'

'I shall remain here and resist Kintyre, if he comes.'

'How will you do that?'

'By all means necessary.'

Looking back, I do not know which was the greater shock, that June day – the discovery that great auks were still alive, that these icons of extinction were still, unbelievably, clinging to existence on a remote Atlantic island; or the realisation that the island's owner was plotting to kidnap them for his own private zoo.

It seemed too outrageous, too improbable for words. It was something an ordinary person not only couldn't undertake, but wouldn't even begin to conceive of. To grab the great auks of Lanna, you had to believe you were capable of grabbing the great auks of Lanna and Rollo Macdonald, Tenth Earl of Kintyre, clearly did. Yet he was matched by Fergus Pryng. The earl might have indestructible self-belief, but Fergus was possessed of a moral force which was as strong or even stronger; plus, he suddenly saw his whole life's purpose being set at naught. When he cried out that Kintyre would have to kill him to get his hands on the birds, he was speaking the literal truth, and as Jenny and I hunched our way back to our hut through the wind and the rain, we were filled with apprehension at what the next day or so might bring – as well as with continuing amazement at what we had already learned. But in different ways. Those incredible survivals persisting on their rocks barely half a mile from us, were what occupied my thoughts; but what gripped Jenny's mind as much, if not more, was this man, this plummy-voiced red-bearded solitary giant who had known about them since God knows when; and had told no one.

'How long d'you think he's actually been aware of the birds?' she said to me when we got in and shut the door against the storm.

'Haven't a clue,' I said.

'Must be a fair few years though, mustn't it?'

I still didn't see the size of the question. I just said: 'Quite the weird guy, isn't he?'

Jenny said: 'I think he's a lovely man.'

'Eh?'

'There's a gentleness about him.'

'Gentleness? This is the guy who beat the shit out of Kenny Lornie. This is the guy who shot the bonxies and when he did that, you said he was a fucking cruel bastard.'

'Yeah, I know. But that was before we'd talked to him.'

'What now then?'

'Now I think he's very … what's the word? I dunno. Righteous, or something.'

'He seems to me to be slightly crazy. And maybe not even slightly. I mean, how long *has* he been sitting on the birds? Why's he not told anybody till now? It's bonkers. He's just been keeping them for himself.'

Jenny said: 'I realise that, but I don't think he's been doing it in a … selfish way. I think he really cares about them. And here all alone.'

'Well that's right,' I said. 'That's bloody weird too. All by himself. Fergus the Solitary. King of Lanna.'

Jenny looked up at me. 'No,' she said.

'No what?'

'Not Fergus the Solitary. That misses the point.'

'What point?'

'That he's said nothing. That he's told no one.'

'So what should he be?'

'I think it will become clear, Miles. I think you will start to see it.'

Fergus takes on Kintyre.

26

In the night the storm swelled to the full and belaboured the hut, battering it with clubs of air, and I realised then the value of the steel cables holding it to the ground; and underneath that unceasing torrent of wind Jenny and I at last were united again physically, she whispering, come to me now, and I whispering back are you sure and she saying, I am sure, and our reunion of the soul was sealed in the flesh, for ever and ever, amen.

And so I come to the last day. I still struggle to believe it happened. I think that for all my life now, I will marvel at the role accident plays in our lives, setting at naught the most determined of our plans, making us fools in the hands of fate.

In the morning I woke before Jenny did and watched her sleeping head on my arm, her ivory stillness contrasting with the gale roaring about us like an endless train rushing through a station, and I lay there thinking about everything, everything that had happened in the last four days, and indeed everything in the last four years, and in my whole life. And then I moved my arm slightly, and she opened her eyes.

I said: 'D'you know where you are?'

She smiled. 'I'm with you.' Then she said: 'Listen to the wind!'

'Some gale it's blowing.'

'We're going back today, aren't we? I've nearly lost track of time.'

'If the storm doesn't stop the boat, I suppose.'

'You think it will?'

'Dunno. Murdo said they would sail in a gale. In an emergency, anyway. Listen, Jen …'

'Yeah?'

'When we get back … can we be together? Would you … come and live with me again?'

The tiniest of hesitations. She said: 'Yes. I will, Miles. Of course. Where would we live, though? I don't think I want to go back to Oxford.'

'Sure.' I understood that only too well. 'And you've got your job in London, haven't you?'

'That doesn't matter. Means nothing.'

'And you did mention … there was a guy …'

'Means even less.'

'Well, I've got under a month left on my contract in Aberdeen and I think I want to get away and make a new start – doing what, I do not know – so we could live in Wimbledon.'

'In the house? With Lotte?'

'Yeah, for the time being.'

'That'd be fine.'

'But first, when we get back to the mainland, I'll have to be there, talking to UKOCA about the auks and stuff … and … you don't have to go right back to London do you, right away?'

'Not really. I'm only working on a freelance basis.'

'I thought we might stay together for at least a few days in Aberdeen. Just to, you know …'

She laughed. 'What, get to know each other?'

I smiled back. 'Sort of.'

'I could do that. You can show me Aberdeen. What's it like?'

'It grows on you.'

And Fergus knocked at the door. The wind was howling around him. He appeared notably red-eyed and I wondered if he had slept. But he strode in and said: 'Something sinister has happened.'

'What?'

'The *Katie Colleen* is not coming.'

'Because of the gale?'

'No. It is for some reason of Kintyre's. I have just spoken to Alastair, the estate factor. He said Kintyre told him last night to phone Murdo and call off the trip. Alastair asked him, what about the people on the island, and Kintyre said, there will be alternative arrangements made, but he did not specify what. And Alastair said, his lordship now seems to have disappeared. But he did not know where.'

'You think he's coming out here?'

'Almost certainly.'

'Does he have a boat of his own?'

'There will be something at Balnay, I am sure.'

'Yes, Murdo said they were building a new modern jetty, in the loch. He'll have a fancy boat, won't he? Plus the equipment, everything. He will have planned it all out. Yes. Of course.' I thought about it. I said: 'Well look Fergus, we're not just going to be trapped here incommunicado, while Kintyre tries to do something desperate with the auks. This is potentially a criminal matter. UKOCA is a major government agency. If need be, I would think they'll send a helicopter. Could we get a message to them over the radio?'

'We could ask the coastguard to relay it.'

'What will we say?'

Fergus said: 'Clearly, we must keep the true nature of things confidential. If it is going over the radio. *En clair*, as it were.'

'That's right.'

'Then some sort of generalised note of concern would seem to be appropriate.'

So we sat down and composed a message to be telephoned from Stornoway Coastguard to Dr Ramsay Wishart, Director of the United Kingdom Offshore Conservation Agency in Aberdeen, which read: *From Bonnici. Urgent: major new developments putting survey at risk. Trapped on island by storm. Can you come out yourself ASAP, or send senior staff, if necessary by helicopter. Repeat, urgent.*

Looking at it now, I think it was wholly inadequate. Ridiculously so. But that's what we wrote, and I said to Fergus: 'We can't really say any more, can we?'

'I believe not. I shall transmit this immediately.'

'We'll just get ready and follow you over.'

When he had hobbled away Jenny said: 'So what're we gonna do, Miles. If Lord Buggerlugs shows up and tries to grab the birds?'

'I think just formally reminding him that he is breaking the law, and we are witnesses, has got to make him stop and think, hasn't it?'

'What if it doesn't?'

'We'll cross that bridge when we come to it. Are you worried?'

Jenny smiled. 'No, Miles, I'm not. I think we should do whatever it takes to stop the fucker.'

When we stepped out of the hut, with the low grey clouds scudding over the island, the wind slapped us both about the face and drenched us with the spray being blown from the western cliffs where the storm waves were breaking. We trudged across heads down to Fergus and I will always remember his words in reply to my asking, as we stepped through the door: 'Any news?'

He was sitting at the radio table. He said: 'As if we haven't got enough to bother about, there is a tanker in trouble.'

I will be able to recite that sentence until the end of my days.

'A tanker?'

'An oil tanker.'

'What, like, near here?'

'Near enough. About fifteen miles away. To the south-west.'

'What's the problem?'

'It has lost power in the storm.'

'How d'you know about it?'

'The coastguard told me a few minutes ago when I contacted them with our message for your director. They said it was not their business to take messages on the emergency channel and anyway they had a serious incident going on in our area which I should be aware of, there was a tanker that had broken down to the south-west of us and was drifting. They had just had the distress call.'

'Is that all they said?'

'They are coming back with more information.'

'What's a tanker doing around here?' said Jenny.

'I believe I mentioned last night, that we are quite near a major tanker route. The deep-water route from the Sullom Voe oil terminal in Shetland, towards the south? They pass very close, in relative terms. Less than twenty miles to the west. I seem to see them more and more. It has become an increasing concern.'

The radio made a noise. It said: 'Lanna base, Lanna base, Stornoway coastguard, Stornoway coastguard.'

Fergus said: 'Stornoway coastguard Lanna, go ahead, over.'

The coastguard told him to switch frequencies for a briefing – away from the emergency channel – and when he had done so the guy up in Stornoway began to tell him about the vessel in distress, which was the Greek-registered motor tanker *Lamprinos* of 103,000 tonnes deadweight, bound from Sullom Voe for A Coruña in northern Spain, with a cargo of 62,000 tonnes of Brent crude.

'Bloody hell,' I said to Jenny. 'That's an awful lot of oil. It's more than double what was on the *Erika*.'

The vessel had encountered engine problems and she was currently without power and drifting in the storm and then there was more stuff that I didn't catch properly about a tug, and then Fergus told the guy we had a serious problem of our own and could they please possibly take a message and send it on to UKOCA, and stressed it was urgent, and the guy agreed then, and when it was finished Fergus signed off and turned to us and said: 'This tanker, the *Lamprinos*, is off to the south-west and everything here *comes* from the south-west – the current, the tide, the swell, and more often and not, the wind. So the tanker is drifting towards us.'

'Right,' I said. I took it in. 'Is there anything that can be done?'

'The coastguard maintains a fleet of big, ocean-going salvage tugs, for just such an eventuality. I know about them. It's as a result of the *Braer* disaster in Shetland. The tanker that ran aground. To stop that happening again.'

'And?'

'They have four of them stationed around the coasts and one is permanently on station in the Minch.'

'Isn't that's a long way away?'

'Luckily, today it is to the south of its area, in the Sea of the Hebrides, and so a lot closer to Lanna. The coastguard have despatched it to come to the rescue. In case the *Lamprinos* cannot restore her power in time. To put a line on her and tow her to safety.'

'That's good.'

'The less good news is the tanker crew estimate their rate of drift at about two point five knots, meaning they could be in this area in about six hours.'

'And how long will the tug take to get here?'

'Five to six hours.'

Jenny and I exchanged glances.

'Right,' I said.

'So we add to the fact that Kintyre is probably coming out to attempt some sort of raid, the fact that a blasted tanker laden with oil is out of control and heading more or less straight towards us.'

'What should we do?'

'We need to keep a lookout, don't you think?'

Fergus showed us how to operate the radios so Jenny and I could take it in turns to maintain a listening watch and monitor the coastguard transmissions. He took us to the store hut to put on oilskins and sou'westers. Then, to our fascination, he led us to the castle, struggling painfully with his arthritis up the slope behind his hut and then up the castle's steep steps, which thankfully had a secure handrail, the building having been restored at the same time as the abbey.

Built on the mini-peak at the bottom end of the island, it overlooked both the anchorage and Lanna's southern tip, Rubha a' Chaisteil, or Castle Point, and it was nothing complicated – just a simple stone tower twenty-five feet square and about sixty feet high. Yet the views from the battlemented platform at the top were spectacular and I found myself thinking, the Lords of the Isles knew what they were about in the siting of their strongpoints, for this one offered a panorama of more than 300 degrees, so that approaching boats could be seen from any part of the compass except due north to north-east, where the view was blocked by the Hill of the Cross – from anywhere else, a raider or indeed any visitor could be picked up very early on.

But more striking even than the scale of the view was the state of the sea, which we were looking over for the first time since the start of the storm: what for the past three days had resembled a flat blue mirror was now a vast undulating pewter-coloured plain streaked with white, a surface pulsing with power, and I wondered about the *Lamprinos*, drifting around in that, and then I wondered even more about Kinytre, if he was trying to get to the island in what would have to be a relatively small boat. I wouldn't want to be out in it, I thought. All the way up the low western side of the island the waves were exploding in white foam, and I looked at the rocks of Sgeir Dubh, fuzzily visible through an endless cloud of spray, and I realised that there was indeed a view directly into the lagoon and up to the rock shelf at the far end. Fergus pointed out the directions we needed to concentrate on, south-west for the tanker, and due east for any boat likely to be bringing Kintyre from either Balnay or Oban, and we decided I would take the first hour's shift with him, and Jenny went back down to monitor the radios, and so our watch over Lanna began.

The image of Fergus staring grimly out to sea that day remains in my mind. It is an image I keep of him – indomitable and unmoving, ready to give his all for the defence of his island and the true treasure it harboured, the treasure which he had found, which the whole world would want to wonder at, and which he had kept from human eyes. I looked upon a granite resolution, a great bearded face impervious to the howling wind and rain whose effects I myself found testing to a degree, with the battlements so wholly exposed that even with the oilskins it was all you could do to keep your concentration and an hour felt very long, and my thoughts were buffeted about as if by the gale. What had happened to Kenny? I couldn't imagine. He knew the secret. Was he going to do nothing about it? And Kintyre, Kintyre almost certainly was going to do something, he was almost certainly heading here to seize the island's wonders for himself.

Would he come, even in the storm?

Yes, given the circumstances, I thought he would.

Would he be alone?

Surely not. I remembered again the sinister penguin-wranglers.

What if it turned violent? Would Fergus bring out his gun?

Christ, I hope not, I thought, and I strained my eyes to the east, looking for the dot on the horizon that would be the first sign of an approaching crisis, while praying that Ramsay Wishart had got our message and realised he had to act on it …

But we saw nothing. No vessel, large or small, appeared out of the gloom where the grey waves merged with the sky. At the end of the hour I suggested to Fergus he might take a break but he simply shook his head and carried on looking steadfastly out to sea, so I went down to the hut and Jenny told me the coastguard had just radioed to say the *Lamprinos* was now about twelve miles off to the south-west, and according to the drift track they had calculated, was on course to pass very close to the island if not actually hit it.

'Christ,' I said. 'That's all we need.' I asked her about our message to Ramsay and she said there had been no response; I suggested she should take a coffee up to Fergus and she said she would do better, she would take him up some soup. 'He seems to live on packet soup,' she said. 'There's packets and packets of it in the kitchen there. Dozens and dozens of them. There doesn't seem to be much of anything else, apart from baked beans.' Then she said: 'You seen the pictures?' She pointed at the shelf of framed photographs I had noticed on our first visit, for the briefing: there were seven of them, two of a younger Fergus with a woman and a very small child, and five more of the same child, a girl, growing older in each one. 'It must be his wife and daughter,' Jenny said. 'That must be Bronwen Pryng.'

I peered.

'Remember what he said about giving up the auks?' said Jenny. 'He said he'd be able to see his daughter on her birthday. That must be her.'

She took him up a mug of his packet soup, and over the next three hours we alternated our watches with Fergus, turn by turn; and it was during this time that we began to shift our thoughts away from Kintyre and focus on the tanker, because there was still no sign of his lordship in any shape or form, but each hour the *Lamprinos* was appreciably closer to the island, eleven miles away, then nine miles, then seven, drifting north-north-east, the coastguard informed us, on a track that continued to put her on collision course with the island. I had found it hard to believe that in the vastness of the ocean the one could actually collide with the other, but I began to see it was a real possibility and that 62,000 tonnes of crude oil really might end up spilling in one of the world's greatest seabird colonies; but more than that, I started to realise that it was the west side of Lanna that would be in the firing line, the side of Sgeir Dubh … which of course would be in the forefront of Fergus's mind.

By the time we learned that the tanker was less than six miles off – though still not yet visible through the murk – Fergus had become very seriously concerned and came down to talk to the coastguard again, now seeming weary from his watch, hobbling slowly down the steps and the slope. Jenny took over on the castle top and I came down with him and listened to him stress to the coastguards Lanna's international importance as a seabird site, and the terrible damage an oil spill could do, and they fully acknowledged the danger, and they said that the salvage tug was proceeding to us with all possible speed and would probably be with us within the hour, and they asked him then if Lanna had a helicopter pad and Fergus said yes and they said they were sending a helicopter which was probably going to take non-essential personnel off the tanker, if it got too close to the island, but it was having to refuel in Benbecula because of the extreme operating range. That detail sticks in my mind for some reason. And Fergus signed off from the coastguard then and he turned towards me and opened his mouth to speak but I will never know what he was going to say because at that moment Jenny ran into the hut crying: 'A boat! A boat! There's a boat coming!'

'What sort of boat?' snapped Fergus.

'A small boat.'

'From what direction?'

'Due east.'

At last, I thought. It had to be Kintyre. Fergus seemed re-energised. He led us back up to the castle and we peered into the driving greyness and there it was, what seemed like a tiny craft being tossed up and down by the waves, heading for us, maybe a mile away, maybe more. Fergus studied it intently through his bins. 'Looks like an old fishing boat,' he shouted. 'Let us ask them.'

We went back down again and on the VHF he said: 'Vessel approaching Lanna, vessel approaching Lanna, this is Lanna warden, please identify yourself, over.'

Nothing.

He repeated his call.

Still nothing. But then a crackle.

'Lanna, Lanna, this is fishing vessel *Western Wave*, fishing vessel *Western Wave*, over.'

'Well well,' said Fergus. And into the mike: '*Western Wave*, *Western Wave*, Lanna, state your intentions, over.'

The voice replying was a Scottish voice. It said: 'Lanna, Lanna this is fishing vessel *Western Wave* out of Castlebay. We have an injured man on board, repeat injured man, he has concussion and needs treatment, we wish to come in to your harbour, over.'

Fergus said: '*Western Wave* Lanna, stand by.'

He turned to us and said: 'Castlebay's on Barra. Barra fishermen don't come here. Not ever. I strongly suspect this is Kintyre, I think he may be coming for the auks and playing a trick to get access to the anchorage. What do you think?'

Jenny said: 'I dunno, Fergus, he sounded genuine enough to me. If they've got an injured bloke on board we ought to treat him.'

I said: 'I think so, yeah. He sounded straight to me, Fergus.'

Fergus considered. 'Very well,' he said. He picked up the mike and said: '*Western Wave*, Lanna. What is your position now, over?'

The voice replied: 'Approximately one mile out, over.'

Fergus asked him if he was familiar with the anchorage and learned he was not and advised him that the entrance was on the eastern side of the island at the south end, and issued further instructions, and asked him if all was received and understood and the boat said it was and Fergus signed off: '*Western Wave*, proceed with caution, out.'

And all this time, the tanker was getting closer.

He got up, and we accompanied him as he shuffled down to the quayside and switched on the winch and the chain rattled out and one of the blocking buoys was sucked under and the other two were pulled to the side and the anchorage was open. 'This had better not be Kintyre,' Fergus muttered. So we trudged back up to the castle to look once more but we still couldn't make out who the boat's occupants were, though as it got closer, we began to perceive that our visitor was a small to medium-sized fishing boat; it was being thrown all over the place by the storm. As it approached the anchorage we went down to the quay to wait for it and when it eventually glided in I saw there was a long-haired guy at the side of the wheelhouse with something dark on his face; as he got closer I realised it was a black eyepatch.

'Fuck me,' I murmured. 'Now it's pirates.'

My surprise increased as the boat approached, for the pirate suddenly called out 'Gotta come ashore, got an injured man on board here,' and his accent was American. He moved to the bows with the mooring rope and stepped on to the quay – I realised it was high tide, and this should really have been the *Katie Colleen* with Murdo, coming to take us back – and as the engine died, a smallish older guy with a white beard came out from behind the wheel.

'Good day to you,' he said. 'I'm Jimmy MacNeil from Castlebay. I'm the skipper. You must be Fergus?'

'I am.'

'We've got an injured man here, Fergus, gonna bring him ashore, OK?'

'Very well,' said Fergus.

So MacNeil and the one-eyed American bent over and reached for this guy lying in the recovery position in the bottom of the boat with his back to us, and they lifted him up, a stocky man, quite heavy, and I helped them bring him out and on to the quay and I looked at his face, which was bloodied, in fact he had blood all over his forehead, and I cried out: 'Jesus Christ Almighty!'

'What?' said Jenny.

'It's Kenny Lornie.'

Injured man — Kenny

27

I don't know which of us was the more astonished to see my predecessor reappear on Lanna, Fergus or myself. Yet the feeling I had, besides the shock, was one of relief, for we knew he'd discovered the secret, and I knew he wouldn't ignore it, and although he had disappeared off the UKOCA radar I had felt in my bones he had to be out there with some sort of scheme; now at least we would find out what.

Fergus felt no such ambivalence. He was filled with fury, realising at once what the situation was, and he turned to the one-eyed American, who was holding Kenny Lornie up with MacNeil, and demanded: 'Who are you?'

'Jus' a friend of Kenny's. He asked me along for the trip.'

Fergus turned to the boat's skipper. 'Why have you brought these people here?'

'They said they wanted to photograph seabirds, Fergus.'

Fergus's eyes widened. 'Have you brought cameras here? Do you have cameras on board?'

'Aye.'

'Where are they?'

'They're below.'

Fergus eased himself painfully on to the deck of the *Western Wave* and ducked down into the cabin, and a few moments later he emerged with a light-brown leather holdall that was full of camera bodies and lenses, two long fat telephoto lenses sitting on top.

'Hey buddy!' shouted the American. 'Waddya doing? Hey! Get your hands off! They're mine!'

Fergus took the bigger telephoto lens and tossed it into the harbour, then followed it with the second one, and then began to throw the smaller lenses and camera bodies over the side.

Jenny and I and Jimmy MacNeil looked on open-mouthed.

'*Motherfucker!*' shouted the American, leaving Kenny to slump against MacNeil and scrambling on to the boat. 'Stop it, you fucking asshole!' He hurled himself at Fergus but he seemed to bounce off him – that's the only way I could describe it – as Fergus emptied the rest of the bag into the water. The American got back up, shouting, 'You motherfucking nutjob!' and swung a punch at Fergus; Fergus blocked it, and pushed him firmly backwards and he fell in a heap. He got up, returned to the attack, and Fergus pushed him over again. I dread to think what would have happened if he had clouted him properly, like he did Kenny. Fergus stood, massive in the boat, glaring at him; the American could see it was a fight he was not going to win. He shook his head and called out: 'You crazy cocksucker. That's twelve thousand dollars' worth. I swear to God you're gonna pay for that! Every last fucking cent.'

Fergus said: 'No cameras are permitted on Lanna. The prohibition is absolute and no exceptions are allowed. Mr Lornie there is aware of the rule. If he did not inform you, you should blame him.'

'Fuck you!'

Jenny and I were seriously alarmed; things seemed to be getting out of hand. 'Fergus,' I called to him, 'come on now, please, for God's sake let's calm down. We have a guy who's unconscious here and we have the tanker to worry about.'

Fergus glared, panting.

I said to the American: 'Listen, whoever you are, if you want to come on to the island, you're going to have to agree to do what Fergus tells you. OK?'

He stared at me.

Jenny said: 'Look, mate. There isn't any alternative. You've gotta do what Fergus says. OK?'

He considered. He said: 'OK.'

'OK, Fergus?'

'Very well.'

So we helped him off the boat and then we helped Fergus off and our two visitors shouldered Kenny Lornie between them, who seemed semi-conscious and was making intermittent groaning noises, and we led them up to Fergus's hut, where they poured him into a chair, as Fergus got out his first-aid kit.

'What happened to him?' he said.

'It was dreadful rough out there,' said Jimmy MacNeil. 'They were both taken bad with the seasick and this one fell and hit his head. Knocked him out cold, it did.'

'Why on earth did you come in a storm?'

'We shoulda been here yesterday but ah had engine trouble just after leaving Barra and ah had to go back in to fix it, so we lost a day.'

We all watched as Fergus wiped the blood from Kenny Lornie's forehead and put a plaster on a nasty cut just below his hairline. Then he wiped his face over with a wet flannel – I could still see the remains of the famous bruise – and Kenny opened his eyes.

He felt for his skull. He said: 'Uhhh, ma heid.'

Then he looked up and started to focus and he said: 'Well if it isn't Fergus.' He smiled. He said: 'The game's up, Fergus.'

We stood around watching him.

'Oh, aye. Ya wee secret. It's coming oot, and there's nothing ye can do tae stop it, not you, nor the fuckin' laird whose lackey ye are.'

Fergus was impassive, his arms folded.

'Ah know what ye're doing. Ah've worked it oot. Ye're keeping them for yaselves, aren't ye, you and Kintyre, for ya own private delectation and enjoyment? The English laird and his English lackey, and they're Scotland's birds! They're Scotland's treasure! Like it was Scotland's oil before you English got ya hands on it! But ye're not keeping the birds like ye kept the oil, ye great lumbering lummock. Not any more. I'm gonna see to that.'

Fergus held his gaze but continued expressionless. It seemed to unsettle Kenny slightly. He glanced around and saw me. 'And look who's with ye here, yet another English man. Dr Bonnici, I presume? Or should I say, Rupert? Are ye no' wondering why I'm here?'

'We know why you're here,' I said.

'You know?'

'We all know.'

Kenny sat up slightly. He didn't seem to register what I'd said. He was still very groggy and he shook his head as if to clear it. Then he saw Jenny. He said: 'Who's she?'

'She's doing the survey with me. The seabird survey, not to put too fine a point on it, that you fucked up.'

Kenny straightened. 'I didnae fuck up any survey, Rupert. What I did was ah found oot what was really here, and him, he put the lid on me – or so he thought. Well ye havenae, Fergus, see? Oh no. Cos me and ma friend here, we're gonna tell the world. D'ye not wanna know who ma friend is, Fergus, hey? Are ye no' interested in who this laddie might be?'

Fergus still said not a word.

'This is Rufus Mehlinger. He's only the world's greatest wildlife photographer.'

Jenny knew who he was. She said: 'You did the snow leopard pictures, didn't you? The ones that were in *National Geographic* earlier this year.'

'That's me, Ma'am.' The American looked pretty grim.

'They were wonderful.'

'Thank you. Good to know you're not all as batshit crazy as your big fat friend. Hear that, batshit? You're crazy.'

'And what are you here for?' I found myself saying, as if I didn't know.

'Well, Kenny informs me you have something here worth photographing.'

'Ah'll tell you what he's doing,' Kenny said, addressing Fergus. 'He's here with me tae blow ya wee secret apart. He's gonna take the pictures and we're gonna give them to the *Scotsman* and the *Herald* first so when they burst on the world, they're coming oota Edinburgh and Glasgow, and nowhere else. That's the agreement. So the world knows they're Scotland's birds. So the ownership is established, right from the start.'

Well, well, I thought. So that was Kenny's scheme. Suppose it made sense, in his terms.

But Fergus looked down on him in incredulity. 'You imbeciles! You think I would allow it?'

'Ye cannae stop us, Fergus.'

Mehlinger shrugged. He said: 'Ocean's a free place, ain't it? Last I heard, it was.'

'You stupid, stupid fools,' Fergus said. 'You would destroy them. If you succeeded, your publicity would destroy them.'

'We'll destroy nothing, Fergus. It's you who'll destroy them, you and ya laird, by keeping them to yaselves, unprotected. It's amazing ye havenae destroyed them already, ye selfish bastards. What ye've done is fuckin' criminally irresponsible. The world needs tae know about them so they can get proper protection. And that's what they'll get.'

I said: 'But why haven't you gone through UKOCA? Through Ramsay, and everyone?'

Kenny said: 'UKOCA's the establishment. The British establishment. Kintyre would know how tae stop it. He'd pull strings.'

Well, you might be right there, I thought. I wondered how on earth he'd got hold of Mehlinger, and persuaded him to come out here. Quite a coup. Gave real credibility to his plan. But then I realised he had no idea of what the new situation was.

I said: 'Kenny. Listen. We need to talk about this. I can understand why you've come, but things have changed. It's not a secret any more.'

'Yes it is. Who knows about it?'

'We do. Me and Jenny here, we've seen the birds. Fergus has shown them to us.'

'Why would he do that?'

'Because he's agreed that the time has come for the world to know about them.'

'No,' said Kenny emphatically. 'No way. Ah dinnae believe ye. No way would he think that.'

'Listen for God's sake, will you. He does, and I'm going to report on them, so it's all going to be official, and they'll get official protection now, they will, but we need to think very carefully about how it's done.'

'No way.'

'You did see what you thought you saw, and it's amazing, it's everything you think it is, but there needs to be to time to consider it, to put together the right conservation plan, surely you can see that?'

Kenny shook his head.

'Think about what you're proposing to do here. You just go and tell the world about them, off the cuff, just like that, there'll be an uncontrolled stampede. It'll be a huge world story, one of the biggest stories ever, that's why your friend here's agreed to come out all this way and take the pictures, but it'll be pandemonium, with all the other photographers who want to make money, plus the twitchers will go crazy, never mind the eggers, have you thought about the egg collectors? We won't be able to handle it. It really will put the birds at risk.'

Kenny blinked, trying to take this in. Then he said: 'Ah no. Ah no. Ye don't get me like that. Ye're on his side. Ye wanna keep it secret. Ye wanna keep it for yaselves.'

'Don't be bloody ridiculous, nobody wants to keep it for themselves, we just have to think carefully about what we do.'

'And what are you proposing tae do, posh boy?'

'I'm going to report on it to the office. To UKOCA. Soon as we get back.'

Kenny shook his head. 'No. Not UKOCA. That's another thing. This is going tae a body with a strictly Scottish remit. It's going tae Scottish Natural Heritage.'

'Who's going to decide that?'

'I am. I'm gonna give it them.'

'You're in a pretty equivocal position here, Kenny. Who are you representing? I represent UKOCA on Lanna. Who do you represent?'

'I'm representing Scotland!' shouted Kenny. 'I'm representing a small country that's been cheated and tricked and conned and swindled, a country that's been defrauded of its own by you and your kind for centuries and ye still are! So ye can fuck right off—'

Then the SSB radio crackled and a voice said: 'Lanna base, Lanna base, Stornoway Coastguard, Stornoway Coastguard.'

Fergus went to the mike. He said: 'Stornoway Coastguard, Lanna, go ahead over.'

'Lanna base, helicopter will be with you shortly,' said the voice. 'Will take non-essential crew members off the tanker and will need to land them on the island owing to extreme operating range, please acknowledge, over.'

Kenny said: 'What's all this about?'

Fergus said: 'Stornoway Coastguard, Lanna, yes that is possible, that can be done, repeat, that can be done. What is the current position of the tanker, over?'

'Lanna Base, stand by.'

Kenny said: 'What tanker? Is this an oil tanker they're talking about?' I realised that the three men from the *Western Wave* knew nothing about the *Lamprinos*.

The coastguard came back and said: 'Tanker now less than four nautical miles south-south-west of Lanna, you should have visual contact soon if not already, over.'

Fergus asked again about the salvage tug and they said it should be on scene in half an hour and he asked again about the helicopter and they said it was due imminently and Kenny said: 'Wha' the fuck's happening?'

I said: 'There's an oil tanker out of control and drifting towards us.'

'A big one?'

'100,000 tonnes. With more than 60,000 tonnes of oil on board.'

'Is it gonna hit the island?'

'It could do.'

Kenny called out: 'See, Fergus? This is down tae you. If the world knew about the birds, they'da kept all tankers clear of here. Ye're criminally irresponsible.'

'Why don't you shut your infernal mouth?' Fergus shouted, with such vehemence that Kenny fell silent. Fergus said to me: 'We need to make sure the helicopter gets in OK, with the gale. We've got some smoke flares in the stores,' and we went and found them, and almost immediately we heard and saw the chopper. It was circling over the island, just below the grey cloud base, a big red and white Sikorsky S61 – as I now know – with red flashing lights on the belly and the tail rotor. Fergus walked over to the edge of the helipad and ignited one of the flares; he held it up and the bright orange smoke blew out in a long train, clearly showing the wind direction, and the pilot started to swing down into the central bowl of the island and came in over the abbey and brought his machine down on the cross in the centre of the pad, and cut the engine. When the rotor blades had stopped he climbed out, a tall guy in an orange suit with a yellow helmet. He called over: 'You Fergus?'

'I am he.'

He came forward and shook hands. He gave his name, but I forget it. He looked concerned as he said: 'Well, you'd better be prepared for the worst. Looks like it's going to be a close-run thing. The tanker's drifting straight for the island and unless we can get a tow line on her she may well hit and it's going be touch and go if the big tug can get here in time.'

'Where is it now?'

'Five or six miles out. We overflew her just now. The heavy seas are slowing her down. Normally she could make eighteen knots but it's nothing like that in these conditions. I reckon about another half hour before she's on scene. So you'd better be prepared.'

'But can I emphasise to you,' said Fergus, 'that there are a quarter of a million seabirds on this island.'

'So we understand,' said the pilot.

'And an oil spill here would be a catastrophe.'

'We get that. But if it's any consolation, your seabirds are all on the cliffs on the eastern side of the island, aren't they?'

'Most of them,' said Fergus.

'Well, if the *Lamprinos* hits, she's only going to hit the western side. Maybe even that reef that's offshore. So you can take some comfort in that maybe.'

I saw Fergus's face tense.

'But we want to stop her hitting anything. First though, we've got to take the non-essential crew off, just in case. Can you put them up here? Just pro tem, of course?'

'How many?' said Fergus.

'Dozen or so, I should think. Twenty max.'

'Very well,' said Fergus. 'That will not be a problem, as long as it is temporary. The tanker is the problem. Can you stop it?'

'We're certainly going to try.'

As he clattered back upwards Fergus bit his hand, as he always did when he was distressed. Jenny and I looked at each other. That the tanker might hit Sgeir Dubh seemed unthinkable.

'Let us continue our watch,' Fergus said. 'There is still Kintyre to be concerned with, God help us.'

'What about these three?' I said, indicating Kenny, Jimmy and Rufus Mehlinger, who were watching us from the doorway of Fergus's hut. 'We can't really leave them to their own devices, can we?'

'They will have to come up with us.' He walked over and said to them: 'We must return to the castle top now to observe and you cannot remain here by yourselves. You must come with us.'

'Yeah? What if we don't wanna come, asshole?' said Mehlinger. He was very upset and I wondered if things were going to turn violent again.

'You will be locked in a hut,' said Fergus. 'Make up your mind at once.'

'Ah think we'd better go with them, Rufus,' said Kenny.

'Aye, let's not have any trouble here,' said Jimmy MacNeil.

So we gave the three of them wet-weather gear and they followed us up the slope to the castle steps and they were duly taken aback by the immense panorama that awaited them on the battlements, and Kenny caught sight of Sgeir Dubh to the north and cried excitedly to Mehlinger: 'There, Rufus! The rocks, over there! That's where ah saw them! That's where they are!'

'Ain't much use you telling me that, with no motherfucking cameras,' Mehlinger grunted at him.

But we were looking the other way, our eyes were fixed on the chopper and its winking red lights heading south-west and we followed them and there, emerging at last from the grey gloom, was the *Lamprinos*. I felt a chill. I saw a long dark bar on the sea, on the grey and white heaving waves, side-on to us; her bows were facing north-west, as if she would sail comfortably past the island from where she was, giving us a wide berth; but of course she had no power and she was not moving north-westwards at all, merely facing that way, and it was north-eastwards that she was being carried by wind and tide and current, directly towards us. She was like a giant piece of flotsam and I thought how strange, how unnatural, that something so big should be helpless and possess no power – for the tanker was startling in her dimensions. Even at a distance, two to three miles away I estimated, I could gauge

her size by looking at the helicopter hovering over her to take off
the non-essential crew, just made visible by its flickering red light;
the chopper seemed like a gnat above the ship and the *Lamprinos*
was at least 150 yards long, I reckoned, though later when I looked
up her details I found the length was actually 268 metres, or 293
yards, which meant an Olympic sprinter going full-pelt would take
half a minute to run from one end of the deck to the other. She
was bigger than any ship I had ever set eyes on, or even imagined.

All six of us on the castle top were sobered by the sight. 'She's
lost power, has she, Fergus?' Jimmy MacNeil shouted against the
wind.

'She has.'

'Which way's she drifting?'

'Broadly north-east. Towards us,' shouted Fergus. 'There is a
salvage tug on the way.'

'When's it due, if ye don't mind me asking?'

'Soon.'

'Ah used to work on tugs.'

If that was a conversational opening, Fergus ignored it. We
watched for more than ten minutes as the chopper winched up
the non-essential crewmen one by one and the tanker, just barely
perceptibly, got closer. Then the helicopter rose and turned and
headed back towards us. Fergus called to me and Jenny: 'Perhaps
you two might meet them?'

'Sure,' I shouted back. 'What do we do with them?'

'Put them in the stores hut.'

So Jenny and I waited at the edge of the helipad as the chopper
swung in and touched down and the pilot cut the engine, and
when the rotors slowed to a stop the cabin door opened and there
was a smiling winchman who said: 'Wotcher! Got a cargo of half-
drowned rabbits here. Can you get 'em a cuppa or something?
They're Filipinos. Don't speak a lot of English.' There were thirteen
of them and they jumped out, small guys soaking and shivering, and
we made room for them in the stores hut as the chopper clattered
back off and got all four of Fergus's mugs and filled them with
Fergus's packet soup for which the crewmen smiled their thanks,
and we raced back up to the castle top. Everyone was looking the
same way, south-west. The *Lamprinos* was much closer, barely a
mile and a half off, I reckoned, and I could see the bridge windows
now and other details of her white superstructure and I cried out,
'But where's the bloody tug?' and Fergus pointed to our left, behind
me, and at last, there it was.

It was white, with a big diagonal red stripe slashed across its hull, steaming in towards us from the east and exuding power, squat and chunky and shouldering its way through the waves which were breaking all over it, almost level with Castle Point now, yet as I turned back to the tanker which was its objective I was dumbstruck by the difference in size. The *Lamprinos* was gargantuan. It was the single biggest object I had ever set eyes on in my life. 'Can that tug really tow a tanker like that?' I called out to no one in particular.

'She's an ETV,' shouted Jimmy MacNeil.

'A what?'

'An emergency towing vessel. She'll have a bollard pull of a hundred and fifty tonnes.'

'What does that mean?'

'Means she can take that tanker and even bigger.'

'You know about tugs?'

'Ah used to work on tugs.'

'So what's going to happen?' I shouted to him.

'They've got to get a line across from the one to the other. With the helicopter.'

It was hovering directly above as the tug steamed over to the tanker and took up station directly ahead of her, stern to bows, and the chopper lowered its winchman and took first one man off the tug and then a second, and transferred them over to the tanker 100 metres away. All this in the surging waves of a Force Eight gale. I was lost in admiration of the courage and the skill.

'They'll take a light line over first,' Jimmy MacNeil shouted. 'What they call a hi-line. And they'll use that to pull over a mooring rope, good strong rope, thick as your wrist. And then they'll use the rope to pull over a towing hawser. Big steel towing hawser,' he shouted. 'Thick as your thigh. Then the tug will get the tanker under way.'

'Hopefully,' I shouted back. If it didn't happen in time the tanker was on course to hit the north-west corner of the island, I calculated, although thank God it looked like it might just go past Sgeir Dubh.

'Och, it's close, but ah think they'll do it,' Jimmy cried, and we watched, as the chopper returned to the stern of the tug and lowered what looked like a bag, and something was clipped on and once again there was a transfer from one vessel to the other, this time of a line. We were gripped by these events, all of us, even Rufus the one-eyed photographer, although I imagined he was more frustrated and furious than ever that he didn't have his cameras to record it all and I have to say I felt a lot of sympathy for him, because I somehow felt he was one of the good guys and he was only doing his job, and he had the misfortune to come up against Fergus at the worst possible time, Fergus the Terrible. I wondered who in the end would pay for his camera gear. Twelve thousand dollars. But even he was transfixed by the spectacle.

'What's the time-frame?' I shouted to Jimmy MacNeil.

'On the tanker they've got to rig up a towing bridle, in the bows,' he shouted back. 'Could take up to half an hour.'

'Have we got that much time?'

'Ah think so. Just about.'

So we watched, which was all we could do, and after a while we were joined by the Filipino crewmen who had found their way out of the stores hut and up to the castle top, eager to know what was happening to their ship, and Fergus was so engrossed in the proceedings I do not think he even noticed them, and so there were now nineteen of us on the battlements; and we saw the mooring rope go across, which Jimmy MacNeil shouted was actually called the messenger, and we saw all the activity in the bows of the *Lamprinos* and eventually we saw the towing hawser itself pulled over by the tanker's winch, and all this time the two ships were moving in line astern in the turbulent sea, closer and closer to the north-west corner of the island and if ever my heart was in my mouth it was now, but eventually Jimmy MacNeil shouted: 'It's there.'

'What?'

'It's on. The hawser's on.'

We watched. We saw the great towing rope come up out of the water as a sagging belly between the two vessels and then tighten as the tug started to move forward.

'Final question is, does he go north about?' shouted Jimmy. 'Or south about?'

'What?'

'Does the tug skipper take the tanker round the north of the island, or to the south? Past us here?'

'What's the difference?'

'He's probably wants to take her to the Clyde, for repairs and that, which is south,' he shouted. 'So south about would be quicker. But you see the tanker is pointing more or less northwards now? So if he goes north, he goes with the wind and the waves. If he pulls her round to the south though, he's going against them. Puts more strain on the hawser. But he's got to do that eventually, anyway. Here we go. Yep. Yep. Well. He's going south.'

We watched as the tug began to turn to starboard, towards us, and pull the *Lamprinos* round, and as we saw her bows begin to follow the turn and we realised she was now under control the feeling of relief was indescribable, and a murmur of contentment ran through her Filipino crewmen; I reckon she was only half a mile from the island and ten minutes more and she would have hit, and if ever there was a great escape this was it and I looked for Jenny to squeeze her hand and in that very moment she cried: 'Another boat! There's another boat coming!'

'Where!' shouted Fergus.

'Right there! Heading for the anchorage!'

We had all been so focused on the tanker on the western side of the island that we had not noticed this approach from the east; we could see it was a fast motor cruiser with a rib hanging from the davits on the stern, now only a few hundred yards out.

'It has to be Kintyre,' murmured Fergus. And it was.

28

He had come with his South African associates, his 'penguin wranglers', and I think his plan must have been simply to head straight for the Sgeir Dubh breeding ledge and seize as many of the birds as they possibly could. But the storm had made the approach to the reef opening impossible, and then the tanker ... I can imagine how horrified Kintyre must have been, as we all were, as he approached his beloved island and saw this oil-laden behemoth about to crash on to it. He must have watched the saga of the tug and the towrope like we did, heart in mouth, and then breathed the greatest sigh of relief of all his years, just like us, as the bows of the monster were swung round and she finally started to move away from the rocks; he must have been, as we were, overcome with thankfulness.

But there was a difference with Kintyre: his mind hadn't stopped working. For he saw not just a deliverance then, he saw a way forward, he saw the solution to everything, and it filled him, it surged through him as his cruiser came straight into the anchorage – Fergus had omitted to reposition the chains after Kenny's arrival – and he leapt off the boat and ran up towards the castle, where we were evident on the battlements and took the steps two at a time crying Fergus! Fergus! Fergus! and he shouldered his way through the Filipino sailors and stood before us and swept his hand out towards the tanker and cried through the wind: '*Now* do you see?'

'See what, Rollo?'

'They cannot remain here! Just then their lives were hanging by a thread! Could anything be clearer? For God's sake, man, is it not obvious? They are not secure here, in the modern world! We have to give them a safe home! We have to give them safety!'

And I have to say, at that moment, I thought he was probably right.

'We can do it together!' Kintyre cried. 'Do it with me, Fergus!'

But Fergus Pryng was not going to have his mind changed, he was not going to fall in line with the Earl of Kintyre just to help him rescue his fortunes. In the gale that still roared about us, he shook his head. 'If you move them, Rollo, you will extinguish them,' he shouted. 'You will make them extinct *for a second time*. You will commit the greatest of all crimes against nature. No, no, no.'

'But do you not see how close they have just come to disaster?' Kintyre shouted back. 'We have watched these tankers together on the horizon and expressed our fears, have we not? How long before the next one arrives, when there is no tug to pull it away? What then for the birds? How long before crude oil destroys them? Is that what you want?'

'What we need is an exclusion zone for the tankers. That must be arranged, when the government takes over their protection. And it will be, Rollo.' He shouted at him: 'I will make sure of it!'

'Stuff and nonsense!' shouted Kintyre. 'How will you police that? How will you stop a tanker skipper taking the quickest way south? Put a fence in the ocean? Can you not see your position has no sense and no logic? It is impossible beyond measure!'

'And your position, Rollo,' Fergus cried back at him, 'is based purely on self-interest, and your professed regard for the birds is nothing but a commercial one! It is a sham!'

The rest of us on the castle top were mesmerised, we were awe-struck by the double spectacle, of in the background the great ship being heaved away from disaster, yard by straining yard, and right in our midst these two men shouting at each other about it – Jenny and I knowing full well what the issue was, but Kenny and his boatman and his photographer at a loss to understand, and the Filipino sailors wholly bemused.

'What they arguing about?' Kenny Lornie called out to me, as Kintyre's two assistants, both noticeably big men, followed their boss on to the battlements. I moved across to him so I didn't have to shout. 'Kintyre wants to take the auks to Balnay.'

'Eh?'

'He's built a special pool for them. At the castle.'

'You mean he wants them for himself? For his zoo?'

'That's right. Be the biggest attraction on the planet, wouldn't it?'

'The fuckin' bastard,' said Kenny.

'Do you think your judgement is infallible?' Kintyre was shouting to his warden. 'Do you think yours is the only view which carries weight? What I see now, Fergus, is that your judgement has been warped, it has been twisted by the proprietorial sense you have developed about the birds, for you think that they are yours, do you not? Admit it! You think they belong to you!'

'You are talking rubbish, Rollo.'

'It is the worst of all betrayals, Fergus! You have been uniquely privileged, you have been allowed unique access to Lanna through my personal favour and this is how you repay me? You are in my service, yet you take it upon yourself to hide the birds from me when you find them, oh yes, I know you did that, for how many years I know not, but I do know it was many, and now you have swelled in your pride and you think that they are yours! They are not yours! They are on my island! I have legal title to them! They belong to me!'

'No they don't!' shouted Kenny Lornie.

Kintyre turned. As he focused on Kenny he reddened and I thought he would burst. 'You!' he cried. 'What in God's name are you doing on my island, you little shit? Get off it! Get off it now! Go on, fuck off!'

'Fuck off yourself!' shouted Kenny, moving towards him. 'You think the birds are like your tenants, don't ye, and ye can move them around as you please, take 'em away from their homes, like ya ancestors did with the poor people they cleared off the land, well ye cannae! The time for you and ya like is finished!'

'My ancestors would have known how to deal with you,' Kintyre shouted back at him, 'and your end would not have been quick, so be thankful you are living today and get you gone, you miserable little man, there is nothing to concern you here.'

'The auks are my concern!' shouted Kenny.

'The auks are *my* concern, and mine alone,' Kintyre shouted back. 'The auks are mine! They belong to me!'

'No they don't!' shouted Kenny.

'I have legal title to them!'

'Away tae fuck wi' ya legal title! They dinnae belong to you, they belong to Scotland!'

'Scotland! The hell with Scotland! They're mine!'

'They're Scotland's auks!'

'You stupid fool!' shouted Fergus. 'They don't belong to Scotland!'

'No? No? Then who do they belong to, ya great laird's lackey? You saying they belong tae you?'

'Of course they don't belong to me!'

'Then to whom do they belong?' Kintyre cried, above the howling wind. 'Tell us, Fergus! You who know so much about them! To whom do they belong, if not the Balnay estate?'

It was like a rumbling volcano finally erupting. 'THEY BELONG TO THE EARTH!' Fergus roared, in the loudest voice I had ever heard from a human being, 'THEY BELONG TO THE EARTH!'

In my dreams I see him in that moment, for although I did not yet understand it, that was when I began to be aware of what had made him do what he had done, and here was the essence of him, it was the climactic moment of everything, and in another way too, because even before his words had died away there was a sharp report, a loud *kerrack!* from the direction of the tanker and Jimmy MacNeil shouted: 'The hawser's parted! The tow rope! It's broken!' We turned, all of us, and saw that it was true: the hawser was hanging limply from the bows of the *Lamprinos*. She was out of control and drifting again – towards the island, now less than half a mile away, as we all instantly realised. We stared together in disbelief.

I understand now what had happened: the tanker had been pulled round by the tug from a north-west heading, at ten o'clock on a clock face, to a north-east heading at two o'clock; she would have swung on further round to face east, then south-east, then due south and away, away from the island and off to the Clyde or wherever; but the moment of maximum pressure just after the north-east heading, when her 103,000 tonnes were being dragged across the full force of the wind and the waves and the tide and current, had proved too much for the hawser.

'I thought that might happen,' cried Jimmy MacNeil. 'The angle was too tight. He should have gone north about.'

It meant that the monster was now pointing direct at the island and in fact, as we saw, she was pointing directly at Sgeir Dubh, and drifting in the direction she was pointing.

'Can they get a line on her again?' I cried to Jimmy.

'It's too late,' he shouted. 'See, the tug's out of position. There winnae be the time nor the space to do it. She's gonna hit. She's gonna hit that reef, looks like.'

'What can be done?'

'All they can do now is try and get the rest of the crew off with the chopper.'

Indeed, that was happening: the big Sikorsky was hovering directly over the tanker and men seemed to be running round on the deck. I fervently hoped they would all get off, of course I did, but the five of us on the castle parapet who had actually seen and knew what Sgeir Dubh housed were consumed with another feeling, a sort of creeping horror at the unhurried but inevitable progress

of the monster toward the rocks, like a gargantuan crossbow bolt
flying forward in slow motion. How long did it take? Five minutes?
More? They were the longest minutes of my life. It was hard to
believe it was taking place, but there it was, in front of our eyes,
the great oil-filled behemoth bearing down on Sgeir Dubh. The
whole company was watching in horrified fascination; but then I
realised Fergus had gone.

I caught up with him at the bottom of the staircase. 'Fergus!'
I cried to him. 'Where are you going?'

He turned. 'I must go to them,' he said. 'I cannot stay here and
leave them in their hour of need. The oil will spill when it hits.'

'What are you going to do?'

'I will try and get in with the rib and bring them back.'

'Fergus, you can't go out in that sea, it'd be suicide.'

'I must go to them.'

'And anyway you can't do it alone.'

Jenny joined me.

'Fergus wants to go get the auks in the rib,' I said.

'In that sea?' she said. 'Fergus, you can't do it by yourself.'

Fergus looked at us, with the wind was howling around our
ears, and we looked back at him, and the question hung in the air.
Then Jenny turned to me. She said: 'I could drive the rib.'

'Jenny, are you crazy, in that sea? In a four-metre inflatable?
It'd be suicide.'

'I think I could do it. I think maybe we have to go with him.
Maybe, after everything, we have to do this, Miles.'

I looked into her eyes. I saw all that had happened and I saw
what she meant. This was part of it too, and it couldn't be avoided.
I said: 'I will go where you go, Jen.'

She said: 'We'll come with you, Fergus. I will drive.'

'Very well, but we must be quick,' said Fergus. 'Suits and
lifejackets at once.'

In the stores we fumbled into them and checked each other and
from a shelf Fergus took a number of canvas sacks and stuffed them
inside his survival suit and we set out for the beach and immediately
saw Kintyre and his two henchmen coming down from the castle.

'Fergus!' cried the Earl. 'What are you doing? Where are you
going?'

Fergus ignored him. I saw Kenny Lornie and his two companions
hurrying down the castle steps in their turn. 'Hey Fergus!' shouted
Kenny. 'Fergus!' Fergus ignored him also. We got to the beach
and untied the mooring rope of the rib and Fergus said to Jenny:

'Listen to me now. Use the power to climb a wave then power off and roll over the top of it. You must not leap into infinity and catch the wind. Understand?'

Jenny nodded.

'I will be in the front to keep the nose down. If there is a big breaking wave, do not hit it straight on, take it at fifteen degrees to your heading, OK? Take it on your shoulder, not on your nose.'

She nodded again.

'Let us go, then. Head for the entrance to the lagoon.'

We wheeled the rib into the water and Fergus climbed in and placed himself in the bows, followed by me and then Jenny, and we pulled up the wheels and pushed down the engine and Jenny started it and I could see that on the quay Kintyre and his guys were climbing on to their shiny white motor cruiser and Kenny and Rufus Mehlinger and Jimmy MacNeil were running for the *Western Wave* but there was no time to bother about them and Jenny opened up and took us through the defile and out into the Atlantic storm and even the pilgrims in their birlinns must have been better protected, I thought, anxiety seizing my whole being. But the sea we surged into was not so terrible, being under the lee of the island, on the sheltered eastern side; it was when we rounded Castle Point that we hit the full force of the storm coming from the west and frankly I was terrified, I had never been in waves like that in a small boat and I never want to be again and every second seemed liked my last; yet Jenny knew what she was doing, climbing the waves then powering off and rolling over the top of them just as Fergus had advised her and we managed to head forward across them towards the *Lamprinos*, starboard side on to us in all her immensity, and as we watched, appalled, the great vessel with its deadly cargo finally slammed into Sgeir Dubh, her bows riding directly into the lagoon entrance itself.

She grounded firmly on the reef, and as we got closer we could see that the breaking waves were pushing her further and further in, making it impossible for us to get through, 'Hopeless,' Fergus shouted above the wind and the water. 'We cannot get in here. We must go round the far side.' So Jenny brought us out around the ship and on her stern I saw in huge white letters LAMPRINOS and underneath PIRAEUS and the coastguard helicopter was hovering directly above us and as we came round we realised she was now stuck in the reef at an angle and her port side was being driven closer and closer in and was actually sheltering the water between the ship and the rocks of the reef. 'She's creating her own lee,' shouted Fergus. 'We can get in here. Put me on the rocks. I will try and climb over to the breeding ledge.'

It was easier said than done, even under the lee of the tanker, and three times we tried, just a few yards away from the hull of the *Lamprinos* with Fergus in spite of his arthritis poised to leap on the rib's upswing and three times the boat was sucked away a moment too soon in spite of Jenny's skill; but on the fourth attempt he leapt and landed on the rocks and managed to cling on; and he began to climb up to the rescue of them, to the rescue of the auks. The rarest and most precious organisms on earth, a short distance away on the other side of the reef. God help them. Without the shelter of the colossal ship he could never have done it because further along the waves were simply breaking over Sgeir Dubh but here we could see he had just a chance of getting up and over the reef and along to the breeding ledge, and he needed to, because now for the first time I smelt the oil, and it was clear that the ship's tanks had ruptured and I realised with dread and dismay that a major oil spill was indeed upon us right here and Fergus had been right to come, he had been right; he began to scale the rocks as Jenny turned the rib round to stand off from them, coming momentarily out from the sheltered water and hitting the waves again, but then as we started to swing back in Jenny cried, *Miles, it's on fire! the tanker's on fire!* and in the corner of my eye I glimpsed bright colour amidst all the grey of the storm and at that moment Fergus reached the top of the rocks and was stretching out both his arms to keep his balance like a tightrope walker and as he did so a great tongue of orange flame shot from the ship with a *whoosh!* and engulfed him and I saw him for a second with his outstretched arms in the fire like a cross, like a burning cross, and Jenny, watching in horror as I was, for the first time took her eye off the waves and powered straight up over the top of one and the gale caught the underside of the boat and I felt it lift, with the weight of Fergus no longer in the bows, I felt it flip right over and we went with it and something hit me a sharp blow on the back of the head and that was all I knew.

PART THREE

29

They called it the Lanna disaster. It was a colossal news story. Usually these oil tanker catastrophes get named after the ship concerned, and yes, it is sometimes referred to as the *Lamprinos* disaster, because who can forget the Greek carrier loaded with Brent crude which ran on to the reef on the remotest of all the Hebridean islands and exploded? But in this case it was the island itself which captured the public imagination, this historic but half-forgotten corner of the world, with its celebrity owner, the Earl of Kintyre. I know that because after I had recovered and we had come back to England I made a special trip to the British Newspaper Library in Colindale and looked up all the headlines, and I found to my surprise that the hero of the whole business appeared to be Lord Kintyre himself. By a remarkable coincidence, said the papers, he was actually present on his island when the *Lamprinos* hit and caught fire, and with his staff he plunged fearlessly into the flames to try to save Lanna's nesting seabirds and was, for his pains, horribly burned, while around him, six other men met their deaths. What a hero. And what an amazing news story.

I scanned the headlines with a sort of detached fascination, reading that the fatalities included the tanker's captain, who had vowed he would be the last man off his ship; a well-known American wildlife photographer; a British government conservationist and three members of Lord Kintyre's own personnel – two from his wildlife park at Castle Balnay in Argyllshire where he famously romped with tigers as if they were golden retrievers, plus his warden on the island itself, a man called Fergus Pryng. And Fergus Pryng only turned out to be the ex-husband of Bronwen Pryng, the superstar green entrepreneur, human rights campaigner and environmental activist! You could feel the journalists smacking their lips. Once that connection was made – it seemed to take about a day and a half – it gave the story a whole new boost and she was pictured grief-stricken on every front page; after a week, as soon as it was safe to do so, she took a helicopter out to the island, reporters in tow, and dropped a wreath into the sea by the wreck of the tanker. Her quote was endlessly repeated: 'Fergus died protecting the environment from those who would despoil it, like he had done all his life. It's a lesson for every one of us.'

But at the time I was aware of none of that: I was unconscious. When the big wave caught the inflatable under its nose and for all Jenny's skill, flipped it right over and the hardened hull base or the outboard or whatever it was struck my head, I was knocked out – I received a fractured skull – and I would quickly have drowned, but for Ms Pittaway, who, almost unbelievably, for the second time in her life found herself rescuing an unconscious lover from an accident in a fizz boat, as she would call it; she kept my head up, helped by our survival suits and lifejackets, and the coastguard helicopter, which was hovering directly over the *Lamprinos* taking off the remaining crew, saw it happen and within a minute or so had picked us up.

Yet we were not alone. When we left the anchorage for Sgeir Dubh, the other two boats had followed us out into the storm, for what choice did they have? From Kintyre's point of view, and from the point of view of Kenny and his photographer, if Fergus was heading for Lanna's secret, they had to be there too. They were close behind us, they had also come in to the lee of the tanker, Rufus Mehlinger taking pictures with Kenny's own camera which Fergus had failed to find in the *Western Wave* (so Jimmy MacNeil told people later), and things happened very quickly: just as the winchman brought us into the helicopter cabin, the tanker below us, on fire at her bows with the flames in which Fergus had been engulfed, was ripped apart by a series of immense explosions along her whole length in which both the other boats were caught up. Jenny saw it happen.

For their actions in the subsequent minutes when they hovered at the edge of the mountain of flame and oily black smoke trying to locate the occupants of the two small craft, the helicopter crew rightly received bravery awards; but for all their courage they only managed to pick up Jimmy MacNeil and Lord Kintyre, both of them badly burned. The two South African marine biologists from Balnay, Nick van der Merwe and Dan le Roux – I somehow feel I ought to record their names – could not be recovered, nor could Captain Spiros Constantinides of the *Lamprinos*. I regret them all, but the captain and the 'penguin wranglers' I did not know, so I cannot in truth feel much for them.

However, I am keenly sorry for the death of Rufus Mehlinger from Burlington, Vermont, who had been a war photographer and lost an eye covering the American entanglement in Somalia in 1993, subsequently turning to wildlife photography, at which he was superlative. I sought out his obituaries, and I have bought his two books, and I hugely regret that my meeting with such a noteworthy and fascinating man was so brief and in such wretched circumstances.

Yet no regret matches that which I have for Kenneth John Lornie, aged thirty-one, Higher Executive Officer, United Kingdom Offshore Conservation Agency. Kenny cared enormously about the natural world and he cared about Scotland, those were his twin passions, and they were noble passions both. He started out in real disadvantage and he would have risen high in conservation, I'm sure, but the heart of my regret is not so much the lost opportunity of his life as the fact that I threw back his offer of friendship, toffee-nosed tosser that I was, and now I can never repair that. I will take the shame and remorse of it to my grave.

None of their bodies could be recovered; and when it was clear there was nothing more they could do and their fuel reserves were dropping dangerously low, the chopper crew flew back to the island and set down the tanker's remaining officers to be with their men; then, with a major emergency operation getting under way, and the salvage tug fruitlessly training a fire hose on the blazing tanker, they flew me and Jenny, and Kintyre and MacNeil, direct to the Western Infirmary in Glasgow. I was in a fairly bad way, as were the other two. I had a serious bleed into the brain cavity and they operated on it to relieve the pressure and put me in an induced coma to let it heal, and I was in intensive care for a week; I eventually came round on a general ward to see Jenny and Lotte beaming at me, overcome with relief.

Jenny had had to deal with everything. She had talked to the police at length and told them about who was there and the approach of the *Lamprinos* and all that happened with Fergus and the others, although she declined to talk to the press (in spite of considerable pressure, as she was the only interviewable direct witness apart from the helicopter crew). That's probably how the narrative arose of the heroics of Lord Kintyre – creative interpretation in the absence of facts. Then the next day she spoke at length to Ramsay Wishart who came down from Aberdeen, informing him – to his bewildered amazement and great distress – that Kenny had been on the island with us, that he had arrived that day with a famous American wildlife photographer, and it looked like they both were dead.

She told him the whole saga of the tanker and how Fergus had set out for the reef with us in the inflatable, to try to save any seabirds which might be at risk there, with Kenny's boat and Lord Kintyre's boat following in our wake.

But *which* seabirds, she didn't say.

She didn't tell Ramsay, or anyone else.

It was just instinct, she told me later. And she thought it was Fergus's business and it wasn't really her place to talk about it. And anyway, she said, she had enough on her plate with me.

I was two more weeks in the Western Infirmary, slowly relearning life skills like walking and using the loo, and then I was another two weeks or so in rehab in a cottage-hospital sort of place somewhere else in Scotland, with a lot of intensive physiotherapy to strengthen my arms and legs; Jenny stayed nearby the whole time. And eventually, it was late July by now, I came out and we went back to Wimbledon, where we had the house to ourselves because Lotte, who was beyond overjoyed at our reuniting, had gone off on another world cruise, once she was sure I was medically on the mend. My contract with UKOCA had finished. We got a removal company to clear the flat in Rosemount and bring my stuff down south: I couldn't face going back to Aberdeen, and the million questions that would follow. For I couldn't have answered them anyway; I had amnesia.

PTA they call it, post-traumatic amnesia, and I was a classic case; everything about the events in the twenty-four hours or so before the tanker hit was a blur. Not only that: I had headaches which built up every day, really bad headaches that laid me low, even with the painkillers I was taking, and I found myself in strange moods, depressed and sort of teary, as if there were something in the background which was not good, which was very upsetting, but I couldn't put my finger on it. I had no idea what it was until, for all my psyche striving to suppress it, on the second night back in the Wimbledon house it suddenly exploded into a dream, the flames, the flames shooting out in a great tongue, a great *Whoosh!* and in the heart of them, a dark figure with his arms outstretched like a cross, was Fergus, and I screamed out loud and I woke.

'What?' cried Jenny who woke at once. 'What is it?'

'Fergus!' I said.

The tears were rolling down my cheeks.

'Fergus burning.'

She put her arms around me and pulled me to her. 'I know,' she said. 'It is terrible. It is truly terrible. But you're here now. You're with me now.' She kissed my forehead.

They were incessant after that, the dreams of the burning cross, they visited me nightly. I remember that the flames had different colours, mostly they were a mix of orange and yellow but sometimes they were blood red. And once Fergus stood on the reef and called out to me, Doctor Bonnici, please to keep these blasted flames away from me, would you be so kind and I called back Consider it done, Fergus, but the flames came anyway, they sort of sneaked around both sides of me as I was trying to beat them back with my hands and they licked towards Fergus and then they engulfed him once again ... I don't think I will ever be rid of them. They still sometimes come to me even now, but they are much less frequent; back then, they arrived so regularly that I was apprehensive about even going to sleep.

I think my head injury made them worse, or at least the aftermath of it did, the migraines and the mood swings and everything; it was a dire combination and it laid me low. Our stuff from the island arrived, including my laptop with the seabird survey figures on it, sent on from the Balnay estate, with a note from Gervase Crinan which said how dreadful it all had been and how thankful he was that we had survived, and informing us that his lordship was still in hospital, but recovering – and I didn't even reply. We turned down flat a talk with a reporter from the *Aberdeen Press and Journal* who had enterprisingly worked out where we lived. There were two interviews we couldn't avoid, though, one to a police sergeant from the Northern Constabulary in Stornoway who was helping the procurator-fiscal with the fatal accident inquiry, and the other to a guy carrying out the separate inquiry of the Marine Accident Investigation Branch. We spoke about them beforehand.

Jenny said: 'You know Miles, with regard to talking about everything, I haven't told anyone ... about what Fergus showed us.'

'How d'you mean?'

'The birds.'

'What birds?'

'Do you not remember?'

'There were lots of birds. Birds all over the place.'

'All right,' she said. 'Never mind. That's fine.'

So when Sergeant Mackinnon flew down from Stornoway to see us, followed a few days later by Mr Baxter from the MAIB, Jenny did virtually all the talking: both men quickly saw that I was in no state to add anything useful and Jenny gave them a full account of what had happened with Fergus Pryng on Lanna, right up to and including his death – with one particular excepted. And then Ramsay Wishart phoned us, more troubled than ever about Kenny's role in the events and his fate, and desperate to learn more and talk to me, but Jenny explained that I was not at all well; indeed, I got worse. A day or so later I had some sort of nervous collapse. The burning dreams had come in the night again, as savage as ever, and in the morning I didn't want to get up. I stayed in bed all day and Jenny came back in the late afternoon and found me looking at the wall with a blank face and took the decision which resolved things.

'Fuck this,' she said. 'This is no good. Come on. We're going to New Zealand.'

We were away more than three months, and in that time, I healed. To go there was the perfect cure: although I was ailing at first, it quickly came to feel like a fresh start in a new land with a lovely light and the southern spring arriving, and the warmest of welcomes from the Pittaway family in Auckland, from Barry the father and Irene the mother and Tim the younger brother; it was a considerable help to be in a household headed by a family doctor, for Barry knew a lot about head injuries and changed my painkillers which brought the headaches under control. The help wasn't just medical, though. Both Jenny's parents could see that for all the trauma of our past we were truly bound to each other now, and they were wholly sympathetic and for the first time in my life I felt part of a happy family, which was enormously restorative; I still had the dreams but I sort of knew deep down I was having them in a safe place, which started to draw their sting; and my memory started to return. In bursts. It was weird. One evening we were in Jenny's childhood bedroom chatting and I suddenly said: 'Jesus, the tanker.'

'What, Miles?'

'The tow rope broke. That the tug had put on it.'

'That's right.'

'It crashed straight into the reef. What was it called? Sgeir Dubh.'

'It did.'

'Wow. And we went with Fergus in the inflatable, right by the side of the ship, didn't we?'

'We did.'

'And it was then that the flames … got him.'

'That's right.'

'Was he killed, Jen? He must have been, surely?'

'He was, Miles. I'm sorry. But your memory seems to be returning, and that's good.'

And she went over the other events of that terrible day, culminating in the fate of the others who had died.

'They didn't make it,' she said. 'I'm sorry, Miles.'

'Including … Kenny? Kenny Lornie?'

She nodded.

It took a minute to sink in.

'Kenny's *dead*?'

She nodded. And that's when I learned of it.

Strange that the last thing that should come back to me was Lanna's secret; but so it was. It returned the next day when I was on a run from the Pittaway home in Ponsonby to the marina where they kept their boat *Windwhistle* and I was going over everything in my mind, the tanker hitting the reef and us bowling out to it with Fergus in that terrible storm … but … there was something else. Knocking on the door of my consciousness. What was it?

I realised. We had gone before, hadn't we? To the reef.

When was that?

We'd gone with Fergus in the inflatable to Sgeir Dubh when the weather was calm, and he had taken us inside …

He had taken us through a gap in the reef into that sort of lagoon … *He idled the motor and let us drift for moment.*

Then he said: 'There.'

I looked past him, and saw it, twenty yards ahead; for a second I could not take it in, as if the connection between my eyes and my brain had failed. But as I registered what I was looking at, in an intense moment of incredulity that suddenly felt like a series of locks flying open all at once, I understood: I understood everything, I understood Lanna's staggering secret, I understood what Fergus was protecting …

I stopped dead. My heart was pounding. I sat down on the pavement.

Jesus Christ.

There are great auks on Lanna.

They're not extinct.

They're still there.

I found I was trembling, trembling at the immensity of the thing. It flooded back into my mind like the bursting of a dam and I saw everything clearly again. And when I got back I took Jenny to one side immediately and said: 'What are we going to do about them?'

'About what?'

'The great auks.'

Jenny threw her arms around me and hugged me. She told me later that this was the moment when she realised that I had fully recovered. She smiled and sat me down. 'You want to talk about it now then?'

'Incredible thing, isn't it?'

'Certainly is.'

'Great auks surviving.' I whistled. I shook my head. 'And Kintyre was going to try and kidnap them, wasn't he?'

'He was.'

'You don't think he succeeded?'

'He barely escaped with his life.'

'And nothing's come out about them ... since the tanker?'

'Not that I'm aware of. I've told nobody.'

'Then what do we do?'

'When Fergus showed us the birds, he said he was showing them to you in your official capacity as the representative of UKOCA, didn't he? And you were gonna tell your boss. Ramsay. I think that's what you're duty bound to do.'

'That's right. I am. But ... it's winter in Europe and the birds won't be there now, will they? Didn't Fergus say, if people from the agency got out there after the birds had left for the winter, no one would believe us? It's just too incredible for words.'

'I think Ramsay will believe you.'

'Why?'

'Because it will explain why Kenny went back there, won't it? With a world-famous wildlife photographer in tow. Which is what he's agonising over.'

I saw the point of that.

Jenny said: 'Ramsay's not the problem, old lad. Nor is Kintyre, really. I think the potential problem is, what did the fire do?'

'How d'you mean?'

'The tanker fire, after the explosion. It was a gigantic fire. I watched it from the chopper, while they were trying to pick up the others and you were unconscious with your head on my lap. Even with everything else I was, er, pretty horror-struck, I have to say. Cos the flames were covering a lot of the reef. Of Sgeir Dubh.'

The implications began to sink in. My brain had been transfixed for so long by the outlandish vision of Fergus's end that I had completely forgotten why we went out to the reef in the first place.

'You think the auks might have been caught up in the fire?'

'Got to be a fairly strong possibility.'

Yet in spite of Jenny's emphasis, it didn't properly register with me, her concern about the fate of the birds on the reef. I don't really know why. I suppose I was too … too bound up in the newly-remembered, scarcely-believable fact of their very existence: that filled my mind, and from then on I thought of virtually nothing else, even though we spent another two months in New Zealand. There was no point in going back to Britain immediately so we travelled a lot, and when we were in Auckland we did a fair bit of hiking, and most weekends we sailed around the Hauraki Gulf with the Pittaway family on the *Windwhistle*; and we talked at length about the future and Jenny said she would like to build a proper career in publishing, though I really had no idea what I would do except that I didn't want to go back into academia; and one night in October I took her out to dinner and went down on one knee and offered her a ring with a sapphire surrounded by diamonds and asked her if she would marry me and she said: 'Wadda *you* think, you drongo?'

But all the time, all the time – I mean, every day – I was thinking of the great auks of Lanna. Not about any harm that might have come to them, but about their presence on their ledge. The latter concern somehow shut out the former. I was gripped, I was properly obsessed, and one of the aspects of it all which began to preoccupy me was, how would the news be announced?

I knew the form only too well; there would have to be a peer-reviewed scientific paper in a major journal such as *Nature* or *Science*, probably followed by a press conference. I could see the paper already, with the simple title which would electrify the world, which would be reported on every national newspaper front page and every TV news bulletin:

Rediscovery of a seabird believed extinct: the Great Auk Pinguinus impennis (L) *persists on an island in the North-East Atlantic.*

But whose names would be on it? That was the question. Those names would become world famous overnight! So would UKOCA be responsible for writing it? Presumably. Would I be one of the authors? I would be bringing the revelation to the agency. But I had left the agency. Would I be excluded? Would I be written out of it all? That would be unbearable!

I confided my worries to Jenny.

We had taken the ferry over to Rangitoto with a picnic and were hiking up to the island summit and I said: 'You know, I've been thinking about how it will all be announced. Eventually.'

'And how might it be announced?'

'Well there would obviously be a press conference, but before that you'd have to have a paper in a major journal like *Nature* or *Science*. And I'm thinking, who would write it? Who would write the paper?'

'Why're you wondering that?'

'Well, pretty big thing, isn't it? To have your name on the paper. It would go round the world.'

'You mean, if you had your name on it, you'd be famous? Would you like that, Miles?'

'I wouldn't mind.'

'And would you be upset if your name wasn't on the paper?'

'Well, I wouldn't be very happy, obviously.'

She nodded. Then she said: 'Miles ...'

'Yeah?'

'What about Fergus?'

'What about him?'

'Don't you think his name ought to be on the paper?'

'Fergus is history, Jen.'

That's what the auk obsession had done to me. I had even ceased to remember the burning cross.

Jenny stopped short. She said: 'Well, he's certainly dead. I'm not sure what you mean by 'history'. If you mean 'forgotten', I certainly haven't forgotten him.'

'Fergus wouldn't be part of it.'

'But don't you think he ought to be?'

'Not really.'

Jenny didn't reply. She said: 'Hmmm.' Then she changed the subject. But she began to watch, she began to watch with a gimlet eye, as the miraculous survival of *P. impennis* began to obsess the mind of Miles Bonnici, just as it had already obsessed the minds of Fergus Pryng and Rollo Kintyre and Kenny Lornie – she watched as it wormed its way into that obscure part of my psyche where there festered still the remnants of my craving for fame, fame to overtop the fame of my bastard of a father, the urge which had been my moral undoing in every way ...

Not that she took issue with me openly. She just went with the flow, and gave no hint of concern when we finally went back to Wimbledon in November, to catch Lotte, who was going to be home for a month in between long cruises, and found a letter awaiting us from Gervase Crinan in Balnay. He said that Lord Kintyre was out of hospital now and making steady progress and was 'extremely desirous of talking to yourself and Miss Pittaway' – so much so that if we would consider coming up to Castle Balnay, the estate would cover the expenses.

'He wants to know if you're gonna tell UKOCA,' said Jenny.

'Should we go?'

'Why not? It's all going to have to be sorted out sooner or later, isn't it?'

So in early December we flew to Glasgow and then drove in a hire car up the side of Loch Lomond to the coast of Argyllshire; now the bracken was russet on the hills and the birches were bare, and on the top of Ben Lomond there was a cap of snow. When we got to Balnay Gervase came out into the chilly air in his fawn waistcoat and tartan cravat and seemed genuinely pleased to see us, bounding up like a red setter and vigorously pumping Jenny's hand and I realised that for his dry wit and his boyish enthusiasm and hopeless indiscretion, I really liked him.

'Appalling business,' he said, shaking his head as he led us through the great hall. 'Well, no need to tell you, you were right in the middle of it, weren't you? I suppose Rollo's lucky, he got away with his life and his penguin pool guys didn't, but his burns are awful. All down one side of his face. And such a handsome man. Please make an effort not to stare.'

It did indeed take an effort, when we met the Earl in his study: his left profile was the chiselled visage I remembered; but the right was hideous, a mixed palette of bright red and dark red, though the brilliant white teeth continued to flash through everything, as they did when he got up from his desk and held out his hand. 'Welcome to my fellow survivors,' he said. Though he was devoid of self-pity. 'Thank you for coming. Gervase, we're going to do this just the three of us, OK?'

'Oh. All right. Very well. Ring if you want anything.' Gervase glided out. We sat down.

Kintyre said: 'A catastrophe of the sort that befell us on Lanna gives one pause, would you not say, Dr Bonnici, Miss Pittaway? Makes one consider what really matters.'

'I think that's true,' I said.

'And as you may well imagine, I have been giving a great deal of thought to the situation, and there is one point in particular I wish to elucidate with you. It is this. If you would take your mind back to last June, I take it that, as you said to me over the radio, Dr Bonnici, in what I confess were somewhat fraught circumstances … Fergus Pryng my warden apprised you of the ah, the true situation appertaining to the island?'

I let the question hang for a couple of seconds.

Some little devil in me just wanted to keep him dangling. *Go on, dangle, I thought. Dangle, you fucker.* He was staring at me. Then I said: 'He did.'

'Hmm,' said Kintyre. 'He in fact, ah, showed you … the birds?'

'That's correct. He showed them to both of us, to Jenny and me.'

'Might I ask, in what circumstances?'

'We went into the Sgeir Dubh lagoon with him in the inflatable on June the eighth and saw the birds at close quarters. We were just a few yards from the breeding ledge.'

Kintyre paused. He looked at us. He said: 'And a wondrous sight, is it not?'

'Absolutely,' I said, meaning it, and Jenny half-smiled and nodded vigorously.

'Yes. An enormous privilege to those tiny number of us who have glimpsed it. So you saw them at close quarters. Very well. And if I recall correctly our somewhat heated words over the radio which must have been exchanged … that same night?'

'I think so, yes.'

'You said to me that … your agency would be minded to take over their conservation.'

'That's right.'

'Yet Dr Bonnici, I have heard nothing from UKOCA.'

'I no longer work for the agency.'

'Ah. Really?'

'I was on a year's contract which expired just after the Lanna trip.'

'I see. I see. So might it by any chance be the case that as of now, you have not in fact communicated to UKOCA, what you saw on Sgeir Dubh?'

The devil in me let him dangle again. It was too good to miss. Dangle, you fucker! He was staring at me once more. Then I said: 'I have not.'

'May I ask, why?'

'I sustained a fractured skull when the rib overturned – when we went with Fergus to the tanker, when he was killed. And because of that I suffered from amnesia for some time. I couldn't remember anything about it. Though I've fully recovered my memory now.'

'I see.'

'And we've been in New Zealand since August. We've only just come back. I've had no direct contact whatsoever with the people in Aberdeen since it all happened.'

Kintyre seemed to breathe out. 'Then there is still a chance,' he murmured, almost to himself.

'I beg your pardon?'

'There is still a chance, Dr Bonnici, that this matter of most surpassing, most desperate importance may be handled correctly and guided towards the appropriate outcome.'

'How d'you mean?'

'The birds cannot stay on Lanna. When's the next rogue tanker going to arrive? When does the oilfield start operating next door? They are critically endangered. They need a sanctuary. They must be taken into benign captivity.'

'Benign captivity where?' As if I didn't know.

'Here in Balnay. Here there is a captive breeding centre specially designed for them. Ready and waiting. Enormous thought has gone into it. No expense has been spared.'

I said: 'And does it by any chance have seats for paying customers to gawp at them, Lord Kintyre?'

He bristled. 'Dr Bonnici, come now, have you thought this through? Do you imagine that wherever they end up, the public will be precluded from seeing these … almost-fabulous creatures? These will be the superstars of the animal world. The megastars. The hyperstars. There will never have been anything like these birds. The demand to *gawp,* as you say, though I would prefer to say, look in wonder, as you have done yourselves, the demand will be global. It will be unstoppable. It will have to be managed, can you not see that? It is essential that the birds be housed in a facility which has been specifically designed with that in mind.'

I was about to throw back in his face the fact that he was up to his ears in debt and money was his true motivation, but I stopped myself just in time, realising that this would betray Gervase's indiscretions. Instead I said: 'But Fergus was convinced that they could only survive *in situ.* He told us that no one had successfully bred members of the auk family in captivity. The chicks always died.'

'Pah,' said Kintyre – that was the sound he uttered, *pah* – 'Fergus Pryng. Allow me, if you please, to maintain a healthy scepticism for the wisdom of Fergus Pryng.'

Jenny said: 'Might I ask you something, Lord Kintyre?'

'Madam, of course.'

'How long do you think Fergus had known about the auks? Before he told you? He told us that he told you in 1998.'

'Did he now?' said Kintyre, visibly irritated. 'Well, that is correct. How long had he known himself? I do not know. I first sent him there in the spring after I inherited, 1983, and I sent him back to Lanna every spring thereafter.'

'D'you think it is possible he might have known from the very beginning?'

'I suppose it is, but I cannot say.'

'Might I ask you then, why d'you think he kept you in the dark? For however long it was?'

Kintyre seemed irritated even more. 'I have no idea, but it was grossly irresponsible.' He considered. 'I rather think the feller may have developed a proprietorial interest, as it were, thinking the birds belonged to him. He came back every summer to look after them like a chap looks after his allotment. Didn't seem to have much else going on in his life. Although I see to my surprise he used to be married to this woman, the other Pryng with all the weird cosmetics and the environmental campaigns and stuff who is always on the telly. She's been making capital out of the situation, milking it for publicity. Outrageous. As if one Pryng were not enough. No, I consider what Fergus did was a very grave breach of the trust I had placed in him, and had he alerted me earlier, the problem might well have been solved by now, and that is the point.' He leaned forward and dropped his voice slightly. 'What I am wondering, Dr Bonnici, is if you would like to join me' – he corrected himself, nodding at Jenny – 'if you would both like to join me, in bringing the great auks of Lanna to safety, in what would perhaps be the greatest conservation operation ever carried out.'

'How?'

'By bringing the birds here, from the island.'

'That would be illegal.'

'I think not.'

'Under the Wildlife and Countryside Act 1981 you cannot legally disturb a wild bird at its nest.'

'Two points, Dr Bonnici. One, I have a legal opinion that says under Scottish law, the birds nesting on my island are my property. Two, the great auk *Pinguinus impennis* is officially extinct. Conservation legislation does not apply to birds that do not officially exist.'

'That's ingenious, but it would be challenged.'

'Not if the government is presented with a *fait accompli*.'

Fergus had warned us of this. I said: 'But why would we go along with you, Lord Kintyre?'

'Because it is the right thing to do. You saw the tanker hit the reef. You watched in horror as we all did. The modern world is becoming too dangerous for such fragile creatures. Yet if you hand over responsibility to UKOCA, they will just keep them on Sgeir Dubh. And for why?'

'Because it's the appropriate place.'

'No. Because *they have nowhere else to put them*. That is why. D'you think the British government, indeed d'you think even the new Scottish government, that bunch of political old lags, is going to sanction the millions it would cost to build a proper captive breeding centre for great auks? No sir. Yet I have already built one, at my own expense. This is where the birds need to come.'

I have to say I thought there was force in his argument, as I had thought when I heard it on Lanna, on the top of the castle, shouted at Fergus over the howl of the gale. I looked at Jenny. She looked back at me. I couldn't tell what she was thinking.

'Dr Bonnici, Miss Pittaway, look,' Kintyre said. 'There are only three people on earth who know that there are great auks surviving on Lanna and they are sitting in this room. I have been … cautious. My wife, God bless her, does not know. My ex-wife does not know. My two boys do not know. Even Gervase, fine young chap that he is who looks after most of my affairs, does not know. I do not think my boatman knows, or my factor, or any of my estate servants. What does that mean? That the thing is still possible. It can still be done in the right way. Once you inform UKOCA, it is possible no longer.'

That was clearly true – from his point of view.

Jenny said: 'But what about the fire? The auks may have been impacted. Perhaps severely.'

'We have not been able to assess that. Since I came out of hospital there has been no weather window. It's been too rough to get into the lagoon to see if there were any effects on the breeding ledge. I think we would have to cross that bridge when we come to it, but proceed on the basis that the enterprise is presumably still viable.'

There was a pause.

I said: 'We will have to think about it, Lord Kintyre.'

'Of course, of course.' He was slightly agitated. 'But might I ask you, that you let me know, within one week, shall we say?'

I looked at Jenny. She nodded. 'Yes,' I said.

'I have your word on that?'

'Yes.'

'Very well. I thank you for your courtesy in travelling here, and I will bid you good day.' He rang the bell for Gervase. We shook hands with him; I forced myself to avoid letting my eyes linger on his face.

Gervase seemed a tad put out at having been excluded. 'What was all that about then?' he said, escorting us through the castle corridors to the car.

'Just future survey work on Lanna's birds, to see if the oil spill has affected them,' I said.

'Don't see why I couldn't have been present at that. I still haven't been to Lanna, you know. Hmph. Maybe the burns are making him tetchy. It's not just the burns though, to be fair he's under an awful lot of strain. I mean, I shouldn't really tell you this, but he's right on the brink now.'

'Of what?'

'Going bust. His creditors are knocking on the door. I'm having to do some fancy fending off. Nimble footwork. It's the blasted penguin pool, see. He was counting on that to put him right then it all went pear-shaped with the tanker and the deaths and everything. He's getting desperate, although he says there's just a chance he might be able to bring it off next spring.'

'What, the penguin pool?'

'Yeah, but I wouldn't count on it.'

'And if he can't?'

We were standing on the gravel terrace. 'All this lot,' said Gervase, waving a hand at the wildlife park, 'goes down the tubes.'

I don't suppose we will ever know if one thing led directly to another and if we played a part in the dramatic fate of Rollo Macdonald, Tenth Earl of Kintyre, the celebrated Tiger Laird. Most people to this day see it as a tragic accident, though some also see a role in what happened for the earlier tragedy which befell him six months before, leaving him horribly burned. We will never know. I mean, the rest of the world *can* never know, since the rest of the world will never be aware of what was in the letter I sent him four days after leaving Balnay, on the morning we got the plane back to New Zealand for Christmas. There was never really going to be any doubt about what the letter would say. I confess I was tempted by his offer, but Fergus had charged me with a task and I saw clearly, in going over everything, that I was duty-bound to carry it out. I say 'going over everything' – by that I mean, rehearsing the arguments, in front of Jenny. Jenny did not offer an opinion. She did not choose to. She did not need to. For I had begun to sense that in all matters pertaining to Lanna's secret, Jenny embodied a moral force which I could not ignore, and so in the end I wrote to Kintyre saying I saw the strength and validity of his arguments but I was afraid that I had been shown what I had been shown as the official representative on Lanna of the UK Offshore Conservation Agency and I felt bound to pass the information on to the agency itself; and in the New Year therefore, I would be contacting the UKOCA director to do so.

I sent the letter on Sunday, 10 December; he would have received it perhaps on the 12th. That week, Gervase told us later, his previous anxiety about the estate and its finances seemed to have passed and he appeared strangely calm; and curiously, he did a great sorting out of his papers, among them stuff from his private safe including, Gervase thought, photographs, which he took himself to burn in the castle's basement furnace. It was Friday, 15 December when he took everyone at Balnay by surprise by announcing that he would be going back in with his tigers; he had had no interactions with the animals since the accident, but he told Gervase he had discussed it at length with the Countess and she thought if he was ready, he ought to go ahead. It was early afternoon when the Earl and his wife, accompanied by Tony Barlow the head tiger keeper, entered the pen of Shura, the magnificent Siberian tigress I had seen them romping with six months earlier, and no one really knows the causes of what happened, though Tony Barlow speculated privately, and others later publicly suggested, that the Earl's facial appearance was so dramatically different from what Shura had been used to that it may have provoked an unaccustomed reaction. Yet perhaps that is nonsense. Who knows? At any rate it happened quickly; in fact it happened almost immediately, and it was terrible, and by the time Tony Barlow, who was himself badly mauled trying stop it with his hands, had reached the high-powered rifle which was always kept just outside the pen, and shot Shura dead, the Earl and Countess of Kintyre lay lifeless on the grass of their wildlife park, both bitten cleanly through the back of the neck.

Whether or not my letter to Kintyre played any part in these events, which we read about open-mouthed in Auckland – Jenny was convinced it did and referred to what had happened as 'suicide by tiger' – their outcome played a decisive role in our own lives, because when we got back to London in the second week of January, there was another letter from Gervase, marked URGENT on the envelope and asking me to call him as soon as possible.

'Miles,' he said. 'Thanks for ringing. Happy New Year to you. Not exactly a happy one here, though.'

'I can well imagine.'

'Yes well, one manages as best one can. Listen. You've left your agency, haven't you? What are you doing?'

'I'm not actually doing anything,' I said. 'I have to work out what my future is. I do know I'm not going back to academia, which is what I did before.'

'How would you like a job? Here at Balnay?'

'A *job*? What sort of job?'

'You're a zoologist, aren't you?'

'I've got a degree in zoology, which isn't quite the same thing.'

'That'll do. We need a zoologist we can trust.'

'Who's we?'

'Sorry. Angela. The Dowager Countess of Kintyre. Rollo's first wife. Who, helped by yours truly, is now running the estate, since it has gone to Roddy, their eldest boy, who is only eight.'

'What do you need a zoologist for?'

'Because everything is falling apart here in the aftermath of Rollo's demise. The estate is bankrupt and the wildlife park will have to be shut down and dismantled. It's even possible the castle may have to be sold. We need someone to supervise the break-up of the zoo. Urgently.'

'I know nothing whatsoever about zoos.'

'That doesn't matter. What matters is that you are trustworthy. Because I hope you aren't embarrassed in me saying this, but I have formed the view that you are a good chap. And that's what we need above all else at the moment, as there are sharks circling here.'

'But I'm committed to Jenny, Gervase. We're engaged. My life is going to be with her.'

'I'm pretty sure she could come up with you.'

I thought about it. 'She's got a zoology degree too. Well. Biology.'

'Then there could well be something for her as well.'

'But where would we live?'

'Here on the estate. There's a very decent estate cottage available right now on the shores of Lower Loch Nay. A super spot.'

I didn't know what to say.

Gervase said: 'Why don't you both come up again to look around and talk it over and meet Angela? You could stay the night. Say, Thursday?'

'You're serious?'

'Never more so.'

'Let me get back to you.'

Jenny was as surprised as I was. 'Go and live up there? At the castle?'

'That's what he's offering. Not live in the castle exactly, but work in it, probably. Live nearby. Says there's a nice cottage.'

Jenny reflected. She said: 'Well, neither of us knows what we're gonna do, do we? What have we got to lose?'

So once again we flew to Glasgow and drove up the side of Loch Lomond, and over dinner Gervase and the Dowager Countess explained how the finances of the estate were in an even more parlous position than anyone had suspected. They knew they had to sack their Chief Operating Officer but they desperately needed a trustworthy replacement right away and would I consider it?

Jenny and I talked it over that night, in one of the castle's flamboyantly splendid but chilly guest bedrooms, and we agreed that we both liked Angela who not only had a tough job on her hands but was devoid of any aristocratic airs and graces; and the next morning Gervase showed us the cottage, which Jenny seemed to be very taken with, but what swung it was when I considered Lanna. I realised that when I informed UKOCA of what was on the island, Ramsay and his colleagues would want to make an expedition there, and if I were the member of the Balnay staff in charge, I could not only facilitate the trip, but *I would have to be part of it*. Which mattered to me a lot. And Jenny saw the point of that; and I told Gervase and Angela that to be also in charge of Lanna, and to be able to take time out to visit it for conservation purposes, would be my condition for accepting the post; and they went into a huddle and agreed; and we said Yes.

For the island and its secret loomed larger than ever in my mind; the year had turned and soon the birds would be back on the breeding shelf on Sgeir Dubh.

I made my call to Ramsay Wishart at UKOCA in the first week of February, just after we had taken up residence in Argyll. He was surprised and moved and pleased to hear from me and I told him about my head injury and my memory loss and how I had spent the autumn in New Zealand recovering and how Jenny and I had now got jobs at, of all places, the Balnay Estate, helping to wind up the wildlife park, and how, believe it or not, after the death of the Earl, the person in charge of Lanna, was now me.

He was astounded.

And I told him I would like to talk to him about the island, and about what had happened with Kenny Lornie.

'I would very much like to talk about that, Miles,' he said.

And I said the subject was strange and it was confidential and I had three conditions: that he told no one else in UKOCA we were speaking; that we met somewhere other than in Aberdeen; and that Callum McSorley also be present.

In the end he agreed, and managed to persuade Callum, and all four of us finally met at the end of February in the house of Callum's elderly mother in Glasgow. Both men were intrigued, Ramsay remarking it was all a bit cloak and dagger, but both were warm, and Callum slapped me on the back. 'Well, bonny prince, ye've been through the mill, eh? Jenny, how are you? Nice to see ye. You too, you been through it, eh?'

When we were settled I said: 'I've asked you both to be here because I know and trust you both and you will both have a very keen interest in what we've got to say, which is very unusual.'

'OK,' said Ramsay, levelly.

I said: 'The real reason Kenny Lornie had the fight with Fergus on Lanna, and the reason he went back with the American photographer afterwards, Mehlinger, was that there was ... something very remarkable about the island that no one was aware of.'

'OK...' said Ramsay.

'It was a secret. Only Kintyre and Fergus knew about it, and it's why they were so touchy and restrictive about access, the no-cameras rule and stuff. But in spite of that, Kenny Lornie found out what it was. He stumbled upon it.'

Ramsay said: 'And it was what?'

'There was a seabird breeding on the island, a bird species that no one knew about, and the news of its being there would have been a sensation. It still would be.'

'What species? Not Swinhoe's petrel by any chance, is it? That's Sidney's pet theory, he goes on about it. That would be moderately sensational, I suppose.'

'It's infinitely more sensational than Swinhoe's petrel.'

Ramsay looked at me. 'So what is it then?'

I found I couldn't utter the English name. It was just too remarkable. I ended up saying: '*Pinguinus impennis.*'

'What?

I said slowly and deliberately: '*Pinguinus ... impennis ...*'

Ramsay screwed his mind to the words. He knew them, of course, but it took him a second or two to make the link. Yet Callum already had, and he sat up straight. He said: 'What are you saying?'

'… was breeding there.'

'Great …'

I nodded.

'… auks?'

'Yes.'

'Were breeding there? Great auks?'

'Yes.'

Both men looked at us in disbelief.

Callum said: 'Ye're saying the great auk is not extinct?'

'That's right.'

'They're on Lanna?'

'Well, they were last summer.'

'How many?'

'A very small number. About six pairs. And some non-breeders.'

'How do ye know?'

'We saw them ourselves. Jenny and I both saw them.'

'And you … you think they were great auks?'

'There is no doubt whatsoever, Callum. Very large, flightless auks, black above, white below, with big bills and big white face patches. Loral spots.'

'How close were ye to them?'

'Ten to fifteen yards from their breeding ledge where they were sitting on eggs. Fergus showed them to us the day before the tanker hit. He wanted UKOCA to take over their conservation.'

'This was last June?'

'Yes. June the eighth. The day before the tanker fire, when he was killed.'

'Why are you only telling us now?'

'Because I was out of it, wasn't I? For months. With my head injury. I had amnesia and all that. The tanker disaster turned everything upside down.'

Callum mulled it over. He said: 'White face patches?'

'Yeah.'

'Flightless.'

'Yeah.'

'How d'you know?'

'Well, they had very small, stubby wings.'

'You notice anything about the tips of the secondaries?'

'I can't remember in that sort of detail.'

'You got your field notes? Any sketches?'

'I didn't make any field notes.'

'All birders make field notes.'

'I'm not a birder, Callum.'

'Yeah. OK. We know that. More's the pity.'

He pondered some more. He turned to Jenny. He said: 'Did you see these birds, Jenny?'

'I did.'

'And what do you think they were?'

'Based on the illustrations I've looked at since, I don't have any doubt that they were great auks.' She said: 'I'm aware of how improbable that is. I have the most vivid memories of you telling us the story of their extinction, on Skarholm. I will never forget it. But I can only tell you what I saw.'

There was quiet in the room. Callum looked at Ramsay and Ramsay looked at Callum. Then they both looked at us. It was as if they didn't quite know what to say. I thought: this is the apotheosis of what is called a *stunned silence*.

At length Ramsay said: 'And ye're saying that Kenny … discovered this situation?'

'He did. The birds are inside the double reef off the western side of the island called Sgeir Dubh. At least, they were. It's the reef that the tanker hit. They were nesting on the other side of the rocks, on a ledge in a sort of lagoon which is sheltered from the sea.'

'So how did Kenny find out about them?'

I told them the story of his discovery and the fight. I added: 'The estate boatman, guy called Murdo Macleod, eventually he came to take Kenny back, and when the boat was leaving, Kenny shouted out to Fergus that he'd discovered his secret. Murdo told me that himself, on the way out there.'

Ramsay thought hard. He said: 'He never said one word of that to me. If this is true, he never gave a hint of it.'

'But you said he behaved strangely, Ramsay. When he arrived back in Oban. You said he appeared not to care that the survey had been screwed up.'

'Aye, that's right.'

'You said he said, 'what's on Lanna will save it'.'

'He did. He did say that.'

'And then he disappeared. Why d'you think he disappeared?'

Ramsay shook his head. 'Och, man, I have never fathomed that out.'

'I'll tell you why. So he could get in touch with one of the world's most famous wildlife photographers, Rufus Mehlinger, and persuade him that he knew of something so special that it was worth going all the way to Lanna to take pictures of it. Quite an achievement, on Kenny's part. How he did it, I don't suppose we'll ever know. I mean, did he go to America? Or what? But you've got to hand it to him.'

Ramsay said: 'What were they going to do?'

'Kenny was going to write a feature article to go with the pictures that Mehlinger would take, and they would be given first to the *Scotsman* and the *Herald*, that was the deal they had, so that the news of the great auks, which would burst upon the world, would come out first from Edinburgh and Glasgow. To show that they were Scotland's birds. They belonged to Scotland. To all of Scotland, and not just to some aristocrat with his English lackey, which is how Kenny thought of Fergus.'

Ramsay and Callum stared at us. I think it was all just too improbable for words. And yet it made sense.

Ramsay said: 'But why on earth why didn't he tell *us*? That would have been the right and proper thing to do.'

'I asked him that when he came back to Lanna. He said he thought that UKOCA was part of the British establishment and Kintyre would be able to pull strings to stop, to thwart any attempt you might make to see the birds. I mean, let's face it, you'd have had difficulty believing Kenny if he had told you, wouldn't you? You'd have said, great auks, yeah yeah yeah, pull the other one, Kenny. Just like you no doubt find it difficult to believe what we're saying now.'

'We do, bonny prince,' said Callum slowly, looking at me intently. 'We do.'

And yet, when they had got over the shock and the initial instinctive disbelief, they agreed that they couldn't ignore what we were saying and they would have to act; and there and then we began to plan an expedition, an official UKOCA trip to Lanna in April – which I, of course, could sanction – to assess what the effects of the tanker fire were on the island's seabird populations, with a small number of senior and trustworthy staff; but with a secondary purpose that would only be known to the four of us – although it was assumed that the real purpose might quickly become apparent to everyone.

When I look back at that time, I see the last remnants of who I was in the first half of my life. What characterised me throughout my early years had been obsession: I was obsessed with surpassing my father and yes, I escaped that, but as Lotte had observed, I was obsessive by nature, and when Lanna's secret entered my life, obsession returned. In the weeks before the second trip to the island it consumed me and I will never be able to thank Jenny enough for the help she gave me in the onerous task of beginning to dismantle the zoo, discussing everything with me and making sure I committed no cardinal or catastrophic errors – while my mind was elsewhere.

Jenny could see clearly where I was. She did not address it openly, then. She made no criticism of me. But she did repeat, twice, that she hoped the *Lamprinos* fire had not done severe damage to the birds on Sgeir Dubh, a sentiment which I pooh-poohed with almost condescending confidence. They would be there, I knew, they were waiting, as the paper was waiting, that scientific paper which would get me on the front cover of *Nature* for the second time – shining in my mind it was, brilliant as a neon sign:

Rediscovery of a seabird believed extinct: the Great Auk *Pinguinus impennis* (L) persists …

My name would be on it, I was sure of that now; it would have to be, wouldn't it? I was part of the team. How would it be cited in the future, the celebrated paper? *Wishart, McSorley and Bonnici?* There was no way I was going first. But even third place would be OK. It was still world fame. I gave no thought to Fergus and his desserts. I had indeed forgotten Fergus. It was not Pryng I was thinking of, it was Bonnici – Bonnici, Bonnici, Bonnici!

The apparent absence of the birds when we got to Lanna on the Saturday after Easter, 21 April, did not disturb me unduly. Fergus had said 'late April' was the time they returned. We were probably too early, and anyway we had our hands full, the five us in the team, Ramsay, Sidney Jeffries and Roddy Baird from UKOCA, Callum and myself – Jenny stayed behind to look after business in Balnay. We went out from Oban in a large seagoing motor cruiser UKOCA had hired with its own four-metre inflatable slung from the davits, and I guided us into the anchorage, trembling with excitement and anticipation.

The others were thrilled to be on the island they had heard so much about, continuously amazed at its extraordinary avian abundance, seabird scientists finding their nirvana; but while Sidney and Roddy concentrated on the main breeding cliffs and were scoping them out, I showed Ramsay and Callum Sgeir Dubh on the other side of the island and the two viewpoints of it, from the castle top, and the rock overhang where Fergus discovered us and fell in the sea. And from them, well, for the moment, no birds were visible. Soon would be, I was sure. The weather was not calm enough yet to take the inflatable into the Sgeir Dubh lagoon itself.

The rest of the team were due to be there a month; I was scheduled to be there a fortnight, initially, and when there was still no sign of what we were seeking by the end of the first week, I began to feel concern. I spent hours – hour after hour after hour – scanning Sgeir Dubh and the waters around it but I glimpsed not a thing. The others were all busy with their formal survey but Ramsay and Callum kept eyeing me, and as the second week went on I began to feel increasingly uncomfortable; finally on the second Thursday, 3 May, two days before I was due to return, the weather settled into a brief window of high pressure and calm, and we took the inflatable – me, Ramsay and Callum – out to the reef.

The wreck of the tanker had been removed in a complex salvage operation in the months after the disaster but we could see that the high-tide gap into the lagoon was the very place where the *Lamprinos* had grounded, that and the rocks to its left, the spot where Fergus had died, which I looked at with a shudder; and even though they were black – that's what Sgeir Dubh means, black rocks – when you looked closely, they seemed to be charred. There was no seaweed on them. It had been burnt off. We passed through the gap and I pointed out where I had seen the first bird, the oldest male, Fergus had said, and we turned the corner, and beheld the flat sloping breeding ledge, and I pointed out the iron rings Fergus had hammered into the rock faces so he could moor his inflatable to observe the birds … that was some evidence, at least. Because on the ledge there was none. Nothing. Zilch. Ramsay and Callum gazed at it intently. 'Right sort of place, certainly,' Callum murmured. 'They could walk out from the water. Aye. Ye can see that. But look, it appears to have been burnt to a cinder. No weed. See? No lichen, no nothing. And crucially, far as I can see, no guano.'

'Why crucially?'

'Cos that would give us DNA evidence, wouldn't it?'

'Of course.'

'But look at it. No other colour. Uniform black. Carbonised. Looks like the oil fire from the tanker has come right through here.'

I looked at it.

I let my eyes linger, I let them pan over the charred emptiness of the breeding ledge.

I felt a chill descend on my whole being.

Even today I don't really have the words describe it. It was as big a shock as the initial encounter. Bigger, even. It wasn't just the death of the birds, it was the death of what their survival might have represented to the world. The death of a wondrous symbol. The death of hope.

It was beyond measure in its tragedy.

And nobody knew. Except us.

Could there be a stranger fate than that which befell Jenny Pittaway and me, to be the sole witnesses of this almost unthinkable calamity – that great auks, driven extinct by human greed, or so everyone thought, in fact survived in tiny numbers on their lost Hebridean island and then *were driven extinct again*? That crude oil, the cursed lifeblood of industrial society, had wrought its most terrible havoc of all upon the natural world? The Lanna disaster, indeed! It should be trumpeted around the globe, it should be the most powerful of all environmental cautionary tales, it should never be forgotten, yet it will never even be known …

I struggled to cope with it, for I realised at once that if even their droppings had been burned away, there was no proof that the birds had ever been there – unless we could find some. I had never seen any photographs. Fergus and Kintyre and Kenny Lornie had seen the birds and could vouch for them, but they were dead. And maybe the 'penguin wranglers' knew about them, but they were dead. And Rufus Mehlinger definitely knew about them, but he was dead. Only Jenny and I were alive, who had seen the great auks, and absent photos, how were we going to persuade the world that the greatest of all wildlife tragedies had in fact taken place? And more immediately, if these most unlikely creatures were nowhere to be seen, how could we prove to Callum McSorley and Ramsay Wishart that they had even existed?

When the three of us bumped back over the grey sea to the anchorage that day, 3 May 2001, it felt very different from that elated return with Fergus, the June before. And just as Jenny and I had had an intense conversation with Fergus then, when we brought the inflatable ashore, so I did now with Callum and Ramsay, though of a very different tenor. I got it wrong. I protested too much. I'd have done better to say nothing. I stood there by the mooring rock and I said: 'I swear to you, they were there. There were half a dozen pairs, maybe more, sitting on eggs. They were only a few yards away from us, on the ledge. I can see them now, as if it was today. Honestly, Callum. Ramsay. They were there. Really and truly.'

Ramsay said: 'I dare say they were, Miles. I don't doubt they were. But they're not there now, are they?'

Callum said nothing.

Over the succeeding weeks I lived in a sort of turmoil. It wasn't just the outrageousness of what had happened; there was a selfish element too, as I felt cheated of the role I would have played in revealing the birds' existence, and I had set my heart upon that. But I think worst of all was simply the fact that we were precluded from speaking of it to anyone. It was mad. It helped that after I got back to Balnay we experienced the most difficult weeks of all in the break-up of the wildlife park and that took my mind off it on a day-to-day basis, but in the background the crazy thought was always there. The world's greatest wildlife story. The world's most appalling wildlife story. They are both bursting out of you. And you can't tell either of them. I think if Jenny had not been the other witness to the birds on Sgeir Dubh, my stability would have been shaken.

But Jenny it was in the end who resolved things. She had feared from the outset for the fate of the auks and she had tried to prepare me for the awfulness of the worst-case outcome, while I had just been focused on getting my name in *Nature*. What she really wanted, though, was for me to see the essence of it all, which, in the mayhem of the discovery and the loss, I was blind to; and eventually she felt she had to intervene.

It was an evening when I was going round in circles, talking obsessively about the photographs Kintyre must have taken of the birds, because a single one of them would be enough, but there was no sign of any of them and Gervase said he had looked and couldn't find any but I didn't think he'd looked hard enough, even though he said he thought Rollo had burned a whole set of photos in the week before he died but there had to be others, I mean, maybe I should look for myself, go through his study, and Jenny suddenly stood up.

'Oh Miles!' she cried. 'Miles, Miles, Miles! Enough! You can't see the heart of all this, can you?'

'The heart of it? What are you talking about?'

She held my arms in her hands and looked at me. 'Fergus Pryng is at the heart of it.'

'How is he at the heart of it?'

'He knew about the birds for years and years. Before Kintyre. He could have told the world about them at any time. And then they would have had official protection, wouldn't they? Like, tankers would have been kept away from the island, or whatever.'

'So ... what are you saying?'

'*Why did he keep it a secret?*'

30

By the time we took the M4 to Cardiff – it was July – we felt we
knew a lot about Bronwen Pryng: certainly, more than just the
fact that she was the world's most famous Welshwoman. After
she agreed to see us we researched her, and I was taken aback by
just how famous she actually was, although that was only because
I had spent most of my adult years, said Jenny, ignoring the life of
normal people while I sat on an island watching seabirds shagging.
Pura Vida, her chain of shops selling cruelty-free cosmetics and
fairtrade products from developing countries was hugely popular,
and had become a global byword for green business, with franchises
around the world; and she herself was not only a millionaire many
times over but a bigger and bigger voice in environment and human
rights campaigning. Climate change was a growing priority – she
was socking it to the fossil fuel companies – as was rainforest
destruction, and she seemed to have a knack for getting rock stars
to back her campaigns. I read a couple of profiles and they both
stressed the role that Ronnie Rhys, her former nightclub-owning
partner from Swansea, had played in getting Pura Vida off the
ground and building up the business. He seemed to be quite a
character. There wasn't a word anywhere about Fergus.

Jenny said she had long thought Bronwen Pryng was an
inspiration to women, and she admired her greatly.

The Pura Vida HQ was a newish, purpose-built block in
Pontcanna; next to the car park was a water garden recycling all
the building's water, a notice told us. While we waited in reception
and gazed at the giant photos of Bronwen with famous faces, we
read another notice describing the building's use of renewable
energy. We were offered a fairtrade coffee. And then eventually,
we were taken up to her top floor office.

She got up and came out from behind a desk to shake hands,
smiling warmly and saying, sorry you had to wait. I think Jenny
was a little star-struck. She was a handsome woman in her forties,

beautifully dressed in a very chic sort of dark green trouser suit. There was something formidable about her.

We sat down and she said: 'Well well. So you want to talk about Fergus, eh?'

Jenny said: 'If that's all right.'

'Sure. I've thought a lot about him, this past year. More than in the previous fifteen, I'll tell you, which is since we split up. And you know what I think? He sort of redeemed himself, by his death. He kind of died a martyr, didn't he? As I understand it.'

I said: 'I suppose you could say that.'

'You said you were with him when he died?'

'We both were, yes.'

'You want to tell me how it happened? Get that over with? I haven't really had a precise account from anybody, except it seems to have been a pretty shitty end.'

I said: 'I think Jenny had a clearer view of it than I did.' I didn't really want to go there.

Jenny said: 'The three of us went out to the reef that the tanker hit, in an inflatable, to try and save what seabirds we could, from any oil spill, and he asked us to put him on the rocks, very near the tanker. And as he climbed up the rocks there was the first explosion and he was caught in it.' She added: 'He would have died instantly.'

'He was trying to save the birds?'

'He was.'

'Like, directly? With his own two hands?'

'That's right.'

'He would be, yeah. That would be exactly him. Kind of heroic death, really. But then, that's what his whole life should have been. And not the failure it bloody was.'

'How d'you mean?'

'Fergus, Fergus Pryng was the original eco-warrior. It's why I married him, for God's sake. Let's face it, wasn't going to be for his looks, was it? I thought he was an amazing guy. When I met him, at least. I thought he would end up saving the world, be running Friends of the Earth or Greenpeace International or something, a huge figure in the environment movement anyway, like, you know, well … like I am now, I suppose. And he gives it all up for this bloody remote island in the middle of nowhere.'

'Can you explain?'

'I don't suppose you know, do you? Fergus did something incredible. He saved a wetland, a very valuable nature site near here, single-handedly. Cors Caewen, it's called in Welsh, Whitefield

Fen. Know how he did it? He sued his own employers. The old
NCC, the Nature Conservancy Council, used to be the government
wildlife agency. Can you believe it?'

'How d'you mean, he sued them?'

'He was an assistant warden for them on another reserve and
he took them to court over Cors Caewen 'cos they could have
protected it but they weren't going to, they were going to let it
become a rubbish tip. They fired him because of it. Well you would,
wouldn't you? But he'd got a judicial review against them going
in the High Court in London, and he won. Correction. *We* won. I
was part of the campaign by then. I was at Cardiff University, see,
I was in my final year doing business studies.'

'When was this?'

'Eighty-one. I didn't give a shit about the environment in those
days. I knew nothing about it whatsoever. I was just going to have
my own business and be rich and independent, that's what my mam
wanted for me, it's what she'd instilled in me, 'cos we'd had such
a bad time from my dad who abused her, when I was a kid, and
then he left us, swine that he was. We lived in Barry, know Barry?'

We shook our heads.

'Ten miles down the road. On the coast. Poor enough place
at the best of times and she had such a struggle to bring me up,
working in Woolworths to pay the rent and put food on the table,
but she was a battler. It's where I've got my tough side from I don't
doubt, and she made me believe that men were bastards and what
I needed was my own career and enough money to be able to tell
any man to sod off. That's what I was set on. And then one day
my friend Karen who was a volunteer for Friends of the Earth told
me about this campaign to save this great wildlife site, it had all
sorts of rare flowers and birds and insects in it and it was going
to be turned into a landfill, and the campaign was run by this
weird-looking huge bloke who was actually really charismatic.
So I went along with her to a meeting of the Save Cors Caewen
group just out of curiosity because believe it or not I was between
boyfriends, and I was always interested in charismatic guys, and
there he was. Funny, wasn't he? Way he looked, way he dressed,
way he spoke. And enormous. You blinked your eyes. Didn't *you*,
first time you saw him?

We smiled. 'We did,' I said.

'I mean, there were only certain cars he could drive. He couldn't
fit in a Mini. But, it was true. He was charismatic. Because he
had this ... unshakeable sense of purpose. He was going to prevent

this wildlife site from being destroyed, whatever it took, and he carried people with him. It became a big campaign, in the papers, on Welsh TV and everything, especially when he sued his own bosses. That was a big story. Thing that attracted me at first was how well organised it all was, almost like a well-run business, and I was fascinated by that aspect of it. Funny isn't it? Never told anyone that. Thing that got me interested in greenery was a business model. I'll use it in the next interview.'

'Must have been exciting, though,' said Jenny.

'It was thrilling. I got involved, really involved, and best of all was the final day when we all went up to London, eighteen of us, to hear the High Court judgement, the judicial review, and when we realised we'd won and the fen would be saved, we all went mad. We were so elated. There were TV cameras and everything outside filming us cheering and we ended up in the pub across the road and got smashed and we carried on celebrating on the train back from Paddington and some of us ended up in my flat pissed out of our heads and when everyone else had gone I got Fergus into the bedroom and I shagged the living daylights out of him. And you know what? I think it was probably the first time he'd ever had sex.'

We smiled again.

'I thought he was fantastic,' said Bronwen. 'And he was. Because … I'll tell you. You know the men's chat-up cliché, *I am not like all the others*? Well, Fergus was not like all the others. But he *really* wasn't like all the others, whereas a man who says to you, I am not like all the others, is going to be *just* like all the others. Fergus had no vanity. And he was completely straight and honest and honourable. I'd never met a man like that. I'd been out with a lot of men and what it was always about for me, was the contest. The battle. They only wanted one thing, but me too, I only wanted one thing, and that was, to win. I never got dumped, but I dumped an awful lot of guys. With him, though, wanting to win was pointless. He wasn't interested in competing. He was interested in something else entirely.'

'What was that?'

'It was the thing that … that awed me, and that really got me properly into the environment. He had this incredible sense of mission.'

'About what?'

Bronwen hesitated, just for a second. She said: 'Well. About the Earth. That was the word he always used. He didn't say the environment, or the planet, or nature, like most of us say, he said the Earth, and he always wrote it with a capital E. As a sort of mark of respect. And love.'

Something stirred in my mind ... something Fergus had said?

'What about the Earth?'

'About saving it. From deforestation and pollution and overfishing and wildlife destruction and everything and now of course he'd be wound up about climate change, like we all are.'

'But isn't that a pretty general feeling?'

'Course it is. I feel it. You feel it, I don't doubt. But Fergus felt it in a particular way. It was very intense with him. More intense than with anybody else I've ever met. It was personal. He had that picture on his wall. You know, the one the astronauts took, coming back from the moon? What's it called, *Earthrise*. The one that shows the world like a blue sphere in space?'

We nodded.

'But also, there was another side to it, see. He had this big down on people. He felt people were naturally destructive. Well. *Man*, he used to say. Man the species. He was convinced there was something destructive in the very nature of human beings. He used to say that Man was the Earth's cursed child. A million species call the place home but only one of them is trashing it.'

Jenny said: 'Why did he feel like that?'

'It went back to his childhood. He tell you about his father? About Sholto?'

We shook our heads.

'He was a clergyman. Church of England vicar. The Reverend Sholto Pryng. He had a church in Suffolk, on the Suffolk marshes, the area that's called the Sandlings. Nice guy. Like his wife, Cicely. Lovely couple they were, both very tall, where Fergus got his height from. And they were old-fashioned posh, you know, no money but well-bred sort of thing, which is where Fergus got his plummy accent. He talked like they did. He was their only child and they were a happy family and Sholto, Sholto wasn't just a vicar, he was an artist as well, he painted wild flowers. He was really good. He was working towards a book and I don't know if he ever finished it 'cos I lost touch after we split, though he's dead now, I do know that. But the thing is, he used to go out into the countryside painting and he used to take Fergus with him, from a very young age. Fergus reckoned he was probably about five when his dad first took him out. And he got to know the countryside very well, he told me he knew at least 200 wild flower species by the age of ten, and he got to love it deeply, every aspect of it. Sholto told him this was the Lord's creation, the Earth was the Lord's creation and it was to be cherished and rejoiced in, and Fergus said, that made complete sense to him.'

I said: 'Sorry, but how did he come to ... have a down on people?'

'Ah. Well. That started with the bittern, I suppose.'

'The what?'

'It's a bird. Sort of small brown heron. Very rare now too, only about a dozen pairs left in all of Britain.'

'What happened?'

'It was the winter of 1963. I was just a toddler, I don't remember it, but it was the coldest winter of the century, apparently the snow started falling on Boxing Day and didn't melt till March. Whole country was frozen solid for more than two months. Took a terrible toll of the wildlife, the birds especially. And one day Fergus, who was out birding in the marshlands in the big freeze, he was thirteen at the time, he found this bittern which was collapsed, at the edge of the reeds. It must have been starving as the fens were frozen over and it couldn't fish. He thought it was dead at first, but then he realised it was still alive, just, so he stuffed it under his jacket and took it home and put it in a box next to the vicarage Aga to warm it up and slowly it started reviving and he and Sholto built a pen for it and they fed it on tinned sardines and stuff, and gradually it got its strength back. And Fergus said, to have it close at hand, to be in intimate contact with it, was the most marvellous experience he'd ever had. He said he thought it got to trust him, at least, it got used to him bringing it its dinner, and he said he loved it more deeply than anything in the world except his parents. And then in March when the snow started to melt, he took it back to the reed bed and released it.'

She paused.

'And?' I said.

'The next day he went back to see how it was doing and he came on a group of lads, three big teenagers, looking at something on the ground. It was his bittern. They'd wounded it with an air rifle, and then beaten it to death with sticks. They were laughing.'

Jenny said: 'What did he do?'

'He put them in hospital. All three of them. Two of them were sixteen and one was seventeen and he was thirteen years old, but he was already six-foot and built like an ox.'

I thought of him smiting Kenny Lornie to the ground. I wouldn't have wanted to be one of those boys, I thought.

'It was touch and go whether he would be prosecuted for assault. Juvenile court. But the police took the view in the end, that he was a respectable kid, son of the vicar and all that, and the older kids were in the wrong in the first place and there were three of them and only one of him and they probably picked on him and they had just bitten off more than they could chew, so they dropped the case. But it wasn't the end of it for Fergus. It was a beginning. It started the way he saw the world.'

'You mean about people?'

'Absolutely. He told me, it wasn't just the pain of it, of his bittern being slaughtered, which was terrible, it was the incomprehension. He was a religious boy then and he told his dad that he couldn't understand how God, if God was a god of love, how God could let people do this. So Sholto explained to him about original sin. He explained how people were basically, not good. Fergus told me his dad had been in the war, he'd been in Germany at the end and he'd seen terrible stuff, he'd been at the liberation of that concentration camp, what was it called? Belsen, that was it. So from then on Fergus had a, had a … what would you say …?'

'A frame of reference?' said Jenny.

'Exactly, yeah, a frame of reference about people and how they might behave towards nature, given half a chance. How they would destroy it. It was the basic belief of his life. It gave him his sense of purpose. To be a warden on a nature reserve. At the sharp end. His words. On the front line. He wanted to be actually physically protecting a piece of the Earth, every day, no matter how small it was. He didn't give a shit about scientific success, or promotion, or anything. He was fulfilled saying, *would you mind not having your picnic in this dune slack, Modom, because there are oystercatchers breeding here.* I've heard him say that. He was always very polite but he was completely uncompromising. And that got him into trouble.'

'How so?'

'Well, after university he got a job with the NCC, the government conservation agency, as an assistant warden on this reserve outside Liverpool. Coastal reserve. Big area of sand dunes. There was quite a lot of public pressure. Not just high visitor numbers, but he told me, sometimes there'd be people letting their dogs chase breeding birds or joyriding with their cars in the dunes or vandalising visitor information signs and that, and Fergus would confront them. Head-on, every time. He had no fear. He was a guy completely without fear. Suppose his size helped. It would, wouldn't it?'

'What was the trouble he got into?'

'He clashed with this gang of blokes. Nasty. They were setting their dogs on the rabbits. Lurchers. Can't do that in a nature reserve, can you? He thought they were basically gangsters. I mean, Liverpool's a pretty tough place, isn't it? And one thing led to another and in the end they had a confrontation and they got the better of him and beat him senseless, it was his turn in the hospital this time. And he'd have been straight back out there as soon as he was on his feet again, but the NCC thought discretion was the better part of valour as he was a marked man now and he'd end up being killed, and they transferred him to south Wales.'

Jenny said: 'I supposed that must have reinforced his sense of … what people could be like?'

'Oh aye, it certainly did. And there was something else strengthened his view even more. He discovered this idea, this theory, which backed up his view about Man the destroyer. And that was the megafauna extinctions. The great beasts of the Ice Ages which all disappeared. You know about this?'

'I've heard something about it,' said Jenny.

'People get it confused with the dinosaurs,' Bronwen said. 'Ever since *Jurassic Park* people've been obsessed with dinosaurs. Kids especially. But the dinosaurs were sixty-five million years ago, and they were wiped out by a comet or whatever, whereas the megafauna, these were the giant mammals of our own time, of the human world, and the modern theory is, they were all wiped out by *us*. As *Homo sapiens* spread out of Africa, this is like 50,000 years ago, 40,000 years ago and so on, right, they wiped out the megafauna in each continent they came to. Australia. Europe. North America. South America. Hundreds of different giant species. The mammoths. The sabre-toothed tigers. The woolly rhinos. The giant sloths. Lots and lots of others. Fergus used to talk about them. All vanished. Amazing saga, when you read about it. It's called the prehistoric overkill hypothesis. It was just starting to be understood then and Fergus said, it showed clearly, that if human beings could drive a creature extinct, they would. He was obsessed with it, with the extinctions. He was reading all about it the summer we were on Skarholm.'

'You were where?' I said.

'Skarholm. An island off Pembrokeshire.'

'I know it. I was a researcher there for six years.'

'Were you really? When was that?'

'Ninety-one to ninety-seven.'

'Ah well, see, we were there in 1981.'

I was taken aback. I said: 'What an amazing coincidence. Jenny's been there as well. How did you get there?'

'After we saved Cors Caewen, that was just before Easter, Fergus didn't have a job, having been sacked and all, so he got this contract as an assistant warden on Skarholm for the summer. It was a three-year contract, end of April to end of September each year. And we were an item by then. I'll tell you, I got some funny remarks from my girlfriends. Me and this giant. But I didn't give a shit. I thought he was great. And in April he goes off to Skarholm and I sit my finals in business studies and then in May I went to join him, on the island.'

Jenny said: 'Did you see the bluebells?'

'Aren't they something? It was a wonderful summer. With the man you love, on an island. You know?'

'Yes,' said Jenny. 'Yes, I do know.'

Bronwen said: 'That was when I got into the environment, properly. Fergus drew up this reading list for me. I started to see the big picture, I started to see what the environment was about and why it was worth saving. And he started teaching me natural history, with all the seabirds and things, well, you'll know all about that.'

The phone on her desk rang.

'I've told them to hold my calls,' she said. 'Must be important. D'you mind?'

Not at all, we said.

She picked up the phone and said: 'Oh hi, how are you. OK. So what's the problem now? Is it? Really? Well, tell them that's not good enough. Tell them I said that, OK? Yeah, bye.' She turned to us. 'Sting's people,' she said. 'We're trying to get him to do a concert with Bono for one of our rainforest projects, but matching schedules is just a nightmare. Where were we?'

'You were on Skarholm.'

'Oh yeah, right. Look, this has been pretty intense stuff, hasn't it? Bringing it all back. I've never spoken about it all like this before and I feel a bit wrung out. I don't mind carrying on talking but shall we stretch our legs? I could take you over to Cors Caewen if you like. There's a monument to Fergus there. You might like to see it. It's only fifteen minutes in the car.'

It was strange to start to realise that Fergus Pryng was more than the caricature he had originally seemed on Lanna, the bogeyman figure of rumour and legend, that he had a past and an interior world of his own that neither Jenny or I had imagined; at least, I hadn't. I think Jenny might well have sensed it. But there was more to come, and it came in Bronwen's Prius. I had never seen

one before. 'World's first mass-produced hybrid vehicle,' she said.
'Only been available in Europe since last year. This is one of the very
first. Toyota suggested it might be a good idea for me to drive it.'

As we slid off – silently with the electric motor – I said: 'So
you were you on Skarholm for three years?'

'No,' she said. 'When we came off the island, at the end of
September, I found I was pregnant, see. Which neither of us had
bargained for. And that kind of changed everything. I wasn't sure
what to do but Fergus wanted the baby and he persuaded me, and
being very traditional and a gentleman into the bargain, he asked
me to marry him, and I said Yes. I suddenly felt very vulnerable.
Sholto married us in his church in the December, in Suffolk. I
think he and Cicely were a bit shocked that I was up the duff, I
don't think they thought their son had it in him to be honest, but
they were very decent about everything. They weren't a problem.
The problem was my mam.'

'Why?'

'She hated Fergus, from the start. She couldn't see he had any
prospects, not in terms of making money and giving me the decent
life she wanted for me. Like, she couldn't work out what he did. I
told her he was a warden on a nature reserve and she said, is that like
a park keeper? And she hated how he looked. I mean, he *was* pretty
freakish-looking with his size, wasn't he? It wasn't too bad while
we were living away from her, Fergus and I had rented a flat here
in Cardiff and Mam was still in Barry, but when the baby came I
thought it would be best if we moved in with her, for support and
that. And Angharad was born on 15 May 1982, and that's when
the trouble really started.'

'Why?'

'All four of us were in the same small terraced house and my
mam was on Fergus's back the whole time. She was awful with
him, do this, do that, why haven't you done the other? He had the
patience of a saint, but I could see it would become impossible.
When Angharad was a month old, Fergus asked me if I would come
back to the island, baby and all, since he was still under contract
at Skarholm and they had kept the job open and I agreed, partly
to get away from my mam and partly because it sounded sort of
romantic. I thought it might be fun. But it wasn't like the year
before. It didn't work. We ran out of nappies. And there was no
doctor, and you can do with a doctor nearby with a tiny baby, and
after three weeks I told him I was going back but I told him to stay
on until September, I thought it would be for the best and I could

manage the baby with my mam, although it just gave her a chance to call him more names, and when he came back it was even worse. He stuck it out for as long as he could, he got a job stacking shelves in a supermarket, but over the winter it gradually started to go off between us too, I was giving him stick, and having me on his case as well as my mam in the end was too much. In the spring I said I thought we needed some time apart and maybe he should look for another warden's job for a bit and eventually he told me he'd answered an advert with some estate in Scotland to go and be the warden on this island for the summer and survey the seabirds, and I said OK. He'd already told the people on Skarholm he wouldn't be coming back. That's how he started with Lanna.'

I said: 'This was when exactly?'

'The spring of 1983.'

'So he went to Lanna?'

'He did. And I missed him, and I remembered all his good qualities. And he came back at the end of July, and we had the long talk, you know, like you do, and he said he wanted more than anything to make it work but he couldn't live with my mam and I could see he was right, so we rented a flat for ourselves back here in Cardiff and we started to make a go of our marriage. And it was great, he got another job for the winter and we were content, we were reading together and everything, and I was starting to kick around my idea of a green business, and we had a happy Christmas and New Year, even with my mam, and Angharad was starting to crawl and make noises and Fergus was a really good dad to her, he was very loving, and then in the March he dropped his bombshell.'

'What?'

'He said he was going to go back to Lanna.'

She was watching the road, she was a careful driver, but she quickly stared at me in the rear-view mirror.

'Can you believe it? For the spring and early summer again. Nearly four months. April, May, June, July. I was incredulous. I said, Fergus, you can't do that, we're just getting settled. He said he had to go. I said, no you don't. He said he was needed, to look after the seabirds 'cos the seabirds were very special and I said, bollocks to the seabirds, seabirds my arse, you're needed here, to look after us. He said, please understand Bronwen, please, I have to go. I said, why d'you have to go, and he said he'd made a bargain, and I said, who with, and he said, he'd made a bargain with himself and I said, but what about your bargain with us? What about your marriage vows, what about looking after me and Angharad in good times and in bad, and he kept saying, he had to go.'

I wondered if he had discovered the auks on his first trip. I said: 'Did he say why, exactly?'

'He didn't explain it to me any more than that. To be honest I didn't really care. I just knew, if Fergus was going to leave me and Angharad for another four months now when we needed him, we were finished. What my shit of a dad did to my mam was engraved on my soul and I wasn't going to stand for it, I was never going to be a doormat for any man and I said to him, Fergus, listen to me, listen to me carefully, if you go back to this sodding island for four months, I will leave you. Read my lips. I-will-leave-you. For good. And he said it didn't have to be like that. He said he loved me and Angharad more than anything in his life, and he begged me to understand he simply had to go back to Lanna. I said is that your final word and he said he had to go and I said, then I'm going back to my mam, today. And I did. I went. And that was the beginning of the end of us. Here we are. This is it.'

She turned to the left off the road into a car park and pulled up by a notice announcing Cors Caewen/Whitefield Fen National Nature Reserve.

'It's the second largest lowland fen in Wales,' she said. 'It's got the fen raft spider and other rare stuff and the dragonflies are fantastic. The birds and plants are pretty good too. Everything you can see around you, Fergus Pryng saved from becoming a rubbish tip. I've spent a bit more time here, over the last year. Since the tanker business. You know. I had the monument redone, with the date of his death on. It was looking a bit battered. Want to have a look?'

She led the way along the path and Jenny said: 'So ... Fergus going back to Lanna for a second year was what broke you up?'

'It sure was. I told him to get lost, and I went back to my mam in Barry. It was a tough time, I had a baby to look after and no job, though to be fair to Fergus, he insisted on giving us money every week, he set up a standing order, I'll give him that. We couldn't have managed without. When he finally got back in the summer he wanted a reconciliation, I mean, he insisted he loved me and Angharad with all his heart and I could see he did, so in the end I said, OK, Fergus, OK, I'll take you back but my condition is, you put me and Angharad first, all right? So no more shooting off to your sodding Scottish island for four months and you know what? He said he would have to go back the following year. Right then and there. I couldn't believe it. I said, *what on earth for?* And he came out with this weird stuff again, about he'd made a bargain with himself to go back there and look after the bloody birds. What a load of bollocks! It felt like he was rubbing my nose in it. He knew full well he had to choose between his island and me, me and Angharad I should say, his wife and his daughter, and he chose the island. It made me very bitter. I mean, wouldn't you be? In that situation?'

Jenny said: 'I would be, yes.'

I said: 'And he never told you anything more specifically about why he felt he had to go back there?'

'Just the birds.'

'He never said which birds?'

'Just the seabirds, on the island. He was going back to look after them. It was very hard to understand. I knew he loved nature with a passion, it was what had attracted me to him in the first place, but I never dreamed it would come between us, he would turn his back on his family for it. Take Angharad. Her birthday is May 15 and he's never been here for it. In her whole life, her father has never been with her on her birthday. When he could have been. Don't you think that's unbelievably selfish? Don't you think that's awful? He's paid the price, anyway. She doesn't think him as her father, it's Ronnie she calls Dad. She just calls him Fergus. I mean, she did. Cos you know what? The last time she saw him, she let him have it. With both barrels.'

'What do you mean?'

'Fergus used to come here with a present for her a month before each birthday. I think he did feel guilty about not being there on the day. He had no idea of what to get her that she might have wanted, like clothes or music, so he got her stuff like books and paintings, and she put them in the back of her wardrobe. She just used to accept it as something a bit odd which was part of her life, you know, like kids do. But after her seventeenth birthday, she asked me about it all, and I told her the full story, of how when she was a baby he started going to this island for more than three months every year and how he wouldn't stop even though I begged him, and how difficult it was for us and how I told him to sling his hook, and even that made no difference. And Angharad was like, you mean he abandoned us? And I said, in effect he did, and she was very angry and indignant, cos she's got my tough streak, that girl, and when he came last year, before her eighteenth, before he went to Lanna for the last time, she had it out with him. She confronted him about leaving us, and she asked him why, why, why, and he couldn't give her a good answer. Correction: he couldn't give her any answer. And she told him what a shit he was and what a failure as a husband and a father and how he'd betrayed us, and he needn't bother ever coming again to see her, and she stormed off. He was very upset. But I mean, what did he expect?'

'So…she's nineteen now?'

'Yeah. She's in London. She's modelling. We've pulled a few strings, but we didn't need to, really. She's stunning. Very tall – that's what she got from Fergus.' She laughed. 'Whereas, the only thing I've kept from him worth having, is my name. I kept hold of Pryng. Much classier name than Jones, which is what I was born with. Much better brand value. I realised that when I started out with the business, even before I met Ronnie.'

Jenny said: 'So you got divorced in the end from Fergus, did you?'

'Yep. I did. And I told him the less I saw of him the better and I'd prefer it if he could keep his visits to Angharad to the bare minimum. And he sent me a letter when it was finalised, he said he was so sorry that he had had to do what he'd had to do, and he would love me and Angharad all his life, and he would never be happy again. That's what he said. And I thought, yeah, well, tough. I was very bitter towards him. I washed my hands of him, and I didn't actually see much of him after that because his mother got ill about that time and he went back to Suffolk to help his dad look after her, and Suffolk to here is a long drive, it's 300 miles. Eventually, he just came in the April each year with a present for Angharad. In the fifteen years leading up to his death that's all I saw of him and I thought about him even less, although I know Cicely died and then Sholto got ill himself and Fergus was looking after him for a few years and the time before last he came, he said Sholto had died as well. And you know what he was doing, Fergus – apart from going to his bloody island, year after bloody year? Shelf-stacking in a supermarket. He said he couldn't get a proper job or resume his career in conservation 'cos he would need four months off every year to go to Lanna and nobody would give him that. So it was supermarkets. He said, they liked him cos he was so tall he could fill the top shelf without needing a stepladder. And the rest of his time, his spare time, he was a volunteer warden on various nature reserves. I think he ended up in Lowestoft. I've got an address for him somewhere, if you want it. This is the monument.'

It was a simple pyramid-shaped plinth about five feet tall at the junction of three paths, and it bore a plaque which read:

In memory of Fergus Pryng
10 April 1949 – 9 June 2000
Who saved this place
And all its life

Bronwen turned to us. She said: 'You know what? I'm glad he died a hero's death.'

'Why?'

'It means I don't despise him any more. He died a martyr, a martyr for nature, and that means he's sort of redeemed. Because otherwise, it was all such a waste. He could have had a top job in conservation, he could have had a stellar career in an NGO, he should have become Director of Friends of the Earth or Greenpeace International, he could have made a real difference to things and he ends up stacking shelves. A total loser. It's so ironic, isn't it? It should have been him, him the huge figure in the environment movement. And it ends up being me.'

She looked at the monument for a last time.

'The thing I just don't get is why he turned his back on it all. You know. The environmental struggle. I will never be able to understand that. He gives it all up for an annual jolly to this bloody island, just to stare at the seabirds.' She shook her head. 'What was really important, he turned his back on.'

Jenny and I exchanged glances.

She said: 'You know, I don't think he did.'

But Bronwen didn't hear. She was already heading back to the car.

31

Bronwen gave us the last address she had for Fergus, which was indeed in Lowestoft in Suffolk, and on the drive back to Wimbledon we agreed we ought to go and check it out … you never know, *there might be photographs* … and the next afternoon we eventually found ourselves in a street running off the Lowestoft southern promenade, looking up at a three-storey Victorian terraced house. On the window over the door was painted in gilt lettering: *Sparrow's Nest.* It seemed like a seaside boarding house, or might have been, once. We rang the bell and eventually the door was opened by a plump middle-aged woman in a kitchen apron. She said: 'Yes?'

'We're sorry to bother you but we're friends of Fergus, Fergus Pryng, who was killed in the tanker disaster in Scotland last year? The very tall chap? And we understand he used to live here.'

She stared at us. She said: 'Fergus? You're friends of Fergus?'

'That's right.'

'Oh, poor man. Come in. You must come in.'

She led us into what I think she probably called her front parlour and indicated a sofa and said: 'I'm Mrs Hazlehurst, Elsie Hazlehurst, I was his landlady. How can I help you?'

I gave our names and said: 'We worked for the Offshore Conservation Agency, and we were doing a seabird survey with him on this island when the oil tanker hit it and exploded, and he was killed. We were with him when we died, and you might think this is a bit strange, but we didn't really know much about him and we're just visiting some people who did know him to sort of try and find out a bit more.'

'Well,' she said, 'he was here for the last two or three years. Since his father died. Except in the spring, when he went away to Scotland.'

I said: 'We wondered if by any chance he might have left any documents or especially any … photographs, behind?'

'Oh yes,' said Mrs Hazlehurst. 'A lot. A lot of pictures.'

'Pictures of what?'

'Birds, mostly. Funny-looking birds.'

My heartbeat began to gallop. 'Might we see them?'

'Well, I'm afraid not.'

'Why's that?'

'I had to clear out his room. After he was killed. I had to throw them out.'

'Did you throw them *all* out?'

'Oh yes. He didn't have any relatives or friends I could give them to, and I wanted to relet his room.'

'So there's nothing left? Nothing at all?'

'Well, I have got one thing,' she said. 'I think I put it in a drawer upstairs.'

'Might we see?'

We held our breath while she clumped about above our heads. Would it be the one remaining photo that would prove everything? That would make history? That would astonish the world?

She came back down holding what seemed to be a book. My heart leapt again. Was it a photo album?

'I kept this because it was too nice to throw away,' she said. 'And to remind me of him. But if you're his friends, I suppose you can have it, if you like.'

There were no photos.

There never would be, now.

Instead it was a leather-bound notebook, clearly expensive, with pages of thick beige artisan paper covered in small neat writing in blue ink.

On the flyleaf was written:

Lanna PI Master Log

By FP

'FP's clearly Fergus Pryng,' I murmured to Jenny. 'But what's PI?'

'Not a clue,' she said.

'Well, thanks,' I said to Mrs Hazlehurst, trying to hide my disappointment. 'We will take it, if we may. It's something to remember him by.'

'You're welcome,' she said.

'And there's really nothing else of Fergus's remaining? No … photos, or anything?'

'That's it, I'm afraid. If I'd thought somebody might have wanted the photos, I'd have hung on to them.'

I didn't want to hear that, but at least the notebook was something. And going through it in the car, we quickly realised what PI must stand for – it was *Pinguinus impennis*, the scientific name. For the first entry read:

1983
Big Hughie the boatman showed me the birds on May 9th. He called them 'the Lanna geese'. He had no idea what they actually were. Plus he is slightly simple. It was the first really calm day of my trip and he took me in the rib into the Sgeir Dubh lagoon. I counted eleven individuals on the breeding ledge, six of them apparently sitting on eggs. I was astonished, not to know at first what they were, but then, my birds are not as good as my wild flowers, and there is no image of PI in the Field Guide. They resembled penguins but they clearly were not and I knew that no penguin species bred in the northern hemisphere. The idea of PI crossed my mind and I dismissed it as ridiculous but as the days went on I began to feel by a process of elimination that it could not be anything else, even though I was only relying on memory of what the true image was. However, I did make sketches and field notes – they are with the notebooks – and I took a large number of photographs and when I returned I at once consulted various sources and there seemed to be no doubt. The matter was clinched by a visit to the bird collection of the Natural History Museum in Tring where there is a mounted skin of PI and the curator, a decent and obliging fellow, was good enough to show it to me. He opened a cupboard and I beheld in front of me a very Lanna goose.

The eggs hatched as far as I can judge on June 18. The chicks were large and were gone, with the adults, by June 21. This astonishingly short fledging period does not seem to figure in the literature. It is not mentioned in Symington Grieve (the monograph, which I have managed to obtain).

I decided for various reasons that for the present the whole business was best kept confidential.

So there it was, the proof. He had known about them ever since he first went to the island. Apart from sharing it with Kintyre in 1998, he had kept the secret since 1983.

That was why he had left Bronwen and gone back.

That was why he had lost his marriage.

'Wow,' I said. 'Long time, eh?'

'A long time,' said Jenny.

We went through the rest of the entries. The next one read:

1984

I came back in late April to anticipate PI's return but the birds were already there before me. There could be no possible doubt about their identity. A quite astonishing situation. They appeared to begin sitting on eggs on May 5th – do they synchronise their laying? There appeared this year to be seven pairs and a total of eighteen individuals. So what is the rate of winter mortality? Where they spend the non-breeding season is a mystery. They must be somewhere – why has no one ever seen one? The chicks hatched on June 19 and once again, were gone after two days. But in that time I observed a bonxie swoop on to the breeding ledge and carry off a chick, despite its size. It is clear that bonxies and all other predators will have to be ruthlessly controlled. Full details in the notebooks.

I have not told Kintyre of this remarkable state of affairs. I have given the matter a great deal of thought. Alfred Newton says, in his account of the last birds in Iceland, wondering if any might remain, in 'some unknown spot': 'it is clear that its extinction, if not already accomplished, must speedily follow on its rediscovery.' I believe this to be absolutely true, and that accordingly the best conservation strategy, Homo sapiens being the destroyer that he is, will be to speak of it to no one whatsoever. Though clearly, the quid pro quo for my silence must be my personal protection. For how long? I do not know. But for the immediate future, certainly.

The entries were very similar, all about 250–300 words, summing up each year in straightforward conservation terms, and referring to various notebooks for more detail. Over time the population of the auks seemed to fluctuate up and down around the 17 mark, with no major dramas until the entry for 1998, a longer one where Fergus detailed how he felt obliged to inform Lord Kintyre of the birds' existence to prevent the survey by UKOCA. It was somewhat agonised but he felt he had done the right thing, and kept the secret.

However, the most striking entry of all was the last, for 1999. Fergus had written out his 300-word conservation report but underneath it, after a space, was something else.

It was in slightly different coloured ink and it was headed: *December 31 1999.*

I thought: he was writing that when Lotte and I were in the Marsden, watching Mum die.

Fergus wrote:

Tomorrow the twenty-first century begins. I am full of foreboding, for I fear it will be a terrible century for the Earth. The dire threat of global warming hangs over us all now and last year was the hottest year ever recorded, by a huge margin: the heat bleached coral reefs the world over and who knows if they will recover? Who knows what is next? What I have for so long feared is becoming real at a faster and faster pace – the scale of human activities is growing insupportable for the planet and it can only get ever bigger as populations continue to explode, populations of Man, the species which has made destruction its own speciality. The lesson is clear for us in the wiping out of the megafaunas – Man is the Earth's cursed child! Man is the species which will destroy its own home, its wondrous home, the blessed blue sphere hanging in the black emptiness of space which gives us everything, the fragile sphere of infinite value, now faced with such a ghastly and undeserved fate.

Poor Earth! Your forests chainsawed, your meadows poisoned with pesticides, your seas stripmined of their fish, your rivers choked with dirt or turned to acid, your tigers slaughtered for their skins and their bones, your elephants slaughtered for their ivory, your great apes slaughtered for bushmeat, your great whales slaughtered simply for the sake of the slaughter and now even your oceans, your oceans where wildness and purity and freedom still persisted, to become factories, producers of filth! That is the worst. I can scarcely bear the thought of it. Poor Earth! Your end is coming! In this century to come Man will destroy you. But I will fight to protect you while there is breath left in my body.

32

It's an isolated spot, where the sea loch meets the sea: the metalled road ends nearly a mile up the shoreline, and there is only a track which carries on down to the medieval chapel on the point, where I sit.

It's a place whose beauty stops the heart. The tide is out, great stretches of sand and seaweed are exposed, and on the waterline, an otter is fishing, porpoising through the small waves; beyond, bobbing on the sea, is a solitary male eider duck, striking in his black and white uniform. Oystercatchers are whistling down the wind. On the far side of the loch are the hills of Argyll, hazy dark blue shadows framed by the milky blue sky.

The three far distant figures walking down the beach towards me appear tiny; they appear black against the pale sand.

It is four years now since I first went back to Lanna with Ramsay and Callum in search of its unique inhabitants, and still they have not reappeared. Every spring since then we have returned with a small UKOCA team to survey the seabirds, officially, and each time we learn more about the life of the island which in the wake of the tanker disaster is now fully safeguarded as one of the great Atlantic seabird colonies; there is a maritime exclusion zone of forty miles around it which tanker traffic is asked to observe. But each year the true purpose of the trip, still known only to Ramsay and Callum and Jenny and me, remains unfulfilled. On the Sgeir Dubh breeding ledge, there is nothing.

For Ramsay and Callum it is an impossible state of affairs. It is not so much the unprecedented tragedy for nature which they find themselves faced with, the possibility that great auks, the western hemisphere's icons of extinction, survived in tiny numbers on a small Atlantic island and *then were made extinct again*, and the distress of carrying such knowledge virtually alone – no, not even that. The principal problem is more basic: whether or not to believe us.

Callum does not. He thinks we are fantasising. Well, he thinks I am fantasising, perhaps because of my head injury and my original amnesia or something. He does not wish to think of Jenny as a liar, but nevertheless, as one of the world experts on *Pinguinus impennis* he simply does not believe that the birds could have survived for 150 years undetected, even in very small numbers, and even in the exceptional circumstances of seclusion offered by Lanna. The fact that all the other people who might have confirmed their existence are dead, he thinks, is just too convenient. Partly, too, I sense he cannot bear to harbour the thought that the lost birds which he made his own special study and cause might have survived, and he did not see them, but one of his former students did. So we are increasingly estranged, which is the greatest of pities. And this year, despite a standing invitation, he did not join the Lanna trip.

Ramsay's position is somewhat different. He too feels confounded by the absolute lack of evidence, but he cherishes the memory of Kenny his protégé and mourns his untimely end, and is still mystified over his conduct in his final days – yet the account we gave of Kenny discovering the birds and his fight with Fergus, and his subsequent return to the island with the photographer, explains his actions perfectly. And if it is not true, what else can explain them? So Ramsay continues, I suppose, in a sort of anguished open-mindedness.

As for myself and Jenny, we have slowly grown accustomed to our bizarre situation, that we were witnesses to a phenomenon which was indeed unique, and then to its catastrophic end, and we are precluded from speaking of any of it in any way to anyone, for if we open our mouths, we will be laughed to scorn. It seems completely crazy. At one stage I found it insupportable and I told Ramsay I was going to write an account of what we had seen and try to get it published, if only for the sake of science, and he urged me not to, in fact, he begged me not to, as he said that in the absence of a single scrap of evidence bar our assertions, it would bring UKOCA and everyone associated with it into ridicule and contempt – presuming it ever did get into print. He said: 'You have no proof, nothing. You will end up in *Fortean Times*, man, along with Nessie and Bigfoot and UFOs.' And Jenny, sadly, said he was right.

I found that very hard. At one stage I even began to doubt whether or not I had seen what I had seen, whether the vivid memory of the old male bird diving and shooting supersonically beneath the inflatable, and then the breeding pairs on the ledge in their awkward ungainliness, which gave them such an appearance of vulnerability, reinforced a thousand times by knowledge of their species' woeful fate – whether these unforgettable sights were mere will o' the wisps of my imagination. I thought I would go nuts. But Jenny suggested I keep my sanity by writing it all out, if only for ourselves; and so this account, this unpublishable account, was begun.

In the meantime, though, we have got on with living, employed and closely involved in clearing up the tangled mess left at Castle Balnay and its wildlife park by the death of its singular owner. We have supervised the dissolution of a large zoo, finding homes for more than 400 animals, and just as important, helping the redundant staff find new jobs. The 'penguin pool' remains an unfortunate white elephant; we have considered turning it into a swimming pool for the Balnay village community, but at the moment, that would simply cost too much, and it stands there forlorn, an empty monument whose true meaning is known to Jenny and me only. The future of the castle itself has also hugely occupied our time: such were Kinytre's debts that at first it seemed certain it would have to be sold, but his widow, Angela the Dowager Countess, with her trusty helper Gervase and Jenny and me in support, was determined to keep the estate together if she possibly could, and after more than two years of negotiations, she persuaded the National Trust for Scotland to take the whole thing over. The agreement was that the Kintyre family could continue to live in part of it; although of course, Castle Balnay is now open to the public, complete with guided tours, souvenir shop, and tearoom.

In this long process, Jenny and I have grown close to Gervase, and also to Angela, a woman who combines a sweetness of nature with a wry outlook on the world which is very engaging. Gervase certainly felt it to the full, in spite of the age gap (she's eleven years his senior); we began to realise there was something more between them in the way that he teased her, especially one day at a summer picnic on the loch side, when he pursued her ladyship along the shoreline, determined to put a squashed plum down the back of her dress, and succeeding, to her squeals. And on a sunny evening a few weeks later he came down to the cottage saying he had some news.

Oh yes? we said.

'I have asked Angela to marry me.'

Jenny and I were open-mouthed.

'And?!' we cried. 'And?!'

'She has accepted.'

'Yes!' we shouted out. We slapped his back and hugged him and Jenny dived into the cupboard under the stairs and came out with a bottle of something called Pelorus, which she said was the Cloudy Bay sparkling wine, and I said I didn't know you had this and she said lots of little secrets you still don't know about me, mate, and in fact she had two of them, and we proceeded to get riotously pissed.

'OK Gervase,' I said. 'Give us the titles bit. Let me guess. If Angela marries you, she will no longer be the Dowager Countess of Kintyre, is that correct?'

'It is.'

'She'll be plain Mrs Crinan, eh? What a come-down for the poor girl.'

'By no means.'

'What'll she be then?'

'She will be Lady Angela Crinan.'

'How so?'

'As being herself the daughter of an earl, she is a lady in her own right.'

'Ah, she's still got a title. Thank Christ for that. Social disaster averted. And does that make you a Sir or a Lord or anything?'

'I remain merely a Mister.'

'Shame!' Jenny and I shouted. 'For shame!' We banged our glasses on the table.

'But with a social position one might describe as, ah, moderately enhanced.'

'Moderately enhanced?' shouted Jenny. 'Wow! Moderately enhanced! Fuck! Fuck me! Moderately enhanced! Yes! Wow! Yes!' And we drained our glasses, until we could drink no more.

They were married in the chapel of the castle. It was hardly a Big Society Wedding: there were nineteen people there (I counted) including the two boys, Roddy, the ten-year-old Earl of Kintyre, and Lord Archie Macdonald, his eight-year-old brother, who strike me as nice young chaps, but – who knows? Will the rogue genes of their father reappear? At least, I thought then, with Gervase for stepfather alongside Angela they can't turn out all bad; at least they'll have a sense of humour. I hope so, anyway. Gervase asked me to be his best man and Jenny was Angela's matron of honour, and Gervase's old Pa was there, purring with pleasure. He had resigned himself to the fact that his son would never now inhabit the lawyer's office in the Georgian terrace in Edinburgh New Town with the perfect scalloped fanlight over the door, and enjoy lunch at the New Club and tea with the partners and weekend golf at Muirfield as he carried on the firm, with the letters WS standing proudly after his name – no, for Gervase that world was lost – yet he had married into the Scottish aristocracy (even if a now somewhat impoverished part of it), so for Sandy Crinan, that would do.

But Jenny and I have built a life of our own. Our cottage is the core of it: Taigh na Mara it's called in Gaelic, the House of the Sea, and it sits on the shore of lower Loch Nay, five miles below the castle, where a burn from the hills above tumbles down and enters the loch; we are at the end of the metalled road, beyond which the track leads down to the ancient chapel on the point, where I sit now, turning it all over in my mind.

Out across the waves I can see a distant white flickering, an aggregation of sharp and slender wings: the terns have found the whitebait shoals on the surface. It means the mackerel must be underneath them, pushing them up.

I sometimes think the mackerel are the sea's most thrilling and generous gift. The gannets will arrive soon to divebomb them.

There is a sole raven circling above – I heard him croak.

The three figures coming down the beach towards me have grown; their silhouettes have lost their blackness and they are resolving themselves now: two of them are large, and one of them is small.

Jenny loved the cottage from the moment she set eyes on it, that dreich January day (as I find myself saying now) when we were debating whether or not to accept Gervase's offer, and move north; it was what swung things for her, just as the chance to go to Lanna swung things for me. I barely noticed the cottage. She told me much later that when she walked through the door she had a sudden sensation of intense happiness, which she couldn't explain, but which was enough for her to make up her mind there and then.

All that first spring, in the run-up to the return to Lanna, and my obsession with what we would find there, I paid Taigh na Mara no heed; it was just somewhere to live. It was only in the summer, when the obsession had been torpedoed and under Jenny's guidance I had begun to understand – when in Cardiff and then in Lowestoft I had started to see into the heart of it all, as she put it – that I began to look around me, and to appreciate, first and foremost, that where we lived was supremely beautiful, and that we had come to a place where we could build a home that would be unusual in its worth. With our love, of course, for which I give thanks every day, at its base: that first Christmas we went back to Auckland and were married. At the reception Lotte played a selection of Joyce Grenfell for Jenny's mum, and had people in stitches, and we honeymooned in Fiordland, walking the Milford Track and sailing in Doubtful Sound.

In Argyll, we are in a Fiordland of our own; I love it beyond words for its beauty and its sweet wild remoteness, this oldest part of Scotland, the ancient kingdom of Dalriada. It's remote but not unfriendly: we are lucky in our neighbours, for they have made our life all the richer and helped give us a sense of belonging. Cameron and Eilidh Campbell and their children run the hillfarm above us, their longhorned highland cattle a sight to see; they were welcoming from the start. Martin McIvor, a single somewhat gruff man in his fifties, who has the croft which is the next house along the road, was a bit slower to accept we were worth knowing, but in the end Jenny's unforced friendliness won him round. He is a decent guy, a part-time fisherman, with a fondness for single malts; we have a bottle of Lagavulin, his favourite, installed on the sideboard in case he calls. And there are others we are friendly with, like Ross and Norma Tanqueray in the big house between us and the castle, and John Ross Macdonald who is another crofter, and we are on Christian name terms with the postman, Davy Erksine, and even with the binmen, Alex, Dougie and Gordon.

But our non-human neighbours have been just as rewarding. The most spectacular are the eagles, the pair of golden eagles which breed on the ridge on the high land above the Campbells' farm; sometimes they float over Taigh na Mara, soaring in splendour. Cameron has pinpointed the nest and we watch them through the telescope on their crags without ever tiring of the sight. The high ridge also holds a herd of red deer and we go up there in the autumn rut to watch the stags fighting and listen to them roaring, all aggressive majesty. Yet there is vivid life much nearer to home. The burn at the side of the house runs down past the edge of the back garden from a wooded glen which is full of birds, and if you put food out on the old bird table which was there when we arrived, finches and tits and woodpeckers and all sorts of stuff will flock to it; and in our first autumn, Jenny put on it some Scotch pancakes she had made on the hot plate of the Raeburn and we were astonished, a few hours later, to glimpse one of them disappearing – we jumped up and saw it was being carried off by a stoat.

It was running across the garden with the pancake in its mouth, carrying it with its head up so as not to trip over it, a remarkable sight, and I dashed for Jenny's camera, but I was too late. The next day, however, which was a Saturday, I kept watch for several hours, and lo and behold the stoat returned, shinned up the bird-table pole, which had been a tree trunk, and grabbed another pancake – I thought stoats were killers, cried Jenny, is this little bastard a vegetarian, then? – and this time, I got a half-decent shot. We showed it to Martin McIvor when he came for a drink a few days later and he said: 'Och, the glen behind you here is full of wildlife. Tom and Isabel, your predecessors, they worked at the castle like you, they saw red squirrels and even pine martens. And once, a wildcat. But they're mainly active at night. Why don't you photograph the otters? You can see them all day long.'

Otters? we said. What otters? Where?

'All along the tideline,' said Martin. 'Otters are ten a penny here.'

It was true; the unimpeded view from the Taigh na Mara front windows across the loch to the distant hills was so breathtaking that we had hardly ever looked closely at the rocky shore right in front of us; but once we did, we realised that otters fished along it, every day, sometimes a dog otter, sometimes a bitch with a cub in tow. There was a mushroom-shaped rock right in front of the house and occasionally they would take the fish they had caught there, to munch. When they were hunting they were so intent on their work that you could approach to within fifty yards; and after taking some fair-ish pictures with Jenny's camera and its standard lens, I went up to Oban and bought a telephoto lens and a book on photography, and the subsequent results, I thought, were really good. I would have continued happily down that road; but Jenny had other ideas. Just before we left for New Zealand at Christmas she said: 'Listen, buddy boy. Photography is my thing, all right? And if you take it over, I'm gonna get jealous and resentful, 'cos I'm like, human, OK? So here you are. Go make some movies,' and she presented me with a digital camcorder.

It was a very fancy-looking piece of kit. It allowed the use of interchangeable lenses. It must have cost her a fortune. She said: 'It's a Canon XL1. It's the video camera NASA takes on the space shuttle.'

Funny, isn't it, the turning points in our lives, which can be as trivial as a Christmas present? There were several reasons it took me down the road I have followed since, that camera. One was, I was determined to master it, and not just leave it lying around. Another was, I got it at the very moment when the digital revolution meant amateurs could start shooting and editing video like professionals, on laptops rather than in an edit suite. And a third reason was, the wildlife on our doorstep was simply waiting to be photographed, most of all the otters, since otters which live in rivers in England are mainly active by night, but the otters which live on the sea coast of Scotland go hunting during the day. So I started to shoot them as often as I could, most mornings before work, in fact, and over the months I began to learn their behaviour, including the times when they would go fishing and the fact that you could get closer to them by moving when they were underwater, and I started to learn their favourite fish, such as octopus, which they adored, chewing the tentacles like spaghetti, and big fat lumpsuckers, which Martin McIvor helped me identify, and which they took fifteen minutes to eat, although the cubs could only catch crabs. And Jenny thought my shots were great, and she said, why don't you email some of this to the BBC Natural History Unit in Bristol, they do all the TV wildlife documentaries?

I picked the name of a producer out at random, a woman called Mary Bannon, and she replied that she really liked my stuff and they were actually in the middle of doing a major otter documentary and if I could shoot a five-minute segment on the animals hunting on the shoreline they would consider including it; and I did that too, and they used it in their film, and she sent me a fee and a note thanking me and saying I seemed to be a natural, and what about sending them some more? So I took time off from work at the castle and spent a fortnight in October filming the red deer rut up in the hills, with the stags roaring through the mist, and the people at the Beeb loved that as well, and then I did another more ambitious film on the seals in Loch Nay, hiring Martin McIvor and his boat as a filming platform, and they accepted that too and when the spring came I made a film about a pair of redstarts – fabulous birds! – feeding their chicks on their nest in the oakwood along the road, and after she accepted that Mary Bannon said had I ever considered doing this for a living? And going professional?

But the idea had already begun to form in my mind, and the main reason, the reason that I thought I might be a wildlife cameraman – that that's what I might do with my life – was because of the beauty and the worth of the world, which we now see fully, since for Jenny and me, always, behind everything, behind all our thoughts, is Fergus.

Fergus Pryng discovered the rarest creatures on the planet and kept them secret for seventeen years. Properly realising that, at Cardiff and then at Lowestoft, was almost as big a jolt as finding the birds themselves. It was more than just hard to credit. It seemed ... the words that first formed in my brain were, *perfectly ridiculous.*

Why would you do it?

Great auks have survived! Why would you not want to tell the world this amazing, inspirational news (and while you were at it, hoover up the international celebrity, the global renown which would be bound to come your way? I certainly would have).

But then, as we looked at it, there seemed to be something not just bizarre but positively harmful about what Fergus had done. For Jenny helped me perceive, almost at once, that the ultimate effect of Fergus's long silence had been to deprive the great auks of Lanna of official security and shelter, and thus make possible their destruction, in the disaster of the *Lamprinos.*

'Wouldn't they have been officially protected? By the government? Once they were known about?' she said. 'The rarest creatures in the world?'

We were driving back down the A12 from Lowestoft to London.

'Sure,' I said. 'Absolutely.'

'Then there'd be two choices, about what to do with them. They might have gone to a captive breeding facility somewhere. Maybe even with Kintyre, at the end of the day. And if so, there could have been no *Lamprinos* for them there, could there?'

'That's right.'

'Second choice would have been for them to stay *in situ.* But if they had, surely there would have been some sort of, you know, shipping exclusion zone put in place around Lanna?'

'Bound to be,' I said.

'Which would keep oil tankers a long way away? Fifty miles, or whatever? So there would have been no *Lamprinos* that way either.'

That night when we got back to Wimbledon, I thought I had thought it through.

'You could make a case,' I said, 'that Fergus Pryng not telling about the great auks on Lanna was the biggest and most ghastly mistake ever made in wildlife conservation.'

Jenny nodded.

I said: 'He presided over the greatest conservation failure there has ever been. Great auks were rediscovered. They were our very icons of extinction. And we couldn't save them. Or at least, we

didn't save them. Because Fergus Pryng had kept them to himself.
For seventeen years.'
Jenny said: 'It was an accident. You gotta remember that, Miles.
The *Lamprinos* was an accident. Fergus had no idea it was going
to happen.'
'Yeah, but he paved the way for it. By keeping official
protection from them. Imagine if the facts were known, Jen.
He'd have been vilified around the world. Selfish, irresponsible,
that wouldn't be the half of it. He'd have been seen as mad. Mad
or evil. Or both.'
'His appearance wouldn't have helped,' said Jenny.
'He'd have been the bogeyman,' I said. 'Fergus Pryng, the
bogeyman of nature. The greatest of all wildlife criminals. There
would never have been such a figure.'
So we returned to Balnay, to Gervase and Angela and the taxing
labour of trying to dismantle a zoo and save a castle, with this
amazing knowledge, this second piece of astonishing information
which only we possessed, now to sit alongside the consciousness of
the great auks and their loss – we were stunned, but also bemused
and perplexed, not only at how to handle it or what to do about it,
but even about how to feel. We did not know why Fergus had done
what he'd done; it didn't appear to be for any material gain, for he
had spurned the opportunity for scientific renown, for genuine
world fame. So why? It seemed mad, any way you cared to look at
it. What he did led to catastrophe.
And yet, over the months that followed, my feelings about
Fergus Pryng began to shift, once again under the influence of Jenny.

Jenny had been fascinated by Fergus from the outset, when,
for me, he was wholly overshadowed by his charges: for me, the
auks were everything, and Fergus was neither here nor there. But
Jenny, wiser than I will ever be, already on Lanna had begun to
discern the outline of something very unusual in what he had
done, and indeed in his person; and although it might seem from
what I have written here that I was the one mainly affected by
the tanker disaster – fractured skull, hospital, amnesia, recovery
on the other side of the world, etc etc, with Jenny's role merely to
be my cheerful carer – in fact she was more deeply marked than
I was by it, by her distress at watching Fergus die. For her it was
more than just the horror of the burning cross; it was the half-
grasped perception of what had been lost in him, and what it had
cost him, to do what he did.

It echoed in her mind through all the months which followed, at her home in New Zealand and then on our return to Scotland, although it wasn't something she chose to speak to me about, since my incomprehension was too dense and my obsession with the birds too fixed; but after she eventually intervened, and we made our pilgrimages to Cardiff and Lowestoft, and we learned what Fergus had done, and saw the awful consequences and I thought I understood it all – one day, some weeks after we came back, she said to me: 'Miles, you know, maybe with Fergus, the best thing might be, to suspend judgement.'

'In what way?'

'We shouldn't just write him off, I think, if we want to grasp who he really was.'

'How d'you mean?'

'Well, for example,' she said, 'he paid a very high price, didn't he, for what he did ...'

And that was how it began, through hours of discussion, of going over everything Fergus had said, and everything Bronwen had told us, and rereading the logbook – our voyage towards understanding. It wasn't that we changed our basic view of his decision; I think today as much as I ever have that Fergus made the wrong choice. I have wrestled with it endlessly and I can only say that personally, I would have made the existence of the birds known, with every possible precaution, so that official protection might have been accorded them. But we started to register the size of what he had done, rather than just his potential culpability for the disaster at the end; we began to appreciate the scale of the sacrifice involved in the decision he took, which was not only to keep the birds secret – easy enough, simply say nothing – but to look after them himself.

We can see now that this stemmed from his honesty, or perhaps it might be more accurate to say, his sense of honour: he clearly felt that if he took this momentous step, as a professional conservationist, to deprive the rest of society of the chance of seeing them – or indeed, of protecting them – he had to give something very substantial back. He had to warden them personally, for the length of the breeding season every year, taking on their welfare as if he himself were a national wildlife body or a government department, and thus in effect, engage his life to them, abandoning all other ambitions and projects for the future. That was the fee he felt he had to pay for staying silent; that was the bargain he ended up making with himself.

As a decision, it can in nowise have been easy, since in taking it, he destroyed his marriage. Fergus faced a choice, and an awful one: he had to choose between protecting the Earth's rarest and most vulnerable living treasures, on the one hand, and Bronwen and Angharad, on the other; and he did not choose his wife and daughter. That is something many would find difficult to accept, and even Jenny, his stoutest defender, finds it very hard to take; but that was the choice he made.

Let me try to be fair; he did not abandon Bronwen.

I look at what I have written.

Did he abandon Bronwen?

He would have been faithful and devoted to her for all of his days. But he did propose leaving her for nearly a third of every year, with no real explanation for such a drastic absence (he obviously felt it had to be that way), and for a young woman with a young child, that was – that is – too much to ask. Bronwen was right to be bitter. She paid the price.

Yet it must have been excruciating for him too. I think it is clear, if only from the parade of pictures in his hut on Lanna, that he deeply loved his wife and his daughter, he was a caring man, and to take such a decision which he knew would hurt them, and which would separate him from them for ever, without being able to tell them why, must have been beyond agonising. Never mind the guilt he must have felt, which was surely terrible in itself. He would never be happy again, he told Bronwen when the divorce was finalised, and it was a sombre insight for Jenny and me to realise just what a burden his choice must have been to him, each day of his life thereafter, what a permanent intensity of misery it must have delivered; Fergus chose a path along which sorrow accompanied his every step.

What could drive him to do it?

Why did Fergus Pryng keep the great auks of Lanna secret, at such a cost to himself?

The idea that he might have done it because he thought human beings were bad, that the species *Homo sapiens* was the enemy of the Earth, we at first did not really consider; but we gradually began to feel there was no other explanation.

Jenny said to me one night: 'You know, Miles, it wasn't just a policy option, was it? It wasn't just a calculation that this policy, say, of keeping the great auks hidden, is probably better for their protection, all things considered, than that policy, of revealing their existence.'

'No?'

'That's just a technical choice. That wouldn't be enough to push you into wrecking your marriage and your happiness, surely?'

'No, I don't suppose it would.'

'It was something far deeper. It was a moral choice.'

'In what way?'

'It stemmed from his whole identity.'

For we started to take on board just how unusual Fergus was in the way he saw the world, even on a day-to-day basis: he looked at it in the round, and he looked at it in a moral way. He saw it as the whole planet itself, this Earth which was exquisite in its beauty, which was our only home and which gave us everything; in his view its worth was limitless and it was thus to be without limit revered, and in his own case, defended. And there was the rub, since he saw the planet's principal enemy in Man himself.

Jenny said: 'You know what Fergus's tragedy was, Miles? Holding the views he did, when he came across the birds. He didn't really have a choice.'

We began to see it: Fergus was convinced that human beings had something in them which was irredeemably destructive in their relations with the Earth, that Man the species was injurious in his essence, and indeed, that now he was on course to destroy the whole natural world. Man had already wiped out the great auk, or so everyone thought; and when Fergus stumbled across the survivors, the miraculous survivors clinging to life on Lanna, he clearly felt he would be damned if he would give Man the chance to destroy them once again.

'He had no choice, being who he was,' Jenny said. 'Once he had found the birds, he had to do what he did.'

'And you could take it further,' I said, 'and say that he was either exactly the right, or exactly the wrong person to have discovered the secret of Lanna. Depending on your point of view.'

Yes, there was the key to it: he was trapped in his character – that clear-sighted, determined persona with unquenchable love for the natural world which had captured the heart of the tough and cynical young Bronwen. That was what propelled him into this scarcely-believable decision which cost him so much, which cost him his felicity and his future, and which ultimately, was wrong, and made possible a disaster.

Wrong or not, though, there was something phenomenal, Jenny and I came to realise, about what he then actually did – about his silence, and its duration. From the summer of 1983 to the summer of 2000, all those years of Margaret Thatcher and Ronald Reagan, of the fall of the Berlin Wall and the collapse of the Soviet Union, of the appearance of AIDS, of the first Gulf War and the release of Nelson Mandela, of Bill Clinton and Tony Blair, of the rise of the mobile phone, the personal computer and then of the internet, not to mention the rise of Bronwen Pryng – through all those seventeen hectic years, every springtime Fergus sailed out to Lanna on his private business and every summer he came back and said not a syllable; apart from letting Kintyre in on it, two years before the end – and he felt he was compelled to do that – he breathed not a word nor a whisper to a living soul. Not a hint, even to those closest to him, for whom a hint might well have been a justification. In this our world where people feel they must speak, our world full of ever-intensifying, interminable babble, our world where trivia is rattling about our ears like a hailstorm, I see it now almost in spiritual terms, as if it were the silence of a Trappist monk, a silence of deep devotion, not to God, but of a similar high purpose, of devotion to the Earth.

That devotion, born of his blessed childhood, accompanying his father to paint the wild flowers of the unspoiled Suffolk countryside of the 1950s, has been the most significant part of Fergus's legacy to Jenny and me, because it has become our lodestar; we have been led by it into our own understanding of the worth of the natural world, here on the shores of Loch Nay. For we are the solitary keepers of his story, of what he did and why he did it, and it is an extraordinary situation to be in, because it is as if we are living, not just in Argyll with its hills and its sea lochs and its otters and its eagles, but inside a special moral universe; almost as if we have a religion of our own which centres around the wonder of the great auks of Lanna and the moral choice Fergus made about them, and which has as its essence the value of the natural world, as Fergus saw it, and as its profoundest image, the memory of watching him die.

It means we have responded in a particular way to what is in front of us here, the richness and beauty of life, with what I suppose you might call an informed understanding. Jenny got there before me; with my long-lasting disregard for nature, which looking back, I think was one of the shabbiest aspects of my career as a natural scientist, I was slower off the mark. But that disregard is gone now; it could not but disappear in this place, where sometimes the beauty is such that it is hard to cope with, as in the winter, when after days of storm and rain there will be a pause, and the wind moves into the north and the cold air comes and scours the sky and the landscape takes on something beyond loveliness, everything you can see is crystal and glistening, the hills and the waters, the shapes and the colours, as it they were new-made this morning by God, you are taken aback by it, you don't quite know how to react. The wildlife all around seems the same, it seems untouched since the Lord made it, so vivid it is in its being and its doing, and the more I looked intensely, especially as I began to film it, the tyro video cameraman, the more I thrilled to it, and the moment eventually arrived when everything came together and I understood the value of it all, and I told Jenny.

It was during the second summer. We were sitting here by the old chapel, which had become our favourite resting place. I said: 'Guess what. I've worked it out.'

'What?'

'All this.' And I swept my hand across the loch and the hills on the far side and out to sea where Jura was resting in the evening sunlight with Islay beyond it and we could even see Gigha, a distant grey shadow on the blue water far off towards the Mull of Kintyre. The oystercatchers were whistling down the wind.

Jenny said: 'What about it?'

'I've worked out what it's worth.'

'And what is that, Miles?'

'It's worth everything.'

And Jenny smiled, and she nodded. And we were there, together. I had followed her into the heart of it.

So it was that, when eventually the idea began to form in my mind that the hobby I had developed from Jenny's Christmas present of a video camera might in fact offer me a future, there was more behind it than my own growing proficiency, and the encouragement of the BBC: there was a value, a commitment, a purpose – that I might record the beauty and the wonder of the world, and perhaps help defend it, as Fergus had done. And I have gone forward into it, the career of a wildlife cameraman, I have moved on from Canon and videotape to Arriflex and sixteen-millimetre, and I have been commissioned increasingly by the BBC, and now I have my first major commission overseas: I am going to Svalbard to film polar bears on their summer hunt for seals, and I leave tomorrow.

It seems a long way to have travelled from my life as a researcher, ruthlessly focused, obsessively striving to outdo my father; a journey via the beach on the Île de Ré with Arty Booboo's contorted corpse, via the bedside of my dying mother, via the castle of the Tiger Laird, and finally via Lanna, and the blessing of Jenny Pittaway.

Lanna, Lanna, lost island, I dream of you incessantly. Even now it is sometimes the nightmare of Fergus's terrible end which comes in the dark, and I have to get up from Jenny's embrace and walk the shoreline to bring my soul to peace; but often it's the good dreams which come to me, of the glorious, bustling monastery of the past, with its pilgrims sighting in their elation the giant Celtic cross on the peak; and of the empty but haunting monastery of today, with its silent ghosts; of Jenny and I, after all our trials, joyfully reunited; and of course, of its staggering, fantastical secret, *Pinguinus impennis*. I still see them, they were not the will o' the wisps of my imagination, they were real, the old male diving and shooting beneath the boat, the breeding pairs gathered in ungainly togetherness on their ledge, seeming to exhibit in their very fragility their burden of history, their evidence of the fateful and terrible destructive potential of Man.

And yet ... from time to time I come down here to the point and stand by the old chapel and look out across the sea towards the Western Isles and I wonder, I wonder hard: have they really all gone? Were they *all* wiped out in the tanker fire, all of them, those miraculous survivors? I thought so, in my despair, when I first saw what the flames had done to Sgeir Dubh; but now I am not so sure. A growing part of me thinks they are out there still, some of them; maybe even a tiny number, but some of them survive. I have no evidence either way; I simply believe it. I feel it strongly. They are out there, the penguins of the western seas, out there in the storm zone with the fulmars and the gannets and the great whales, and one day, we shall see them again.

Fergus, though, could not have such a thought. He went to his death fearing all was lost. And it was worse than that, really, because in our final perception, Jenny and I came to see that towards the end, he had perhaps begun to understand himself that there was a problem at the heart of his enterprise. We had a hint of it when he came to the door of our hut on Lanna to signal he was about to tell us everything, which we did not then understand; there, just for a second, was a glimpse of the creeping feeling that maybe after all, either in denying the birds official protection, or in doing so, destroying his marriage – that in either of these matters or in both, in spite of all his superlative intentions, he had been wrong.

I often wonder now what that final night must have been like for him, after the row over the radio with Kintyre, I mean, after we left him. At the time I was far too bound up in myself and Jenny, and of course in the birds, even to conceive of such a thought, but now it seems to me that the cost for him of the isolation which came with the role he had chosen on Lanna might that night have been at its steepest. So many thoughts must have crowded into his brain, and no one to share them with! He was giving up his life, his life's project, and there was no friend or partner he could discuss it or debate it with, and more than that, as he thought back over it all, intensely as he must have done, there was no one to reassure him against that terrible scintilla of doubt which was briefly visible when he knocked on our door; for we remember his words then, and now of course we understand them: *I have begun to think it has all been a mistake.* And what followed: *Which is a dreadful prospect to contemplate.* Because you can take the privations, can't you, you can take the troubles and the suffering and the sacrifice that the choice you make throws at you, you accept all that as part of the deal, but what you can't accept is having been wrong in the first place. It's like Christ on the cross, crying out at the end, when the pain is unendurable, My God My God, why have you forsaken me? ... the most moving thing in the whole Bible, that doubt, *maybe I'm not divine after all* ... Did Fergus have that doubt, the night of the storm, did it loom large for him, did he feel that the sacrifice he had made of his own happiness was not noble and worthwhile, merely mistaken? It was the last night of his life. Was it the dark night of his soul? I will never know, though I will wish to the end of my days we could have been there for him.

Worst of all, I think that with the tanker the next day, after the towrope broke and the *Lamprinos* and its sixty thousand tonnes of crude oil surged unstoppably towards the Sgeir Dubh reef and what it was sheltering, maybe then, as he watched in unbelieving horror, he was suddenly certain: he had been wrong. Did he feel that? We have no way of knowing. But I think that he may well have done, and that if he did, such certainty was something he would not have wanted to survive.

The three figures coming down the beach are separate entities now: I can see the detail of their faces. They will be upon me soon.

It was Jenny who first suggested there should be a memorial to Fergus. She did so one evening in Taigh na Mara, when we were playing chess after dinner, and she suddenly said: 'You know, I don't want Fergus to be forgotten.'

I said: 'How d'you mean?'

'At the moment he's lost, isn't he? He's lost to the world, with everything he tried to do. And everything he believed in. And his end was terrible, wasn't it? I just don't want it to be, sort of ... capped, by, by oblivion.'

Might we put up some sort of monument to him on Lanna, she said, where he had spent all those incredible secret years, and I said, fine by me, though that would need the co-operation of Angela and Gervase; but when I broached it with the latter he said: 'A monument to Fergus Pryng? Why? What did he ever achieve?'

'He gave his life trying to save the island's seabirds.'

'But so did four other people. Plus the captain of the tanker also died. Not to mention Rollo being permanently disfigured, God rest his soul, like that other chappie, the old fisherman from Barra. I think a monument to *all* those who were killed is a good idea, in fact. Why don't you get on it, Miles?'

Gervase was right, of course; it was an appropriate measure, and so a year later the monument to the victims of the *Lamprinos* disaster was installed: a semi-abstract seabird by a young sculptor from Lewis whom Angela had patronised, which was pretty good, I thought. I made sure it was placed on its plinth, which bore the names of those who had been killed, just in front of the rock overhang from where Fergus had watched over his charges, so it looked across to the exact point where the tanker had hit the reef, and we invited relatives and friends of those who had died to a ceremony marking the installation. They came out by helicopter on a fine clear day in July, more than a dozen of them in the end, including the woman from Vermont who was the partner of Rufus Mehlinger the photographer, and the Greek wife of the tanker captain, and Kenny Lornie's old mother, God bless her, and Ramsay and a couple of others from UKOCA, though no one made it on behalf of the two South Africans, I don't know why. Most notably, Bronwen came, accompanied by a reporter and photographer from the Press Association. I thought – I hoped – she might have brought Angharad with her, but she did not.

So Fergus shares his island monument, and I am sure he would not for a single second have complained; yet Jenny and I still wished strongly for a memorial that would be his alone, because with every day that passes, we see more reason to commemorate him. Yet we are caught in this bind, this fantastic bind, of being the only people alive who know the story of the great auks of Lanna and the story of their protector, and we cannot make either public. We have discussed it interminably, but we always come back to the fact that if we tell but one person, such as Bronwen, for example – and there, we have been strongly tempted – then the secret of the island

and of Fergus's involvement with it will eventually see the general light of day, and it is so exceptionally implausible that evidence will at once be demanded; and evidence there is none. Not a jot. And then all will be ridiculed as mere fantasy, as a mad invention; and we will not let that happen.

Thus it goes unacknowledged by the world, as if it had never taken place, the tragedy of the ocean's unique survivors, and their loss, and of the man who tried to save them. Was Fergus responsible, for the loss? Maybe. Even though it was an accident. That was the first thing we saw, when we realised he had kept them hidden. But subsequently, suspending judgement, as Jenny suggested, we saw so much else: we saw what he had gone through, and what he had lost, and the effort he had made to preserve the birds single-handedly over seventeen years on the remotest corner of all the British Isles, which can be described by no other word than heroic, and we saw him give his life for them. And finally we saw his reason for acting: simply the way he looked at the world. What he did was outlandish, but was it unreasonable? Well, Jenny and I both think, he had no choice. He did what he did, with all its consequences, because of who he was; because of his character. And there, perhaps, is the meaning of tragedy.

I still do not know if Fergus was correct in his view of *Homo sapiens* as the greatest of all threats, to view Man above all as this single one of the planet's millions of radiated species which alone carries the gene of wanton destruction. *Poor Earth!* That would be my cry as well as his, if I thought he was right. Was he right? Was he right about people? Was he right about us? I shake my head. These days I think about it more and more. Sometimes it seems to me Fergus was merely a man with a very big misanthropic side, he was the naturalist reincarnated as Scrooge; at other times, and I have started to think this recently, the more I have begun to witness of the destruction assailing the forests and the meadowlands and the rivers and the oceans and all the living creatures within them, the destruction which I realise now is going to grow beyond all bearing, I think that he was simply more clear-sighted than the rest of us.

But I do not know.

What I do know is that the other side of him, the side that came from love rather than the side of distrust, was indomitable. The original eco-warrior, Bronwen called him, the saviour of Whitefield Fen 'and all its life' – the fearless, confident, uncompromising warden who had sued his own employers to save a bog, who had taken on a bunch of thugs to save a few rabbits, who had conceived so deep a love of the Earth and its nature that his commitment to protect it knew no qualification. It was what made Bronwen give her heart to him, and the greatest regret I have in all this business is that we cannot reveal to her that her first love was not the loser she eventually came to take him for. It may be true, that Fergus lost everything; but he wasn't a loser. He went down fighting.

Yet he went down very alone, his spirit, very possibly, broken by self-doubt. Fergus, you might have been wrong, but I say to you now, that if you were, you were wrong for the right reasons. Indeed, one of the purposes of the memorial we gave him in the end was to try to lessen the icy solitude of his final agony, as if to say, *Look, Fergus! You're not alone! We're with you! We're here!* An illusion of course, though perhaps we may be allowed it. But it does mean that he will not be forgotten, his memory will not be lost to the world as Jenny feared. We have been determined that although his story cannot be told, the memory of Fergus Pryng should not die, and it will not. It will not. That's what I am thinking, as the three figures walking down the beach are upon me now, thinking that in the end we made your memorial not in a bronze casting or a stone sculpture but out of our own love, Fergus, the most precious thing we have, that we travelled so far to find – Fergus the King of Lanna, Fergus the Solitary, Fergus the Sacrificial, most of all Fergus the Silent, oh, Fergus, Fergus, Fergus, I say, thinking of everything, and now I am calling it out, Fergus! Fergus! Fergus! And the smallest figure of the three detaches himself from the other two, Jenny and Lotte who is staying with us, smiling both, and he starts to run, to run as fast as his small feet will carry him – Fergus Bonnici, two years old, tearing over the sand with his head thrown back in laughter and his arms outstretched towards me, as my own arms open to receive him.

Acknowledgements

This story was inspired by the lives and actions of three men I knew well who cared deeply for the future of the natural world and fought to save it, and who are now dead: Reg Arthur, Jon Castle and Andrew Lees. I honour their memory, and I pay tribute to them here. But it has also been informed by the wisdom and insight of friends who are still living, and foremost amongst them are Tim Birkhead and Jeremy Mynott, who have been infinitely patient and generous with their time and support over an extended period; I owe them more than I can repay. I also owe a great debt to my agent, Andrew Gordon, who has always believed in the worth of this story, and most of all to the unwavering support of my wife, Jo Revill, over the long time that it took for it to come to fruition.

My thanks are further due to members of Britain's biological community, with at the head of the list, the staff of the Seabirds and Cetaceans Branch of the Joint Nature Conservation Committee in Aberdeen, in particular Mark Tasker, Caroline Weir and Andy Webb; and to Andy (now with HiDef Aerial Surveying) I owe a separate note of thanks for taking me on the seabird cruise of the *Poplar Explorer*, with Ben Dean and Claire McSorley (now Mrs Claire Shaw.) Other leading ornithologists I must thank include Mark Avery, Andy Clements, Mark Cocker, Euan Dunn, Peter Marren, Ian Newton and Paul Stancliffe. And I owe a special debt of gratitude to John Aitchison, most inspiring of wildlife cameramen, who with his wife Mary-Lou and their children Freya, Kirstie and Rowan (now a wildlife cameraman himself) welcomed me into their home on the heart-stoppingly lovely, otter-animated shores of Loch Nay (as it were).

The others to whom I am indebted are alas too numerous to thank in detail but I must give their names: Nigel Ajax-Lewis, Scott Baxter, Bernard Cadiou, Rochelle Constantine, Peter Cresswell, Nick and Janet Cowie, James and Lesley Cowie, Alison Duncan, Kate Farquhar-Thompson, Mark Fricker, Erroll Fuller, Chris Green, Geoffrey and Ellen Green, Hamish Haswell-Smith, Julie Kerr, Julian Luxford, Ian Lyall and Ewen Lyall, Kester Macfarlane, Angus MacIver, Murray Macleod, Roland Philipps, Mark Pilgrim,

Robert Pirrie, Hugh Raven and Jane Stuart-Smith, John Regan, Fiona Reynolds, Michael Rodgers, Chris Rose, Ben Sheldon, Jeremy Thomas and Andy Wightman. I apologise for any unwitting omissions. More recently, I owe a particular debt to Bob Fowke and Russell Wall. Finally, and most enduringly, I would like to thank Carol Cromie of Ruby Bay, for reasons which will be obvious to her.